TAIWAN TRAVELOGUE

Yáng Shuāng-zǐ is a writer of fiction, essays, manga and video game scripts, and literary criticism from Táichūng, Taiwan. In 2020, she was featured in *Wenshun* magazine's Rising Stars of the Twenty-First Century and *Unitas* magazine's Twenty Most Promising Young Novelists. In 2021, she was the youngest-ever nominee for the *United Daily News* Literary Award, and her novel *Taiwan Travelogue* was awarded the Golden Tripod Award, Taiwan's highest literary honor. In 2022, Yáng was voted Representative Author of Twenty-First Century Taiwanese Popular Literature.

Lin King is a writer and translator from Táipěi, Taiwan. Her writing has appeared in *One Story, Boston Review, Joyland,* and *Far-Near,* among other publications, and has received the PEN/Robert J. Dau Short Story Prize for Emerging Writers. Her translations from Mandarin Chinese and Japanese have appeared in *Asymptote,* the *Margins,* and *Columbia Journal.* She is also the translator of the Taiwanese historical graphic novel series *The Boy from Clearwater,* by Yu Pei-Yun and Zhou Jian-Xin.

TAIWAN TRAVELOGUE

A Novel

YÁNG SHUĀNG-ZǏ

Translated from the Mandarin Chinese by Lin King

PICADOR INDIA

Originally published in Mandarin Chinese as 臺灣漫遊錄 by
SpringHill Publishing, Taipei City, Taiwan in 2020
Published by arrangement with And Other Stories Publishing, UK

First published in India 2026 by Picador India
an imprint of Pan Macmillan Publishing India Private Limited
707 Kailash Building
26 K. G. Marg, New Delhi 110001
www.panmacmillan.co.in

Pan Macmillan, The Smithson, 6 Briset Street, Farringdon, London EC1M 5NR
Associated companies throughout the world
www.panmacmillan.com

ISBN 978-93-6113-910-9

Map by Jeffrey L. Ward

3 5 7 9 8 6 4

Book design by Ann Sudmeier

Printed and bound in India by Thomson Press India Private Limited

This book is dedicated to Yáng Jò-hūi, the younger of the twin sisters known jointly as Yáng Shuāng-zǐ.

TAIWAN 1938

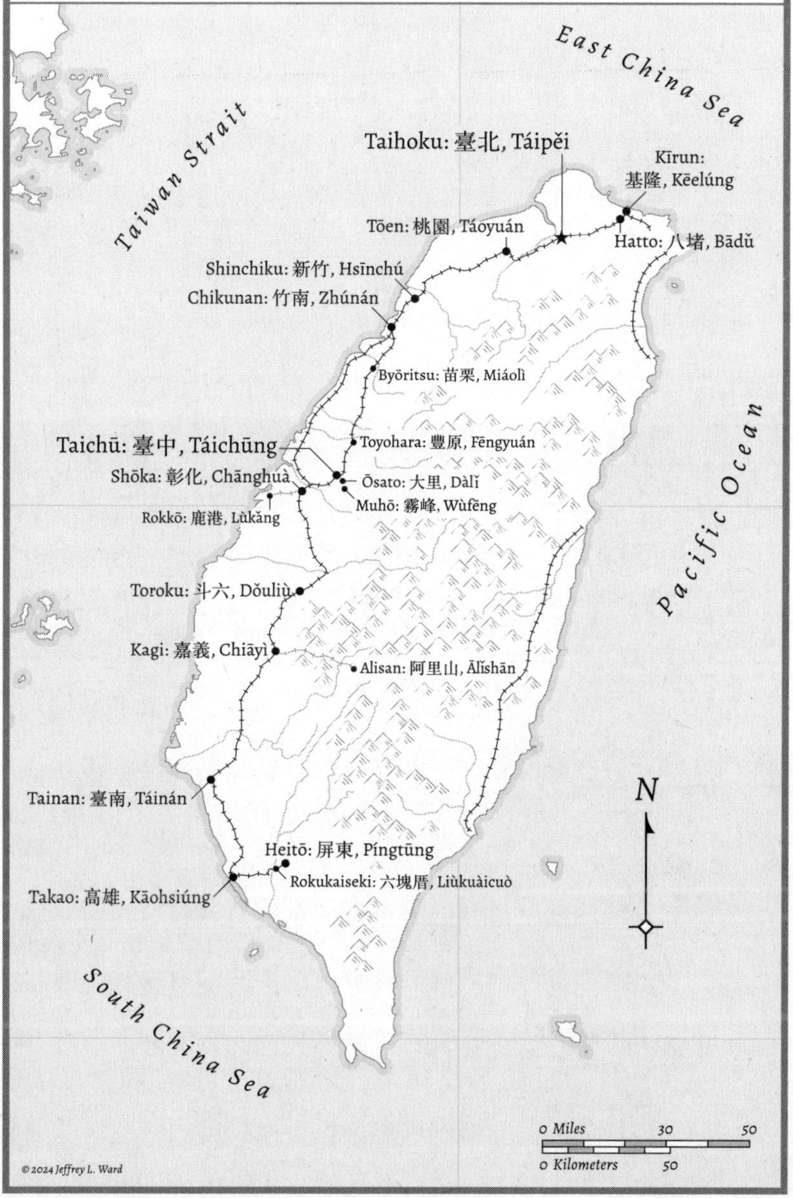

East China Sea
Taiwan Strait
Pacific Ocean
South China Sea
Taihoku: 臺北, Táipěi
Kīrun: 基隆, Kēelúng
Hatto: 八堵, Bādǔ
Tōen: 桃園, Táoyuán
Shinchiku: 新竹, Hsīnchú
Chikunan: 竹南, Zhúnán
Byōritsu: 苗栗, Miáolì
Taichū: 臺中, Táichūng
Toyohara: 豐原, Fēngyuán
Shōka: 彰化, Chānghuà
Ōsato: 大里, Dàlǐ
Muhō: 霧峰, Wùfēng
Rokkō: 鹿港, Lùkǎng
Toroku: 斗六, Dǒuliù
Kagi: 嘉義, Chiāyì
Alisan: 阿里山, Ālǐshān
Tainan: 臺南, Táinán
Heitō: 屏東, Píngtūng
Rokukaiseki: 六塊厝, Liùkuàicuò
Takao: 高雄, Kāohsiúng
N
0 Miles 30 50
0 Kilometers 50
© 2024 Jeffrey L. Ward

CONTENTS

Introduction to *Taiwan Travelogue*, New Mandarin Chinese Edition, 2020

A Truncated Dream, a Foreign Splendorland

Hiyoshi Sagako

My affiliation with this new translation of *Taiwan Travelogue* began in 2015, when I heard via word of mouth that Ms. Yáng Jò-hūi, a translator, was seeking a copy of the first Mandarin translation, published in 1977. I found this an unusual quest, considering that the book had been out of print in Taiwan for many years and even academics had difficulty securing a single copy. As it happened, I was in possession of not only the first translation but also the Japanese original; I therefore asked a staff member at the National Museum of Taiwan Literature to pass along my contact information to Ms. Yáng. At the time, it did not occur to me that my actions would catalyze the birth of a new translation. The tributaries of fate have met and merged into a coursing river, one that enabled this book to be reintroduced to the world at a time when the world needed it most.

Interestingly, I did not learn until the Taiwanese publisher asked me to write an introduction that the museum staff had described me to Ms. Yáng as a "Japanese scholar." When I heard this, I did not know whether to feel amused or offended. The word that I would use to describe myself, 灣生, is pronounced wānshēng in Mandarin Chinese, wansei in Japanese, and uan-sing in Taiwanese Hokkien. Being catalogued as simply "Japanese" seemed to exclude me from Taiwan entirely. However, perhaps my unusual origins make me unusually suited to introduce this novel to contemporary readers.

The term wānshēng originated when Taiwan was under Japanese colonial rule, and its meaning is exactly what the Han characters imply: Japanese people born in Taiwan. By blood we belonged to the great Yamato race, but as Japanese citizens we were "subpar"; growing up on the subtropical island, our use of the national language, Japanese, was often nonstandard, and few of us had ever seen snow or truly experienced the four seasons. Even if our bloodlines were "pure," many Japanese argued that we could not possibly possess the true "spirit" of the Japanese people. Thus, the wānshēng were often regarded as inferior.

No matter how much the Japanese administration in Taiwan promoted their official stance that all Taiwanese peoples were as much the children of the Emperor as any Japan-born person, the reality was that Taiwanese "Islanders" were second-class citizens compared to Japanese "Mainlanders," and the wānshēng drifted somewhere between the two classes with no means of finding belonging in either. Some of us regarded Taiwan as home, whereas others abused the Islanders all the more ruthlessly for their own inferiority complexes.

In many senses, the wānshēng are homeless, casteless ghosts. However, there are perspectives to which only ghosts are privy. For instance, there are certain things that only we ghosts would notice within Aoyama Chizuko's novel.

Let us now turn to the novel's background. Aoyama Chizuko, the author of *Taiwan Travelogue*, was born in Taishō Year 2 (1913) and made her literary debut at the age of nineteen. She became an instant star, with her first novel adapted for the silver screen. In Shōwa Year 13 (1938), the Japanese Government-General of Taiwan invited this renowned writer to Taiwan for a lecture tour. While this seemed at first glance a tasteful proposal, in reality tensions were already building toward the Second World War, and imperialist and expansionist propaganda was no doubt one of the government's primary motives for sponsoring Aoyama-sensei's trip.

During her stay in Taiwan, Aoyama-sensei published dispatches from her travels in Mainland newspapers and magazines; these essays and articles were presented as a series titled Taiwan Travelogue. However, this Taiwan Travelogue has little overlap with the novel *Taiwan Travelogue,* and was instead a precursor to the novel. The novel *Taiwan Travelogue* was published in Shōwa Year 29 (1954), fifteen years after Aoyama-sensei's trip. Presented as fiction, it forsook all traces of nationalist agenda and instead focused on the relationship between Aoyama-sensei and her interpreter, Ms. Wáng Chiēn-hò (Ông Tshian-ho̍h in Taiwanese, Ō Chizuru in Japanese).

I will admit that, back when I first read Aoyama-sensei's serialized essays, I had assumed that Ms. Wáng must have been a fictional character. These articles were inextricable from their propagandistic undertones, and Ms. Wáng's presence in them seemed too conspicuously *counter*propagandistic. I therefore deduced that Ms. Wáng must have been a clever metaphor, a vessel through which Aoyama could imply her true views under the veil of patriotic writing. This was not unheard of as a technique: Satō Haruo, well known for his writings on Taiwan, once created a servant-girl character in his "Tale of the 'Precepts for Women' Fan" as a metaphor for the inequality between the colonizers and the colonized.

Today, there is no longer any doubt that Ms. Wáng was very real indeed; those who attended Aoyama's lectures testified to seeing Ms. Wáng at her side. But while Aoyama's motives for publishing the book were rooted in her relationship with the real Ms. Wáng, she ultimately chose to present the work as fiction, and the novel's very premise rests on the fictionality of Ms. Wáng as a character. For better or worse, Ms. Wáng *has* become a metaphor—one without which the novel *Taiwan Travelogue* cannot stand as a work of literature.

There is also the interesting matter of the book's twelfth and final chapter, "Mitsumame / Fruit and Jelly Ice." For the novel's reprint published in Shōwa Year 45 (1970), Aoyama Chizuko's adopted daughter, Aoyama Yōko, writes in an afterword that there was no chapter twelve in the original manuscript that she first read. Why would this critical conclusion have been excluded from the first draft? Why was it added?

I present a conjecture: maybe Aoyama-sensei did meet with Ms. Wáng in Shōwa Year 14 (1939), but that encounter may not have been as neat as what was depicted in the novel. At the very least, Aoyama-sensei left the conversation feeling that she still needed to apologize. She may have therefore added the twelfth chapter, intending it as a letter of repentance specifically addressed to Ms. Wáng. Through this chapter, she asks: If I had been able to reach these conclusions back then, would things have been different? Would Ms. Wáng acknowledge that this different outcome was possible? Aoyama-sensei must have sent this love letter of a novel with much anxiety over its reception, even if it was too late to turn back the clock.

If my theory is correct, then the majority of "Mitsumame" has been fictionalized. But there is no need to chastise Aoyama Chizuko, for the lofty barrier that stood between these two women was not only the power imbalance between the colonizer and the colonized, but also Japan's loss of the Pacific War and the subsequent division of Taiwan and Japan from one country into two. This is a cruel fate that perhaps deserves a happy modification. "Mitsumame" is a dream that had the potential of becoming reality, yet this dream was cut short.

I will not divulge much more out of consideration for first-time readers; I do not wish to begrudge readers of the right to form their own interpretations of the text. However, I would like to draw attention to one crucial point: that power imbalance is more subtle and delicate—as well as more ubiquitous—than most people imagine. Therefore, when reading this book, please remain cognizant of Aoyama Chizuko's status as one of the colonizers within the story.

I have made the bold choice to publish this bumbling memorial to my travels, which I hereby dedicate to:

Madame Takada Sumako, formerly of the Taichū Prefecture Nisshinkai in Taiwan

Mr. Mishima Aizō, of Taichū City Hall, Taichū Prefecture, Taiwan Government-General

and

Miss Ông Tshian-ho̍h, of Chōkyōshitō, Taichū City, Taichū Prefecture

Your hospitality and generosity will never be forgotten.

Aoyama Chizuko
January, Shōwa Year 29

Sketches of the Yana River cottage by Aoyama Chizuko

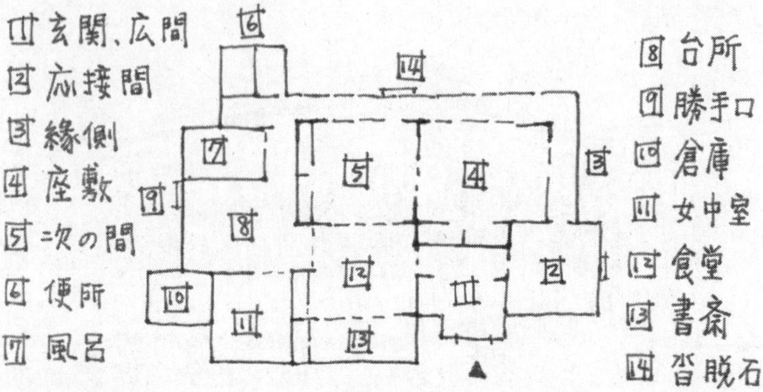

Floor plan of the Yana River cottage by Aoyama Chizuko

1. Foyer
2. Drawing room
3. Engawa veranda
4. Zashiki main room
5. Tsugi secondary room
6. Toilet
7. Bathroom
8. Kitchen
9. Side door
10. Storeroom
11. Servant's room
12. Dining room
13. Study
14. Garden stepping stones

TAIWAN TRAVELOGUE

CHAPTER I

Kue-Tsí / Roasted Seeds

"Hold on. What's going on here?"

I couldn't help but voice the thought out loud.

For, in that moment, I seemed to have been transported back into the midst of Shōkyokusai Tenkatsu's Magic Troupe.[1]

I'd crossed paths with Tenkatsu's troupe long ago, before I'd started high school. They had been on tour, and on the day they arrived in Nagasaki, my aunt Kikuko and I happened upon the opening parade.

The procession comprised a majestic formation of rickshaws, rows and rows of them with no end in sight—enough to rival an army regiment. The band rode at the frontmost rickshaws, performing with remarkable gusto; after them came the women magicians, beaming and waving at the crowd in exquisite maquillage; they were followed by the male magicians in top hats. Other troupe members went on foot, encircling the rickshaws and ushering them along. They held up long poles with brightly colored flags—streaks of crimson, white, violet, and azure that were no less commanding than the band's spirited music. My chest thrummed and lifted, as though something had been strung from my navel all the way up into the sky.

And here I was, decades later, on the outpost island of

---

1. Yáng Shuāng-zǐ (Mandarin Chinese translator of the 2020 edition): Shōkyokusai Tenkatsu (1886–1994) was a Japanese magician known for her modern stage magic derived from Western illusionist methods. Known as the Queen of Magicians, she became a popular phenomenon in the prewar period.

Taiwan, reliving this old reverie. It was May, in the thirteenth year of Shōwa,[2] yet the sights and sounds coursing before me were just like those of Tenkatsu's Magic Troupe.

Rows of red-brick Shina-style[3] buildings stretched endlessly into the distance.

Round vermilion lanterns hung from the roofs alongside sunset-colored ones shaped like seeds.

Squares of white tarp blossomed overhead.

Kanji signs of all colors and patterns flashed past my sightline.

And then the stalls: vegetables—utterly alien to me—piled into green, yellow, white hills.

Blood-red meat carved into strips, hanging from hooks like flesh tapestries.

Mud-brown and swamp-green herbs bound into bundles, or else scattered in wicker baskets, or else stewed into inky, emerald concoctions.

One vendor had an imposing spread of large glass jars that glinted in the light. Each contained treats I could not name: pale red, dark red, light yellow, deep yellow, pitch black, bone white.

There were several stalls where people stood eating desserts from soup bowls, which contained nugget-like delicacies. Some were white and soft and others yellow and semitransparent; still others were like the darkest of pearls.

Inside one greengrocer's shop, bunches of bananas dangled over tea-green and lacquer-red fruits. I was only able to identify a few of them—watermelon, peach, and something that was perhaps namuka.[4]

My eyes did not know where to turn first.

---

2. Yáng: 1938 in the Gregorian calendar.

3. Lin King (English translator): Shina is a now-obsolete Japanese term for China; it came to be regarded as derogatory in the twentieth century.

4. Yáng: Namuka is an archaic Japanese name for bell apple, known as lián-wù in Mandarin.

Outside the stately Taichū Station,[5] the ribbon-like Midori River threaded its way across Tachibana District. On the other side of the riverbank stood First Market and Taichū Hotel. The crowds, too, were like water; I'd come here, to Kanjō Bridge Avenue,[6] because I'd been told that it was where the Islanders gathered, and the sheer number of pedestrians proved my source correct. Thick willows lined the river on both sides, and the stream itself glittered with undulating ripples. I felt dizzied and dazzled—the May sun was a wheel of searing light that made every color more saturated and every scent more fragrant. The smell of the river, plants, raw meat, herbs, fruits—everything teemed and surged toward me under the cobalt sky.

There was something else mixed into that current: voices, speaking an Island language that I couldn't understand.

"XXXXXX XXXXXXX XXXXXXXX?"

"X XXXXXXXX XXXXXXXXX!"

"XXXXX XXXXXXXXXX."

My gut somersaulted to my chest. The corners of my mouth couldn't help but curl with glee.

Ah—so this was Taiwan, Land of the South!

No matter what, I must visit Taiwan at least once in my life.

I'd first made this resolution while standing out back on the deck of a large passenger ship heading home to Kyūshū

---

5. King: Taichū is the Japanese pronunciation for the place known in Mandarin Chinese as Táichūng. In both languages, the name is written with the Han characters 台中. This English translation uses Japanese pronunciations of Taiwanese place-names for conversations taking place in Japanese (e.g., Táipěi is referred to by its Japanese name Taihoku). Place-names in the current Mandarin Chinese and their corresponding Japanese colonial pronunciations can be found on the map at the front of the book.

6. Yáng: Kanjō Bridge Avenue is now Chénggōng Road in Taichung City's Central District. Kanjō Bridge is now Chénggōng Lyù Bridge.

Island from Okinawa. I'd been wondering whether the hazy shore I could see in the distance was Miyako Island or Ishigaki Island—or was it in fact Taiwan Island, right there, just across the water?

After my novel was adapted into a film, my royalties saw a notable increase. Leading up to my Okinawa trip, magazines I'd never worked with came to my door offering, quite literally, handfuls of cash.

"If Aoyama-sensei is amenable, you can feel free to leave all the arrangements to us—the travel expenses, everything. We would *love* for you to write a serialized novel set in the South Pacific," said Editor F of a certain magazine, flashing an eager smile. "I have heard that Aoyama-sensei is an avid traveler. This is a wonderful opportunity, is it not?"

"A story set in the South Pacific . . . is that meant to complement the Southern Expansion Policy?"

"I—I am not quite sure what Aoyama-sensei means."

"I beg your pardon. I only mean that, if the premise of the novel is to promote the Empire of the Sun, I am afraid I will be a poor candidate. You see, I do not believe I can produce any interesting work on the subject, which would be a shame for the magazine as well as for its readers—do you not agree, sir?" I pushed the neat stack of bills back toward Editor F's knees. "Besides, I have already purchased tickets to my next destination, Okinawa, which would mean delaying your project—that is, unless you are interested in serializing a historical tale of the Ryūkyū Kingdom."

"Ah . . . but if Aoyama-sensei is fond of Okinawa, then would you not consider visiting Taiwan in the future? It is also an Island of the Southern Country."

I didn't wish to continue this pesky song and dance and put an end to the meeting without making any promises. But ever since that conversation, Taiwan, Island of the Southern Country, became a small seed in the field of my heart.

As fall deepened into winter that year, I concluded my brief trip to Okinawa. Ryūkyū, the chain of islands that stretched from Kyūshū to Taiwan and a Kingdom of the South in its own right, boasted a warm climate, and as I stood homebound on the deck, the salt-laced sea breeze brought no chill to my skin. Taiwan was even deeper in the South—what was it like in November? I recalled the large cargo ships that passed through Moji Port in Kyūshū, bringing crates of bananas from Taiwan day in and day out. The memory was enough to fill the air around me with that fresh yet fragrant scent.

A thought germinated and took root. *The next time I travel, it will be to Taiwan.*

Once I returned to Nagasaki, I began researching for this future journey. I'd learned my lesson from an earlier trip up north to Hokkaido that, to be sufficiently immersed in any locale, the stay must be substantial—half a year or more, ideally. But six months' worth of transportation, lodging, and, most important, dining expenses was no negligible sum. After completing an estimate, I clutched my head in frustration.

"Aunt Kikuko . . ."

I entered the earthen-floored kitchen, where my aunt and our young servant Haruno were hard at work. Steam was wafting from a clay pot; from the scent alone, I could tell that the white rice cooking within was of a caliber that would be delicious with a sprinkle of sesame salt and nothing else. Watching the pot was enough to make my stomach groan.

"Chizuko-san, dinner is not ready yet," Haruno said, giving me a knowing smile.

Hmph! As if I was here to ask about dinner!

"Aunt Kikuko . . . do we have five hundred yen for me to go to Taiwan?"

Haruno's jaw dropped.

Aunt Kikuko looked at me sedately. "What are you talking about, silly child?"

"I hardly look like a *child*, dear aunt." Age aside, I was tall enough to walk shoulder to shoulder with the foreigners in Nagasaki's streets. My nickname back in my school days was the Great Cedar.

Aunt Kikuko gave a gentle "hmm" and said, "Didn't that magazine editor say they'd be happy to finance you?"

"But all that Southern Expansion stuff—I can't write about something like *that*."

"Then go to Kumamoto and make an appeal to the head family."

"The head family! Forget about going to Taiwan, the Aoyamas in Kumamoto will be dragging me to the altar."

"It *is* high time you got married."

"Please oh please—"

"What a bothersome child. Maybe you should visit the shrine and ask the gods for your travel funds."

Now *here* was a conundrum. I hadn't anticipated that my babyish begging would have absolutely no effect whatsoever. Sighing, I said, "Can it be true? Is it possible that Suwa Shrine is my only ally? Ah! But they do sell *delectable* Castella cakes and Siberia cakes over there.[7] Surely the gods cannot refuse me—not with such offerings!"

"Chizuko-san is just naming her personal favorites," Haruno said, blowing my cover.

"Oh, dear gods, why oh why is our Chizuko such a hopeless glutton?" Aunt Kikuko asked.

Despite such ruthless attacks on my strategy, the gods did appear to accept my bribe of desserts. Not long after, at a time when I wasn't expecting it, I received an invitation from the Government-General of Taiwan and a Taiwan-based women's group.

---

7. Yáng: Castella cake, now called Nagasaki cake in Taiwan, is a popular sponge cake. Siberia cake is Castella cake with a layer of yōkan jelly (red bean paste, agar, and sugar) in the center.

As it turned out, Taiwan, like Mainland Japan, was going through a film craze. My timely invitation came thanks to the film adaptation of my novel *A Record of Youth,* which had premiered in Tōkyō two years before and had made its way to Taiwan, whereupon members of the Nisshinkai women's organization based in Taichū Prefecture were so moved that they funded the film's wider release. This apparently received such a warm reception from viewers that the Nisshinkai decided to invite me on a lecture tour. The Government-General of Taiwan had always been fond of bringing Mainlander authors to Taiwan, and thus the two parties sent a joint invitation, naming Taichū City Hall as my official host. Even without the lectureship compensation, their offer to cover transportation, housing, and dining immediately dispelled all of my financial woes. After a number of telegrams and telephone calls, I set off in the beginning of summer.

Departing from Moji Port in the north of Kyūshū, I took the Domestic Taiwan Route passenger ship and docked at Kīrun Port. I'd declined the Nisshinkai and Taichū City Hall's offer to have one of their staffers meet me at the port, and instead made my own way into Taihoku City, spent the night, and boarded the train from Taihoku Main Station down to Taichū alone. The express only took three and a half hours. I thought to myself: *Now this is what traveling is all about.*

The train departed at 9:30 and I simply could not wait until Taichū to have lunch. At Tōen Station at 10:05, I saw someone on the platform selling railroad bento boxes and bought one. Inside, I found pearly white rice, deep-fried fish, pan-fried fish, pickled radish, and unagi burdock rolls. It was hardly discernable from what I could get back home on the Mainland.

11:01, Shinchiku Station. I bought something from a platform vendor called bí-hún-tshá.[8] I asked a lady sitting next to me what

8. King: Taiwanese Hokkien for stir-fried vermicelli noodles.

it was, and she explained that it was something akin to yakisoba. (In fact, it was utterly different.)

About twenty minutes later, we arrived at Chikunan Station, and I carefully appraised the remaining capacity of my stomach.

11:47, Byōritsu Station. The bento here also seemed of the Mainland variety, so I only bought five salted duck eggs and a couple of plain onigiri. People boarded and alighted the train as we chugged along. The farther south we went, the more I heard my fellow passengers speaking the local language—I was fascinated, and looked forward to the journey ahead even more.

1:03, Taichū Station.

Sparrows darted in my chest.

I had an appointment to meet a City Hall staff member at 2:00, but I couldn't bear to just sit and twiddle my thumbs. From the window at the station's waiting area, I could see the sun beating down on the glossy leaves of palm trees, setting the green alight with gold. The day was far too hot; people made their way down the street by shuffling from one pocket of shade to another. Western automobiles and man-powered rickshaws passed by, as well as hefty wagons dragged by water buffalo. A little farther off, under the shelter of some trees, stood a row of vendors' carts.

"Excuse me. Is there some shopping area nearby where the Taiwanese go?"

The ticket collector was momentarily stumped by my question. "The Taiwanese . . . do you mean the Islanders?"

"Islanders—yes, the Islanders."

He gave me instructions that brought me to Kanjō Bridge Avenue—the thoroughfare that so vividly evoked Tenkatsu's Magic Troupe for me.

Without being too aware of what I was doing, I found myself buying some unknown, prickly fruit, a transaction made through charades-like gesturing that I decided to count as an auspicious beginning to my communication with the locals. Just as I thought the purchase complete, however, the baby-faced youth selling me the fruit began repeating—slowly, deliberately, and very seriously—a series of words. "X, X, X, X, X?"

"I'm sorry, I don't understand Taiwanese! What do these words mean—what on earth do you mean?" I waved my hands and wagged my head.

The boy looked equally defeated. "XXXXXXXXX," he said, and brought over a wooden container with a label on top. With impressive dexterity, he bundled the fruits into a charming gift box.

"Ah, I see! You were asking if I'd like them wrapped?" I hurried to take out some coins. "Say, is ten sen enough for the packaging?"

He looked at the coin in my hand, then back at me. "X, XXXXX? XXXXXX?"

I pointed at the box in his hand, then back at the coin. "This—is—for—the—packaging."

"X, XXXXXXX, XX!"

"Pack—a—ging!"

"XX! XX!" The boy's face reddened with effort.

"Oh, what can this mean?" I, too, grew flushed.

Hehe. A gentle chuckle to my side.

"I beg your pardon—would you like any assistance?"

I followed this flawless Japanese to its source: the face of a petite young woman who came up to around my jaw. Silken cheeks like an infant's—and two dimples that punctuated them when she smiled.

"The boy means to say that the wrapping is free of charge. He asks that you kindly put the coin away."

"You speak the national language! Oh, fantastic! Would you kindly tell him for me in dialect that I'd like him to keep the ten sen—for his time and trouble?"

She looked at me with some surprise.

The back of my head warmed with embarrassment. "You see, I've been badgering this poor boy for a *very* long time!"

The young woman chuckled and turned to exchange a few words with the boy in Taiwanese. He, at last, relaxed his face and broke into a smile. He pressed something into her hand, which she then passed to me. It was a thin paper packet; I peeled it open to find a handful of small, black, shard-like objects.

"He wishes to give this to you as thanks. Perhaps they will help you pass the time on your journey."

"I am very grateful, but—what is it?"

"Ah," the young woman tilted her head, grinning. "I forget that it is not something familiar to Mainlanders. We call it kue-tsí."

"Is it edible? How do you eat it?"

When it came to food, my enthusiasm soared higher than most people's. I leaned closer to the paper packet, which immediately filled my nose with a salty yet sweet scent. I picked up a few pieces and squeezed the hard surface between the flats of my fingers. Could one really eat this?

"No, not like that. In order to eat the kernel inside, you must first crack the shell with your teeth."

"The shell? With your *teeth*?"

The young woman took a piece from my hand. "Like this." With fingers that looked blue-white against the pitch-black kue-tsí, she raised the shard to the corner of her mouth and bit down gently with dainty, gleaming teeth. With a ringing *clack* the shell broke cleanly in two. The young woman fished out the ivory kernel and showed it to me. "I must warn you, cracking kue-tsí requires quite a bit of practice for a novice."

"Amazing!" I exclaimed. "What a marvel!"

She smiled. Her cheeks grew even rosier.

"Excuse me, would you be Aoyama Chizuko-sensei?" A man's voice, in Japanese.

He was young and wore a summer suit. He had thick eyebrows, thick eyelashes to match, and a broad forehead adorned with heavy beads of sweat.

"I am Mishima, from Taichū City Hall."

I let out a low "Ah."
2:00 at Taichū Station.
I had completely forgotten.

Mishima explained that he'd been informed of my physical appearance beforehand and, unable to find anyone of my description at the train station, had asked the ticket collector. Once he arrived at Kanjō Bridge Avenue, he had spotted his target easily: at one hundred sixty-five centimeters, I, the Great Cedar, stood taller than most men.

"The automobile is right around the corner," Mishima said, picking up my luggage and gesturing ahead. "This way, please."

"I am *so* sorry."

"Please do not apologize," he said with a perfectly straight face, patting away sweat with a handkerchief.

It wasn't until I was seated in the taxicab that I felt again the thin paper packet in the crook of my arm and recalled the young woman. When had she disappeared? I hadn't even thanked her properly.

My attention was redirected toward the new world speeding past the car window: the Shina- and Western- and Japanese-style buildings, the occasional interlude of rice paddies and banana fields, the bright reds and deep greens. Warm Southern Country breeze wafted into the car, bringing to my mind again the market, the crowds, the young woman's dimples, the young man's flushed face.

"Mishima-san, the Island is truly a picturesque place! It is so full of life!"

"Indeed."

"And the Islanders are so friendly, so kind!"

"Very true."

"I saw so many fascinating things in the market earlier—I am positive now that the rest of the trip will be *most* enjoyable."

"Most certainly."

Even the flatness of his textbook responses could not diminish my good mood. What an enchanting place!

Mishima launched into an explanation of logistics. First, we would head to the Takada residence in Muhō outside the city, where Madame Takada, the representative of the Nisshinkai women's group, awaited us. While my invitation had nominally been issued by Taichū City Hall, in practice my true host remained the Nisshinkai.

"Whenever Aoyama-sensei is traveling, there will be a local government staff member assigned to be your guide, which includes arranging lodging and dining as well as any of your other needs," Mishima said, twisting toward me as much as the front passenger seat allowed and bowing formally. "While you are in Taichū, I will have the privilege of acting as your interpreter and guide. However, your room and board here have already been arranged for by Madame Takada."

"Thank you so much for your trouble." After a beat, I asked, "If Mishima-san is to act as my guide, may I also ask you general questions about the Island?"

"Yes, of course."

"In that case, what exactly is this fruit that I bought?"

"It is a pineapple."

"And what do the Islanders call it?"

"In the Taiwanese dialect, it is called ông-lâi."

"What about the concoction that people were drinking next to the herb vendor? Is it Shina medicine? Do the Islanders go to the market instead of the doctor when they are ill?"

"No, that is not medicine. It is a local beverage called tshenn-tsháu-à tea."

"I also saw people eating a half-translucent, yellowish dessert. What might that be?"

"That would be either ò-giô or hún-kué."

"Are the two similar?"

"They are similar in appearance but not in taste."

"What about those small, black, pearl-like beads?"

"That would be hún-înn."[9]

"Mishima-san knows so much about Islander culture! Have you been working in Taiwan very long?"

He hesitated for a second. "I was born on the Island."

"Ah, I see! Excellent!" I grew even more excited. "I would love to taste all those Islander foods. Could you arrange that for me?"

When he turned to me this time, his thick eyebrows were slightly furrowed. The man was likely grumbling *What is this impertinent woman going on about?* in his head. But I didn't care—I was used to such reactions from others.

Soon enough, he neutralized his facial expression and said, "I will do my best."

"Can I get some by tonight? Maybe the herb tea—the tshenn-tsháu-à tea."

"Aoyama-sensei need not worry. We have arranged a first-rate dinner to welcome you."

Madame Takada had prepared a large, orderly Western-style room for me. In the afternoon, she hosted a tea party where I met some of the Nisshinkai's core members. After that, we all headed into bustling Taichū City for a banquet that S-san, a high-ranking member at the City Hall, had arranged at an establishment called

---

9. King: Tshenn-tsháu-à tea, or qīng-cǎo tea in Mandarin Chinese, is a tea brewed from many herbs, including Chinese mesona and mint. Ò-giô (Mandarin: ài-yù) is a jelly made from a type of fig. Hún-kué (Mandarin: fěn-guǒ) is made from potato starch and gardenia seeds. Hún-înn (Mandarin: fěn-yuán) is the tapioca product now popularly known in English as bubble or boba. (Note on transliteration: Taiwan uses several different romanization systems of Mandarin Chinese, including the more traditional Wade-Giles system and the Hanyu Pinyin system developed in 1950s People's Republic of China. This translation uses Wade-Giles for proper nouns typically written in Wade-Giles in Taiwan and uses Hanyu Pinyin for all other Mandarin words.)

Baishunen—a restaurant of Taiwanese cuisine catered toward Mainlander guests.[10]

Mishima had spoken the truth. I was indeed treated to a luxurious feast that night.

A luxurious feast indeed . . .

Salted fish roe, fried sausage, braised pigs' feet, stewed shark fin, soft-shelled turtle, sea snail soup, steamed crab over sticky rice, followed by a lush stir-fry of carefully selected vegetables, meat, and seafood. Desserts were almond tofu and something called Eight Treasures Rice, a pudding of sweet glutinous rice, dried fruits, and red bean paste. The meal was topped off by coffee and Taiwanese oolong.

Everything was perfectly delicious and, also, perfectly catered to a Mainlander's palate; I had no doubt that the recipes had been tailored or even invented to suit Mainlander tastes. I ate such an astounding amount of food that S-san, who sat near me, burst out laughing.

But no—this was not the Taiwanese cuisine that I craved!

Before getting into Madame Takada's car, I raised a complaint. "Mishima-san, whatever happened to my tshenn-tsháu-à tea?"

He observed me quietly.

"Please, Mishima-san. Even if it's not tshenn-tsháu-à tea, I'll be happy just to try any Islander street food."

"I will do my best," he said, his brows drawing close together once more.

The following morning, feeling energized from a good night's sleep, I gave my first lecture in Taiwan. It was a smaller event, held specifically for members of the Nisshinkai at the Takada

10. Yáng: According to the staff registry of the Taiwan Government-General, S-san was likely Shimasawa Jirō, special aide to the mayor.

residence's spacious lobby. There were familiar faces from the tea party the day before, as well as younger women who seemed to be relatives of the older ones. I spoke for two hours on the topic "*A Record of Youth* and Me."

Before that, I broke fast with white rice, pickled vegetables, seaweed, a raw egg, and grilled fish, along with miso soup with tofu and fish—the type of meal I would have had back on the Mainland. This dampened my spirits somewhat, and I did not fill my stomach, which in turn filled my head with thoughts of sweets as lunchtime approached. Fried bread sprinkled with sugar, cream cookies, yōkan jelly, red bean buns—those delicacies *were* appetizing, but all were things that I could have eaten in Nagasaki. Taiwan, with its heat that brought torrents of sweat down my back, called for some more hydrating desserts. Cold ò-giô, hún-kué, hún-înn, tshenn-tsháu-à tea, and tropical fruits teeming with juice—how I longed to try them!

After my talk, Madame Takada kindly declined the other women's lunch invitation on my behalf. "May on the Island is already very hot for someone unaccustomed to the climate," she told them. "The heat can easily lead to exhaustion."

Madame Takada, who was nearing her fifties with a dash of silver in her hair, was a rotund woman broad in stature as well as in heart. I'd heard that she was from a former samurai family in Kagoshima—a Kyūshū native like myself.

To me, she said, "Let us skip those formalities for today. How about going into town with my family? The entertainment center in Taichū shows American films and has air-conditioning—it's a very popular spot in the summer."

"Air-conditioning?" I cried. "The Island really *is* incredible!"

Madame Takada chuckled. "Mainlanders always seem to think of the Island as a primitive backcountry! If even Chizuko-sensei thought this after your travels to Ezo and Ryūkyū, then we really don't stand a chance."

I grimaced. "I beg your pardon. I only meant that, before

arriving in Taiwan—I mean, the Island—I had only read some scattered travel literature. My knowledge must be incomplete. I even assumed that, being based in Taichū, I would be able to easily travel to all the cities on the western coast via railroad, even if I am not able to reach the east coast. Was it presumptuous of me to think so?"

"Chizuko-sensei is very well prepared, and not, as you say, presumptuous. Beginning with Kīrun in the north, there are thirteen major stations that end with Takao in the south. We can certainly hold lectures in all thirteen cities. But before we discuss any more logistics," she said, grinning, "shall we eat first?"

"Ah," I pressed my hands to my loudly growling stomach. "How embarrassing. I confess that I am quite the glutton."

"Please don't apologize. As your host, it brings me great joy to see how much you enjoy the food." Her smile deepened with a layer of mystery. "Mishima-san informed me that you would like to try the Island's foods, so I arranged for a special meal to be brought from Taichū City—something my family normally forbids me to eat!"

Is that so! My heart lifted. I hurried into the Takadas' Western-style dining room and saw, on the beautiful mahogany table, an exquisite black lacquer box laced with gold. The box was surrounded by small plates and bowls. A wholly Japanese place setting.

The shock of disappointment left me stiff-limbed.

"Unagi over rice! Made from wild eel native to the Island!" Madame Takada lifted the lid as if opening a present, a childish grin on her face. "It's my absolute favorite. Does Chizuko-sensei like unagi?"

What could I say?

"Yes—I love it."

"Ah, you're even getting teary-eyed!"

"Yes, I suppose I am."

I spent the following week by Madame Takada's side. But because the Takada residence was in the town of Muhō the family relied on automobiles for transportation to Taichū City. I didn't want to be constrained by their driver's schedule, yet my hosts always kindly dismissed my proposals to take public buses or handcars. When I confessed these feelings to Madame Takada, she said, laughing, that I was lionhearted. She began taking me to see places for rent in the city proper.

On my eighth day in Taichū, Mishima made a second appearance on the occasion of my lecture in nearby Toyohara, to be held jointly by Taichū City Hall and the Toyohara District Office. I scanned his taxicab from front to back without spotting anything that vaguely resembled tshenn-tsháu-à tea.

"Mishima-san, I heard that there's a famous Maso temple on Toyohara Street that acts as a religious and cultural hub for the Islanders."[11]

"That is correct."

"I heard that they sell a beverage made of pickled pineapple there."

"Yes, that is true."

"Can I have some of that today?"

"Yes, I will try to arrange it."

I gave him a long look. "Mishima-san, you really have no intention of getting me any Islander food, do you?"

"That is not the case. I will do my best," he said, lying with a straight face.

Insufferable!

As expected, I did not have pineapple juice that day. Likewise

---

11. King: Maso is the Japanese name for Mātsŭ (Taiwanese spelling) or Māzŭ (Hanyu Pinyin), one of the most popular deities worshipped in Taiwan as a goddess of the seas. The Mătsŭ Islands, an archipelago of thirty-six islands, are so named because the goddess is said to have been buried there.

as expected, our lunch in Toyohara was at a restaurant run by Mainlanders. Egg-drop udon topped with fishcake, pan-fried burdock, konjac yam, and white radish.

When the taxicab arrived back at the Takada residence, I headed straight for Madame Takada and began spilling my grievances as though upending a jug of water. "Madame Takada, why, in your opinion, does Mishima-san insist on denying my every wish?"

She could not stop chuckling while I ranted on. She said, "Mishima-san is a rather inflexible young man. I believe that he once took charge of Mainlander guests who insisted on trying kiâm-lâ-á,[12] but they got sick from it and ended up at the hospital. Poor Mishima-san was terrified!"

My attention had already shifted. "But what is kiâm-lâ-á? Is it very delicious?"

Madame Takada laughed so hard that she bent over. "Chizuko-sensei, unfortunately, we will not be able to prepare kiâm-lâ-á for you in this house. Only Islanders can determine the quality of Islander food like that."

"I see." My shoulders drooped.

Madame Takada clapped me on the back encouragingly. "I understand Chizuko-sensei's frustrations, so I've taken the liberty of arranging something that will surely cheer you up."

"Oh—if it is unagi, I am quite full."

"Ha! No, not unagi!" She laughed for a long time before wiping away the tears of mirth and continuing. "It's an Islander interpreter, Ō-san. Since you are traveling to so many cities, it would be much more convenient to have one consistent guide who travels with you. She's a young woman like you, so I imagine you will be able to get along better than you do with Mishima-san."

"Is that so!"

---

12. King: Kiâm-lâ-á is a dish made from salted river clams.

"She comes recommended by members of the Nisshinkai. She used to be a Japanese-language teacher in a primary school and proved herself extremely capable, but has left her position in preparation for her marriage, which is to take place at the end of next year. Oh, and this is a fun coincidence—Ō-san's given name is Chizuru, the same as the first kanji characters in your name. I have no doubt that Ō-san would be able to determine the quality of kiâm-lâ-á."

"But that's—that's fantastic!" I was almost jumping for joy. "When can I meet this Ō-san?"

"Chizuko-sensei would do well to cultivate more patience," she said, holding back laughter again. "If you hadn't been so urgent in communicating your objections to Mishima-san, you would have met Ō-san already."

"What?"

"She's been in the waiting room for some time now."

"Ah!" I made my way to the waiting room in my largest strides. The doors were open; inside, the afternoon sun set the whole room aglow. There was a woman seated in the Western armchair; she had evidently heard my approaching footsteps and was rising ceremoniously to her feet.

A young woman. Pinkish cheeks. Dimples when she smiled. Eyes that glittered with sunlight.

The sudden swelling in my chest made me choke on a lungful of air. "*You . . .*"

"Are you in need of assistance?" Her voice was gentle and amused, with a slightly teasing note.

My teeth and tongue felt like a knotted jumble. "You! That day—the fruit stand—ông-lâi—kue-tsí!"

"Yes. My name is Ông Tshian-ho̍h, or Ō Chizuru in Japanese. It is not our first time meeting, but it is my pleasure all the same."

"Wait, why are you not surprised at all? Besides, aren't you supposed to be a schoolteacher? You look like a student yourself!"

I shook my head, trying to organize my thoughts. "No, sorry, I ought to introduce myself first. I am Aoyama Chizuko. Our names share the same kanji characters—that must be what the Buddhists call en![13] But does that make addressing each other confusing? What on earth should I call you?"

She giggled. I cut myself short.

"Aoyama-sensei is as fascinating as ever," young Chizuru said. "That day, at the fruit stand, the gentleman who came to fetch you had said your name. Later, I heard from my sister that a certain Aoyama-sensei was seeking an interpreter, and made the connection. Please do sit down."

"Oh . . . right . . ." I felt stunned out of coherence.

"Has Aoyama-sensei mastered the skill of eating kue-tsí?"

I shook my head.

Chizuru nudged a plate in my direction. I looked down at the Western tea table to see a plate full of kue-tsí: black, white, and black streaked with white.

"The black ones are the same as the ones roasted in soy sauce from the other day, though one can also use licorice and salt instead of soy sauce. They are made from watermelon seeds, while the white ones are pumpkin, and the striped ones are sunflower. If we get the chance, Aoyama-sensei might also try raw sunflower seeds, which can be found in the countryside."

"And what if I wanted to try kiâm-lâ-á?"

"Kiâm-lâ-á? That is only available at the market at dawn. Perhaps I can bring it to you tomorrow?"

"What about ò-giô, hún-kué, hún-înn, tshenn-tsháu-à tea? Can we get those today?"

"You are quite the student of Taiwanese." She said, dimpling.

13. King: En is Japanese for the Mandarin yuán, the Buddhist concept that translates roughly to fated connections or coincidences between people.

"Lunchtime has only just ended. How about heading to the market at around three o'clock?"

"You—you—are you an angel?"

Chizuru couldn't contain her laughter this time. My head felt so hot that I was sure steam was rising from my scalp. "In that case, for now, please teach me how to eat kue-tsí," I said.

She nodded, smiling.

The ivory teeth cracked open the petite seed.

CHAPTER II

Bí-Thai-Ba̍k / Silver Needle Vermicelli

"Is there something good to eat around here?"

"Hm?"

"Is that not what Aoyama-sensei was thinking?"

"Oh—did I say it out loud?"

I'd been so busy scribbling away in my notebook that I wasn't even aware of having voiced the thought. I stopped writing and looked up at Chi-chan across the dining table.

Chi-chan was the nickname by which I referred to her in the privacy of my mind; in reality, I called her by the more proper Chizuru-san, but I found it disorienting to think of her as such given the overlap in our names. Since she was born in the sixth year of Taishō[1] and therefore was four years younger, I used my seniority as an excuse to nickname her as endearingly as I pleased. *Chi-chan it is!*

Chi-chan's dimples appeared. "No, Aoyama-sensei did not have to say so out loud. Perhaps you are not aware of this, but 'Is there something good to eat around here?' is rather a pet phrase of yours."

"Ha! A glutton can't hide her true colors!" I put down my pencil and began snacking on the deep-fried fava beans on the table between us.

The notes that I'd been so diligently taking were on Taiwan's railway system as explained to me by Chi-chan. Kīrun Station in

1. Yáng: 1917.

the north, Takao Station in the south. At Chikunan Station, which was located in the south of Shinchiku Prefecture, the rail forked into two lines—the Coastal Line and the Mountain Line—that then merged again at Shōka Station. To reach Taichū Station as I did on my first day, one had to take the Mountain Line, which is also known as the Taichū Line.

I hadn't quite decided whether any of this admittedly dry information would be useful for writing fiction, but my hands were quicker to act than my brain, and soon I was filling page after page with smudged pencil script. A writer's reflex, I supposed.

Chi-chan had also been telling me about some recent history. In the tenth year of Shōwa, almost three years before I arrived in Taiwan, a disaster known as the Great Shinchiku-Taichū Earthquake led to countless casualties and collapsed buildings, including one of the major bridges and a tunnel on the Taichū Line. The current railway was an emergency replacement. Despite this, I hadn't noticed anything out of the ordinary on my first ride. No doubt it was thanks to the tireless recovery efforts of people all across the Island that I could enjoy the scenery from the train that day.

Ah, Taiwan!

I felt in awe of the resilience and vitality that coursed through this formidable colony.

"The damaged Gyotōhei Bridge[2] is located between Jyūroppun Station and Taian Station, and used to be known as the Artistic Treasure of the Taiwan Railroad. Nowadays, you can see the remains of the old bridge when taking the train south from Jyūroppun Station. Perhaps Aoyama-sensei missed it because you did not know to look for it."

---

2. Yáng: The Gyotōhei Bridge, still kept in its ruined state as a monument to major earthquakes, is now known as the Yúténgpíng Bridge Ruins or the Lóngténg Bridge Ruins.

"Jyūroppun, you say? I really must have missed it, then! Next time, I'll be sure to pay attention."

From north to south, the Taichū Line consisted of Chikunan, Yokoe, Zōkyō, Hokusei, Byōritsu, Nansei, Dōra, Mitsumata, Jyūroppun, Taian, Kōri, Toyohara, Tanshi, and finally Taichū. My pencil scratched away while my brain whirred. When I first took the train down to Taichū in May, I hadn't bought a bento at Byōritsu Station and instead had two plain onigiri; when I was passing Jyūroppun Station, I would have just gotten started on the five salted duck eggs. Ah—no doubt I'd missed the ruined bridge while I was peeling the eggshells.

Speaking of which, is there something good to eat around here?

This was the inner dialogue I'd arrived at right before Chi-chan voiced my thought out loud.

And now I was stuffing a handful of freshly shelled fava beans into my mouth.

The deep-fried beans were exquisite in texture as well as taste. The thicker ones were airy and crumbly, the thinner ones crisp with a satisfying crunch; the garlic was quite simply addictive. I was worried about eating too quickly, being two handfuls in and already craving a third. It wasn't embarrassment for myself that concerned me, but the fact that Chi-chan, who'd been shelling the beans, did not seem to have eaten a single one.

Alas, the fava beans proved to be the collapsed bridge that disrupted the railway of my professionalism.

"Aoyama-sensei?"

"Huh? Oh, yes. Please continue!"

"The Chikunan and Byōritsu region is known for its Hakka population. The local cuisine and language are very different from here in Taichū. But it might be too early to go into specifics—perhaps I should save the explanations for when we visit in the future."

"Yes, please!"

Chi-chan could be as electrifying as she could be caring. She now nudged a small plate of shelled beans toward me, and I gratefully took my third handful.

Hm? Hold on a second.

"Chizuru-san, you spoke of the Hakka population just now. Do you mean the Mountain Peoples? Come to think of it, after my train passed Byōritsu, I felt like I started to hear different types of Islander dialects. I couldn't understand any of them, of course, but it sounded to me like they were different from what the young man at the fruit stand was speaking."

"Aoyama-sensei really is very attuned to linguistic differences. It must be because you grew up among so many foreigners in Nagasaki," Chi-chan said, continuing to shell fried beans. "In Taichū, the Islanders speak what we call Taiwanese. The Hakka people speak the Hakka dialect, and they refer to the people who speak Taiwanese as Hoklo people and sometimes refer to Taiwanese as the Hoklo dialect, or Hokkien. The indigenous peoples are distinct from both and generally divided into Mountain Peoples and Plains Peoples, but they are in fact composed of many tribes, and each tribe has its own traditions, language, and culture. There are the Tayal and Vonum tribes, for example. In fact, designations such as Mountain Peoples, Plains Peoples, and the umbrella term Bannin are all inaccurate, and there are now some scholars who only refer to these tribes by their original names."

"I see! So Taiwanese doesn't actually refer to the aboriginal languages."

"No. Even before the Japanese Empire received Taiwan, the majority of the population here has been Han people, who are originally from Shina and speak Hokkien. So their dialect has long been referred to as Taiwanese."

"In that case, which ethnic group do you belong to, Chizuru-san?"

Chi-chan's hands stopped. She raised her face and gazed at me quietly. "What a trick question, Aoyama-sensei."

"Hm? Why do you say that?"

"We are all the children of the Heavenly Sovereign. As one family across the seas, there is no division of race—"

I raised my hand to stop her. "Sorry. My mistake. I won't pry any further."

Chi-chan smiled and relaxed her voice. "The Ō family is Hoklo. Specifically, we are Hoklo people from the Zhāngzhōu region in Fújiàn in Shina. In Hokkien, our name is pronounced not Ō but Ông."

"Huh . . . it's all so complicated . . ."

"Anshi[3] said, 'A hundred li's distance breeds different habits, a thousand li's distance breeds different ways of life.' It is not because of such differences and complications that Aoyama-sensei needs an interpreter like myself?"

She managed to quote the ancient philosopher with a perfectly natural expression.

I crushed my fourth handful of fava beans with my molars and released the tension in my shoulders. "I see now that one mustn't underestimate the Island's public education. The erudition of one schoolteacher alone is enough to leave me speechless!"

It was Plum Rain season in Taiwan. The downpour deluged the green willows outside my window; the teeming river coursed day and night.

The rain and roiling river made for a water song that, in the dark of night, pierced through the earthen roof tiles and wooden awning to serenade me in bed. Several times, on the verge of sinking into a dream, I thought about how this music of rain would surely become one of my vivid memories of Taiwan.

3. King: Anshi is the Japanese pronunciation of Yànzǐ (578–500 BCE), a Chinese philosopher and state minister who was a contemporary of Confucius.

In June, I bade farewell to the Takada mansion in Muhō and moved into a Japanese-style cottage next to the Yana River in Kawabata District of Taichū City.

We called it "the cottage" not because it was small, but because it was the smallest among the many houses owned by the Takadas. Madame Takada had shown me several two-story, Western-style houses, but each time I'd felt that they were too large and luxurious for my needs. Eventually, she brought me to this one-story, Japanese-style abode, explaining, "Kawabata District was only developed recently and is still considered a fringe neighborhood in Taichū. Look at all the paddies! How could we let you stay at a place like this? One positive is that the house is new and well built. My son is the only one who comes sometimes when he is visiting Taichū—usually just for a short break and not to spend the night. But it occurred to us that maybe Chizuko-sensei would actually prefer the quiet. Well, what do you think?"

The entrance to the southeast of the house led to a four-tatami foyer; to its right was a Western-style drawing room, to its left a Western-style dining room. The earthen-floored kitchen was eight tatami in size. The study was four tatami, the servant's room six tatami, and the zashiki main room was, impressively, ten tatami. The secondary tsugi room was, like the kitchen, eight tatami. The bathroom was equipped with a full tub and a traditional Japanese toilet as well as a Western toilet. The engawa veranda ran along the house's north and northeast, with excellent natural light and ventilation; it looked out into a garden of magnolia trees, sweet osmanthus trees, and a hedge of golden dewdrop shrubs.

In short, it was compact but perfectly comprehensive.

"This is *beyond* ideal, Madame Takada!"

A resounding laugh rang out from her ample body. "The Takada family has always prided itself on being good hosts."

A true descendant of the Satsuma aristocracy, Madame Takada was quick with her promises and true to her word. She announced that I was to have the house free of charge for the duration of my stay. I returned her generosity of spirit by accepting the offer as resolutely as she proposed it.

"I'll take it!"

Madame Takada's smile was so wide that her plush cheeks squeezed her eyes into crescent moons. "With *this* disposition, Chizuko-sensei will no doubt be somebody of great importance one day."

Even if she was being sarcastic, I could only accept the compliment.

After I moved into the cottage on the eighth of June, Chi-chan began coming over twice a week. Before I knew it, she'd fully equipped me for my new life: lightweight dresses and hats befitting Taiwan's climate; leather oxfords and wooden geta; parasols for sun and umbrellas for rain; mackintosh coats that accommodate my stature; brand-new mosquito nets and lightweight summer blankets. The Takada family had arranged for staff to assist me with such things, and such tasks were not within the purview of an interpreter's job description, but meticulous Chi-chan put everything in order herself. This included securing me a library card at the Prefecture Library, maps of the city and its bus routes, and a list of restaurants suited to dining alone. Everything was done before I could even think of asking for it.

"Chizuru-san is beyond competent—you are omnipotent!"

"Aoyama-sensei exaggerates."

"No no, I really mean it!" I raised my voice to convey my sincerity. "Not only are these fava beans shelled to perfection, even the tea you make tastes better than other tea!"

"I cannot take credit for that—it's just that the tea leaves here are superior," she protested, furrowing her brows.

Ah—so she had *this* expression up her sleeve, not only the imperturbable smile!

Perhaps because of her childlike face, Chi-chan looked sweet-tempered even when she was frowning. She was wearing a nondescript Western dress of a muted color, but even this office-worker attire could not dim her glow.

Earlier that day, she'd arrived at the cottage with a bag of garlic fava beans and patiently answered my various questions. We left at 10:30 for the local girls' high school, where I was to speak on my usual topic, "*A Record of Youth* and Me."

This was Chi-chan's first time accompanying me to a lecture. In the preparation phase, I'd protested that a two-hour lecture was far too long. When she'd proposed two class periods instead, I'd replied childishly—as though making one of my appeals to my aunt Kikuko or Haruno—*Aw, wouldn't one hour be plenty?* Chi-chan had smiled, shook her head, and said she would try to convince the school. Later, we managed to settle on a lecture that was one class period.

One class period—the last before lunch.

I felt hungry already.

The taxi pulled up to the gate of the school and we proceeded on foot, kicking at the rain as we walked.

"Chizuru-san must be pleased to return. This is your alma mater, is it not?"

"It is. Yes, I suppose I should be pleased."

"Are you—not?"

"Well, I have only been gone for three or so years."

It was then that I noticed something unusual in her smile.

A row of six people awaited us at the school's door. We changed into indoor slippers in the midst of small talk, and the principal began leading the way while the others surrounded me.

"Oi, Ō-san," came a clipped, low voice from the shoe cupboards behind us. "You're the personal assistant, yes? Then I'll leave Aoyama-sensei's shoes for you to clean."

What?

I stopped walking and turned back. A middle-aged man who hadn't even ranked high enough to introduce himself to me was lording over Chi-chan. "There's mud here and here, see? You can manage a simple task like this, no?"

The impudence!

I marched over. "Ō-san is my interpreter."

"Ah! Aoyama-sensei, I . . ."

"Please do not make such unreasonable requests of my interpreter."

I took Chi-chan by the arm and tugged her close to me. She stumbled a step and looked up at me with the same curious smile that I'd spotted before we entered.

My chest ballooned with rage. It felt like a sealed barn of burning hay. I had not been this upset since arriving in Taiwan—not even Mishima's bureaucratic manners had roused so much distaste.

When the school bell sounded for lunch, I declined the school's invitation and, without so much as asking for a taxi, stormed out with Chi-chan's wrist in my hand. When we reached the exit and saw the continuing rain, I stomped back to ask for an umbrella but insisted on leaving again immediately.

"Are you not angry, Chizuru-san? If someone had insulted me that way, I would have smacked his face with the shoe!"

"That does sound like something Aoyama-sensei would do."

"The nerve of the man! I can't believe it! Ah—you know what the best cure for anger is? Food! Is there something good to eat around here?"

Hehe. Chi-chan's chuckle rang out as clearly as ever.

"Let us go to Shintomichō Market. Aoyama-sensei enjoys sashimi, yes?"

Emboldened by my anger, I declared, "I can eat a whole tuna by myself right now!"

"I look forward to witnessing it."

Chi-chan seemed at ease, looking more amused by my reaction than displeased by what had occurred. Meanwhile, I charged forward as though I could tear through the curtain of rain. I didn't, couldn't understand: Why did Chi-chan have to suffer this kind of treatment?

"*Technically,* yes, but—in the end, a privately hired female Islander interpreter is not so different from an odd-job worker, no?"

The speaker was I-san, an administrator at the local university's agriculture department. There was no trace of shame on his face as he said these words.

He spoke in Japanese, but it sounded to me like an unknown language.

Thanks to Madame Takada's and the Nisshinkai's local networks, I was invited to event after event in the Taichū area. Shortly after the lecture at the girls' school, I visited the Taichū branch of Taihoku Imperial University and, assuming that my experience at the high school had been a disagreeable anomaly, complained of the incident to my host, I-san. He, however, looked bewildered. "Women interpreters are rare in the first place, and she is an Islander on top of that . . . besides, how would you rank her professional abilities, Aoyama-sensei? She used to teach the national language, but it was only at a public school[4] after all . . ."

Was this some sort of disease spreading across the Island?

It wasn't as though I'd never met anyone who disliked "ca-

4. Yáng: Under Japanese rule, Taiwan's early education system was divided into elementary schools (shō-gakkō) for Japanese Mainlanders and public schools (kō-gakkō) for Taiwanese Islanders. The elementary schools shared the same curricula as schools in the Japanese Mainland, whereas the public schools had courses in both the national language (Japanese) and local dialects. Seeing as the nationwide exams were conducted exclusively in Japanese, elementary school students had a greater advantage. Here, I-san is implying that since Ō Chizuru taught at a public school, her linguistic abilities may be inferior to those of a professional interpreter.

reer women" before. After my book was adapted into a movie, I'd heard my fair share of disparaging comments at literary events. *Why do they call her a "woman writer"? Emphasizing the "woman" is probably just a way of soliciting patrons, if you catch my drift!* And, *With the holy war ahead of us, a woman's only duty is to head on home and make a kid! Or better yet, two!* But I-san was polite and attentive toward me, and his prejudice did not seem to be directed toward working women generally.

In my confusion, I'd somehow missed the opportunity to object to his last statement. "But where is Ō-san?" I asked. "Is she already waiting at the restaurant?"

"Since today's event will not require an interpreter, we have asked her to go home."

"Go home?"

"Yes."

I pressed at my stomach to contain the growing conflagration within. "If that is the case, you must excuse me from today's luncheon as well."

I-san looked at me with unconcealed shock. "Aoyama-sensei? What—?"

"When I first arrived on the Island, my assigned interpreter was Mishima-san from Taichū City Hall. I wonder, I-san, if it had been Mishima-san here with me today, would the school have asked him to 'go home'?"

"Of course not," I-san said, his confusion sincere. "But Mishima-san is a city employee."

Am I *the one missing something here?*

Either way, I did not have the equanimity to accept this arrangement. I-san, looking beleaguered, bowed me off in a taxi. Back at the cottage, I entered through the kitchen and, as I expected, saw Chi-chan sitting at the Western-style table in the dining area.

"Have you eaten, Chizuru-san?" I asked.

"Yes."

"Well, *I'm* starving!" I called out, feeling suddenly as though I, too, had been wronged.

Chi-chan laughed.

How can she laugh at a time like this?

But it was then that I noticed the smell of broth, soy sauce, and chives. It was a scent that I recognized from walking through market stalls.

What's that?

"It's bí-thai-ba̍k," Chi-chan said, "noodles made from ground rice. Savory bí-thai-ba̍k is served with pork bone broth, topped with minced pork stewed in soy sauce and chives."

"But that sounds *unbearably* good!" I cried, kicking off my shoes.

"Islanders usually eat bí-thai-ba̍k as a small dish meant for snacking, and I bought some thinking that you might not have enjoyed the banquet. I got back not so long ago—the soup is still hot. But perhaps Aoyama-sensei would prefer me to reheat it?"

Who could make a fuss over reheating when something looked so delicious? I slurped up the bí-thai-ba̍k as quickly as I would soba noodles. Whenever I neared the bottom of my bowl, Chi-chan would serve me another ladle, again and again until the whole pot was emptied.

"Are you full, Aoyama-sensei?"

I nodded, then shook my head.

She laughed. "What can that mean?"

"Chizuru-san."

"Yes?"

"Taiwan is a colony."

"Yes, indeed."

"Before the Nisshinkai invited me, there was a Mainland publisher that offered to pay for my travels in Taiwan so long as I agreed to write articles promoting the Southern Expansion

Policy. I turned them down. The idea of using my pen as a weapon for war—ha! I think it a laughable and petty tactic for a nation that calls itself the Empire of the Sun. Of course, I could never explicitly say anything like that in public. But there is nothing I dislike more than social etiquette at the expense of reason—including irrational ideas like *women must marry*. It drives me mad." I could not stop myself once I'd gotten started. "*If*, one day, the war reaches a stage when writers *must* wield their pens like guns, I would probably toss mine and run away. And *if* the day comes that I must marry, I would shave my head and become a nun. Can you understand how I feel, Chizuru-san?"

"I believe that Aoyama-sensei is capable of all these things, yes."

"Chizuru-san," I said formally, "I would like to be friends with you."

The rain had let up for the moment.

The awning was folded away and the glass sliding doors pushed aside, letting daylight and fresh breeze into the room.

Chi-chan and I sat eating lychee on the engawa veranda.

"Are we not going to Kappan Mountain[5] today?" Chi-chan asked. "Or the sugar factory?"

"Those are just attractions designated by the Taiwan Government-General."

The *Travel Guide to Taiwan's Railways* that Chi-chan had brought me included a "Map of Highlights," which I felt were not so different from the landmarks advertised by tourism companies on the Mainland. I told Chi-chan that I wasn't interested in such sights, and she didn't seem at all surprised.

"I feel that I am beginning to understand Aoyama-sensei's approach to things."

5. King: Present-day Jiaŏbǎnshān (Jiaŏbǎn Mountain).

"But don't you agree? Rushing to catch a bus or a train, rushing from one attraction to the next—that kind of 'touring' is just moving around, not 'traveling.'"

"Then how would you define traveling?"

"Traveling is *living* in a foreign place."

"Living?"

"As in, experiencing all four seasons of normal life in a foreign place. Leaving behind a home environment where one's habits have settled into old, tired ways and spending one's days somewhere else, trying to find some new feeling in the mere act of being alive in this world. In this sense, traveling is a way of cleansing one's body and mind—starting afresh."

"Ah, I see. Madame Takada did say that you are staying on the Island until next year."

"Oh, yes! It was originally meant to be half a year, but thanks to Madame Takada's help, I can now stay for a whole year by publishing more travel articles and giving more lectures. Then, after I go back to Kyūshū, I can reorganize the dispatches into a book—maybe something titled *Taiwan Travelogue*. If I were to write something like that, it would be much more holistic to cover all four seasons, don't you think?"

Anybody else would have scoffed. A man would have scolded me—*It's a travesty, letting a good-for-nothing woman run wild abroad for a whole year.* Even Aunt Kikuko, who had raised me, was stern and cautionary in her telegrams: "Forget not home stop. Awaiting your return full stop."

But Chi-chan only smiled. "Yes, much more holistic."

I chuckled. The sun shone bright after the rain. Mottled light danced on Chi-chan's fingers as well as on the lychee fruit that gleamed white when they were relieved of their red armor. She'd brought them over in the morning, snipped off their black leaves, washed and wiped them dry, and laid them out on some newspaper. Sitting on the veranda, she made an incision at each stem with a small knife, gave it a twist, and nimbly extracted the pearly fruit from its spiked skin. She quietly piled these into a small hill in a glass bowl.

Soshoku,[6] the famed poet from Northern Shina, once wrote, "The promise of three hundred lychee a day / would make me a willing Southerner." I thought, if sensei had Chi-chan by his side, he would probably have had six hundred a day. Perhaps he would have even written a poem just for her. I, on the other hand, was a bumbling fool by comparison. I could neither write in verse nor peel my own lychee—despite enlisting both my fingers and my teeth, I could barely fish out the seeds, and my hands were soon coated in sticky juice.

"Please eat," Chi-chan said, pushing the pile of peeled fruit toward me. She neatly bundled up the lychee debris in the newspaper and headed toward the kitchen. When she returned, it was with hot tea on a tray.

Thorough, thoughtful, impeccable Chi-chan.

The light notes of Taiwan's fragrant oolong are, without a doubt, the best possible companion to the nectar of lychee. One sip of tea, two bites of lychee—this burst of perfection on my palate was enough to make me plagiarize Soshoku-sensei: "In Taiwan, all seasons are spring / fruit grows anew day after day. The promise of daily lychee / would make me an unwilling busy tourist."[7]

Chi-chan laughed. "What on earth was that?"

"All I'm saying is, is it not much better to eat lychee here like this than to visit Kappan Mountain or whatnot? Sweating through our clothes just to catch a glimpse of a sight that humans have arbitrarily dubbed 'famous' can make us forget that we are surrounded by wonderful things every day. What a shame."

---

6. King: Soshoku is the Japanese name for Sū Dōngpō (1037–1101).

7. Yáng: The original poem reads, "All seasons are spring at the foot of Luófú Mountain / fresh loquats and ripe plums morn after morn. The promise of three hundred lychee a day / would make me a willing Southerner" (English translation by King).

"Madame Takada was right—Aoyama-sensei will no doubt be somebody of great importance one day."

"Do I detect some sarcasm?"

"No sarcasm—and not mere politeness either."

"Think about it. I have yet to spend two months on the Island, but I already have enough business cards from lectures and tea talks and luncheons and banquets to make a deck of playing cards—admit it, we could basically play karuta![8] Now *this* type of day, lounging at home, *this* is what I call living."

Without waiting for her to reply, I continued pontificating on what I saw as "real living" and "real travel": not just socializing and making business connections, but eating, walking, sleeping—the things that one would normally do at home. That was the way in which I wanted to gain a deeper understanding of the Islanders' lives. Chi-chan nodded and smiled while I talked on.

"But, Chizuru-san, are you not eating any of the lychee? Please don't tell me you peeled all these just for me!"

"I had some at the market earlier. Lychee is an inflammatory fruit in Shina medicine terms—with my constitution, I am not supposed to have too much at once."

"Oh, I see . . ."

"But I really did assume that Aoyama-sensei would want to see Kappan Mountain."

"This again! Why would you think that? Because of the aborigines who live there?"

"No, because of the handcars. Have you ever ridden one? They

---

8. Yáng: Karuta, also known as uta-garuta, is a competitive card game traditionally played during the Japanese New Year. A common form is based on *Ogura Hyakunin Isshu*, a collection of one hundred poems written by one hundred poets. The cards are divided into a hundred "reading cards" and a hundred "grabbing cards." One poem is read out loud, and players compete to identify and "grab" the corresponding card as quickly as possible.

run on rails, but are pushed manually by the drivers, who hop on board after they set the car in motion and hop off to push again when the car slows down. The handcars on Kappan Mountain are said to be exhilarating going downhill. I have heard many visitors say that it left a deep impression on them."

"Aha. And to you, I seem like the thrill-seeking type?"

"Perhaps I should put it this way: *had* Aoyama-sensei wished to visit Kappan Mountain, I would have tried to persuade you out of it."

"And why is that?"

"It is an old tale, but I once heard that there was a young police officer posted on the mountain who, whether out of impatience or a sense of adventure, always asked the drivers to push the handcar with all their strength even when going downhill. The drivers all tried to talk him out of it, but to no avail."

"And?"

"Once, it was going far too fast. There was another handcar on its way uphill, but the speeding car could not brake in time and they crashed. The young police officer flew off the car."

"Flew?"

"Yes. He soared across the sky until he landed on the rail and rolled to a stop."

Her tone was quiet and serene, but I, picturing the scene, burst into laughter. "What a tragic tale!"

"But you are laughing," she said, though she, too, was showing her dimples.

"What a bizarre story! Where does one hear such things?"

"But such stories are why you want a local interpreter like myself, Aoyama-sensei."

I wagged my finger. "As I said before, you are not to be underestimated!" I picked up a lychee and prodded it into Chi-chan's mouth. She wasn't quick enough to dodge it and scowled at me with bulging cheeks.

"Aoyama-sensei, I told you I cannot."

"But is it not incredibly sweet? Lychee inflames, but in Shina medicine, watermelon tempers, which counters inflammation, am I right? We will just have to eat some watermelon later."

Chi-chan looked at a loss in the face of my rascally logic.

"But how will you be able to eat lunch?"

"Are we not having your homemade bí-thai-ba̍k vermicelli for lunch? When it comes to good food, I will forever have room in my stomach."

I'd asked Chi-chan many questions about the making of bí-thai-ba̍k since first eating it. The method went: grind Taiwanese long-grained rice into a thick pulp, drain the water, knead it into balls of dough, cook some of it partially, knead the semicooked dough together with raw dough until it becomes one large, soft mass, then push it through the lattice of a metal sieve to create long strips. Sweet bí-thai-ba̍k could be eaten hot or cold, and was popularly eaten cold in the summer, topped with mung beans, red beans, and the sweet jellies that I'd been pining after: sian-tsháu[9] and ò-giô. The thought of all these treasures in one great bowl was more dazzling to me than any jewelry box.

But that was the dessert version. That day, for lunch, we were again to have savory bí-thai-ba̍k, which could be eaten with pork bone broth or seafood broth. While the one I ate last time had minced pork and chives, there were other choices of toppings such as fried red onion, soy sauce–braised egg, or meatballs. Farther south, in Tainan or Takao, they tended to add fish or fresh oysters.

In short, Chi-chan explained, there was no set recipe for bí-thai-ba̍k, meaning different regions could distinguish themselves with different flavors. On this note, I immediately exclaimed, "Then I want to try Kyūshū-style bí-thai-ba̍k!"

Which would be what, exactly? A sweetish, soy sauce–heavy flavor?

---

9. King: Sian-tsháu, or xiān-cǎo in Mandarin Chinese, is commonly referred to in English as grass jelly. It is made from Chinese mesona, a type of mint.

We won't know until we try!

"Aoyama-sensei, you *claim* to have unlimited room, but I bought two whole kin[10] of bí-thai-ba̍k this morning, and it isn't something that can be left sitting, so you have to finish it all in one meal."

"But I will have Chizuru-san to help me."

"I am not nearly as talented an eater as you—my stomach is already full from dealing with your antics."

"Haha! What a conundrum!"

The feigned anger on her cherubic face was wholly ineffective as a scare tactic.

"The way I feel right now, I can eat two hundred kin of bí-thai-ba̍k!"

She broke into a smile. "Then, once again, I look forward to witnessing it."

The last time she said this, after that unpleasant day at the school, I didn't end up eating a whole tuna after all. That said, I did manage to wolf down a box of sushi rice, a banquet-sized plate of sashimi, stewed sweetfish, grilled mushrooms, fried burdock roots, bamboo shoot salad, tamagoyaki sweet omelet, grated yam with salted seaweed, steamed chawanmushi egg custard, clear clam broth, and, finally, unagi. I'd devoured all this in front of Chi-chan with the bearing of a sumo wrestler.

One of my sisters once said—and I really had to concur with her—that I had a monster's appetite. But Chi-chan had barely batted an eye. This in itself was strange, and even I, undiscerning as I was, could see that she was unusual in an elusive yet noticeable way.

Despite being a Japanese teacher at a public school and a graduate of a women's high school, and hailing from a family well-to-do enough to associate with the Nisshinkai, Chi-chan

---

10. King: One kin is approximately half a kilogram or one pound.

had no airs or arrogance about her. On the other hand, she did not simply swallow everything that came her way, either. She protested and stated her opinion, but even when she was protesting, she was somehow still amiable.

With her, I felt as though I had fallen off a cliff and was plunging through cloud and mist.

When I'd expressed the desire to be friends, she had neither consented nor refused. She had simply looked at me for a while, then smiled, then said, "I see."

That smile was like a Noh mask.

Inscrutable.

"Chizuru-san."

"Yes?"

"Do you not think that my appetite is like that of a monster's?"

A dimpled smile—still a perfect mask. "According to *Shǐjì*, 'The emperor is sustained by his people, the people are sustained by food.'[11] A large appetite is a blessing, I should think."

As always, her response was watertight. I clapped my hands together, laughing.

"Perfect composure even when you are face-to-face with a monster! I *must* have you as a friend. From this day on, please allow me the privilege of calling you 'Chi-chan'!"

11. King: *Shǐjì*, also known in English as *Records of the Grand Historian*, is the definitive history of ancient China written in the first century BCE by the Chinese historian Sīmǎ Qiān.

CHAPTER III

Muâ-Ínn-Thng / Jute Soup

People who are good with their hands look graceful even when they are shelling peanuts.

Chi-chan's left thumb and index finger pinched the softened skin while her right hand sliced into it with a small silver spoon, and the glistening kernels tumbled down into the plate waiting below. The motion was as seamless as the drifting of clouds or the flowing of water. I was faster at peeling peanuts than I was at lychee, but even so, I couldn't hold a candle to the speed and elegance of her movements.

I'd been tempted into buying ten sen's worth of salt-boiled peanuts by the scent wafting down the street. The young vendor had been calling out at customers as if singing a song.

Chi-chan passed a heap of kernels to me on a plate. I poured a handful into my mouth.

"Chi-chan, have you heard of Izumi Kyōka?"

"The one who wrote *The Holy Man of Mount Kōya*?"

"I heard that Izumi-sensei also has a serious case of germophobia."

"I am not a germophobe, Aoyama-sensei."

I chomped on my second handful of peanuts as a cow or horse would, thoroughly relishing the taste. "But seriously, you take so much care with cleanliness, I can't help but wonder if you secretly aspire to become a doctor."

"That would be impossible."

I shook my head and sighed dramatically. "Wrong again!"

We were in Shōka. There had been a screening of *A Record*

of Youth at Shōka Theatre, followed by a discussion over tea. For lunch, we were treated to a full Taiwanese-style banquet at Kōhinkaku, a newly opened restaurant: steamed shrimp, scallion-roasted chicken, vegetable fish broth, almond tofu jelly, and candied lotus seeds.

I never managed to truly eat at such ceremonious events, and Chi-chan, knowing me, took me to nearby Shōsei Street after we bade farewell to our patrons. We stopped by different vendors to taste various street foods: steamed pork buns, barley malt candy, ò-giô, as well as taiko manjū[1] that had been introduced here from the Mainland.

Shōka's streets gave me the impression of traveling through time. Under Qīng rule, what was now Shōka City used to be surrounded by a tall brick rampart and multiple gates. Shōsei Street connected the West and North Gates; for centuries, Islanders have worked, fallen in love, made families, and created daily routines in this vibrant neighborhood. The old city walls had been torn down when the city was replanned during the Taishō era, and Chi-chan showed me where the city gates used to be.

Throughout all these changes within the city, its view of abutting Hakke Mountain had remained unchanged. Under the cobalt sky and summer sun, the mountain looked like a floating green pond. Without context, it seemed to me but an unremarkable, smallish hill, and among tourists it was primarily known only for its hot springs, yet it was designated in the Qīng period as one of the Eight Great Sights of Shōka, named the Stockade Overlooking the Sea because its former name was Dìngjūn Mountain, which meant something like "Settled Army Mountain" due to its militarily advantageous position.

---

1. Yáng: Taiko manjū is one of many names for what is now known in Taiwan as red bean cakes or wheel cakes.

I paused to wonder what the Islanders of the past felt when they were looking out at the waters from the military mountain. The heat drenched my clothes and diluted all emotions. I distracted myself from the discomfort by thinking of another poem—Toho's lament from over a thousand years ago: *The nation shattered, mountains and rivers remain.*[2] The poignancy hardly applied to my own situation at the time, but even so, the idea of it made my chest swell.

In the end, however, even the literary greats could not shield me from the pulsing midday sun for long. Soon, I was dragging Chi-chan into a tearoom to seek the relief of electric fans. Sparkling water and iced coffee displaced Toho in my mind.

If we'd been in a café instead of a tearoom, I would have opted for two cold beers—that was what the weather and the boiled peanuts called for.[3] Alas, alas! As women, the inability to simply waltz into a café was yet another inconvenience we had to endure. When would such inconveniences come to an end?

My monologue was interrupted by the arrival of jam sandwiches, ham sandwiches, and cream puffs. Everything was seventy sen each; as on the Mainland, tearooms on the Island were not cheap, though the bill would have no doubt doubled or tripled in a café. In this sense, the tearoom wasn't so bad a

---

2. Yáng: From Tang dynasty poet Dù Fǔ (Japanese pronunciation: Toho)'s "Spring Prospect": "The nation shattered, mountains and rivers remain; / city in spring, grass and trees burgeoning. / Feeling the times, blossoms draw tears; / hating separation, birds alarm the heart. / Beacon fires three months in succession, / a letter from home worth ten thousand in gold. / White hairs, fewer for the scratching, / soon too few to hold a hairpin up." (English translation by Burton Watson.)

3. Yáng: The tearoom here refers to a kissaten, a type of Japanese establishment founded as distinct from cafés, which were known at the time for nightlife and having female waitstaff who served a male clientele. By contrast, kissaten tearooms did not sell alcohol, and their entertainment-free service was reflected in the lower prices.

choice—or so I told Chi-chan, rambling as I toweled the sweat off of my face and neck.

"With Aoyama-sensei's ambition, I am sure you can open a tearoom that sells beer one day."

"But there are the wartime restrictions on alcohol, too. Wait, no, what am I saying? I *have* no business ambitions!"

"Very true. You explained all of your ambitions in the film, after all."

"Oh, that?" I laughed. "Movies are movies. Novels are novels. I am me."

"Yes, I know," Chi-chan said. Her long eyelashes fluttered like a movie's flickering title cards.

The film *A Record of Youth* only captured a portion of the novel of the same name.

The female protagonist had been a large baby whose size led to a difficult birth that took her mother's life. Her father did the closest thing he could to abandoning her by sending her off to a tertiary branch of his large family, to be raised across the sea and out of sight in Kyūshū: "The child is cursed." Despite wagging tongues, the girl's uncle personally taught her to read and write. When she was nine, however, the kindhearted uncle died in a horse carriage accident; if his wife hadn't insisted on keeping the girl, she would have been sent off to a convent.

And thus, despite being born into wealth, the girl had been dismissed from the esteemed "head family" and relegated to a "branch family" in Nagasaki with no male heirs or prospects. At a young age, she had lost a parent as well as a beloved parent figure, and her short life was filled with malicious gossip. The only two things she could depend on were her noble-hearted aunt and the enormous collection of books in her aunt and uncle's home. She questioned whether there was any meaning to the fact of her being alive—whether both she and the world would be better off if she threw herself off Nagasaki's port. But she found solace in literature, and officially launched her career as a writer the year after graduating from high school.

It made me blush to talk about my own work in this way, but the truth remained that, with their detailed description of a girl's thoughts and feelings, both the novel and the film *A Record of Youth* were known to bring tears to women readers and viewers of all ages. One image in particular was widely distributed on movie posters and postcards: Y-san, the leading actress, standing at Nagasaki Port in her high school sailor uniform, the profile of her face turned toward the sea. The image came from the film's most critical scene, with the camera trained on Y-san's face, which transformed from disorientation to agitated outrage, then to a visible effort at restraint that morphed into silent tears of frustration, then, finally, to an expression of hardened determination. The title card read: "My life will *not* end here." As she turned resolutely and walked away from the sea, the cinema inevitably filled with applause.

After the novel was published and the film released, I often received encouraging comments in letters and in person: "Aoyama-sensei, thank goodness you are alive and well," "Thank you for continuing to write," et cetera.

Movies are movies. Novels are novels. I am me.

But this much was true of both my protagonist and myself: my ambitions had always been literary. I turned the question around on Chi-chan and her ambitions.

"Schoolteacher?"

"I have already resigned."

"But that might've been because you plan on taking your own studies further! Hmm. Musician?"

"No, I have no talent in playing or singing."

"Typist?"

"You do not have to keep guessing, Aoyama-sensei."

And it wasn't doctor either, apparently.

My fingers were soon oily from the peanuts, sandwiches, and cream puffs. Chi-chan leisurely wiped down her own hands without touching a single peanut herself. Instead, she used her clean, pale hands to flip through her notebook. Though Chi-chan never ate much at those crowded banquets, she nevertheless ate *something*. What was the difference, I wondered, between those occasions and these with me?

Never mind. At least she drank some iced coffee this time.

"It's still early. Would Aoyama-sensei like to visit the ancient town of Rokkō? There is a train thirty minutes from now. Although we would not return to Taichū until the evening in this case."

I recognized the name as one of the three great towns of Taiwan: Fujyō, Rokkō, Banka.[4] Of *course* we had to go!

I set down my dirty towel and rose to wash my hands in the restroom. When I returned, there were two women standing next to our table. Chi-chan sat shrouded in their shadows; they had their backs to me, though I could deduce from their dresses that they were young. Shōka was only a forty-minute train ride from Taichū—perhaps they were acquaintances of Chi-chan's.

"To think that even someone who grew up on XXX can dine in tearooms now!"

"XXX" was said in Taiwanese. I couldn't understand it.

The other woman's shoulders shook slightly as she laughed. "Don't say *that*. Maybe she's a waitress here!"

I placed one hand on each of their shoulders. They jumped at the sudden touch and, due to my height, took several steps back to look up at me.

I mustered all my strength to beam at them as cheerfully as

4. King: These three Qīng-period financial hubs (Mandarin: Fǔchéng, Lùgǎng, Měngjiǎ) are located in modern-day Táinán, Chānghuà, and Táipěi, respectively.

I could. "I beg your pardon, but I must ask: Why might two civilized ladies such as yourselves behave so rudely to my guest?"

Whether it was because of my stature or the Tōkyō accent that I exaggerated, the effect was immediate: the two women flushed and, without saying another word, scurried away with their heads lowered. I sat back down in my seat.

I gazed at Chi-chan. She looked back at me, her two sweet dimples visible. But that wasn't a smile—it was just an arrangement of facial muscles that showed her dimples.

I did not wish to back down in the face of her unwavering Noh mask. "So—you won't explain?"

"Thank you, Aoyama-sensei, for your help."

"That's not what I mean."

"What do you mean?"

"Who were they?"

"They were my distantly related sisters."

"Can *sisters* say such insolent things?"

"To be fair, there *are* high school graduates who work as waitresses in tearooms." The perfect, seamless mask.

My shoulders collapsed. "What was it that they said? XXX?"

Chi-chan chuckled. "You have remarkable hearing, Aoyama-sensei. Muâ-ínn-thng is a soup made from newly grown jute leaves."

"I would like to have this muâ-ínn-thng when we get back to Taichū."

"Muâ-ínn-thng does not taste good. Nor is it sold in markets."

I feigned surprise. "Oh, really? It doesn't taste good?"

Curled lips. "It is very bitter. Forget Mainlanders—even most Islanders would not think of drinking it."

"In other words, it's poor people's food, correct?" Without waiting for her reaction, I pressed on. "As for why the markets don't sell muâ-ínn-thng, that's because jute is used for making bags and ropes, so the jute leaves used in this soup must be a by-product of the processing done on jute farms, correct? Which means that other than families who plant jute, only very poor families would make this soup, correct? I've heard of similar practices in Hokkaido and Ryūkyū. No—I'm sure that if I did some research, I would learn that people in Tōkyō do the same thing."

"Aoyama-sensei is very knowledgeable on—"

"No, what I'm trying to ask is, why would they say that you grew up on muâ-ínn-thng? You got this interpreter position through your sister, who knows Madame Takada, which must mean that your family, the Ō family, has similar rank as the members of Nisshinkai. And, as far as I know, the women members of Nisshinkai all hail from socially or politically important families in Taichū. Am I wrong?"

"I am surprised to hear how much Aoyama-sensei cares about the birth of her interpreter," she said, her smile shallowing. Then, softly: "I will ask Madame Takada to find a more suitable replacement."

"Chi-chan," I said, taking care to enunciate each word, "I only care because I care about *you*."

She stopped smiling. I grinned. "I care about *you*, my Islander friend, and so I did a lot of research on the Island. How can I make you understand, Chi-chan? I truly, sincerely wish to be friends with you."

After the tearoom, we took the train to Rokkō.

Looking back on the rest of that trip, I have only a vague recollection of the old, atmospheric streets—even the famous temple[5] barely made an impression. This wasn't because Rokkō was forgettable, but because our conversation made the streets of the ancient town recede like a low tide. In their stead, the

5. King: This refers to Lúngshān Temple.

wave that surged toward me was the complicated story of a Taiwanese Islander family.

Early under the rule of Qīng's Emperor Jiāqìng, the Ō family, or the Ông family in Taiwanese Hokkien, traversed the sea from Shina to Taiwan as one of the "ancestral pioneer families." To this day, the family remains influential and wealthy agricultural landowners based in Chōkyōshitō, Taichū. When Japan received Taiwan, the Ō family pledged loyalty to the Empire.

Chi-chan's father was the sixth head of the family in its long lineage. He had three sons and three daughters by his wife and concubines, and Chi-chan was the daughter of one such concubine.

Large Islander families had complex relations, I learned. Chi-chan's mother was born to a poor farming family, and while she was an adolescent became a gē-tòa—the Island's take on the geisha profession—to earn her keep. It was there that she caught the attention of Master Ō, who took her as a concubine. Though the Ō family was well off and had plenty of resources to spare, they regarded concubines as lowly and therefore neglected their children; while the sons received some priority treatment, the daughters of concubines were so overlooked that they sometimes went hungry. Thus, Chi-chan was at one point sent to live with her mother's jute-farming family, hence the pejorative of being someone who "grew up on jute soup." Luckily, her precociousness was soon noticed and encouraged, which eventually earned her favor with members of the Ō family.

I was confused. "What do you mean by 'favor'?" Islander and Mainlander women all shared the fate of being treated as their families' property. What difference could favoritism make?

Chi-chan chuckled. "I meant that I grew close to my sister. It was thanks to her favor that I became Aoyama-sensei's interpreter, remember?"

"Chi-chan, you're being evasive again."

"Ah—Aoyama-sensei is beginning to see through me."

Hmph.

"My fiancé is an accomplished man who has lived on the Mainland since he was young. Our two families are eager to form a business partnership—which, in a way, has successfully begun with our engagement."

"What? Is *that* what you mean by favor?"

"A concubine's child usually cannot escape the fate of concubinage herself, you see."

"In the Qīng period, you mean!"

"Not quite—the Island still maintains old customs. But even if they are not concubines, such daughters are often married off to rich but old widowers. A more brazen family might even marry them to long-serving laborers, trading daughters for a more dedicated workforce. All in all, I have been quite fortunate. Thanks to the Empire's advocacy for the national language, my position as a Japanese-language teacher qualifies as a coveted dowry among Taiwanese families. That was how I managed to secure such a distinguished fiancé."

My brows were so furrowed that my whole face felt puckered. "I still can't quite accept this."

"My father and sister arranged the marriage for me despite objections from others. Given my fiancé's modern education on the Mainland, we are likely to complement each other and have a happy marriage. That was my father and sister's way of showing their love for me, I believe."

"But shouldn't you refuse this sort of arrangement altogether? There must be other paths aside from marriage!"

She cocked her head as she looked at me, her eyes like crescent moons. "Most women in the world share similar fates. Seeing as there is only one general path, the choices that allow one to walk the best possible specific path are the best choices."

"I can't understand it. Oh, hold on, I see—does Chi-chan aspire to run a large family? As a matriarch?"

"Alas, my ambitions are not nearly so bold."

Wrong again.

But I was happy to be wrong with this particular guess. Fussing around with the minutiae of family politics in a dark mansion—that would have been far beneath her!

I added a spring to my step as we walked on, and it took me one kan[6] to remember the discrepancy in our strides. I stopped to wait for Chi-chan, who had fallen behind.

"Chi-chan, you said that your family has three sons and three daughters, but this sister whom you're closest to is—a half sister? Not one of your mother's children?"

"Ah—Aoyama-sensei is very perceptive."

"In reality, you aren't close to any of them, are you?"

"Does Aoyama-sensei aspire to become a detective?"

"I take that question to mean that you, too, read detective novels. In which case, hear me out on my deduction: Seeing as this distinguished fiancé was educated on the Mainland, your sister thought, why not let her interpret for a Mainlander since she's not doing anything before the wedding anyhow? If nothing else, it'd help her pick up Mainland customs. Am I right? In this case, even though Chi-chan supposedly volunteered to be my interpreter, it was actually your sister's wish—was it not?" I looked at her rather aggressively.

"Aoyama-sensei, I did not lie to you," she said. "I simply did not reveal the whole truth, see?"

"Doesn't that count as lying?"

"And by following my sister's wishes, I managed to make a rare friend like Aoyama-sensei. Do you not think congratulations are in order?"

I felt, suddenly, that I had lost the argument. I could only grumble some meaningless noises in reply.

We walked for a while, side by side.

---

6. Yáng: One kan is approximately 1.8 meters or six feet.

"If that's the case, don't call me 'sensei' anymore!"

"Aoyama-san, then."

"Yes."

Islander names often carried more layers of meaning than Mainlander names, which I found fascinating. In order from eldest to youngest, Chi-chan's siblings and the literal meanings of their names were: eldest sister, "surpassing valiance"; eldest brother, "illustrious skies"; second brother, "ten thousand miles"; third brother, "sagacious skies"; Chi-chan, "a thousand cranes"; younger sister, "surpassing vigor." I could see from the characters alone that the children of the wife were imbued with heavenly blessings and high hopes, whereas the children of the concubine—the second brother and Chi-chan—were bestowed a number character paired with an auspicious character. The numeric diminution from "ten thousand miles" to "a thousand cranes" perhaps implied a wish for the concubine not to have any more children.

Chi-chan's older brothers had each been allocated different sections of the family's land, real estate, and businesses to manage. Her older sister was married to a man from a banking family in Taichū, and already had children. I asked and Chi-chan confirmed that it was this half sister who was friendly with Madame Takada, via her husband's connections.

As for the younger half sister, it turned out that she was studying at a music conservatory in Tōkyō and was expected to graduate the following spring.

"In that case, she must be very close to Chi-chan in age."

"Yes."

"In that case, if that fiancé of yours is so exceptional, why is he not betrothed to your younger sister instead? They're both already on the Mainland—wouldn't it be easier for them to marry?"

"Because the characters of their names clash. My fiancé's name is Hideo, and my sister shares the 'o' character of 'vigor' with him, except her name literally means 'to surpass o.' Both families thought it an inappropriate match."

"Hm . . ."

We'd been walking the ancient red-brick roads for a long time and chose to rest our feet at a street stall in the market. Its main offering was a meatball soup—all of the hand-rolled meatballs were different in shape and spiced with fragrant cilantro. Despite the unsavory nature of our conversation, I nevertheless managed to devour three whole bowls, and bought some more to take home.

Before I knew it, we were clutching bags upon bags of bamboo-wrapped rice dumplings,[7] meatballs, taro balls, and an impressively wide variety of desserts. We had no choice but to set them down on the floor of the station platform as we awaited the train back to Shōka.

Chi-chan hadn't objected to my aimless itinerary, perhaps in part because I'd bought her a Han-language[8] novel in the market as a gift.

On the Island, daylight lingered even after six in the evening. Thread by thread, the blue-and-white light turned yellow, orange, red. On the platform, the glimmer of sunset traced the profile of Chi-chan's face as though etching her silhouette in gold. It was nothing less than a movie poster—just like the image of Y-san at Nagasaki Port.

---

7. King: This refers to zòngzi, a traditional Chinese dish made of glutinous rice stuffed with different fillings, including pork, mushrooms, water chestnuts, peanuts, and egg yolks, and wrapped in bamboo leaves, often eaten during the Dragon Boat Festival.

8. King: Han language refers to Chinese. Aoyama uses the Japanese term kanbun, which literally means "Han writing," and is a written form of classical Chinese that was also used in Japan until the twentieth century.

Or perhaps I was just projecting myself onto Chi-chan.

"So what's this fabled fiancé like?"

"I have only met him once, so it's hard to say."

"And you're really all right with that?"

"Is that not the case with all matchmaking? Has Aoyama-san's experience been different?"

"You're right. I can't argue against that." I myself have often had my sister and aunts bombard me with photographs from matchmakers in recent years. "But I just can't bear watching Chi-chan endure this sort of arrangement!"

"I'm grateful that Aoyama-san wishes to protect me," she said, chuckling quietly. "But practically speaking, it is much easier to accept the fate of such arrangements than to resist. On the other hand, whether on the Mainland or the Island, some men claim to be 'modern' and 'civilized' and boast about believing in free will and love. These men complain about feeling suffocated by arranged marriages, yet they can also abandon their arranged wives after the wedding and continue pursuing their studies or their jobs. The so-called marriages they object to only span the few weeks between the wedding and the moment they go off to do whatever they please. But it is different for women. For women, marriage is always a division between her past life and the rest of her life."

"Oh? Is Chi-chan confiding in me at last?"

Chi-chan chuckled. "What I'm saying is, I know that it is easier to accept the arrangements in theory, but thoughts like these completely soured the meal with my fiancé. How is it that no novelist has captured a woman's feelings in these situations?"

"True, true!" I cried. "With such a big family on the Island, Chi-chan's life is full of exotic theatricality. I'm no poet, so I can't compose poems for you, but I ought to write a novel for you!"

She said nothing. In the sharpened shadows of the setting sun, I could hardly make out her features.

"Hold on. Is it your ambition to become a writer?" I asked.

"Ah—" she dragged out the sound, her tone teasing. "No."

"Wrong *again*!"

"There's only one guess left, you know."

"What? Is there a limit?"

We transferred at Shōka and headed back to Taichū Station.

The sky had become a layered curtain the color of red bean paste. The lamps turned on inside the car of our train. The steady vibrations of the tracks were like the rocking of a cradle. I leaned against the window, watching things and places and people flash by.

The Southern Country. The Island. Taiwan. Ah—

The sun had sunk completely, giving rise to a sadness with no clear cause.

Fleeting light, fleeting light, I beg you drink this cup of wine![9]

I drifted off on the train. When I woke, Chi-chan was reading the Han-language novel I'd bought her under the train's lamplight. She seemed entirely absorbed.

---

9. Yáng: From Táng dynasty poet Lǐ Hè's "Lament That the Days Are So Short": "Fleeting light, fleeting light, I beg you drink this cup of wine. / I know not how high the blue skies, nor how rich the yellow earth, / I see only the cold moon and hot sun wearing away our human years. / We eat bear paws and grow fat, we eat frog legs and grow thin; / where is the spirit goddess, where is the supreme god? / A sacred tree grows east of the sky and below it a dragon roams with a torch in its mouth. / I will sever the dragon's sacred feet and chew on its sacred flesh, / so that it cannot bring about the day nor conceal in the night, / so that old men will never die and young men never cry. / Why swallow gold or white jade for immortality? / Who has actually seen Rèn Gōngzǐ soar to the clouds on his donkey? / Even Emperor Liú Chè lies in his Mào Lǐng tomb, a mere pile of bones. / Even the Emperor of Qín lies in his catalpa coffin, buried with wasted abalone." (Translation by King.)

"Is it interesting?"

"Mm."

"You seem like you're enjoying yourself, even with the poor lighting."

"Mm."

"What kind of story is it?"

Her soul seemed to slot back into her body. She raised her smiling face. "It's a fantastical novel based on the mythology of deities in Tainan's temples. I imagine it would bore Mainlanders who are not familiar with these gods."[10]

"Not at all. Please, tell me about them."

"If you say so." She flipped back to the first page. "The story begins at a small temple for Shàngdì, the First God, near Chìhkǎn Tower—Senkan Tower in Japanese. The temple had few visitors and, up in heaven, Shàngdì and his marshal gods were left in poverty as a result. One July, a typhoon razed the temple, and the god was forced to ask two of his marshals to pawn his holy crown . . ."[11]

"Typhoon? In July? Does that mean there will be typhoons soon?"

"This uses the lunar calendar, so July translates roughly to August in the Gregorian calendar. But yes, it's truc, the typhoons will come soon. Aoyama-san will certainly have a front-row view of Yana River at its most violent, given where the cottage is situated."

I nodded, and Chi-chan continued translating the story aloud.

---

10. Yáng: According to Chi-chan's ensuing description, the novel mentioned is likely *Little Deities*, a collection of stories by writer and cartoonist Hsú Pǐng-tīng, originally serialized from 1931 to 1932.

11. King: Throughout this scene, proper nouns have been transliterated according to their Mandarin Chinese pronunciations (instead of Japanese pronunciations as in most of this translation) because Chizuru is translating directly from a Chinese text.

"The two gods sent on the unpleasant task were Marshal Kāng and Marshal Zhào. On their way home from pawning the crown, they passed by the goddess Mātsǔ's temple—the goddess Maso, in Japanese—and saw two of her guardians, Qiānlǐyǎn and Shùnfēngěr, gambling at the gate. They asked to join, reasoning that they could use their winnings to buy the crown back from the pawnbroker. Yet they had failed to consider that Qiānlǐyǎn was known as the Far-Seeing God and Shùnfēngěr the Far-Hearing God; the two marshals were no match against them.

"The marshals returned home penniless. Too afraid to report the truth to Shàngdì and hoping to frame Qiānlǐyǎn, they claimed that they had been robbed by a large, bucktoothed man in front of Mātsǔ Temple. Furious, Shàngdì made for Mātsǔ Temple with his sword, came across a large, bucktoothed man, and immediately seized him and bound him to the gate of his own temple as punishment. Alas, this bucktoothed gentleman was not the guardian Qiānlǐyǎn, but the God of Stars, Kuí Xīng, from the Wénchāng Temple next door—"

I suppressed my laughter to avoid interrupting Chi-chan. Listening to her gentle yet ringing voice in the dim lamplight felt like submerging in warm spring water. I lowered my eyelids. "And then?"

"The gods of Wénchāng Temple, who represent Culture and Literature, were outraged that Kuí Xīng was suffering such humiliation for no reason. They went to Confucius Temple to ask that justice be served. Confucius stated simply that one should avoid direct confrontation. However, his three thousand disciples were dissatisfied with this conclusion, and Confucius had no choice but to visit Guān Yǔ, God of War, and ask him to talk sense into Shàngdì. The righteous Guān Yǔ immediately headed to the Shàngdì temple on his crimson steed. The conversation began well, but as soon as Guān Yǔ pointed out that Shàngdì had mistaken Kuí Xīng for Qiānlǐyǎn, Shàngdì's embarrassment boiled over into anger . . ."

There were many sounds on the train: people's chatter, the wheels rolling over the tracks, the rumbling of the engine. Amid all this noise, only Chi-chan's voice was like the string of an instrument, plucked to play a translucent melody.

A flash of inspiration struck me. My eyes flew open. "Wait, I know what your ambition is! It's to become a professional translator—of novels, isn't it?"

She smiled at me under the faint light. Her eyes, embedded in that impassable Noh mask, shone with a brightness I had never seen in them.

A soup made from young jute leaves.

When I first heard the description, I thought that one simply had to pick the newest leaves from a jute branch and throw them into boiling water. The reality was far more complex.

First, there was the task of breaking off the upper stem—the part that had yet to harden into stiff fiber—and picking off the edible leaves. While experienced jute pickers could distinguish the usable, tender leaves at a glance, novices could not necessarily tell the difference even when touching them. Even in a new leaf, the mid rib took up most of the surface area, and the actual tender areas were scant. By the time the rib was extracted, only two small half moons of leaf remained. Only a quarter or so of the original jute remained by the end of this process.

But the true test of one's skills was only just beginning.

The first tools required were clean water and a woven bamboo pan. A very specific amount of force was required for crushing the leaves into small pieces against the pan; water was then poured across the bamboo to wash away the bitter sap. This process continued for quite a while, with the goal of ridding the leaves of their bitterest juices without destroying their taste and nutrition. Applying too much force would overpulverize the leaves, and they would wash away with the water, leaving behind only sparse veins.

Chi-chan spent roughly twenty minutes on this kneading process. Rather, I should say that she *only* spent twenty minutes, whereas someone as clumsy as I would conceivably have spent an hour or more. The task was considered complete when a large, blue-green ball of crushed leaf formed at the bottom of the bamboo pan. The volume had decreased again, but we were at last ready for the cooking stage.

We heated a large vat of water and added as many cubed yams as we wished. After it reached boil, we loosened the leaf ball with our fingers and placed it in the pot, where the jade chunks immediately dissolved. We kept up the high heat, stirred clockwise occasionally, and removed any white foam that formed on the surface. The unique and refreshing scent of jute grew gradually denser. Here, we added anchovies and a pinch of salt.

Oh, yes—we also washed and cooked rice while all this was taking place. One curious tip was that one had to add more water than usual when making the rice, even at the expense of diluting the taste, for it was necessary to collect a few spoons of the semiwhite water that formed on top. Adding the rice water to the muâ-ínn-thng made it smoother and sweeter.

"It might be called 'poor people's food,'" I cried, plopping down on the wooden floor and stretching out my feet on the cool stepping stone, "but the number of steps it takes to make muâ-ínn-thng is no less involved than a banquet dish!"

Chi-chan, without responding, passed me a towel that she'd cooled with water from the well. The towel, pressed to my face, was a lifesaver.

Muâ-ínn-thng was a summer dish, but the picking, kneading, boiling, and stewing had taken over two hours in the heat of Taiwan's July. My nails were blue, green, and black from the effort, and sweat had been pouring from my head ever since the boiling phase began. The ordeal of transforming jute into jute soup had proven both mentally and physically draining.

Chi-chan checked on the soup. "About five more minutes will do. Muâ-ínn-thng is excellent for cooling down the body, and some people prefer to drink it after leaving it out to cool. Aoyama-san can try the hot version first and the cooled version later."

"Whoever came up with muâ-ínn-thng must have been quite the gourmet!"

She smiled. "As far as I know, you are the first Mainlander ever to taste this soup. I warn you—it's very, *very* bitter. Please do not expect anything delicious."

She began taking bowls out of the cupboard and I jumped up to help. We scooped ourselves large bowls of rice and drizzled the muâ-ínn-thng onto the rice.

Yes, two large bowls. Mine—and Chi-chan's.

Earlier, while we were just beginning to pick the jute leaves off their stalks, I'd asked her more about the meal she shared with her fiancé.

"Was it one-on-one?"

"Yes."

"But that's strange."

"What do you mean?"

"How come you can share a table with your fiancé but not with me?"

I'd assumed she would simply deflect the question, but no. To the contrary.

"Ah—so you've found me out."

"So it *is* intentional! But why, Chi-chan?"

"Well . . ."

"I want to hear the whole truth!"

Her hands stopped working.

"I decided from the beginning that I wouldn't presume to explain if Aoyama-san didn't ask. But now that you *have* asked, I will answer honestly."

"So? What is it?"

"No matter Aoyama-san's stance on the matter, as an Islander interpreter, I *am* expected to act as your personal assistant. In this sense, I am subordinate staff, and it would not be appropriate for me to dine at the same table as a Mainlander writer."

Seeing her solemn expression, I tried my best to suppress my emotions until she finished speaking.

"I am unwilling to dine at the same table with you as an inferior. People should eat at the same table only if they are of equal rank. This is why I can eat with my fiancé, and can eat at a large banquet where there are people of all ranks, but cannot eat one-on-one with you."

I slowly exhaled the breath I'd been holding.

"Perhaps not with Aoyama-sensei the Mainlander writer, but what about with Aoyama Chizuko the human being?"

Chi-chan laughed. "That is true. We can dine together now that you are Aoyama-san, not Aoyama-sensei."

And so there we were, with two large bowls of muâ-ínn-thng over rice for lunch.

For the side dishes, we had the large variety of meatballs and taro balls that we'd bought in Rokkō, which we reheated by steaming them in a pot. In addition, we had kiâm-lâ-á clams and some pickled radish that Chi-chan had brought along with the jute.

We opened all the shōji sliding doors in the cottage to let in fresh air, making the dining room brighter and breezier than usual. We then loaded the table with pots, bowls, plates, chopsticks, and spoons. The meatballs and taro balls we divided evenly between us. Inside the large bowls, the white rice looked like small hills, surrounded by a greenish sea in which yam and anchovies swam.

"Chi-chan, is this too much food for you?"

"I'm more worried about *you*, Aoyama-san. You still haven't tasted the bitter soup."

I immediately delivered a spoonful into my mouth.

How should I describe this taste?

Another spoonful, followed by another.

Another, then another.

"Please don't force yourself."

I finished the final piece of yam and raised the bowl to drain the rest of the soup, then let out a long exhale. "The bitterness has a sweet aftertaste, so in that sense it's quite similar to tea. This one bowl probably isn't enough for me to truly understand the taste of muâ-ínn-thng, but no matter—I can have multiple bowls of this!"

Chi-chan said, in a low voice, "Now I feel that I mustn't lose to you."

"Yes, it's your turn! It's like that poem: 'Gift me a sweet fruit, and I shall give you jade—not merely to reciprocate, but to feel our shared affection'!"[12]

We'd bought five types of meatballs in Rokkō: one had pork filling on the inside and a skin made from yucca starch and potato starch, which turned semitranslucent when it was cooked; the second kind had a skin-of-pork paste; the third had no skin and was made from pork marinated in sauce; the fourth had pieces of minced fruit mixed into the ground pork; the fifth was made from shaved taro, marinated pork, and starch—they were the size of a toddler's fist and had to be cut into pieces.[13]

Chi-chan picked up her chopsticks. Beginning with the translucent meatballs, she ate one of each in the order I described. Then she went for round two. Then round three. She sipped some

---

12. King: From *Shījīng*, the oldest existing collection of Chinese poetry.

13. Yáng: Based on these descriptions, in present-day parlance these foods are referred to as crystal dumplings (shǔi-jīng-jiǎo), swallow dumplings (biǎn-shí-yàn), steamed meatballs (zhēng-wán), water meatballs (shǔi-wán), and taro meatballs (yù-wán).

soup, ate some pickled vegetables, then went for round four, then five, then six . . .

My jaw dropped.

Somehow maintaining both speed and grace, Chi-chan cleared her entire plate of meatballs.

A monster's appetite.

And to think I'd sometimes wondered: Where in the world would I find a fellow monster?

"Chi-chan, we must have been destined to meet!" I jumped to my feet, raising my voice. "We must eat our way across all of Taiwan Island!"

At first, she only blinked in surprise. But, the next moment, she nodded and grinned.

Sunshine set the room aglow.

Ah, the Southern Country! Ah, the Island! Ah, Taiwan!

CHAPTER IV

Sashimi / Sliced Raw Fish

Six-sided, four-cornered, and carved from bone—dice were the same on the Mainland and the Island. A simple and popular gambler's game here was to throw three dice into a bowl: the lowest number of points was three, the highest was eighteen, and the dealer and player competed for the higher or lower number.

I placed a bowl on the table—the same bowl from which we'd eaten muâ-înn-thng all summer. Chi-chan stood on the opposite side of the table.

"Hoho! Let us begin!" I swung my shoulders dramatically.

Chi-chan watched my theatrics mutely, a slight smile pinching the corners of her lips.

She was to be dealer, and we were competing for the highest number. However, we were not gambling with money, but over whether or not Chi-chan would move into my little cottage by Yana River.

At this point, I'd been living there for approximately two months, with Taichū City as my base. During this time, Chi-chan continued to visit me on a regular basis. I'd noticed that she was often red in the face from the harsh summer sun but didn't ask her about it until many weeks later, and only then did I learn that she commuted on foot.

"But why walk when there are buses in the city?"

"So that I can buy things to bring here along the way, of course."

Which meant that I, who so often pronounced on a whim that I would like to eat this or try that, had been adding to her troubles.

I unfolded the map and found that the Ō residence, which was located in Chōkyōshitō, was south of even Akebono District, which was the southeasternmost district in Taichū. Meanwhile, Kawabata District, where I lived, was the northwesternmost. From her home to mine, Chi-chan had to walk approximately twenty chō[1] along Taishō Bridge Avenue.

Twenty chō, with the Southern sun overhead and packages in hand? No—if she had to take detours to buy the desserts and groceries requested by her gluttonous employer, she must have been hauling these bundles for more than twenty chō! Even I, who prided myself on being stronger than most of body and spirit, felt that this was more a chore for a Buddhist monk undergoing ascetic training than something suited to Chi-chan.

And so—was it really so unreasonable for me to make the suggestion?

"Chi-chan, you must live *here*!"

Her response, however, wasn't nearly as forthright as my proposal.

"It's a perfectly normal distance to walk, even for a delicate young woman."

We were thus at a stalemate.

"Why won't you stay here?"

"Why must I stay here?"

"Answering a question with a question will only plunge us into a whirlpool of questions!"

Chi-chan nodded. "Very true. But, Aoyama-san, seeing as you were the one who proposed the idea, I believe that you ought to answer first."

"Well, first of all, would it not make things much easier on you? You wouldn't have to commute, nor would you have to deal

---

1. Yáng: One chō is approximately 109 meters, twenty chō approximately two kilometers or 1.4 miles.

with your family. Oh, and you love to read! The bookstore that specializes in Han-language texts is right around here, is it not?[2] You can go all the time! And, and, we would be able to go to the market together. Whatever you want to eat, we can buy as much of it as we like! You wouldn't have to get permission from anybody, and—and, if we wish, we can go to restaurants and order whatever we desire!"

"I appreciate your kindness and generosity, and it is true that these would all be great advantages, but they are not exactly reasons for why I *must* live here."

"Th—that's true enough."

I acquiesced, but struggled to give up the idea once it had taken hold.

It would definitely be more fun *if Chi-chan stayed!*

Yet even I did not have thick enough skin to voice a thought as willful as that.

Instead, I lay down on the tatami.

"Aoyama-san, you'll wrinkle your skirt."

"I can't think of a good reason right now, but I can't give up on the idea just yet."

"Is that so?" Chi-chan sat quietly for a second, then asked, "How about a game?"

We promptly went outside to buy dice. On the way, we saw a young man hand-pulling sugarcane sticks and ended up buying a large package—but that was beside the point.

There we were, standing on two sides of the large bowl. Chi-chan, the dealer, would throw first.

"I'm warning you in advance, Chi-chan, I tend to have very good luck with these things!"

---

2. Yáng: Aoyama refers here to Central Bookstore, which was established in 1927 and is the largest-scale Chinese-language bookstore in Taiwan under Japanese rule.

"What a coincidence—so do I."

She tossed the dice into the bowl. The clacked around and around and stilled one by one by one.

All three showed six.

"Eighteen!" I cried.

The dimples surfaced. "I told you, Aoyama-san. I have good luck when it comes to these things."

"But this—this—"

Gamblers on the Mainland sometimes cheated by imbuing powdered gold into one side of a die so as to make it heavier. But these were dice we'd just bought impromptu. How could she possibly have cheated?

I threw the dice and immediately proved that they had very much *not* been tampered with: three, four, five, for a total of twelve.

It wasn't an unlucky throw per se, but it was entirely powerless against eighteen.

"Fine, then, have it your way . . . oh, I know, at least ride a bike instead of walking! What do you say? I can teach you if you don't know how!"

"Aoyama-san, how about we pose this question to the dice as well?"

"Yes, let's! I'll go first this time!"

I rolled nine.

She rolled twelve.

Oh dear, oh dear! I had no choice but to admit defeat and return to my work.

I had been taking many notes at my writing desk in the four-tatami study.

What drove me to write was neither political agenda nor money, but a simple desire to record my observations whenever

I saw or heard anything interesting, or whenever I felt moved to reflect on something. If I didn't have a notebook at hand, I would use pages from a calendar, packaging paper, or old newspaper instead. Over time, piles of notebooks and scraps covered my desktop and drawers, and slowly consumed the study's bookshelves, windowsills, and floors.

Some of my notes were inevitably lost in this disorderly system. There was also one time when a grain of rice had dried between two pieces of paper, gluing them together in a way such that I lost both when trying to peel them apart. And yet I was not a totally hopeless sloven. Every once in a while, I would straighten out the papers, organizing and rewriting the penciled scribbles into a leatherbound notebook with a fountain pen. In doing so, I would receive renewed inspiration from the various notes, which I often incorporated into travel articles. The short articles I sent to *Taiwan Nichinichi News* in Taihoku, and the longer essays I sent to *Taiwan Kōron* magazine. After moving into the cottage, I generated on average six articles per month. When things were going well, I could produce two articles in one go.

On writing days, I always felt that I had to ride one wave to the end, so to speak. I would start working after lunch. The first half of the work included categorizing the notes, organizing my thoughts, and transcribing; after a simple dinner of neko-manma[3] or else store-bought sushi or soba noodles, I'd continue transcribing, then start structuring and finally drafting, all the way into the small hours.

By the time I laid down my pen, my stomach usually felt like an empty city. My eyes would see stars. If I was lucky, there would be a mī-tê vendor honking the whistle of his little cart

---

3. Yáng: Neko-manma literally translates to "cat rice" in Japanese. This is a simple Japanese household fare made by drizzling miso soup over rice, or adding bonito flakes and soy sauce over rice.

outside—there was nothing quite like downing a steaming hot bowl of the sesame and nut porridge while the nighttime summer breeze stirred the wheat fields and my hair. If I was unlucky, however, I could only munch on the white toast set aside in the kitchen specifically for nights like these. Though I was more often than not out of luck in these situations, I felt no inclination to change my routine.

Chi-chan was quick to see through my bad habits.

The study was connected to the dining room, divided only by a shōji sliding door. Taking into consideration ventilation and lighting, I always left this door open. Sometimes, my stacks of notes would spill their way onto the dining table, and Chi-chan would restore them to the study without a word. Soon, my toast cupboard began to see additions of yōkan jellies and red bean buns.

Shortly after our trip to Shōka and Rokkō, Chi-chan sent over several ceramic urns and tiered lunch boxes.

Stray pieces of paper could easily blow away, but they were safe inside the Shina-style urn with its large round belly and small mouth. Small notebooks could be stored inside the lunch boxes. Although I still lost some notes now and then, these modifications greatly reduced the amount of time it took me to find and sort them.

Improvements were made on the matter of my dinners also. Chi-chan began staying until evening on my writing days. If I happened to see the word "noodles" in my notes and called out that I wanted noodles, by dinnertime she would deliver clam and egg noodles along with grated yam noodles. In the Christian Bible, when God said "Let there be light," there was light. When I said, "Let there be vermicelli noodles, rice noodles, thick starch noodles, egg-drop udon noodles," Chi-chan would light up the dining table with my fulfilled wishes.

One time, I mentioned that I would like to try the jūn-piánn rolls that Kataoka-sensei had mentioned in his book,[4] and Chi-chan arrived earlier than usual to prepare the dish.

Fresh powdered peanuts; fish floss from the market; ink-black seaweed to be shredded right before the dish was served; two varieties of Taiwanese pickled cabbage, sour and salted; bean sprouts, garlic chives, fresh cabbage, wild rice shoots, bamboo shoots, lotus roots, soybeans, and whole peanuts, all of which were to be boiled. Some of this had to be julienned, whereas the beans and nuts were individually shelled. There was river shrimp, which had to be gutted, cleaned, boiled, and peeled. Braise-dried tofu, Taiwanese sausage, and pork were to be sautéed at specific temperatures and cut into slices. Carrots and burdock roots were to be peeled and stewed in a mixture of soy sauce and sugar. Cucumber, celery, scallions, garlic sprouts, and cilantro, which did not need to be cooked, still had to be washed thoroughly.

I could not help sneaking glances as Chi-chan worked.

"I love eggs. Can we add eggs? Omelet-style or shredded, anything."

"Yes."

She oiled and heated the wok, beat some eggs with salt, poured the mixture into the wok through a funnel, and used long chopsticks to swirl the eggs that floated up to the surface so that they dispersed in tiny, foam-like pieces. The pieces quickly browned, and Chi-chan removed the wok from the heat.

I was enthralled.

"It's like an egg version of tempura crust!"

---

4. Aoyama: Kataoka Iwao published *Notes on Taiwanese Customs* in Taishō Year 9. In the chapter "The Food of the Taiwanese," he explained that jūn-piánn involved making a thin crepe on a hot steel plate and wrapping bean sprouts, peanut powder, pickled daikon, pork, tamago floss, and algae within the roll.

"We call it egg crisp.[5] It's an important component in traditional Taiwanese cooking—never the main character, but an indispensable supporting character in many dishes."

"And all the steps it takes to make it! How extravagant!"

"Aoyama-san, are you only now realizing what a luxury jūn-piánn is?"

I laughed.

That evening, sitting across from each other at the dining table, we kept rolling up the ingredients of our choice until we finished one and a half kin[6] of the jūn-piánn skin.

An idea struck me. "We can also use this to wrap karasumi!"[7]

Chi-chan, wearing her Noh-mask smile, said, "Aoyama-san, you may as well use it to wrap gold foil."

"But gold foil tastes terrible!"

". . ."

Thanks to Chi-chan's homemade dinners, I began to take more and more writing days during August.

On the day that Chi-chan made jūn-piánn, the Takada family's housekeeper, Sae-san, happened to be cleaning the cottage. Afterward, she made a point of saying to me while Chi-chan was absent, "That Ō-san is so hardworking, I can hardly tell if she's a personal assistant or an interpreter. For all that work, she ought to have two salaries!"

The clam shells fell from my eyes.[8] Her words pierced me like an arrow.

---

5. Yáng: Egg crisp is, in fact, the same as the tamago floss that Aoyama quoted in her footnote on Kataoka Iwao; she did not seem to realize this.

6. King: About 1.6 pounds.

7. King: A delicacy of salted, cured mullet roe. Iterations of it are popular in Japan, Taiwan, and Korea.

8. Yáng: Likely an exaggeration of the idiom "the scales fell from my eyes" commonly used in Japanese.

I immediately invited Chi-chan to dine with me at a traditional Japanese restaurant.

Sashimi, nigiri sushi, maki sushi rolls, chawanmushi egg custard, tofu stew—I didn't skip out on a single dish. I asked for the ice-cold, paper-thin slices of fish to be served first.

I watched Chi-chan put the sashimi into her mouth and, as she chewed, asked eagerly whether she liked it.

"It isn't so much a matter of liking or disliking . . . an Islander cannot truly understand the taste of sashimi. Aoyama-san should not have treated me to such a luxurious meal. It is wasted on someone like me."

"No, no—it's not that Islanders can't understand sashimi. It's just because it's summer right now! Sashimi is best in winter and spring. Hm, how can I explain it . . . ah! There's a place between Kyūshū and Yamagushi called Shimonoseki and it's got the best pufferfish sashimi anywhere in the world. *That* taste is something that anybody anywhere can understand as soon as it touches their tongue! Chi-chan, you must come to Kyūshū sometime."

She cocked her head. "The next lecture will take us to Kagi—the Futai Port there is famous for its seafood. Wouldn't Aoyama-san like to try one of the Islanders' raw dishes?"

I immediately said yes. But then: "Wait, is it kiâm-lâ-á clams again?"

Chi-chan's dimples appeared at this question. "I suppose it's similar, but not quite the same. It isn't kiâm-lâ-á, but geh."

Geh?

I asked her to specify the pronunciation and description and took meticulous notes.

Geh: Fresh fish and shrimp, etc. from the sea, seasoned with large quantities of salt, sugar, cooking wine, and vinegar, stored in a large urn until fermented, then cured under the sun for over one month.

Our conversation took place on the third Saturday of August. We were to go to Kagi the following Saturday. Even as I was flicking through the notebook, the aroma of the sea seemed to waft from the pages and make my mouth water.

"Chi-chan, for dinner tonight, I'd like miso soup with lots of fresh fish and seaweed!"

Kagi didn't make much of an impression on me—and I daresay many other Mainlanders would have felt the same.

Chi-chan gave me a thorough introduction to the city on the train there: The most famous sights for tourists, she explained, are Kagi Shrine, Kagi Park, and Alisan,[9] which includes the popular "fantasy forest railway" whose train departs from Kagi Station and terminates at Alisan Station. Originally built by the Empire for logging, the train affords views that have become renowned far and wide, for Alisan Station is a whopping two thousand meters above sea level.

Picture it: A heavy mist weaves its way across a thick-leaved forest, and, out of the blue, a steam train penetrates this white carpet, wailing its long, heartrending whistle. The wheels cling firmly to the rails below, inching up the steep mountain with steel resolve. Poking one's head out the window in the brief moments when the mist eases, one sees rows of sacred trees crowding the railroad like soldiers fallen into rank, stretching far into the opaque skies.

Then there are the flower-lined paths in sakura season: Taiwan cherry, Chishima cherry, Yoshino cherry, Fuji cherry, and finally the eightfold Yae cherry, whose fallen petals mark the arrival of summer. It was truly as the poem went: *The eightfold cherries of ancient Nara / today bloom inside the ninefold palace.*[10]

---

9. King: Alisan is the Japanese pronunciation of Ālǐshān, a mountain range in the central-southern region of Taiwan in present-day Chiāyì County. Known for its railway, high-mountain oolong, and hiking trails, it remains one of the most popular scenic attractions in Taiwan.

10. Yáng: From poem 61 of the *Hyakunin Isshu* Japanese waka poetry collection. The poet expresses amazement at how the sakura that had been relo-

It was an August day, and all the flowers had long gone. The train car rocked and clacked, Chi-chan's voice was as delightful as ever, and I indulged in picturing those high-mountain cherry blossoms: lacquer red, coral red, blush pink, blush white, white laced with red undertones, red laced with white undertones.

"Now I'm really craving red seabream!"[11]

"You've just finished two bento boxes, Aoyama-san."

"Bah! I can't believe the nerve of them, calling onigiri and plums a 'patriotic bento.' They still had *proper* railway bento not so long ago, with a wide range of dishes and—whatever happened to those vendors selling bí-hún-tshá on the platforms? You see, *this* is why war is—ah, never mind, never mind. There's no use complaining about these things. I'm only souring my own mood."[12]

Our train would arrive in Kagi at 2:00. Just as a steam locomotive needs coal to move forward, humans cannot move through a day without food to burn in their stomach. Chi-chan, however, ignored my food-related grievances and continued introducing me to Kagi.

Kagi's historical name is Tirosen, named by indigenous peoples. Despite including the "mountain" character of "sen," the name referred to the urban area. Kagi was also one of the earliest cities to be planned and built on the Island under Qīng rule; some referred to Kagi as the Island's first "architectural city."

Was there any truth to this? I, a foreign traveler, was in no

---

cated from the former capital of Nara to the new capital of Kyōto continue to bloom as always. Here, "nine-fold palace" refers to the nine layers of gates at the new castle. (Japanese to English translation by King.)

11. Yáng: The color of red seabream sashimi is similar to that of sakura blossoms, which may be the reason for this leap.

12. Yáng: After the July 1938 Lúgōu Bridge Incident, which launched a war between Japan and China, the Japanese government limited Taiwan's railways to selling only "patriotic bento" with onigiri and pickled vegetables. When Aoyama first arrived in May 1938, the wartime regulations were not yet in place.

position to offer criticism or praise. I thought only of how the saying "even an old broom is cherished by its owner" held true everywhere I went, and that the love shown by Kagi residents for their hometown was endearing.

I told Chi-chan what was on my mind. Her dimples appeared.

"Aoyama-san, would you like to hear another story about Kagi?"

"Of course."

"Over a century ago, there lived a Tirosen boy named Wáng Té-lù. Wáng first fought on a battlefield when he was seventeen, when a man named Lín Shuǎng-wén started a civil uprising and laid siege to the city of Tirosen. Young Wáng volunteered to lead Qīng soldiers to crush the rebel forces. After this, Wáng, the prodigy general, fought nearly one hundred more battles against Lín Shuǎng-wén's rebel forces."

"A boy war god! It's like the plot of a kabuki show!"

"The following year, Emperor Qiánlóng sent reinforcements, and Wáng continued fighting alongside top Qīng generals until Lín Shuǎng-wén's forces were completely pacified. Emperor Qiánlóng admired Wáng as the leader of Tirosen's peoples and renamed the region Chiāyì—the Mandarin pronunciation for Kagi. Chiā means 'to commend' and yì means 'righteous,' so the city was renamed 'commendation for a righteous deed,' and seventeen-year-old Wáng was promoted to a fifth-rank general. I should explain: the Qīng system divided officials into nine ranks, the same as Japan's system before the Meiji Restoration, which is further divided into 'lower nine,' 'upper nine,' all the way up to 'upper first.' In other words, from unranked to 'lower fifth,' Wáng skipped not five, but eight ranks in one leap."

I could almost picture him: the glorious boy-general. "It really *is* theater material! Or a novel? I'd only heard of Koxinga.[13] Who knew that there was also a General Wáng?"

---

13. King: Koxinga (1624–1662, Mandarin name: Zhèng Chéng-gōng) was a Later Míng general known for defeating the Dutch colonial outposts in

Chi-chan flashed a fleeting smile. "Later, Emperor Dàoguāng promoted Wáng to the rank of Crown Prince Tàibǎo, the highest official title in Taiwan at the time. Wáng's home village in Kagi thus became known as Tàibǎo Village. Now you know. Wáng Té-lù's legendary life of victorious battles began right here, in Kagi."

"Ah! Not to be underestimated—never to be underestimated!"

"Further, Kagi's famous Maso Temple and Hosei Taitei[14] Temple both date back two to three hundred years."

My interest was roused. "Now that you mention it, I haven't had the chance to visit any Islander temples! Where in Kagi are these two temples, exactly?"

"Sorry, Aoyama-san, but I must remind you that we have to be at the venue by three o'clock today, so it would be impossible to visit."

I hadn't even managed to get out the question! I leaned against the train window and let out a deep exhale.

Chi-chan showed me her notebook. There was a chart; the top row and leftmost column had kanji, and the rest was filled with Arabic numerals.

"What are these times for?" I asked.

"Kagi Station. It's located at the cusp of the mountains and the plains, and connects the Taiwan Railway, Logging Railway, and Sugar Railway. It is perhaps the only train station on the Island where these three railways meet."

"Oh, uh, I see—very impressive, eh?" I didn't see what she was getting at, but thought I couldn't go wrong with praise.

Chi-chan chuckled at this, then tapped one of the times on

Taiwan and claiming Taiwan for China. Interestingly, in the context of Aoyama's story, Koxinga was born in Nagasaki to a Japanese mother and a Chinese father. He is worshipped as a deity in Taiwan and parts of southern China.

14. King: Hosei Taitei is the Japanese pronunciation for Bǎoshēng Dàdì, a deity of medicine popular in Taiwan and Fújiàn, China.

the chart. "The two ancient temples are in Shinkō, which is accessible from Kagi via the Sugar Railway, but as you can see, there are no trains there after your lecture. Why do we not go tomorrow morning, when Aoyama-san can be at leisure? As for our hotel tonight, I have contacted them to ensure that there is an Islander chef willing to prepare oyster and saltwater clam geh for Aoyama-san."

I bobbed my head up and down eagerly. At the mention of this forthcoming dinner, my shoulders actually shook with excitement. "Chi-chan, you're like the thousand-armed Kannon Bodhisattva! How much time have you spent taking care of all these logistics? Since we can't visit the goddess Maso today, I ought to worship at your feet instead!"

"Aoyama-san exaggerates."

"Not at all. There's no greater human happiness than being able to eat the food that one craves."

At this, Chi-chan couldn't suppress her laughter. "Now Aoyama-san is *really* exaggerating."

"In Buddhism, the 'three poisons' are greed, hate, and delusion. I don't believe I'll make it to Nirvana even if I shave my head and move into a monastery tomorrow—not with this obsessive monster in my belly!"

Perhaps my exclamation was a little too heartfelt. Chi-chan's face clouded with concern.

I hesitated. "When I was a child," I said, "there was a summer when I spent two months at a small shrine in the mountains. I ate only plain rice with a bite of pickled vegetables every single day."

"Every single day?"

"Yes."

"Did the others do the same?"

"There were no others. I was the only one there, in charge of keeping the Buddha's lamp burning. The little shrine was several ri[15] of mountain roads from the main temple, so I was virtually forgotten. Every ten days, somebody from the main temple brought lamp oil along with some rice and salt. I was fortunate in that I was surrounded by a forest with a water source, so I could collect wild vegetables and pickle them with the salt. Even so, by the end of the two months, I was diagnosed with severe beriberi."

Chi-chan mumbled something under her breath.

"Pardon?"

She said, "There wasn't anything about this shrine in the novel."

"Chi-chan, have you read *A Record of Youth*?" I cried, smiling. "That's why I keep saying that novels are only novels, not real life. In any case, I developed a fervent obsession with food after that. My gluttony isn't limited to exquisite or expensive foods, either—whenever I start craving something, *anything*, my stomach burns with this insatiable greed until I get my hands on whatever it is. *That's* the monster in me. And that's why I'm so very grateful to you! Ever since I arrived in Taiwan, you've been the only one to appease this monster."

The noise she made was something like a sigh. "Aoyama-san is exaggerating still." But the Noh mask had melted like warmed ice. Behind it, her face was neither joyful nor sad. The hint of something unreadable lifted the corners of her mouth. "But," she said, "I'm very glad to hear you say so."

Was that a breeze?

It couldn't have been, but I felt it all the same.

Within her gentle words there was a cooling breeze. It rose from a valley creek and penetrated the summer heat pent up in my chest.

I could only sit there, silent and incognizant of time and space, for as long as that breeze wafted through me.

---

15. King: One ri is 3.927 kilometers, or 2.44 miles.

Until the train's whistle sounded in the depths of the valley.

Until we pulled into Kagi.

The lecture was at Kagi High School for Girls. We arrived via taxi on time, and likewise concluded the event on time. We stayed for a brief reception but graciously declined the school's invitation to dinner. My mind was preoccupied with the meal awaiting us at the hotel, and Madame M, a foreign music teacher, detected my distraction while we exchanged business cards.

"You are quite an open book," she said, plainly amused.

I opened the book even more. "That is because I will get to enjoy delicious Islander dishes tonight!"

She seemed surprised at first, but her face relaxed into a broad smile. "You will definitely enjoy it, because Kagi is a very good place."

Madame M only spoke basic Japanese, but the topic of good food traversed language barriers, and she quickly added a string of fast-paced English to match the enthusiasm I'd shown. My grasp of English was poor despite growing up in international Nagasaki, but thankfully Chi-chan spoke some; they twittered back and forth for a while, and Madame M seemed to grow more and more delighted. She shook my hand again before taking her leave and said, "You are very lucky to have such an excellent interpreter."

This compliment pleased me more than any praise she could have given on my lecture.

Chi-chan and I walked back to the hotel. Though it was already evening, the hotel room was still tepid with residual heat. Still in an excellent mood, I asked the waitress to bring us two iced Calpis before dinner.

"Is Aoyama-san not curious about what Madame M said to me?"

"What did she say?"

"Only bad things about you."

I laughed. "Liar. It was about food, wasn't it?"

"Ah, nothing gets past Aoyama-san after all. It's true. Madame M recommended food local to the Hakka people in Kagi."

"Huh! Chi-chan, you said before that Shina descendants on the Island are divided into Hoklo and Hakka, but how come we didn't hear any Hakka on the train coming here?"

"Hoklo and Hakka peoples do not live in separate neighborhoods here in Kagi. I have heard that many Hakka people here speak in Taiwanese Hokkien, the Hoklo dialect."

"I see."

The shōji door slid open. The waitress served us two glasses coated in beads of condensation.

I immediately began gulping down the sweet drink, but Chi-chan was in no hurry. She opened her notebook instead.

"Madame M recommended that you try lug-tong-qi, a Hakka mochi dessert. During festivals, or during busy periods like planting or harvest seasons, landlords would roll mochi into flat rounds and add them to a sweet soup made from peanuts and ginger for everybody to share . . . hm? Is Aoyama-san not interested?"

I downed the rest of my Calpis and let out a long exhale. "Ah—that's because the monster isn't craving dessert right now!"

"And yet you finished your sweet drink in one go."

"Oh, but that's because I'm in a good mood!"

Chi-chan looked as though she would laugh at me, but when she spoke, her eyes were ineffably gentle. "You really *are* an open book."

I felt effervescent, as though I'd had beer instead.

We had yet to see much of the city, but in that moment, I felt deeply that Madame M had spoken the truth: Kagi was indeed a very good place.

The table in my hotel room was loaded with dishes.

The hotel was managed by Mainlanders, which was duly reflected in its dinner menu: white rice, sashimi, miso soup, fishcake, tofu, mountain vegetable salad, chawanmushi egg custard, plus grilled bamboo shoots and marinated fish, as well as shrimp and vegetable tempura. Though these looked Japanese on the surface, the fish chosen for sashimi were of Island varieties—it was my first time having fourfinger threadfin and white pomfret, and I couldn't believe it possible for sashimi to taste so flavorful in such hot weather.

Likewise, the usual pickled tsukemono appetizers had been exchanged for pickled Islander foods: oyster geh, saltwater clam geh, shrimp geh, clam geh, and whitebait fish geh. Chi-chan had been right that geh was nothing like kiâm-lâ-á salted clams. The geh had been fermented over such a long period of time that the seafood itself had become half-solid, half-sauce. (What could I compare it to in terms of Mainlander food? Perhaps shutō?)[16] In addition, there was cabbage, mustard leaf, and daikon radish that had been not only pickled but also sun dried. These reminded me of Kyūshū's takana mustard greens, though instead of dark green they were jet black.

I thought: *Might as well order some beer!* After all, there was no need to worry about other eyes when one was dining in the privacy of one's own hotel room.

Chi-chan poured me a glass.

I poured Chi-chan a glass.

The savory geh went just as well with alcohol as it did with white rice, and so I ordered some warm rice wine, too.

We switched between pouring and being served as though

16. Yáng: Shutō is made by curing the entrails of fish, sea cucumber, and sea urchin over a long period of time. Shu means alcohol and tō means robbery, a reference to how the strong flavor goes well with alcohol. While shutō and geh are produced through similar processes, geh, which was originally made to preserve seafood in seaports before refrigerators were popularized, is not limited to entrails and has a much wider variety of ingredients. Since refrigeration became common, geh has all but disappeared, and can now only be found in very few seaport areas.

playing a game of table tennis. Our conversation, too, felt like a ball being passed back and forth.

"The wasabi here tastes fresher and airier than in other places."

"They said that it's grown in Alisan, that its flavor is the taste of the high-mountain soil. It's cultivated in small quantities, so you can't find it anywhere else."

"Chi-chan, did you try the tempura yet? It's *unbelievably* good!"

"I believe those are chayote sprouts.[17] It's a rather rare vegetable."

"Isn't it also rare to see pickled vegetables this black? It's much saltier than the usual tsukemono, too. And the texture is really intriguing."

"These are Hakka-style pickles. Perhaps this Islander chef is of Hakka descent."

"What are the differences between Hakka and Hoklo cuisine? Do restaurants that advertise themselves as Taiwanese serve a mixture of Hakka and Hoklo foods?"

"Hmm . . ."

"That's all right, you don't have to answer. I don't know why I'm interrogating you like an examiner."

"Not at all. I just needed some time to think. Compared to Hoklo people, Hakka people tend to live in slightly mountainous areas. This has made it harder for them to cultivate land, which has fostered in them a spirit of leaving nothing to waste and making use of every possible ingredient. Most Taiwanese restaurants focus on Hoklo cuisine. In terms of Hakka dishes, there are often appetizers of pork gallbladder or liver, and the main course of fung-ngiug, which is a type of braised pork belly like Shina's Dōngpō pork and comes in very large portions."

"We also have a version of that in Nagasaki, you know. We

---

17. Yáng: Chayote sprout is what is now known in Mandarin as lóng-xū-cài, literally "dragon whisker vegetable."

call it pork kakuni. But, Chi-chan, I still haven't made out what makes Hakka cuisine distinct."

"I've heard people say that most Hakka dishes evolved from food originally made for worshipping the gods. Hoklo food's origins are quite different. In Tainan, there is something called a-sià dishes. A-sià means a young gentleman from a wealthy family, and a-sià dishes are meticulously made delicacies that abide by the motto 'no grain can be too refined, no meat sliced too thin.' By comparison, Hakka food is more pragmatic, with a wide variety of pickled and cured dishes—vegetables, seafood, foraged foods—I've heard that there are hundreds of options. I've heard that whereas Hoklo people only use one word for marinading, sīnn, Hakka people have four or five words, each with different nuances."

"Chi-chan really *is* an aspiring translator! How impressive!"

"On the contrary, I only know a little. Oh, I just remembered—there is a special technique in Hakka cuisine that involves mincing frogs or birds, complete with the bones, which is then made into meat pies or meatballs. This, too, reflects the Hakka tradition of letting nothing go to waste."

"I see. Do they simply call them meat pies and meatballs?"

"In Hakka, frogs are called guai-er. When they are chopped and pan-fried, they are called jien-guai-er, which is something like fried frog meat pie. Hakka seems not to differentiate between different birds, and I believe all meatballs made from poultry are called diau-ien."

"You baffle me, Chi-chan! Why on earth does a teacher of the national language know all of this? How does one even begin to go about learning about things like this? Is it all for translation? As a novelist, I'm absolutely ashamed!"

"Aoyama-san, I do believe you're tipsy."

"Well, maybe I am! I feel wonderful. Let's go up Alisan tomorrow! We can drink in the misty mountain forests, see the sacred trees . . ."

"I'm afraid that's impossible. The railroad tracks were recently damaged by a typhoon."

"You've looked into *everything* ahead of time!"

"Not at all. I was told this by one of the teachers at Kagi Girls' School. The students were originally meant to go on a hike, and it was because they had to cancel their plans for the day that they invited you to give a lecture. Aoyama-san, you really ought to listen to what other people say once in a while."

"Oh dear, oh dear."

"I do believe you've gone from tipsy to drunk."

"Chi-chan."

"Yes?"

"I'd like to try the lug-tong-qi Hakka dessert tomorrow."

"Ah. I'm not surprised by the request, but even so . . ."

"It's all right if we can't tomorrow, but what about the day after tomorrow?"

"Either day would be very difficult. But there are also famous desserts in Shinkō, where we're headed tomorrow. Nītaka candy, kin-chio cake, and more."[18]

"Ack! Is it really, *absolutely* impossible?"

"If I said yes, what will the monster in your stomach do?"

"It'll cry."

"It will?"

"Because its heart will be crushed—crushed! It'll bawl and bawl like a child!"

"You are *quite* drunk."

"Chi-chan!"

"Yes?"

---

18. King: Shinkō (Mandarin: xīn-gǎng) candy is made by mixing crunchy peanut candy with sticky malt candy and adding glutinous rice. Kin-chio cake is the Taiwanese name (Mandarin: gōng-jiāo-gāo) for a chewy glutinous rice candy with banana flavoring.

"Out of all these geh, the oyster one is the best! You must have more of it!"

"Please don't worry about me. Do have some more yourself."

"I can't, I can't! Because it's the best—and I must save the best for you."

"You are quite *thoroughly* drunk."

"Oh dear oh dear oh dear!"

"Aoyama-san, you really shouldn't drink any more. I'll ask the waitress to clear away the food and set up your bed."

"Chi-chan—Chi-chan!"

"Yes, Aoyama-san."

"The sakura on Alisan. Let's go see them. Together. Next spring."

". . ."

"Ah, how unwilling you seem! Oh, I know—let's roll dice and see who wins! I'll go first. Here! Hah! A whopping seventeen!"

"Very well . . . ah, what a shame. I rolled an eighteen."

"Hahaha! Even your dice-rolling skills are not to be underestimated."

"It was only luck."

"Oh dear! Luck is also a type of skill."

"Here, have some water."

"Chi-chan."

"Yes?"

"It's brutish, isn't it, to transplant Mainland sakura and force them upon the Island's soil? You think so, too, don't you?"

"I never said that, Aoyama-san."

"But I was watching your face closely on the train, and I don't believe I misread your expression."

". . ."

"It's true that the Empire's coercive methods are unpleasant, but the beautiful sakura are innocent of any crime. It would be a dream for me to go see sakura blossoms with you, Chi-chan.

You know, I've never had any friends to go flower-viewing and picnicking with . . ."

"..."

"Chi-chan?"

"Aoyama-san."

"Hm?"

"To be honest, I'm at a total loss with you! Ah—I apologize, I've spoken out of turn. Perhaps I am tipsy as well."

"That's no matter. Oh dear oh dear."

"Oh dear oh dear indeed."

CHAPTER V

Bah-Sò / Braised Minced Pork

There was a monument in Kagi that marked the Tropic of Cancer. Everything south of it was officially "the tropics."

The monument was built in Meiji Year 41,[1] the same year the railway was completed. But even without it, the scorching sun was telling enough; the Taiwanese heat showed no sign of easing even in September. Taiwan was, without a doubt, a Southern Country of the Tropics.

Chi-chan and I were again on our way south, this time past Kagi and down to Takao. Not far from the train station, we saw a vendor shouldering a pole with a small cabinet tied to one end and a large basket to the other. Even with the sun roasting my brain and stirring ripples in the air, I couldn't ignore the bucket of chopsticks tied to the cabinet.

"Is that a vendor heading to the market?" I asked Chi-chan.

She stopped in her tracks and looked in the direction of my gaze. "No, not to the market. That's a street vendor—probably of lóo-bah rice."

"Lóo-bah rice?"

"Remember when we talked about Hakka-style braised pork belly—fung-ngiug? You said that Nagasaki had a similar pork kakuni. Lóo-bah is the Taiwanese Hoklo take on the same concept. We often put lóo-bah on a small bowl of rice, a dish we call lóo-bah-pn̄g, literally 'braised pork rice.' It's a very popular small

1. King: 1908.

dish among laborers, but because lóo-bah is on the expensive side, it's also a bit of an indulgence. Come to think of it, that vendor may be selling bah-sò-pn̄g, because the pork used for bah-sò is cheaper than the pork for lóo-bah."

"I see. Well, can we have some of that?"

"Aoyama-san, you just finished two bento. Granted, they were bare-minimum 'patriotic bento,' but you also finished the side dishes we brought."

By side dishes, Chi-chan meant the pickled daikon that were called tshài-póo in Taiwanese and could withstand the formidable heat, as well as a type of dried fish called sì-phuà-póo, which were salted mackerel stir-fried with soy sauce, ginger, and garlic. These fish were just slightly burnt, and had a texture somewhere between meat jerky and typical dried fish that was simply irresistible.

"I would have offended the sì-phuà-póo if I hadn't finished it. It was just that delicious."

"You would have offended the fish?"

"Precisely."

"But may I remind you of all the snacks you bought at the dagashi[2] store? The soy sauce rice crackers, the milk rice crackers, not to mention the sugared wheat puffs."

"And the roasted soybean candies and the karintō fried flour."

"Yes, all those kinds."

"Well, I bought those because it's the most awful thing to find oneself hungry and without snacks while spending the night in a strange place."

"And yet you've finished all of them."

---

2. Yáng: Among Japanese confections, known broadly as wagashi (literally, "Japanese confection"), there is a subcategory of snacks made from cheap materials that were designed to be long-lasting and easy to carry. These snacks, intended for "commoner" consumption, are called dagashi.

"*That's* because it's offensive to the delicious snacks if I didn't finish them in one go."

"Mhm."

"So—can we go get some lóo-bah rice now?"

"Aoyama-san." Her smile was immaculate. "The answer is no."

Oh dear.

We were scheduled to spend three days in Takao. On the first day, we took the express train from Taichū to Takao, which took four hours. It was ōmagatoki,[3] roughly five in the evening, by the time we arrived. On the second day, we would have a film screening with support from the local Women's Cultural Lectures Association, which would be followed by a talk. We would return to Taichū on the third day.

The Women's Association was to hold a banquet on the night of our arrival. Chi-chan knew my dislike for banquets, and had arranged for dishes that I hadn't tasted before to appease me. The menu included Hakka-style fung-ngiug; a chicken dish that involved three steps of frying, braising, *and* steaming; winter melon broth; egg-coated fried shrimp scramble; silver carp steamed with radish and cucumber; eel broth; and a final addition of the mangrove crab steamed rice that Chi-chan specially ordered because she knew how much I loved it. I understood her concern: it would've been a pathetic waste of all the effort that had gone into orchestrating this banquet if I'd filled my stomach with lóo-bah rice beforehand.

"Don't worry about it, Chi-chan. Even with lóo-bah rice, I can still eat two, three crabs—with room to spare!"

Chi-chan looked as though she did not know whether to laugh or cry. "Aoyama-san, you misunderstand me. You see, there

---

3. King: Ōmagatoki is Japanese for the time of day when the sky grows dark. The kanji characters technically mean "the time for meeting spirits and monsters."

are no seats at street vendors. Do not say you plan on eating rice while standing shoulder to shoulder with men."

"What, it's tachigui[4] only?"

I turned and saw that, while we'd been talking, the vendor had pulled to a stop at the street corner, hailed by a middle-aged man who had brought his own bowls, followed by a few boys wearing student caps. They clustered around the vendor like butterflies sharing a petal.

Looking more closely, I saw that there was an iron pot secured inside the short cabinet, which seemed to contain a charcoal stove. When the vendor removed the lid, hot steam tumbled from the iron pot. He then opened the large basket at the other end of the bamboo pole, revealing a clean cotton cloth that in turn unveiled pearly white rice. He was unbelievably speedy; in no time at all, he had filled the bowl with rice and drizzled two ladles of meat sauce on top, encircling the rice as though it was a small hill.

And ah! How delicious it looked!

The middle-aged man, with a bowl in each hand, hurried away with a grin on his face. The students, on the other hand, began shoveling the pork and rice into their mouths standing next to the vendor.

Could I really join them, burying my face in a bowl side by side with teenage boys? Even I, the Great Cedar, had to blush at such a thought. It seemed as though I could only give up on the overpowering urge. I groaned miserably.

Chi-chan said, "There will be pork belly at the banquet. I will ask the chef to make part of it into lóo-bah for Aoyama-san."

"No, no, that's not how it works." I sighed dramatically. "You see, Chi-chan, dagashi and jōgashi are entirely different

---

4. King: Tachigui, literally "eating while standing," is a popular style of casual dining in Japan.

things.[5] And why bother traveling at all if one only plans on eating jōgashi?"

She hesitated. "I see. Aoyama-san prefers dagashi over jōgashi because in order to be truly immersed in the local environs, one ought to favor street food over restaurant banquets, is that right?"

"That's exactly right. You understand me perfectly!"

"Then seeing as we cannot have lóo-bah at the moment, I will have to ask Aoyama-san to make do with daga—" she stopped speaking and flashed an apologetic smile. "I beg your pardon. The dagashi is all in your stomach. Ah, what on earth can we do? I suppose our only choice is to make haste for the restaurant!"

"Chi-chan, are you making fun of me?"

"Oh dear. And if I am?"

"Hmph . . ."

"If I am, that is only because Aoyama-san is noble-minded enough to permit her interpreter to tease her. I am very fortunate to find myself by your side."

"What a sly thing to say! Now I can't possibly argue against you."

I hunched over, putting on an exaggerated look of defeat. Chi-chan gently bent my shoulders back to place and said, laughing, "Let's go."

I turned to see her smiling at me. Her dimples looked as sweet as though they were made from honey. I felt almost faint.

Oh dear oh dear oh dear.

---

5. Yáng: Jōgashi are exquisitely crafted Japanese desserts developed through tea ceremony culture. The discrepancy between jōgashi (literally, "upper/superior snack") and affordable dagashi (literally, "lower/trivial snack") is not unlike the dichotomy of the upper and working classes.

By the time we went to Takao, I'd been living in Taiwan for almost six months.

I had no habit of keeping a diary for day-to-day matters. I did not document the endless speeches and tea parties—roughly eight to ten a week—and could only revisit them through whatever made it into my Taiwan Travelogue essay series. I also couldn't keep count of the many, many people I met.

As the Empire's southern colony—and, for that matter, the Empire's first colony—Taiwan was a fascinating place to observe in terms of the interplay between Japanese and local cultures. There were many subtle differences among the Mainlanders who remain in Japan, the Mainlanders who had moved to the Island, the Mainlanders born on the Island, the Islanders who grew up within the Empire's modern civilization, and the Islanders who had pursued schooling or work on the Mainland. These differences revealed their respective upbringings and the ways in which they were taught to carry themselves, but, seeing as these were difficult to summarize in a few words, I had yet to write about them.

I had, instead, been entirely engrossed in observing the Island's peoples.

As a young person and as a novelist, I had neither the talents nor the ambitions of politicians and academics. All I could manage was to record what I saw and heard, as well as my true feelings of the moment.

And as for what those so-called true feelings were—

The Empire's Southern Expansion Movement and so-called National Spirit Mobilization Movement had taken shape as imperial assimilation movements here in the colonies. Were they not, in essence, brute acts of erasing the distinctions of individual cultures? I couldn't help but feel resistance and disgust whenever I considered the matter seriously.

In the face of war, there is no distinction between man and woman.

This was a tune that I'd heard some sing. I was unconvinced.

It would have been more accurate to say *When it comes to hurdles faced by women, there is no distinction between Mainland and Island.*

Yet I did not openly disclose these cynical views. At the banquet, when a Madame K of the Women's Cultural Lectures Association asked me about the roles that women and writers ought to play in the Holy War, I replied by quoting Mencius:[6] "When out of favor, attend to one's own virtue; when favored, attend to the virtue of the world." I told her that tending to the things immediately in front of us seemed enough to me—that the key lay in our awareness and our actions. Madame K then asked what some concrete examples of such "actions" might be. I replied that we ought to care for the disenfranchised and encourage those who aspire to learn, so as to cultivate strong hearts and minds in our people and thus enable every individual to become a pillar of our homeland.

All around the table, people expressed their admiration for my little speech.

I couldn't betray so much as a blush as I said these things. Ah, to think that even I couldn't escape the fate of regurgitating these polite platitudes!

Chi-chan and I declined the Women's Society limousine after the banquet and set out for our hotel on foot. On the road lit by streetlamps, a breeze wafted toward us. The heat had finally diminished a little in the night. I watched Chi-chan's profile from the corner of my eye and felt as though there was a mirage obscuring her face; I couldn't read any trace of "true feeling" in it.

She had worn her Noh mask the whole night.

Yes, she was impeccable in her secretarial work; yes, she was a remarkable cook. But those things aside, what I found even

6. King: Mencius (Mandarin: Mèng-zǐ) was a Chinese philosopher who lived from 372 to 289 BCE. His influence is commonly considered second only to that of Confucius.

more extraordinary was her extreme social maturity—her flexibility and infallible propriety—given her young age. Should I call it empathy? At times I even felt as though she could read minds, effortlessly detecting the most minute changes in other people's moods and attitudes and quickly offering an appropriate response in kind. Even when she was faced with open hostility, she could restore harmony with a few quick strokes. Was this all thanks to her aspiration to become a professional translator?

I could not help but feel in awe. Hers was not only a vocation, but a craft—an art.

Speaking of which, even in the strictly linguistic aspect of this work, Chi-chan had deeply impressed me. Not only was she skilled in the national language, Hokkien, Hakka, and English, she also seemed to have some knowledge of French.

The first hint of this was on our train ride to Takao. There had been a Westerner couple in our car, and after they left, I made casual conversation about how I'd heard that English tourists particularly enjoyed traveling in colonized places. Chi-chan replied, "That couple was from France."

"Oh? Could you tell from their facial features?"

"From when they spoke. When they rose to leave, the husband let the wife pass first, and she said 'Merci,' to which he said 'De rien.' That means 'thank you' and 'you're welcome' in French."

"Chi-chan, you speak French!"

"Just a few basic phrases."

"Bonjour, good morning! Bonsoir, good evening!"

"Indeed. Merci beaucoup, de rien, au revoir, je t'aime—just some phrases I've picked up here and there."

Where in the world would one pick up such French phrases? I didn't probe any further.

This concubine's daughter born in a colony—albeit to a wealthy family—had been more difficult for me to sum up than any government official or literary scholar I'd met. What would Chi-chan have been like had she been born to Mainland aristocracy? No doubt someone formidable! In this sense, an Islander's identity *did* inhibit her fortunes. She was an overlooked jewel.

"Aoyama-san."

Her voice was soft and seemed to melt into the Takao night air, but was nevertheless enough to return my mind from its meandering. "Aoyama-san once said that the purpose of travel is to live someplace foreign, which also means you wish to document your life abroad, correct? You seem to have made plenty of progress on the Taiwan Travelogue project you've been working on. But what exactly are the kinds of things that you would like to document here on the Island?"

"Hm . . ."

After a moment, she said softly, "Please forget that I asked."

"No, you've asked a great question. In the past two years, I've made brief trips to Hokkaidō and Okinawa. Hokkaidō has the Ainu people and Okinawa has the Ryūkyū people, but both their native ways of life are gradually disappearing. And to think that the Empire's development of these places only began in the first year of Meiji![7] Under the Empire of the Sun, all children of the Holy Emperor must become part of the Yamato race—no doubt that's what the Empire aspires to."

Chi-chan looked as though she wished to say something. She did not, however, and I continued: "No doubt the colonies in Taiwan, Chōsen, and Manshū[8] will go down the same path as Hokkaidō and Okinawa. How tragic is that! At least that's what I think. As you saw at the banquet, I didn't wish to say anything that went against my beliefs, but even I couldn't avoid saying a few accommodating things about the war. I'm powerless against

7. King: 1868.

8. King: Chōsen is the Japanese name for Korea, per its earlier Korean name Joseon; the Korean Peninsula was under Japanese control from 1910 to 1945. Manshū is the Japanese name for Manchuria, where the Japanese established a puppet state from 1932 to 1945.

the state of the world. So, as a novelist, what can I do? I can come to Taiwan, write down what I observe, and preserve the state of this island before it's changed forever."

"But Taiwan has already gone down the same path."

Her footsteps stopped. I looked at her. The streetlight haloed her slender figure and made the seashell buttons of her chōsan[9] dance with warm light.

"What does Aoyama-san think of my attire today?"

"I think it looks wonderful."

"You are very kind."

"It's the truth. If you think I'm lying, I'll swallow a thousand needles to prove myself."

At this, her expression relaxed a little.

"But you did notice, did you not, that it was because of my Islander chōsan that Madame K asked such a pointed question? What she wanted from you was not a quotation from a Shina classic. If the occasion hadn't called for extreme decorum, Madame K would no doubt have said, 'Please ask your interpreter to stop dressing like a Qīng slave!'"

"There's no need to pay notice to someone like that."

"Aoyama-san is right. One day, people will no longer remember the Islander way of life. But during the Qīng period, the Hoklo people also did the same thing to the native tribes' ways of life here. How far back should one go when lamenting such cruelties? But the absurd thing about humanity is that we only feel pain when we're on the receiving end. Ah, I beg your pardon. These are the words of a drunk person, and I do not even have that excuse."

"Then let's drink. Let's order some wine when we get back to the hotel."

---

9. King: Chōsan is the Japanese pronunciation of the Mandarin cháng-shān, literally "long shirt." This is a long tunic typically worn in the early 1900s, and is a looser and more "masculine" equivalent of the cheongsam (Mandarin: qí-páo).

"It isn't a Western hotel. I do not think they have wine."

"Then beer! Ice-cold beer!"

I hooked her arm in mine and marched forward with big strides. We stepped out of the ring of light and into the dark, then again into the light of the next lamppost.

Light then dark. Clarity then obscurity.

The wind was so strong that it seemed capable of blowing our very shadows away.

"Will they serve food at this hour, do you think? Oh dear, if only we had some sì-phuà-póo!"

"We do. All the mackerel is stored in your stomach."

"Ahaha!"

"It's nothing to 'ahaha' about."

"Oh, before I forget, Chi-chan, let's go see the iron bridge before we go back to Taichū!"

"Iron bridge?"

"I saw it on some postcards in a store. It's called the Katansui River Iron Bridge.[10] The view looked so vast, so boundless! There's nothing like a great view to clear out pent-up gloom."

"We are scheduled to be on the 12:45 return train. If we miss it, the next one isn't until 4:15, and it will be the dead of night by the time we get back to Taichū. We won't even be able to get a taxi at that hour!"

"Oh, don't fuss over something like that! Ahaha!"

"There's nothing 'ahaha' about it . . ."

Our arms were linked and our footsteps were a dance. The night wind tousled our hair.

Apparently, postcards of the Katansui River Iron Bridge were rather rare in Takao. This was because the bridge was south of

10. Yáng: Katansui River is present-day Kāopíng River, and the bridge is now commonly known as Old Kāopíng Iron Bridge. It was put out of commission in 1992 and named a Grade II National Monument in 1997.

Takao in the direction of Heitō, located between Kyūkyokudō Station and Rokukaiseki Station. On the postcards I saw, the imposing-looking bridge was titled Katansui River Iron Bridge: Number One in the East or The Great Iron Bridge of Katansui River in Ako District, Over One Kilometer Long (Number One Longest Bridge in the Orient). I found it all quite appealing, especially the charming parentheses. Akō was an older name for Heitō, so the postcard had likely been printed long ago. I checked the hotel's copy of *Travel Guide to Taiwan's Railways* and saw that Katansui was the second-longest river on the Island, originating in Mount Niitaka.[11] Was that not all the more reason to see it in person?

Chi-chan thought not.

"I am very sorry. I had not anticipated Aoyama-san's interest in the bridge and my preparations are sorely lacking . . . would you kindly allow me to arrange for us to visit the bridge on our next trip to Takao?"

"Why wait for the next time? Traveling is more interesting when it's spontaneous!"

"Aoyama-san, Rokukaiseki Station was built specifically for horse racing. I have heard that it is bustling during races, but seeing as there are no races now, I'm afraid you will find Rokukaiseki very dull indeed. We could easily arrange to visit during a race on our next trip."

"Chi-chan, I have no wish to watch horse racing. I only wish to see the magnificent river and bridge!"

"Did you not hear the announcement earlier? There is a typhoon approaching. The bridge is over one kilometer long. It would be unsafe to ride a train across it during a storm."

"If the typhoon gets that bad, they would stop service anyway."

---

11. King: Mount Niitaka was the Japanese name for present-day Mount Jade (Mandarin: Yùshān). It is the highest mountain in Taiwan and, while Taiwan was under Japanese rule, was the highest mountain in the Japanese Empire. The kanji characters for Niitaka mean "new high."

"Aoyama-san . . . the ancients said, 'A person of great worth does not sit under rundown roofs.' You ought to protect yourself from harm."

"Chi-chan, the ancients also said, 'One cannot capture a tiger cub without crawling into its den.' No risk, no reward."

"I'm sorry to be so blunt, but a professional interpreter would not let her employer crawl into a tiger's den."

"Oh dear."

The hotel did not provide beer this late at night. After our baths, we ordered rice and green tea for chazuke, as well as bran-fermented vegetables for side dishes. We discussed our itinerary for the following day over the modest meal.

"Besides, I could not find a timetable for the Chōshū Line, and I cannot risk having Aoyama-san travel all that way for nothing. Please, Aoyama-san, allow me to decline your request at this time."

Her back was extremely straight, her expression extremely resolute.

I had no choice but to acquiesce.

That night, I fell asleep listening to the howl of the wind. The following morning, I rose early to a gloomy sort of dawn. At this, I thought that the typhoon must really be nigh, but after taking a turn around the hotel, I saw sunshine pierce the corner of the sky where some clouds had begun to disperse.

I ran into Chi-chan in the hotel's hallway. She said, "They have the onsen poached egg you like for breakfast."

"Let's go!"

"Go? Go where?"

"To Rokukaiseki! I was told that the typhoon won't make a landing until much later. I also found a timetable for the Chōshū Line! There's one about thirty minutes from now. If that's too much of a rush, we can still make it back by noon even if we take the next train."

"Aoyama-san, you still haven't given up . . ."

"Ahahaha!"

I took her hand and made for the table. My breakfast consisted of onsen egg, white rice, sashimi, and miso soup with ganmodoki fritters.[12] Chi-chan's was toast, a French omelet, ham slices, and hot coffee. I tipped two drops of soy sauce onto my onsen egg, swirled the egg into the rice, and downed the whole thing in a few slurps. The sashimi and fritters, however, deserved slower and more thorough savoring. Chi-chan sandwiched her omelet and ham between the toast and finished it in a few bites, but slowed down when she was sipping her coffee. Perhaps she was pacing herself to my rhythm, or perhaps the coffee was just too hot.

"Isn't the ham better eaten on its own?"

"Thanks to Aoyama-san's speed, I can barely taste anything."

"Then let's ask the waitstaff to pack us some ham to eat slowly on the train!"

"I can never keep up with you."

"You flatter me."

"No," she said, smiling and shaking her head, "I did not intend it as praise."

Her exasperation, mixed with a wisp of amusement, was far tastier than the fritters.

"Oh, come, come," I said, appeasing and playful.

Chi-chan stared for a while at my broad grin, then her shoulders dropped.

"Oh, go, go," she said.

Was she impersonating me? The mischievous tone suited her so poorly that I couldn't help but laugh.

---

12. Yáng: Ganmodoki is a Japanese fritter made of mashed tofu and minced vegetables such as carrot, lotus root, and burdock, which are balled up and deep-fried.

By the time we finished eating, our taxi was waiting for us in front of the hotel. When we arrived at the station, the train was due to depart in five minutes. Everything was going as well as possible. There was even a vendor in front of the train station with a cart full of namagashi.[13]

On the train, I leaned against the car window, but Chi-chan sat ramrod straight.

"You must be good at mental arithmetic, are you not?" I asked.

"Is Aoyama-san demonstrating her detective skills again? No, I would not presume to live up to such praise."

I couldn't believe it. She had put on her Noh mask.

"Hmph! Let me test you on the desserts we just bought, then. The dorayaki pancakes—both the red bean and cream-filled flavors—were ten sen per piece, or five for forty sen. The yōkan jelly—both the red bean and mung bean flavors—were twelve sen each, or six for sixty sen. The red bean dango, runner bean dango, and red bean mochi were all ten sen each, no discounts."

"Very well."

"Right now, in this bag I'm holding, there are three red bean dorayaki, three cream dorayaki, three red bean yōkan, three mung bean yōkan, three red bean dango, and three red bean mochi."

"Very well. And?"

I handed the bag to her. "What is the total cost of what I just gave you?"

"Two yen."

"Ah! So close and yet so far!"

---

13. Yáng: Namagashi is a subcategory of wagashi desserts that contain more moisture, such as mochi, yōkan, and red bean paste. Many luxurious jōgashi are namagashi, but Taiwan had developed affordable namagashi that were often sold on the street. Though fewer in number now, there are still namagashi carts in Taiwan to this day.

"Hm?"

"Alas, alas! Wrong answer."

"How so? Six dorayaki is five for forty sen plus one more for ten sen, which is fifty. Six yōkan is six for sixty sen. The dango are sixty, and the mochi is thirty. Fifty plus sixty plus sixty plus thirty is two hundred sen, or two yen. I wasn't wrong."

"You are indeed, because this is a present from me to you, and so the cost is exactly zero sen."

Chi-chan looked dumbfounded.

Her adorable lashes flickered up then down then up. I watched the immaculate Noh mask melt—ever so slowly, just like the thawing of ice—into an expression of grudging fondness.

"I can never keep up with you, Aoyama-san," she said.

I smiled. "I would not presume to live up to such praise."

Before I knew it, the train had departed Kyūkyokudō.

Outside, the wind tore through the scenery. It seemed capable of thrusting the train faster, or even lifting it into flight. The view outside our window unfurled like a movie. In all directions, the streets appeared and receded in the blink of an eye.

Then, a mere second later, the train was on the Number One Longest Bridge in the Orient. The iron trusses flashed by on both sides like frames in a roll of film. The glimmering waves of the river only flared in intervals.

I squinted. Something trembled at the bottom of my heart.

"It's beautiful. Taiwan."

Chi-chan seemed to feel the same thing I was feeling. She said, as gently as though she was merely exhaling, "Yes, it is."

See? There was nothing like an open view to clear a gloomy mind.

The train arrowed forward. The trusses, in breaking the wind, made a rhythmic roar. Still squinting, I looked all around. On the forests of both shores, the deep green of old trees was interspersed with the bright green of young ones. A few beams of golden light penetrated the sieve of clouds and danced on the tips of the leaves. White flowers were blooming on a sandbank in the middle of the river. As the wind blew, their petals undulated like ocean waves.

"Are those reedbeds?"

"No, they aren't reeds. In Taiwanese, we call them kâu-tsià, monkey sugarcane, or iá-tsià, wild sugarcane. They aren't actually a variety of sugarcane, but we call them that because the roots taste slightly sweet."

"Oh, you can eat them! How nice."

"Well, people sometimes use them as an ingredient in tshenn-tsháu-à tea, but I've never heard of anyone eating the plant by itself."

My stomach growled. I'd only eaten one bowl of rice for breakfast, after all.

Chi-chan said, "Let's make some bah-sò-pn̄g when we get back to Taichū. Or would Aoyama-san prefer lóo-bah-pn̄g?"

"Both! Bah-sò *and* lóo-bah! Merci beaucoup!"

"Je vous en prie, mademoiselle."

"Aha! You *do* speak French!"

Chi-chan did not deny it. The gentle light in her eyes was just like the river's shimmer that flashed between the trusses of the bridge.

Merci beaucoup. *Thank you very much.*

Je vous en prie, mademoiselle. *You're very welcome, miss.*

What had Chi-chan said? "Merci beaucoup, de rien, au revoir, je t'aime—just some phrases I've picked up here and there."

Au revoir. *Goodbye.*

Je t'aime. *I love you.*

Really, in what context would one "pick up" French phrases like these?

I was no detective, and the only mystery I managed to solve was about bah-sò and loo-báh.

When Chi-chan first saw the street vendor, she'd guessed that he was selling lóo-bah-pn̄g; it was only later that she deduced he was selling bah-sò-pn̄g. Her only explanation then had been "because the pork used for bah-sò is cheaper than the pork for lóo-bah," which meant that the two dishes must be extremely similar. How could one tell the difference?

The day after we returned to Taichū, Chi-chan came armed with pork and answers. She brought not only pork belly, whose meat was intact with skin, but also—separately—pork skin.

"When put into words, both lóo-bah and bah-sò are pork braised in soy sauce or a specialized marinade, which makes them sound extremely similar. If you only tasted the sauce from the stew alone, the taste would be almost the same as well. But the biggest difference between the two is their forms. As I said, the way to make lóo-bah is the same as making Dōngpō pork: braising chunks of pork belly with skin. Bah-sò, on the other hand, is braised minced pork. You've actually tasted it before, Aoyama-san. Do you remember?"

"Oh! Now that you say it—was it when we had bí-thai-ba̍k? I even wrote it down in my notes! Ah, I see—so if you drizzle bah-sò on rice, pn̄g, then you get bah-sò-pn̄g. What a no-fuss way of naming a dish! I like it!"

"Bah-sò is used in many dishes, not just bí-thai-ba̍k and bah-sò-pn̄g. We eat it with rice noodles, vermicelli noodles, and Taichū's extra-thick wheat noodles. Oh, and the hand-rolled meatballs we had in Rokkō also had bah-sò as the filling. But, even though all these are called bah-sò, they're not necessarily made in the same way. Every family has its own bah-sò recipe depending on their financial means and dining habits."

"Really? Wow. Islanders must really like their bah-sò!"

"Indeed. One might even say that Islanders like our bah-sò as much as Mainlanders like their sashimi."

I pointed at the piece of pork skin on the cutting board. "But this—I don't remember seeing this before."

This wasn't to say that I'd never seen the skin of pork. Dōngpō pork, pork kakuni, and feng-ngiug pork all came with a thick, oily, tender layer of skin. The slab of pork belly meat that was also lying on the cutting board also had its skin. Yet *that* piece of pork skin was, extraordinarily, skin only. The meat had been removed. All that remained was the thick, rubbery-looking skin cushioned by a thin layer of white fatty tissue.

"Pork skin is the cheapest part of pork. Poor families sometimes use it when they're making bah-sò—mincing the skin and boiling the fat off of it using low heat, which also generates lard as a by-product. Lard is not only useful as cooking oil that adds flavor to other dishes, but can also be drizzled by itself over rice for a simple dish that both the rich and the poor enjoy. Once the lard has been removed, you add soy sauce, cane sugar, and fried shallots to the remaining minced pork and scramble it thoroughly until the aroma of the pork grows strong and rich. You then add a small amount of water and stew it until the juice of the meat is reduced into a thick, viscous, fragrant bah-sò. So long as you are willing to spend the time, homemade bah-sò can be just as delicious as the ones at the vendors' stalls—though it can take half a day."

"Oh my. It's as complex as the jute soup! Both dishes were created by true gourmets."

"No—unlike muâ-ínn-thng, bah-sò with pork skin is *actually* gourmet cuisine."

"You're right," I said. "I can tell how delicious it must be just from listening to Chi-chan's explanation."

She looked at me with some surprise.

"Aoyama-san," she said. "You really are very kind."

"Not that again."

"The pork I used for bah-sò last time was of better quality than what I brought today, so today's pork skin bah-sò will most definitely be inferior. A true gourmet like Aoyama-san will certainly know the difference."

"The only thing I know for certain is that everything you cook is delicious."

She was silent for a long time. "Aigh, I really, really cannot keep up with you, Aoyama-san."

"If you think I'm lying, I'll swallow a thousand needles to prove myself."

She laughed brightly. But when she spoke, it was not in response to my words and instead about lóo-bah. "In the word lóo-bah, the verb lóo means to braise with soy sauce and marinate until all the flavor is absorbed by the meat. There's a similar term called khòng-bah, where the khòng means to braise the meat so thoroughly that it becomes fluffy and tender. Islanders refer to the dish as either lóo-bah or khòng-bah depending on the region."

"Oh! But that means bah-sò also uses the lóo technique, does it not?"

"It does. I've heard that chefs for wealthy families cut up pig shoulder to make bah-sò. Because they take into consideration the ratio of fatty versus lean meat, the bah-sò they end up serving still looks less like bah-sò and more like lóo-bah."

"How erudite national language teachers are these days."

"Now Aoyama-san is mocking me."

"That is because Ō Chizuru-san is noble-minded enough to permit her friend to tease her."

"Oh dear." Chi-chan glared at me with mock anger and turned away from our conversation. She went to the sink and began washing her hands meticulously. I watched the soap bubbles run from her hands.

"When it comes to both lóo-bah-pn̄g and bah-sò-pn̄g," she said, "the other main character is the pn̄g—the rice. The Island's traditional long-grained zairai rice is delicious, and one can also steam it together with glutinous rice for a different texture. Short-grained hōrai rice has more elasticity and can better absorb the juice from the meat, and nowadays, both lóo-bah-pn̄g and bah-sò-pn̄g vendors use hōrai rice.[14] I've prepared hōrai rice from Toyohara for you today. I hope you will have the chance to try zairai rice in the future."

She turned off the tap. Her voice and the sound of water stopped at the same time.

She turned to look at me.

Probably because, on a usual day, I would have moseyed off to wait for dinner at my writing desk already.

"I'm afraid that's the end of my presentation," Chi-chan said. "I'm going to start cooking now. Are you not writing today?"

"I'd like to watch. Is that all right?"

"Lóo-bah and bah-sò take a long time to prepare. You will be bored, I'm sure."

"I won't be."

"If you say so."

She turned on the tap again, letting the water fill the pot. With the water still running, she placed the pork at the bottom. The water overflowed from the pot, rinsing away the minuscule particles on the surface of the pork. Chi-chan then deftly removed the meat and patted down the excess moisture with a clean cloth.

Picking up a pair of tweezers, she removed the remaining hairs from the piece of pork skin. She then returned her attention to the pork belly, cutting it into cubes. After that, she chopped up the pork skin. Every movement was measured and composed; even the mincing of meat looked graceful.

"Aoyama-san."

"Yes, ma'am."

---

14. King: During Japanese rule, Japanese agricultural scientists modified short-grained japonica rice to grow in Taiwan's climate. This new species was named hōrai (Japanese) or péng-lái (Mandarin) rice. To differentiate, long-grained indica rice native to Taiwan was renamed zairai (Japanese) or zài-lái (Mandarin) rice.

"The pork skin bah-sò."

"What about it?"

"Surely you know."

"I assure you that I don't."

"When I was young—when I was living with my mother's family on the farm—we could only have pork skin bah-sò on special occasions."

"I'm sure it made for wonderful memories."

At this, she lifted her face and smiled at me. "When I was young, I thought that pork skin bah-sò was a rare, luxurious dish. I had a dream back then: that one day, when I grew up, I would eat as much bah-sò-pn̄g as my heart desired."

"Well, then, I suppose today is that day."

She said nothing.

"Oh, bah-sò-pn̄g probably goes well with beer, doesn't it? We can have the beer that we didn't get to drink in Takao. I'll go send for some cold beer. Since we're in the city, we can order wine too. Red wine and pork would be *delectable*!"

"It's quite official," Chi-chan said. "I can never, *ever* keep up with you. You have utterly defeated me." Chuckling, she returned to the kitchen counter and sorted the chunks and mince of pork in separate bowls.

The squeak of the tap. The splish-splash of water.

Chi-chan began washing the cutting board, and the splatter hushed to a trickle.

"Chi-chan, you really don't have to use keigo with me."[15]

---

15. King: Keigo, literally "respectful speech," is the Japanese system of honorific speech used to address one's superiors and elders. The system is expressed through both vocabulary and grammar, altering conjugation and sentence structure. As this is impossible to reflect in English (and, for that matter, Mandarin Chinese), I have tried to express this through different degrees of tonal formality, e.g., having Mishima from City Hall speak with more formality and stiffness than Aoyama, who often speaks casually.

"That would be—nice."

"Wouldn't it?"

I gazed at her profile. Her soft, warm, sweet face.

"The typhoon's making its way to Taichū. Why don't you spend the night here?"

"You know that I will do no such thing."

"But we'll be having beer and wine."

"Would you like to play dice for it?"

"Oh dear oh dear. She never lets her guard down!"

CHAPTER VI

Tang-Kue-Tê / Winter Melon Tea

"Lí-ya!"

A slur for Islanders, used by Mainlanders.

Half a year into my time on the Island, Chi-chan and I found ourselves trailing behind F-sensei, a woman teacher and dormitory supervisor at the Tainan County First High School for Girls, who was giving us a tour of the campus founded in the sixth year of Taishō.[1]

The school gates opened to a passage lined with flower patches on both sides. The first row of buildings along the path were administrative offices, followed by a row of educational facilities—including a newly completed building equipped with an art classroom and an exhibition space for scientific specimens. The remaining three rows were student quarters. There were two dormitories and a third building that held the bathhouse, cafeteria, kitchens, and other communal spaces. The area was bookended by a swimming pool to the east and four tennis courts to the west.

According to F-sensei, those who seek to provide an education for the modern woman must nurture students into well-mannered, well-informed, multitalented *persons* of excellence first and foremost, and only *women* of excellence second—

"Furthermore," she concluded in a voice that rang with authority, "any one of our students or faculty members can say

---

1. Yáng: 1917.

with their heads held high: our school's hopes for our students are thoroughly reflected in our architecture."

Hm. The "First" Girls' School certainly lived up to its name.

I said, "Seeing as there is a First Girls' School, there must also be a second?"

"Indeed. The Second High School for Girls is but two streets away."

"I see. And how are the two different?"

"The Second Girls' School mostly takes Islander students, and the campus is roughly half the size of ours. Indeed, some local residents have objected to this division, but you see, all of Tainan's female students who excel in their studies name *our* school as their top choice. There is no Islander student who does not take pride in herself for testing into *our* school—and that, in the end, is the proof of our excellence!"

Excellence, excellence, excellence.

I glanced at Chi-chan, who stood next to me wearing a smile as immaculate as white jade.

"F-sensei," I said, "would you say that even within this community of all-around excellence, there are still Mainlander students who would call Islanders 'lí-ya'? I only learned about the word very recently, you see."

F-sensei stopped walking. She turned to first look at me, and then at Chi-chan.

"I would very much like to say that such ill-mannered words are not uttered within our school, but—Aoyama-sensei, if you intend to write on this subject, please do make it clear that the school dealt with the matter fairly!"

"I have no intention of targeting the school. It was just something I happened to hear about on my travels."

"Hm. What a coincidence." F-sensei evidently found my explanation unconvincing. Nevertheless, she took it upon herself to elaborate. "Recently, an incident took place between two fourth-year students in the same class, Ōzawa Reiko of Mainland citizenship and Tân Tshiok-bi of Island citizenship. Both are very popular students who, over time, unwittingly attracted something like two opposing camps among their classmates. That said, the two used to be very close friends! I suppose a bit of friction is inevitable when young women are at the peak of adolescence. They have since reconciled, however."

"Really? The opposing camps disbanded so easily?"

"Well, dividing into cliques is common for students their age, no? Some Islander students protested that Ōzawa-san had addressed Tân-san as lí-ya. The school took the complaint *very* seriously and was able to resolve the conflict *very* quickly. In fact, it is only because the school has *no* tolerance for such poor behavior that this small affair was ever regarded as an 'incident' at all. I only say this because, after the uproar died down, some of the students came to us privately to say that it had all been something of an inside joke."

Inside joke.

A Noh mask took extraordinary skill to maintain. I couldn't emulate Chi-chan, and instead stared directly into F-sensei's eyes.

F-sensei gave a small chuckle.

"Of course, whether or not it was in jest, the school addressed the issue with an appropriate response. In fact, we hoped to reconcile the two students through a suitable educational approach, and therefore arranged for them to share the responsibility of receiving Aoyama-sensei on your visit. Ah, there they are."

She gestured toward the path between the classrooms and the dormitories. At the dormitory doors, a bougainvillea tree teemed with plum-red and violet-purple flowers.

Two students stood shoulder to shoulder under the tree, both gazing up at the resplendent bloom.

It was like a scene out of a shōjo novel.[2]

---

2. King: Shōjo, translating roughly to "young woman," is a literary genre popularized in Japan beginning with the Meiji era in the early 1900s. The novels were serialized in magazines that targeted an adolescent female readership.

A slow breeze rose, brushing some of the blossoms off their branches.

One of the girls, who had the build of a star athlete, raised a hand to brush the fallen petals off the shoulder of the shorter, slighter girl.

I could not wrap my head around it: one of these two shōjo novel characters had called the other a lí-ya.

Allow me to start again, this time from the beginning.

I first heard someone use the term lí-ya the day we arrived in Tainan.

While the Taihoku Railway Hotel was the premier Western-style hotel on the Island, I was much more interested in the newer Tainan Railway Hotel in the south. In the former, the attractions are pretty much limited to: one, good Western food, and two, guest elevators that save you the effort of stairs. Although its Tainan counterpart was also Western, fully equipped with a restaurant, bar, entertainment center, and telephone room, it boasted an additional distinction of being located within the train station itself. The hotel had just nine guest rooms total, and its lobby was right past the ticket gate on the second floor of the station. I looked forward to what I thought would be a delightful experience of drinking my fill, falling into a boozy sleep, then waking up to the noise of an engine and wheels hurtling across the tracks as the first train pulled into the sunlit station.

With this in mind, I'd asked Chi-chan to arrange a trip to Tainan. Our itinerary would be much like the one in Takao: arrive on day one, give a lecture on day two, return to Taichū on day three.

Despite its being October, there wasn't one trace of autumnal cool in Tainan's air. By the time we got past the ticket gate, I was much more invested in getting my hands on an ice-cold soda than in seeing the hotel.

"But Aoyama-san, you can get a soda anywhere—would you not be interested in Tainan's winter melon tea instead?"

"Oh! What's that?"

"There are a few traditional Islander beverages for combating the heat: tshenn-tsháu-à tea, plum tea, lotus tea, and tang-kue-tê—winter melon tea. This is made by stewing winter melon with sugar until it boils down to concentrated blocks, which are then dissolved in cold water. For those of us living in the tropics, winter melon not only cools us down but also replenishes our energy. Mainlanders have a hard time getting used to tshenn-tsháu-à tea, but they tend to be very fond of the sweet winter melon tea."

"By winter melon, you mean the green gourds with the white spots? You make that into *sweet* tea?"

"Precisely. You should definitely have a taste."

"But of course!"

I was ready to head straight out of the station in search of this wonderful drink, luggage and all. But Chi-chan touched my arm and began steering me toward the staircase that led to the hotel's check-in.

Alas.

I suppose I should give an accurate account of the hotel. In keeping with its low room count, Tainan Railway Hotel had but a petite staircase. Only the lofty arched window that flooded everything with sunlight possessed the grandeur of a high-end hotel. Heading up the stairs, one is faced directly with the front desk. To the right is a long hallway, whose main source of light is a row of smaller arched windows along the western wall rather than the glass chandeliers overhead.

I walked over to the main window and looked down at the train terminal. Countless heads crisscrossed below: panama hats, floppy straw hats, fedoras, as well as baseball caps, military caps, and student caps. There were women with intricate updos and boys with clean-shaven, monk-like skulls. I could not tear my eyes away, thinking that this was perhaps the most entrancing view of Tainan Station one could find.

It happened then.

"Lí-ya!" A deep, gruff voice.

I turned and saw Chi-chan standing not far from the reception desk. Her profile was backlit and therefore obscured from me. Her silhouette was stiff and straight-backed—her shoulders rose and fell ever so slightly with each breath.

She walked toward the desk.

I hurried after her in time to see the receptionist's disgruntled face.

"We're full. Now get out of here."

It was impossible to believe that such spiteful words could come from the staff of a luxury hotel. Chi-chan, however, was calm.

"Would you kindly confirm the reservation for Aoyama Chizuko-sensei under the Nisshinkai Organization?" She presented her business card to the glowering man. "I am her Islander interpreter. Aoyama-sensei is a writer visiting from the Mainland at the invitation of the Taiwanese Government-General itself. If you have any questions, you may direct them to Mr. Mishima Aizō at Taichū City Hall."

I did not possess her patience. "Enough! There's no reason why we should take this boorish treatment. So *this* is the best that the Tainan Railway Hotel has to offer!"

I began pulling Chi-chan away, but the receptionist darted out from behind the desk and gave a deep bow.

"Please accept my deepest apologies. It is my fault entirely. We have heard from City Hall earlier—you may access your rooms immediately if you wish." When he raised his face again, it had transformed from the scowl of a Niō warrior to the jolly grin of Ebisu.

The sudden transformation stunned me into silence. Was this part of some avant-garde play?

While I had my guard down, several of Ebisu's servant boys

materialized to take our luggage away. The goddess Benzaiten—who, until moments ago, had simply been a woman attendant blatantly ignoring our presence—greeted us with a broad smile, as though we were honored patrons who had just donated a large fortune to her temple.[3]

"Did Aoyama-sensei arrive on the last train? The journey must have been exhausting in this heat! Ah, here is Aoyama-sensei's suite, and Interpreter-san's room is just across the hall—very convenient. We will arrange for you to dine at the railway restaurant tonight. Dinner is at six, but please just say the word if you would like to have it earlier or later. We will bring you cold beverages in a moment—would you prefer fresh juice, soda, or milk? Shall we bring the beverages to your rooms separately?"

Her enthusiasm was so over the top that it was almost comedic.

"Dinner at six is fine. And please bring two glasses of juice to my room."

The chilled drinks soon appeared on an ornate tray.

Inside the suite was a Western mattress with springs, curtains with elaborately woven patterns, and chairs with curved armrests. Chi-chan and I sat at opposite ends of the room and finished our juices in silence. The farce and chaos that had pummeled us since we set foot in the hotel only now began to recede.

A leftover ice cube gave a small crackle from the bottom of a glass.

Chi-chan sighed quietly. "I am so sorry to have caused Aoyama-san alarm."

"It wasn't your fault at all."

---

3. Yáng: The Niō warriors, Ebisu, and Benzaiten are all folk deities in Japan. The Niō warriors are guardians of Buddhist temples, who are often represented with menacing expressions. Ebisu and Benzaiten are two of Japan's Shichifukujin (Seven Gods of Fortune), who are known for their smiling expressions.

"But it was. Wearing a chōsan was negligent on my part."

It was then that Chi-chan explained it to me.

Lí-ya!

The word meant "You there!" in Taiwanese. While at first it was simply a crude way of addressing Islanders—implying that they could be ordered around at will—somewhere along the way it had become a derogatory slur in itself.

Chi-chan and I had checked out of Tainan Railroad Hotel before traveling to the campus. At my request, Chi-chan had made prior arrangements with the school for us to spend the night in their dormitories following my lecture, hence F-sensei assigning students to serve as our hosts. Under the bougainvillea tree, F-sensei transferred us into the care of Ōzawa Reiko and Tân Tshiok-bi, two young women who lived up to their respective names. Ōzawa, like the kanji characters for "vast waters" and "beauty" in her name, was broad-shouldered and full-bosomed, with a comely face and a grounded carriage. Tân Tshiok-bi, like her kanji characters for "sparrow" and "slight," was as delicate and spindly as a prepubescent boy.

"Does Aoyama-sensei stay in dormitories when lecturing at other schools as well?" Ōzawa asked.

"To be honest, yours is the first school where I'm staying overnight."

"Oh! But that must mean Aoyama-sensei is interested in our dormitories specifically. Why is that, may I ask? Are our housing facilities particularly well known?"

I grinned. "Well, before I came to the Island, I read a book written in the Taishō era by an English traveler who visited a girls' school in Tainan—which I think must be this one—and noted that the dormitories housed three students per room. Why an odd number? Generally speaking, even numbers are much easier to manage from an administrative standpoint. You see, mine is the type of idle mind that fixates on such trivial details, so I wanted to witness the mystery for myself."

"I see! Did they have three people to a room during Taishō? But the dormitories we use now were only completed recently, and there are eight people to a room—an even number! Has Aoyama-sensei heard of the Second Girls' School? Their housing is also eight to a room, and seeing as we are both prefecture-run schools, it makes more sense for us to share the same system, I think. Oh, but that means Aoyama-sensei's mystery will remain unsolved. What a shame!"

Ōzawa had a manner of speaking that radiated openness and candor. Sparrow, next to her, nodded and smiled, affirming everything that came out of Ōzawa's mouth. It was impossible to detect any sign of friction between the two.

No, that wasn't all. Let me put it this way: as we made our way across campus and the South Country sun climbed higher overhead, I saw Ōzawa reposition herself multiple times in order to shade Sparrow from the harsh sunlight with her own body.

Could this same Ōzawa Reiko really have called this Tân Tshiok-bi a lí-ya?

The two of them gave Chi-chan and me a thorough tour of the living quarters. Ōzawa explained, "The boarders have free time after dinner, then study hall from eight to ten. Lights out is at ten, after which there is no talking allowed until six in the morning. Oh, but since Aoyama-sensei and Ō-san are not familiar with the buildings, please feel free to come to me if you have any concerns after lights out. My room is directly next to yours."

It was Chi-chan who responded first to this curious afterthought. "Ōzawa-san, are there any specific concerns that we should be aware of?"

A tactful yet incisive question. Chi-chan never disappointed.

Sparrow chuckled before Ōzawa could reply. "We would advise against going to the lavatory outside Building One after curfew, if possible."

"Oh? And why is that?"

"No real reason," Ōzawa cut in, but I gestured for Sparrow to continue.

An intriguing smile danced on Sparrow's lips. "There are tales about a mythical dimension in that lavatory."

"Mythical dimension? Do you mean to say that a student was spirited away or something like that?"

"Yes, something like that. At least that is the rumor among the boarders. After curfew, an unknowable space opens up there, and people disappear into—"

"Tân-san," Ōzawa said firmly.

Sparrow shrugged, her expression as cheery as ever.

Huh. *Huh!*

A shōjo romance? Or a supernatural thriller?

My lecture concluded at the end of second period, but the students did not have lunch until after third period, so Chi-chan and I politely declined the administrators' invitation to a luncheon and hailed a taxi to the famous West Market.

Lóo-bah over glutinous rice, ricefield eel and vermicelli noodles thickened with corn starch, soup with hand-molded fishcakes and oysters—we filled our stomachs with an exquisite feast. Dessert was fresh fruit: plates and plates of sliced watermelon, mango, tomato, papaya. Standing by a vendor's cart on a street corner, we downed winter melon tea and star fruit juice from coffee cups—sweet, unrivaled nectar. Ah, the flavors of the South!

Seeing as we were in Tainan, Taiwan's historic capital and cultural center, there was a sense of obligation to visit some famous tourist attraction like Senkan Tower, but this felt too much like being told what to do.[4] Instead, we ambled over to the nearby bustling neighborhood known as the Ginza of Tainan, which included both the Tainan Shrine and the Tainan Confucius Temple. We concluded our stroll at a department store, where I bought a new fountain pen and some pencils while Chi-chan picked out two novels.

On our way back to the First Girls' School, I sneaked glances at Chi-chan's profile. The Noh mask seemed to have relaxed a little after she'd found the books that she wanted. I instantly felt more relaxed as well.

"I didn't expect to find such different ways of eating braised pork over rice between Tainan and Taichū! We've had lóo-bah with hōrai short-grained and zairai long-grained rice before, but the *sticky* rice!"

"Aoyama-san seems to have enjoyed all three."

"Because all three were delicious! If I *had* to be critical, I'd say that long-grained rice is rather too dry and loose for this dish. Most of the broth ends up pooling at the bottom of the bowl, so you'd have to add more rice to soak it all up—but once you add more rice, you'd have to add more lóo-bah, too. In which case, don't you fall into an endless spiral of pork and rice and pork and rice?"

Chi-chan chuckled. "I've heard of a local dish called bah-kué, where they grind the rice down to a pulp and steam it into a palm-sized savory cake, which is then fried and drizzled with lóo-bah. I'd hoped that we would come across it today, but no such luck."

"My goodness, Chi-chan, where on earth do you get all this information? I've never found such detailed accounts of the Island in any newspaper or magazine!"

---

4. King: Senkan Tower (Mandarin: Chìhkǎn Tower) is also known in Dutch as Providentia. The structure was originally built in 1653 during Dutch colonization of Taiwan (1624–1662, 1664–1668).

"An interpreter never reveals her secrets."

"Ah! I *do* beg your pardon," I said, laughing.

Chi-chan, too, laughed—the kind of laughter that made her shed her Noh mask altogether. "Aoyama-san."

"Yes, miss?"

"I've heard people say that Mainlanders think lóo-bah has a displeasing stench. I have also been warned that Mainlanders only eat sashimi. But Aoyama-san seems to regard lóo-bah and sashimi with equal esteem."

"Bah! Anyone who can discriminate against lóo-bah must be completely incapable of appreciating good food."

"The demarcation between the Islanders' lóo-bah and the Mainlanders' sashimi is the distinction between the dirty and the pure," Chi-chan said, her voice low. "The same applies to the Islanders' chōsan and the Mainlanders' kimono."

"I . . . have never felt that way."

"That is because Aoyama-san is a good person."

"No—I don't know why or what or how. This is much too difficult for a simpleton like me." The train of thought twisted into my mind knots that took a few more silent steps to straighten out. "Perhaps I should put it this way, Chi-chan: lóo-bah and sashimi are both delicious, chōsan and kimono are both beautiful. To me, the essence of a thing is by far the most important. I'm sure there are plenty of people who choose not to understand the beauty of lóo-bah and chōsan, but there are also plenty of people who do."

Without replying, Chi-chan raised her purse to cover her own face.

"Why are you doing that?" I asked.

"Because it isn't fair—how Aoyama-san always manages to say the exact thing that people want to hear . . ."

"Is it what *you* want to hear, Chi-chan?"

She said nothing. I took the purse from her hands. Behind it, Chi-chan's dimpled cheeks had a subtle flush. I saw neither the sweet yet impenetrable Noh mask nor the coy grin she sometimes wore when she was chastising me. It was, instead, the expression she once bared to me in the kitchen at the Yana River cottage: a softening as gradual as the thawing of frost in early spring. It was also the smile that she once gave me when our train crossed the Katansui River Bridge—with true warmth shining out from the depths of her eyes.

I laughed and laughed, hooking my arm around hers.

"What a tease you are!" she cried, nudging me with her shoulder. I dug my elbow into her side, still laughing with a bounteous mirth that seemed to overflow from the core of my chest. *Ha! Ha! Ha!*

As we walked arm in arm in this merry mood, wind brushed against our cheeks—a wind strong enough to lift bougainvillea blossoms off their branches. Did that mean we, too, were characters in a shōjo romance?

If we'd been standing under that same tree, I, too, would have brushed the vivid petals off of Chi-chan's shoulders.

No—that wasn't all. Let me put it this way: had arrows showered down on us instead of flowers, I would have shielded Chi-chan's body with my own.

We had dinner that night at the dormitory cafeteria along with the faculty and students. We also washed ourselves in the dormitory bathhouse, soaking in the same public tub as the young girls. Ōzawa and Sparrow stayed by our side for most of these evening activities, all the way until the nighttime roll call at lights out.

Chi-chan and I slept in the same room on traditional futon bedspreads laid out on the tatami floor. Lying there in silence, I suddenly thought of the "myth" Sparrow had mentioned. I said, in a small voice, "Chi-chan."

She laughed. "Can it be that you need to visit the lavatory?"

"Hahaha."

"And, specifically, the one outside Building One?"

"Do you plan on stopping me?"

"There's no need to stop you from doing something that isn't dangerous."

"Can it be that you actually want to go with me?"

She said nothing. But when I climbed out from under my blanket, she did too.

Moonlight permeated the room, lighting up her grin.

Ha.

The dormitories were two-story buildings; we were staying on the first floor of Building Two. The lavatories were housed in two freestanding structures to the northwest of Buildings One and Two.

The dormitories were silent. I lowered my voice. "Isn't the northwest the direction of the so-called demon gate?"

"Is Aoyama-san a believer in fēngshǔi?"

"No, but the students must know about this, too."

"Sometimes it's hard to tell whether you're a novelist or a scientist."

"I am Sherlock Holmes, the great detective."

"Does that make me Doctor Watson?"

We were fast approaching the Building One lavatory.

The lavatories were the only sources of light in the dark mass of the dormitory buildings. Their solitary brightness on the pitch-black campus gave them an otherworldly air. The buildings were all made of wood, and the floor beneath us creaked softly with every step. Everything about the place screamed *It's scary in there!* I was surprised that there was only *one* supernatural rumor rather than a whole host. Chi-chan, however, seemed completely unaffected.

We went around the staircase and stepped onto the path to the lavatories.

Lí-ya. A small yet bright voice coming from inside.

"Lí-ya, why didn't you come sooner?"

Chi-chan and I stopped in our tracks and exchanged a quick look. "Who's in there?" I asked at the top of my voice.

Silence.

I began to walk farther toward the lavatory, but Chi-chan held on to my arm. "I can't let you go where there's danger."

"Aren't you curious?"

She nodded, then walked in before me.

I hurried after her. Inside, there were multiple stalls, and all of the doors stood open. Spotless sinks stood to the other side of the stalls. There was no door on the opposite wall—the one through which we'd come was the only means of entrance and egress. Yet the room was empty.

The only thing that stood out from the ordinary was a piece of paper on the floor under the sink counter. I picked it up and immediately felt from the texture that it was a photograph. The image had been taken indoors, against a backdrop of a tea table with a vase of blooming lilies. A young woman stood in the photograph's center, as lean as a young boy. She looked masculine and strapping in a double-breasted suit jacket, riding pants, and long boots as well as a beret angled to cover one of her eyebrows, which together with her crooked grin made her look rather mischievous.

It was Sparrow—Tân Tshiok-bi.

Neither shōjo nor horror, but a mystery.

"What are your thoughts now, Holmes-san?"

As always, Chi-chan's mind was on the same page as mine. I put on an aristocratic voice. "Jolly good question, Watson." I had no clue. *Where would a detective start investigating?* The answer came to me immediately: examine every inch of the lavatory.

Unfortunately, that was when F-sensei, who was on her rounds as the dormitory supervisor, appeared. She was instantly suspicious. "Aoyama-sensei, Ō-san, why are you here? The Building Two lavatory is much closer to your room . . ." But then she seemed to cotton on. "Ah, there must have been a line! You see, there is a strange rumor about this lavatory, so many of the students now opt to line up at at the one near Building One . . . it's been quite the headache."

Chi-chan and I both kept quiet about the "mystery" we'd just witnessed. Chi-chan, her eyes wide and brimming with innocence and concern, asked, "Sensei, what do you mean by 'strange rumor'? Is it something frightening?"

"No, nothing frightening. Please do not worry."

"I see . . . but I suppose it's human weakness that makes us more afraid of the unknown than of the things we know for certain. The students probably misinterpret the facts all the more because they have few facts to go on." Chi-chan then added in an appeasing voice, "Oh, but I apologize. We would not wish to hold up F-sensei's rounds. We will return to our room and ask Ōzawa-san about the tale tomorrow."

F-sensei sighed. "It really isn't anything horrific at all. To tell you the truth, it's something of a heartwarming story." She seemed to let down whatever guard she had up and grew more talkative. "There were once two students who each told their respective roommates that they were going to the lavatory at lights out, but neither returned for a long time. Their roommates each felt uneasy and went searching for them separately, which led them to run into each other at the bottom of the stairs. That was when one of the two missing students came out of the lavatory. The roommates asked her if she'd seen the other missing student, and she said no. They all went inside to search, but there was nobody there. In fact, there was no need for them to search—the two so-called missing students did not get along, and would no doubt have argued had they been in the same place."

I couldn't help but interrupt. "What can possibly be heartwarming about this?"

F-sensei smiled ever so slightly. "The rumor that spread among the students was that the second missing student had been hidden by the gods. As in, the gods hid the two students from each other in order to foster peace and harmony in the dormitories."

"That would be quite an outrageous thing for the gods to do just for maintaining peace in the dormitories."

"Yes . . . well, that is the gist of the story. Do you remember the way back to your room?"

I'd already scanned the whole lavatory as we were speaking, and since F-sensei now looked ready to usher us all the way back to our rooms, we had no choice but to follow her.

But what *had* happened in there? In the bedroom, Chi-chan and I sat cross-legged facing each other. A moonbeam struck the photograph that lay on the floor between us.

"It couldn't have been supernatural."

"Does Aoyama-san have any theories?"

"It was Ōzawa Reiko who spoke."

"Oh? And what is the reasoning behind that answer?"

"When we got near the lavatory, the person inside said 'lí-ya,' correct? 'Lí-ya, why didn't you come sooner?' They were waiting for somebody. But when they heard that it was us, they rushed out of the bathroom and dropped the photograph. As for the other party involved in this lí-ya incident—that would be Tân Tshiok-bi, the subject of the photograph."

"Hm—indeed, out of the hundreds of students here, Ōzawa-san might not be the only one who would refer to an Islander student by that word, but it seems too great a coincidence that the photograph is of Tân-san."

"Yes, and it seems to be quite a personal photograph. So, the photograph somehow came to be in Ōzawa's possession, and she made a secret arrangement to meet with Tân-san in the lavatory tonight. As an upperclassman who is familiar with campus legends, she cleverly used everybody's fear of the 'mythical dimension' to give them privacy. But how did Ōzawa exit the lavatory?"

"To leave that aside for a moment. If Aoyama-san is correct and the person inside was Ōzawa-san, then what was her intention in asking Tân-san to meet her tonight? Was it blackmail?"

"Hm—"

Our gazes met, and we fell silent at the same time. I couldn't get the earlier image out of my head: the falling bougainvillea blossoms, and Ōzawa gently brushing the petals off of Sparrow's shoulder.

Plum-red and violet-purple petals swirled in the wind. Slowly, slowly, they drifted to the earth . . .

"Aoyama-san."

At Chi-chan's voice, I woke from the reverie.

When had I drifted off? I sat up and rubbed my eyes at the gentle light in the room. What time was it?

"Aoyama-san, let's go to the lavatory again."

I couldn't help but laugh. But Chi-chan tapped my shoulder playfully and said, "I'm not asking because I'm scared to go alone."

"All right, all right."

We retraced the now familiar path. Once we got there, Chi-chan placed the photograph on top of the sink counter and pulled me toward the stairs. She sat down at the staircase's landing.

"Chi-chan?"

"Shh . . . Aoyama-san, I believe that *she* will come back for the photograph."

"Huh?"

Her whisper was so low that I had to lean my ear toward her lips. She said, "The wake-up time in the dormitory is six o'clock. Since there was a nighttime roll call, there must also be a morning roll call. The student in charge of taking roll would rise before six. It is now 5:30 a.m., and recently sunrise has been around 5:50 a.m. Whoever *she* is, she would definitely come retrieve the photograph before it gets bright outside."

I looked at her and saw that she was watching me with serene eyes. There was no trace of sleepiness in her face, though the skin under her eyes was darker than usual; she must have spent the whole night dwelling on the mystery while I slept.

Who said that she was Watson?

Birds were beginning to trill and chirp. The gray sky grew whiter by the minute. Chi-chan's dark-circled eyes were brighter than both the birdcall and the sunrise.

It happened then.

Creak, creak. Steps on the wooden floor in the midst of birdsong. Creak, creak. Nearer and nearer to the staircase. Creak, creak. Past the staircase. Creak, creak.

Chi-chan and I stood up at the same time and peeked through the gap between the staircase and the building. A young woman was walking into the lavatory.

"But that's—"

I almost cried out with shock, but Chi-chan looked unfazed—as though she'd predicted everything. She counted from one to five under her breath, then strode purposefully down the stairs, her footsteps loud against the wood. I hurried to keep up with Holmes-san.

We entered the lavatory just as we did earlier in the night. The lights were still on, the stall doors ajar, the sinks spotless, the opposite doorless.

It was empty.

And yet, *and yet*, the photograph on top of the sink counter had disappeared. Chi-chan put a finger to her lips, took my hand, and slipped back out of the door.

We returned to our room. No long after, the six o'clock bell rang. The whole dormitory sprang to life, drowning us in the buzz and hum of chatter and movement. The din blended together with the calls of the birds. After listening for a moment, Chi-chan smiled at me. "You can speak now."

"It was Tân Tshiok-bi! How could it have been Tân Tshiok-bi?"

Per our itinerary, we left on the 11:40 a.m. train back to Taichū. On our way, we bought two bags of black water caltrops from a street vendor. After the train departed from Tainan Station, we unfolded the newspapers that contained our water chestnuts and spread them on our knees.

The water caltrops looked like bats with their sharp, pointed ends—and seemed entirely impenetrable to me. Thankfully, Chi-chan came to the rescue with her ever-nimble fingers.

Nimble fingers, nimble mind.

How could it have been Tân Tshiok-bi?

Back in the bedroom, Chi-chan had grinned. "I guessed it. An incredibly lucky guess, don't you think?"

Naturally, I wasn't about to let her off with such a cursory explanation. When I pressed, she asked, "When we first met Tân-san and Ōzawa-san, did you notice how Ōzawa-san used her own arm to protect Tân-san from the falling bougainvillea flowers?"

"Yes, of course."

"The two of them were walking in front of us as our guides. Once, when turning a corner, I noticed a magenta blossom adorning Ōzawa-san's hair, just behind her ear. That same flower was originally tucked inside Tân-san's uniform collar, where it had been barely visible. But I am roughly the same height as Tân-san and saw the flower early on. From what I saw, I believe that between the two of them, Ōzawa-san is the protector, and that Tân-san as the protectee sometimes commits small acts of rebellion."

"Huh . . . rebelling against her defender, eh?"

"Indeed. Therefore, the slur of lí-ya has also been reversed between them, becoming an endearment that Tân-san uses on Ōzawa-san. In this sense, 'the lí-ya incident' between them may have been a total misunderstanding."

"*That* Tân? Calling *that* Ōzawa lí-ya?"

"I cannot guess at what passed between them, but Tân-san asking Ōzawa-san to meet her in the 'mythical dimension' on a night that outsiders like us are staying on campus was likely also a form of mischief. But I don't believe that it was blackmail. Both of them will be graduating this coming spring, and it's common for students to exchange personal photographs in girls' schools. For *those* two particular students to exchange photographs, however . . . well, let's just say that the minds of young women are the most unsolvable mysteries in the world."

"But that's hardly enough information to deduce that it was Tân!"

"You're right. The first clue was that Ōzawa-san lives in the room next to ours. She was responsible for the nighttime roll call, which meant that she returned to her room late, and perhaps did not have time to step out again before *we* left for the lavatory. She would have heard us leaving, and would have waited to avoid running into us. With eight roommates to one room, there are bound to be one or two people visiting the lavatory at night. If it had been Ōzawa in the lavatory on our first visit, she would have returned to the bedroom after us. But I listened for movements next door the whole night, and there was always the sound of someone leaving before the sound of someone returning. Which meant that my hypothesis was right: Ōzawa must have been in her room at the time of the first incident."

"But isn't there also the possibility that Ōzawa—after vanishing from the lavatory through unknown means—managed to return to her room before we got back to ours?"

"It would be extremely difficult not to make any detectable

noises in a silent dormitory, and even more so for someone of Ōzawa-san's stature. We would have definitely heard *her* steps on that wooden floor had she been rushing back to the room."

"That's true—she's got quite the athlete's build! Then why was there nobody inside the lavatory?"

"Well, this is another clue. None of the stall doors were closed, which made it look like they were empty. But this was a blind spot. I agree with Aoyama-san that there is no mythical dimension, which makes the answer simple: the person did not vanish; she was simply hiding in the stalls. Back in public school, some of the bolder students used to hide right behind the lavatory stall doors during hide-and-seek. Ōzawa-san couldn't have, not with her stature—but Tân-san, who is as petite as a child . . . I made a lucky guess."

"Chi-chan, Chi-chan, Chi-chan—"

"Yes?"

"You are neither Watson nor Holmes." I announced in my most serious voice: "You are Chi-chan, the Great Detective!"

The room was flooded with golden sunlight. Chi-chan sat cross-legged on top of her futon; her face was radiant—even more so than usual. I felt dizzy.

"Aoyama-san," came her voice. "Please have some."

I snapped out of my daze, my mind returning to the first-class car of the northbound express train. Chi-chan had, I saw, stacked a small pile of cream-white water caltrops—freshly extracted from their sharp-ended black shells—into my palm. When had this happened?

"You struggle with peeling these kinds of things, do you not?" she explained cheerfully. "Water caltrops have to be cracked between the teeth, and extracting the flesh also takes some skill. It's no easy task for a novice."

"Huh. I feel that we've had this conversation before."

"Ah, indeed. When we first met. It was kue-tsí that time."

"Ah, kue-tsí! I still struggle with those."

"And that is why Aoyama-san needs me."

Her smile reached her eyes.

I pinched a water caltrop between my fingers and offered it to her. She put it in her mouth, still smiling.

I could not say why, but in that moment I thought of the emptied glasses in my suite at Tainan Railway Hotel. The left-over ice cubes. Their gentle crackle.

The drinks they brought us had been winter melon tea, but its sweetness seemed to have eluded me until that train ride.

CHAPTER VII

Ka-lí / Curry

A flower whose name I didn't know had bloomed in the cottage garden.

The autumn showers had been falling for days, and at last the Southern Country breeze now carried a hint of coolness. I opened the glass sliding doors at dawn to let in the fragrant wind. Just three months prior, the scent that filled the air had been that of ripe melons; in the blink of an eye, it seemed, we were in sweet osmanthus season. The Island's osmanthus blossoms were a milky white, whereas the ones on the Mainland were a bright orange. The ones on the Mainland bloomed in September, whereas the ones here did so in November. Ah, Taiwan was truly the tropics!

I stepped off the engawa veranda to better immerse myself in the scent.

On a whim, I decided to leave my geta sandals by the door and proceed barefoot. The grass, made damp by rain, felt itchy on the bottom of my feet. It was then that I noticed the row of unknown flowers along the perimeter of the garden.

Should I even call them flowers? At their base were crisscrossing green leaves that lay flat against the soil; each leaf was roughly the size of a palm; from within them, long, arrow-straight stems stretched upward, then split into branches that sprouted tiny blossoms and buds of a light magenta color as well as clusters of small berries.

When Chi-chan arrived, I asked her about them. "It sounds

like wild ginseng." She walked to the veranda and looked out. "Yes, it's wild ginseng."

"Ginseng? As in Shina medicine?"

"No—it *can* be an ingredient in Shina medicine, but it isn't the rare ginseng that you are thinking of. Wild ginseng is treated as a weed in cities—I imagine the Takada family's gardeners will remove this. But, in the countryside, people sometimes pick the leaves to eat. The medicinal part is the root, which tastes quite similar to the rare ginseng. I've heard of vendors cheating their customers by selling rare ginseng mixed with wild ginseng."[1]

"So—does it taste good?"

She began chuckling as soon as I raised my question.

"Chi-chan, this isn't pure gluttony, you know. It's for the sake of documenting the Island."

"Whatever you say, Aoyama-san. Although—it's been so long since I've seen wild ginseng that it feels like a waste to eat it all up." She turned to me with her head tilted. "It was the first plant that I learned to identify as a child."

Her expression made it seem like she *was* a child, asking me for a favor with pointed sweetness. I grinned. "In that case, we'll spare it for now. We're having Yanagawa pot for lunch today!"

"I'm very much looking forward to Aoyama-san's cooking."

"I wouldn't get my hopes up if I were you!"

While I often fixed myself neko manma or broth with crushed seaweed, neither of these could be considered real dishes. Yet I was to be our chef that day.

Yanagawa pot is, put simply, a hotpot dish made with dojo loaches. In the summer, these little fish would come with a bonus of caviar. We could not hope for this in autumn, but there were fish vendors in Shintomichō Market who could provide

1. King: What is known in Taiwan as wild ginseng is also known as fameflower, Jewels-of-Opar, and pink baby's breath in English.

fresh dojo. I'd bought some first thing in the morning and boiled them as soon as I got home.

To prepare the dish, burdock root had to be julienned and soaked in a mixture of water and rice vinegar. This was then spread evenly across the bottom of a clay pot, and the dojo were layered on top. This was followed by anchovy broth—stewed ahead of time—as well as soy sauce, mirin, rice wine, and sugar. I went heavy on the sugar and decided to skip aji-no-moto[2] and salt. I heated the pot until it boiled. Back on the Mainland, we usually covered the ingredients with a wooden drop-lid to prevent the dojo from disintegrating in the boiling broth, but because the Islanders didn't seem to use drop-lids, I improvised and covered the fish with a large strip of Hokkaidō konbu that I cut into shorter pieces. This was an extravagance, to be sure, but since the taste of the konbu would also sink into the fish and the broth, I did not consider it wasteful.

When the dojo had changed color and the burdock root had softened, I removed the konbu and cracked a few eggs into the center of the pot, then stirred the yolks and whites toward the rim of the pot in circles.

By the time the eggs reached a semisolid state, the pot would be ready to serve.

We'd prepared the other food while the pot was stewing—two bowls of white rice, plus side dishes that I'd also gotten from Shintomichō Market: bran-fermented vegetables, pickled cucumber, eggplant, and yellow radish, plus Kyōto-style fermented shiso, which was rare on the Island. I also made winter melon and clam soup with a generous topping of green scallions.

"Actually, what I really wanted to make was stew with winter melon codfish sticks."

"Codfish sticks? I don't believe I've ever heard of it."

---

2. King: Aji-no-moto literally means "essence of taste" in Japanese, and is a product name for MSG coined by the brand eponymously named Ajinomoto.

I couldn't help but smile at the thought of this hometown delicacy. "It's essentially dried cod—a common gift to give during the Ghost Festival. Every July, my family's sharecroppers would bring us batches and batches of them, which would last us all the way into autumn. I looked forward to it so much every year. They're a hassle to prepare, but they're extremely delicious. Just seeing them reminds me of autumn!"

"Dried fish? Are they a hassle because it takes time to soak them?"

"Time, and also energy. Codfish sticks are completely different from normal dried cod, which is sliced ahead of time. The fish sticks, on the other hand, are as hard as rocks. I'm not joking! Before eating them, you have to pound them with wooden sticks, then soak them in rice water, then dry them in the sun, then repeat this whole process several times before you can make them tender enough to chew. But they taste infinitely better than your average dried cod, so I really can't complain."

"A true gourmet's dish."

"Quite right! Then you take the tenderized codfish sticks and stew them with cubed winter melon, and sometimes with potato as well. Wait for the winter melon to turn translucent while taste-testing the soup, adding ginger juice, salt, and soy sauce. I could never help sneaking in bites before the dish was even done! Every time, my aunt would yell at me to wait until the food was on the table."

"Sounds like a wonderful childhood memory."

"Ah . . . it's not so much a childhood memory as . . . a continuing phenomenon in my adulthood."

She laughed. "That does sound like you!"

"Doesn't it? You know, I'd been missing codfish sticks and winter melon stew ever since we had winter melon tea in Tainan. And since Chi-chan made bah-sò-pn̄g for me, I wanted to share the taste of my childhood with you in return. But since I couldn't find codfish sticks anywhere, I settled for Yanagawa pot."

The Yanagawa pot seemed about ready, so I beat five eggs into the pot in one go. Chi-chan's voice filtered through the clicking of my whisking chopsticks. "Codfish sticks and winter melon stew for autumn, Yanagawa pot for summer—is that so?"

"Precisely so!" I was seized with nostalgia. "My uncle and aunt, the ones who raised me—we ate so many codfish sticks and so many dojo loaches together! Both dishes bring back many happy memories. I wanted to eat them together with you, too."

She made a soft "mm" sound. I turned to see her twinkling eyes watching me.

My cheeks began to burn. I must have left the gas stove on too high.

I filled a small bowl and placed it next to Chi-chan's hand.

I was in no hurry to touch my food. Across the table, Chi-chan picked up her chopsticks, put her lips to the bowl, and scooped both egg and dojo loaches into her mouth. She chewed in a ladylike manner, picked out some fish bones with her chopsticks, then scooped another mouthful.

She was probably the only person in the world who looked this elegant eating loaches.

"How is it? Islanders seem more partial to preparing dojo with a medicinal flavor, isn't that right? You're probably not used to the sweet and salty broth of Yanagawa pot, but—ah, if it doesn't taste good, that's because of my poor cooking, not because Yanagawa pot is—"

"Aoyama-san."

"Mm."

"I think it is delicious."

I broke into my widest grin and immediately slurped up a big piece of dojo, picking out the small bones with the tip of my tongue.

Between bites of the fish, egg, and tender burdock root, I took bites of pickled vegetables to add texture, then swallowed big gulps of white rice. How thoroughly wonderful everything was. If only we could have a drink—sadly, it was the middle of the day.

"Let's have this for dinner next time! Dojo goes great with a bottle or two of warmed rice wine, don't you think?"

"Except Aoyama-san doesn't stop at one or two bottles. It feels dangerous to let you drink unaccompanied."

"It's not *dangerous.*"

"The last time Aoyama-san got drunk at dinner, I got you to go to bed, did I not? But after I left, you went to take a bath, did you not?"

"That's because the bathwater was already heated up."

"And then you fainted in the tub."

"Ahaha—I didn't faint, I just wasn't quite able to climb out of the tub!"

"*Just* wasn't *quite* able?" She was smiling.

Oh dear. That was the evening Chi-chan had walked past a mī-tê sesame porridge vendor on her way home and returned to the cottage to fetch a container so as to buy me some. But instead, she found herself tasked with dragging the large, clumsy Great Cedar out of the bathtub. I'm afraid that night left her rather the worse for wear. "Heh, see? Everything would be better if Chi-chan were to live here."

"Aigh, how like you to say something like that in response to something like this!"

"Isn't it?"

"I do not intend that as praise."

"Chi-chan, do you remember asking me for a legitimate reason why you *must* stay here?"

"Preventing the great writer from fainting in her bathtub doesn't qualify."

"Of course not. But I finally thought of one recently. The Ō family wishes for Chi-chan to grow accustomed to the Mainland way of life by taking this job, correct? For that, uh—that fiancé who grew up on the Mainland. And if you were to stay here, you would gain a deeper understanding of *and* grow more used to the Mainland's domestic life."

She said nothing, but her dimples deepened. Did I say something odd?

"I understand, Aoyama-san."

"What?"

"I appreciate how much thought Aoyama-san has put into the future happiness of my fiancé. You are right. The Ō family still lives in a Shina-style courtyard house. I imagine my lifestyle will be completely different if I move to the Mainland. I'm afraid I don't even know how to properly fold away a futon bedspread—"

I slapped my chopsticks down on the table. "Ah, I still can't accept this! A man whom you don't know at all! A man who doesn't even know whether you prefer rice or bread! How can you *marry* somebody like that?"

She continued smiling at me. "In that case, there is no reason for me to stay here."

"Argh—"

"We can play dice for it again."

"Let's!"

She went to fetch the dice and a large bowl. I stopped her before she rolled. "Hold on. We've always competed for the higher number. Let's compete for the lowest number this time."

She consented, then tossed the three dice into the bowl. They clattered and tumbled.

Three.

I grabbed them and tossed.

Eighteen.

"Do you have personal guardian gods living in these dice?"

Chi-chan laughed for longer than usual at my exasperated cry. Her laughter dipped and flared like a musical phrase. The sound of it sapped me of my ability to complain. I picked up my chopsticks and begin shoveling dojo, pickles, and rice into my mouth again.

"Aoyama-san is behaving like a blatantly sore loser."

"Argh—"

"How about this? I'll give Aoyama-san a special voucher."

"A voucher? For what?"

"For something small that I can do for you—so long as it's within my ability."

A voucher special enough to make me forget all the wrongs I have suffered. I mulled the proposition over and over as I chewed.

"Only something within my ability, Aoyama-san. And you don't have to decide on it right away."

"No problem! I've got it already. It's simple enough—the next time we travel, I'd like Chi-chan to wear a Western dress."

"A Western dress . . . why this particular request?"

"No, that's not the request—my full request is for you to accept my invitation to spend one night at Taihoku Railway Hotel! Dinner would be a formal Western meal, so I, too, would attend in a Western dress. Ah, how about we go get a new dress made for you? I wonder if we'd have enough time . . . and, of course, I would pay for everything. That's my request."

She watched me in silence for a while. "But that would be *you* giving *me* special treatment."

"Ahaha!"

"Why the Taihoku Railway Hotel?"

"Because I didn't find the Western dinner we had at the Tainan Railway Hotel very authentic."

"The critique of a true gourmet."

She shook her head at me, wearing her usual expression of *Good grief, what am I to do with you?*

Something small that I can do for you—so long as it's within my ability.

If Chi-chan was actually willing to do any one thing for me, I would have asked her to answer this one question: *Who are you?*

Ông Tshian-hȯh, of Chōkyōshitō in Taichū, the daughter of a wealthy landowning farmer and his sharecropper concubine. A graduate of Murakami Public School and Taichū High School for Girls. After school, she spent one year in an intensive training course, then at age nineteen began working as a public-school teacher of the Japanese national language. She left the position this spring, and is now twenty-two years old.

She had few interactions with her siblings and no elders in her family to rely on. It was true that girls could choose to study foreign languages in high school, but was it normal to be able to converse easily in English from just four years of study? As for the "national language"—it took me some time to realize that, even in Taiwan, there were fewer people who could speak Japanese effortlessly and elegantly than I'd imagined. Besides, how on earth did one learn French, which was far less common on the Island than English or Japanese?

Learning languages took time. Gaining true erudition took even *more* time.

Chi-chan so often revealed pieces of knowledge that fit neither her age nor her upbringing, especially when it came to her thorough and nuanced grasp of the geography and customs of the Island's different regions—at least all the places we'd traveled to on the West Coast Railway.

Her understanding of the cultural differences between the Island's many ethnic groups clearly exceeded the information that a schoolteacher would have been taught. Her referring to the aborigine Bannin as "indigenous peoples" alone placed her in the realm of a scholar. She read widely and diversely, both in the national language and in the Han language, and I assumed in English as well. From her conversation, it was apparent that her reading encompassed classical Shina poetry and texts, informational magazines, essays, and literary novels, as well as popular fiction—specifically, some rather intense detective fiction.

She was blessed with either an abnormally good memory or extraordinary talent. She excelled in technical work like arithmetic, accounting, shorthand, and reciting, as well as cleaning and organizing—everything from collecting data to paring fruit. Every imaginable task had been completed to perfection. This included her cooking: her miso soup and chirashi sushi bowls could easily compare with those served in restaurants. Whenever I said that I'd like to eat some delicacy we had on our travels outside of Taichū, she could almost always recreate the dish.

There were also some bizarre aspects to her.

For one thing, she was extremely well versed in Western dining. The night that we dined at the Tainan Railway Hotel, she didn't commit a single faux pas with the row of big and small knives and forks. Could it be that girls' schools on the Island taught Western etiquette? Even if they did, surely such lessons wouldn't go as far as to affect one's food preferences; yet Chichan enjoyed coffee as well as bread, neither of which was common in the Islander diet.

I couldn't shake the feeling that I'd missed a clue somewhere. How did a child who was given no family support and sent to live with tenant farmers grow up to be this erudite, multitalented, high-achieving woman?

If I'd asked her outright, she would no doubt repeat her confounding response from when I questioned the source of her knowledge about the Island's customs: *An interpreter never reveals her secrets.*

If I wanted a real answer, I needed to ask the right question. It was like how she wouldn't admit to refusing to dine alone with me until I pinpointed and articulated the problem. *I wouldn't pre-*

sume to explain if Aoyama-san didn't ask. But now that you have asked, I will answer honestly.

That had felt like finally locating the right key to a confounding door.

I had yet to find the key to this other door.

"I'd like to ask Chi-chan some questions," I said. We were on the train to Taihoku.

"Very well."

"When did you first decide that you want to become a translator?"

"Oh . . . I thought you meant questions about Taihoku."

"Am I prying?"

"No, not exactly. Um, I suppose it was when I was in high school."

"But why a translator of novels?"

"Why did Aoyama-san want to become a novelist? Ah—if I asked you that, we would only get sucked into an endless cycle of questions with no answers. But it isn't quite fair that I am the only one who has to answer."

"How about this? We'll trade a question for a question."

"Oh."

"She shows no interest, ladies and gentlemen!"

"That's not true. In that case, please answer my question first."

"All right! I first had the idea of writing novels when I was left in charge of that Buddha's lamp in the mountains. I was alone and had nothing to do. Naturally, I felt lonely and afraid of the forest, so I thought up a lot of stories as a way to comfort myself. That's about it, really."

She was silent.

"Your turn. Why a translator of novels?"

"If I had to explain, I would say it's because I love to read."

"That doesn't count as an answer."

"I suppose it's because the worlds inside books are so vast. Through novels, I can see Tōkyō, or London, or the hillsides of Los Angeles. Novelists use words to create worlds. I don't possess that generative ability, but if I could translate their words, then I can share this scenery with others."

"Ah, that's a far more magnanimous reason than what motivates novelists, I think. How did you find out about translation as a career option when you were only in high school?"

"You're not following the rules of the game, Aoyama-san."

"Oh, sorry. It's your turn to ask a question!"

"Then you must allow me to save my question until next time, because we're pulling into the station now."

I hadn't made as much progress as I'd hoped with my oblique probing, but thought it still counted as a step in the right direction.

The first thing on our agenda in Taihoku was lunch. Thanks to the conveniences of modern civilization, we managed to reach Taihoku in the northern tip of Taiwan before noon by getting on the earliest train at dawn. Even so, the five-hour ride had left me half in starvation mode long before we reached our destination.

The treat that we'd brought for the train ride was called be̍h-á-tsienn, literally "wheat pancakes," which Chi-chan told me were a street food dish originally from Fújiàn. I thought of them as a variety of taiko manjū, which I'd eaten at the market on our earlier Shōka trip and which the Islanders now called imagawa-yaki, likely due to the influence of Tōkyō vernacular.[3] These

3. Yáng, King: Taiko manju is commonly known in the Kantō region of Japan as imagawa-yaki and in Taiwan as kóng-á-kué (Taiwanese, literally "tube cake") or chē-lún-bǐng (Mandarin, literally "wheel cake"). See chapter III.

bėh-á-tsienn pancakes were made by first pouring one layer of dough into round, palm-sized pans and heating it slowly; after the dough rose and turned golden, it was loaded with a generous serving of unrefined sugar, peanut powder, and sesame powder; the whole pancake was then folded in half and removed from the pan, and the delicious semicircle was cut into triangular slices. Other than peanut and sesame, which was the flavor I liked best to accompany the wheat-heavy dough, one could also opt for red bean paste or cream.

The steaming pancake was crisp on the outside and fluffy on the inside. In the morning, Chi-chan and I had each eaten a slice in the market, then taken four slices with us on the train. When they were cooled, the pancakes lost their crispness and developed a slightly springy texture that the Islanders called khiū in Taiwanese.[4]

We'd finished the pancakes before we even reached Shinchiku. Clutching our empty stomachs, we entered a yōshoku restaurant right outside Taihoku Station. I ordered pork cutlet katsu curry rice and juice, Chi-chan ordered potato croquette curry rice and coffee, and to this we added meatballs, fried shrimp, fried chicken, seafood cream stew, and a leafy salad. Though the word yōshoku technically meant "Western food," the cuisine has evolved so much since arriving in Japan during the Meiji Restoration that it is now neither Western nor Japanese, but something in between. It would not take away from the "real" Western food we were having for dinner.

"Chi-chan, you like yōshoku, don't you?"

"You sound quite confident. Have I mentioned it before?"

"No, but whereas most people order pork katsu, the king of yōshoku, you went for potato croquette, which tells me that you must be very well-versed in yōshoku."

---

4. Yáng: The word khiū, still commonly used in Taiwan, is now written simply with the English "Q."

"Aoyama-san's powers of observation can be quite formidable."

"In a way, yōshoku is a product of changing times," I said. "If one thinks about the origins of what one eats, it really feels as though a small dining table holds the multitudes of whole oceans and continents. Take Nagasaki—our shippoku cuisine is a hybrid style of cooking that evolved from Shina food. Maybe it's because I'm from Kyūshū that I feel the breadth of Japan's culinary culture so acutely!"

"Aoyama-san speaks with so much enthusiasm that I cannot help but feel that you have other motives in bringing up the subject."

"Chi-chan's powers of observation really are formidable."

"Please. You can speak frankly with me."

"Um—to put it simply, I'd like you to consider coming back to Kyūshū with me next year."

Her dimples were shallow, her smiling eyes like moons.

"You're not taking me seriously."

"No, I am not, because you did not speak in the tone that you use for serious requests," she said, watching me closely. "But this is rather sly of you, Aoyama-san. First, you make a request that I cannot possibly agree to, then after I refuse, I am obliged to grant your second request. Isn't that right? Which is to say, there must be a second request that is your true wish."

"Aigh! Not to be underestimated!"

"So—what is the true request, Aoyama-san?"

My eyes, too, curved into crescent moons.

The table was covered in a white tablecloth; at its other end, Chi-chan sat in a similarly white Western dress. The stiff cloth was embroidered with white flowers and trimmed with a cream-color lace; the three golden buttons at her throat somehow accentuated the steadfastness in her gaze. I said, "Well, since the Western dress suits you so well—"

"Thank you, Aoyama-san, for your generous gift," she said, her eyes still watching, waiting.

"Next time, Chi-chan, I'd like to have a set of kimono made for you."

Is Aoyama-san scheduled to attend some formal occasion where even your interpreter needs to be dressed in a kimono?

No, I'm not.

In that case, why have a set specially made?

Because I bet Chi-chan would look fantastic in a kimono! No, you definitely *would!*

Please allow me some time to think it over.

You don't have to worry about the cost. Leave all that to me!

We stayed at Taihoku Railway Hotel that day. The building, completed in the Meiji era, was a sprawling three-story structure whose grandeur lived up to its reputation. The VIP guest elevator was likewise impressive. The second floor, where the ladies' room was located, had a striking view of the major avenues built in the European style.[5] One could see well-dressed gentlemen ambling down the sidewalk and ladies standing in clusters. I'd heard this area of the city referred to as the Little Paris of the East.

But I hadn't come all the way to Taiwan to see Little Paris.

We spent the sunny afternoon taking a leisurely stroll in Eiraku District's Islander market. That evening, we returned to the hotel's restaurant for a meal prepared by a French chef: vegetable chowder, fig salad, baby asparagus, foie gras, and roasted chicken, all of which did indeed taste more authentic than the food at the Tainan Railway Hotel. After that, we went out again

---

5. King: These refer to four avenues designed and built by the Japanese government after tearing down the Táipěi city walls built during the Qīng dynasty. The avenues are distinguished by the barriers in between the lanes, which are lined with trees.

to the New World Theatre in Seimon District[6] to see a film while enjoying ice cream cones. The following day, after a simple breakfast at the hotel, we went to Kensei District's En Park to visit its many food stalls, feasting on oyster pancakes, shredded chicken soup noodles, and sticky rice dumplings wrapped in bamboo leaves. Later, for lunch, we went to the restaurant floor of the Chikumoto Department Store, where we had impressively authentic Indian curry—Taihoku wasn't the Island's capital for nothing. Finally, we bought some crispy egg roll cookies for our afternoon train back to Taichū.

It was only on the rumbling train that I woke from what had felt like a two-day reverie. "Weren't we playing a question-for-a-question game on the way here? It's your turn to ask a question, isn't it?"

"It is, but I have not thought of any good ones."

"Hmph."

"Ah, you look displeased again."

"Really?"

Chi-chan sighed. "Aoyama-san, how exactly do you regard me?"

"As my friend, of course. Wait, did that count as a question? Aigh, forget about the game. Why do you ask that?"

"Are we really friends from your perspective?"

"Are we *not* friends from yours?"

"Friendships are between equals, are they not? I, on the other hand, am always on the receiving end of Aoyama-san's generosity with no means of responding in kind. On the other hand, the relationship between an author and her secretary has a clear

---

6. King: Seimon District is the Japanese pronunciation of present-day Táipěi's Xīméndīng, which continues to be a popular shopping district and subculture hub. The other districts mentioned in the paragraph are all defunct. Chikumoto Department Store, the first department store in Taiwan, is now an office building owned by Cathay Group. En Park is now Jiànchéng Traffic Circle.

hierarchy, and it would be an honor for the inferior party to receive the—"

I held up my hands to cut her off. "Chi-chan, remember what the Confucian disciple Zǐlù said: 'My wish is to share with friends my horse, cart, and clothes; were they to break and tear, I would have no regrets.' I feel the same way! These are not 'gifts' to be 'received.' This is just sharing."

Chi-chan was silent.

"I'm sorry—I've put you in a difficult position, haven't I? But you, too, have done far more for me outside of your interpreting work! All the cooking, for instance—I only made Yanagawa pot once! Does *that* not make us even?"

"Aigh . . . I can never win an argument with you, Aoyama-san."

"That's because I'm on the side of reason. Speaking of equality, I call you Chi-chan, yet you still call me Aoyama-san. That's hardly equal."

"That's because you are Chizuko and I am Chizuru. I can hardly call you by the same nickname."

"Call me Chiko, then."

"That's—a strange contraction."

"Or Yoshiko."

"Why Yoshiko?"

"You know, 'yoshi, yoshi.' As in 'very well, very well.'"

"W-what? What on earth is that supposed to mean?" She laughed. "You make it impossible to have a serious discussion, Aoyama-san!"

"I do no such thing!"

I put on a straight face. Chi-chan turned away from my self-righteous expression and bit her lip as she giggled.

I relaxed my furrowed brows. "So . . . we're friends, are we not?"

She hesitated. "If you consider us to be friends, then I will do the same."

"Ah, you translators and your word games."

"A novelist can hardly complain."

Very well, very well! Seeing her openly protesting my antics put me at ease. I said, "Are you still willing to cook for me when we get back?"

She said nothing for a moment. The silence was a string that tugged my heart higher and higher into the air until, at last, she nodded. "Yes—when we get back, let's make curry."

The rich scent of spice engulfed us.

I'd heard that, though India was widely regarded as the birthplace of curry, there was in fact no dish called curry there. It was an umbrella term that English colonizers had coined to refer to all Indian dishes that used a large number of spices. As one idiom went, "the untended bud blossoms"; so-called curry was brought from colonized India to England; then, after Commodore Perry forced Japan to end its era of isolation, it was imported to Japan under the misnomer of yōshoku, Western food, and from there made its way to another colony—Taiwan.

The day following our return to Taichū, Chi-chan filled the dining table with curry dishes.

These were not the Japanese iterations of pork katsu cutlet curry or potato croquette curry, nor were they the Indian originals.

Chicken curry: a whole chicken and cubed potatoes stewed on low heat until they were tender and fluffy, then seasoned with curry powder, soy sauce, and black vinegar, then further simmered until the liquid was reduced to a chowder-like consistency.

Shrimp curry: shelled and gutted shrimp ground into a paste, mixed with potato starch and egg, shaped into shrimp balls, then steamed; water chestnuts and mushrooms sautéed in a separate frying pan; stock boiled from shrimp shells and seasoned with curry powder, turmeric, and salt. When topped with chopped scallion, it looked like a golden sea with a green archipelago drifting on top.

Fish curry: Spanish mackerel cut into strips, coated with egg and flour, then deep-fried; bamboo shoots, wood ear fungus, yellow daylily, carrots, and chili peppers julienned and seasoned with curry powder, pepper, brown sugar, soy sauce, and a pinch of vinegar, all of which was drizzled over the fried fish.

All were called curry, yet each was distinct. The chicken dish, with its substantial meat and potato, had a thickness somewhere between gravy and soup. The shrimp ball soup, meanwhile, contained a diverse array of textures. The fried curry fish had a particular sour-and-sweetness from the vegetable medley. None of it was strictly yōshoku, and of course it wasn't Indian cuisine or Qīng-style Shina cooking, either. This was, quite simply, Taiwanese food.

"Did Aoyama-san not say so yourself? A dining table can hold the multitudes of oceans and continents. Mainland Japan gave birth to yōshoku, but the Island has its exclusive take on yōshoku as well."

I was busy stuffing my mouth with chicken curry and white rice. I chewed hastily and swallowed. "Chi-chan, are you trying to imply something?"

"I am sure that your hometown Kyūshū is a wonderful place. But, to me, the Island is wonderful enough. I feel no need to travel far."

"Is this a formal rejection of my invitation?"

A pause. "By this time next year, I will be married and living in Tōkyō. Therefore, while I am incredibly grateful for Aoyama-san's kindness, I cannot feasibly travel to Kyūshū for fun."

"What a distressing conclusion to draw."

"I hope you can understand."

"Ack, don't be so formal."

I put a chunk of fried fish in my mouth, then followed it with yet more white rice, gulping down all the words threatening to spill out of my mouth along with the food.

Chi-chan picked up her chopsticks and helped herself to some rice and potato.

"Aigh," I sighed, "let's talk about happier things."

"Aoyama-san probably hasn't heard of koa-á books, have you? Next time, I'll bring the koa-á book of the 'Song of a Dozen Dishes' for you."

"What's the 'Song of a Dozen Dishes'?"

"An Islander folk song. Koa-á books of these lyrics are written in Taiwanese Hokkien, and this one is a story about a woman hosting a banquet, creating her menu of twelve dishes, and serving the dishes to her guests. One of the dishes is curry chicken."

"Oh, I didn't expect curry chicken to make it into a folk song! It must be very popular."

"The 'midbanquet small dish' and 'finale small dish' are taro dates and thousand-layer cake, respectively."

"Both sweet?"

"Yes. Taro dates are made by rolling taro paste into date-sized chunks and deep-frying them. Thousand-layer cake is also called nine-layer cake on the Island, which is the Shina way of saying it—because koa-á actually originated in Xiàmén. It involves grinding white rice into a paste, adding brown sugar to half and confectioner's sugar to the other half, then steaming them layer by layer, alternating between brown sugar and confectioner's sugar. It is a dessert that looks as good as it tastes, with its pretty clear stripes."

"That does sound delectable!"

"They are both Taiwanese banquet dishes. I will try to make arrangements."

I tried my best to look happy and claimed that I was looking forward to it.

She only smiled.

After we finished eating, we opened all the sliding doors in the cottage, even the glass doors along the engawa veranda. The breeze diluted some of the thick scent of curry and brought inside the fragrance of sweet osmanthus blossoms. The wild ginseng had spread all along the veranda toward the sweet osmanthus trees, dotting the garden with petite purple flowers.

Chi-chan seemed to notice them only then. "They're all still here."

"You like them, right? So I asked the gardener not to weed them out."

She looked at me, a bit surprised. Perhaps even *pleasantly* surprised. She thanked me in a low voice, then added, "When I look at them, I almost feel as though I'm looking at myself. I can't help but feel fond of them."

"Is that so? Maybe we'll build a little flower bed for them."

"You always manage to say such kind things."

"I'll take that as a compliment."

She gave a chuckle. "Wild ginseng has another name: fake ginseng. Some people in the world regard me as the child of a well-to-do family, but most people see me only as the daughter of a concubine, an Islander girl like any other . . . I am but the eye of a dead fish pretending to be a pearl. I am but fake ginseng."

I was solemn. "Chi-chan, you're no fish eye. You *are* a pearl, and those people are blind."

"Shakespeare wrote, 'a rose by any other name is just as sweet.' Is that what Aoyama-san thinks?"

"Yes, of course. A name is only skin deep. What really matters is the beauty of something's essence. No matter what Chi-chan seems like from the outside, Chi-chan is, essentially, Chi-chan."

"Such kind words again. I do not know whether I am a fish eye or a pearl, but what I do know is that even wild ginseng has its own sense of dignity."

"Meaning . . . ?"

"I've accepted my status as wild ginseng and have every plan to continue living my life as such. But Aoyama-san sees me as a pearl—and, if I'm understanding correctly, hopes that I can dress up as a more realistic ginseng." Her smile did not waver. "Is that not what you think? That it would be better for me to wear a kimono rather than a chōsan."

My confusion left me momentarily at a loss for words. I felt as though I was trying to capture wind with my bare hands.

"No. No, that's not what I think." I had to force my voice out of my throat. "It's not that I think that a kimono would be better. You look wonderful in a chōsan and you look wonderful in a Western dress. Only, for people whose eyes are only capable of seeing ethnicity in clothes, wouldn't a kimono act as a form of a protection for you?"

"But . . . to me, such protection isn't necessary."

"Of course it isn't necessary—because you are strong. But, can we not think of it as a token of my wish to protect you? As a friend?"

She gazed at me in silence.

I looked into her eyes.

The autumn breeze whistled between the panels of the shōji doors. The scents of curry and sweet osmanthus mingled in the room. Dimples gradually appeared in Chi-chan's face.

She sighed and said, "I can never keep up with you." The dimples deepened. Her voice was honeyed when she added, "In that case, please allow me the honor of accepting Aoyama-san's gift."

The change was incredibly subtle yet utterly unmistakable. I blinked several times before I could confirm it: Chi-chan had put on her charming yet emotionless Noh mask again.

CHAPTER VIII

Sukiyaki / Beef and Vegetable Hotpot

Chi-chan peeled the steaming sweet potato in three swift motions, wrapped it in wax paper, and placed it in my hand.

The season for eating roasted sweet potatoes was also the season of hot springs.

I'd documented trips to the Shōka and Tōho onsens in my Taiwan Travelogue article series, which also discussed the famous Bathhouse Route in the Island's railway system. That was a small branch off the Tansui Line in the suburbs of Taihoku and had only one stop, New Hokutō Station, in an area also known as the Onsen Village.[1] Because of this, the train tracks themselves had become known as the Bathhouse Route. How adorable! I couldn't help but be drawn to the route and its destinations despite their being tourist attractions, which I generally avoided.

One clear winter morning, we took a train that departed Taichū before the sun had even risen. Our itinerary was to transfer at Taihoku Station and head to New Hokutō Station, spending one night at an onsen hotel. I would give a lecture at Taihoku First High School for Girls the next day, and we would return to Taichū on the third day.

The scenery from the train window was like a liquid light, or like passing time. I took one large bite of sweet potato and finally

---

1. King: The Shōka onsens are present-day Chānghuà hot springs; the Tōho onsens are present-day Dōngpǔ hot springs. Hokutō is the Japanese pronunciation of Běitóu, a mountainous suburb of Táipěi (Taihoku) famous for its hot springs.

looked away from the window. Chi-chan had peeled a second potato and was eating it slowly and meticulously. She smiled slightly when she noticed me looking at her, but the smile did not reach her eyes—it was but a twitch of the muscles around her mouth.

There it was. The Noh mask.

She had continued dining at the same table as me and sharing food with me on trains, but the ways in which she spoke and acted were different—or, rather, they had regressed to an earlier stage of our dynamic.

Chi-chan was by nature a discreet person, and even her change in attitude was inconspicuous, but I knew for certain that it had taken place. I watched her and wondered: Did she *know* that she was wearing a Noh mask?

The kimono she wore was persimmon colored with a pattern of snowflake-like wheels; both this and the dark blue obi belt were plain and elegant. Only the haori jacket, which was long and patterned with countless birds, gave off an air of decadence. Its black color contrasted with Chi-chan's skin, making the latter look even milkier than usual.

As I'd predicted, the kimono suited Chi-chan impeccably.

Despite the formal clothing, she still performed quotidian tasks without the slightest hiccup, whether it be peeling the skin of a potato for me or eating her own neatly, cleaning her hands on a small towel afterward. I thought again about how someone with her innate self-possession—had she been born into another situation—would have been regarded as an elite among elites.

I took my time chewing, mulling things over in my head.

"Chi-chan, have you gotten used to the kimono?"

"Hm . . . it's so expensive that I feel it to be a rather heavy burden."

"Huh?"

"I am joking." She chuckled and looked at me through slightly narrowed eyes.

I stared back, knowing that her lightheartedness was but a pretense.

"Aoyama-san, your gaze is quite piercing."

"If you're not comfortable wearing it . . ."

"Please don't trouble yourself. I often wore kimonos as a student, just never with such luxurious fabric."

"Oh, so you *have* worn one before. That's what I assumed, because it's quite a different thing to walk in a kimono and geta sandals versus in a Taiwanese chōsan or in Western clothes, but Chi-chan walks and moves very elegantly."

"Aoyama-san, you were saying? If I'm not comfortable wearing it . . . do I not have to?"

"That's right. If that's the case, then don't wear it anymore!"

She was quiet.

"I don't want to force you."

"And yet you did not say so earlier."

Her tone was rather hard, and I felt my chest tighten. But she immediately softened her voice to add, "I intend to wear it and take good care of it in the future, and not only because of its cost, but because of the care that Aoyama-san put into selecting it for me. I was even thinking that, if I were to have a daughter, I would give it to her as a coming-of-age present."

"A daughter? That's a bit too far in the future, no?"

"No, not that far. I'm getting married next year, after all." She laughed. "My fiancé is quite a few years older than I, and his family is eager for heirs. Following Islander customs, the heir must be a boy, and sometimes even one boy is not enough. After all, a woman only has one job after marriage. Statistically speaking, I am bound to have at least one girl."

"Chi-chan."

"Yes?"

"Are you intentionally trying to provoke me?"

"Why do you say that?"

"Because you know that I don't want you to marry that fellow."

"Why do you not want me to marry?"

"The better question is, why do *you* accept this fate? You have things that you want to pursue—things that have nothing to do with marrying a man. If that bastard only wants a wife in order to have children, then he should find a woman whose only goal is to marry."

"Are you angry?"

"No, I'm not. But isn't it your dream to be a translator? I don't plan on marrying either, you know. My goal is to spend my whole life writing. In that case, wouldn't it be perfect for you and me to go back to Kyūshū together? Your family will agree if I propose it to them directly, won't they? Well, it wouldn't necessarily matter whether they agree or not. Once you move in with the Aoyama family, you won't need to rely on the Ō family. You'll only need me."

Ha.

Chi-chan grinned. "That is quite brazen. Are you by any chance asking me to elope with you?"

"I'm not joking."

"Mm. Aoyama-san, you once said that you regard me as a friend. Are you saying these things now because you regard me as such?"

"Because I regard you as my *best* friend."

I had kept my expression serious, yet Chi-chan said softly, "Best friend, huh." Her smile was unbearably sweet.

"Chi-chan, I believe *you're* the one who's angry."

"Oh? And why do you say that?"

"I don't quite know how to explain it."

"Is that so."

"That's right. I don't know why you are angry, and I don't know how to explain my feelings, yet I feel quite certain of your displeasure. I am a clumsy, obtuse, tactless woman. I want to cherish this friendship, but I seem to have made some mistake along the way and made you unhappy. If you aren't straightforward with me, I'm afraid I'm simply too stupid to know what I did wrong."

Nothing.

"Is it because you dislike kimonos?"

"No, I do not dislike kimonos. From Aoyama-san's point of view, perhaps it seems as though I always wear a chōsan out of some sort of principle, but that's not the case. You call yourself obtuse, yet you must remember that I also wear Western clothes quite frequently. Given the Island's heat and humidity, a chōsan is simply more comfortable than a kimono as far as formalwear goes. That is my only consideration. You yourself have always worn Western clothes instead of kimonos since arriving on the Island, isn't that right?"

She spoke gently, yet that gentleness was only further proof of the Noh mask.

"You're not lying, are you?" I asked.

"No."

"But you're not telling me the whole truth, either."

She chuckled. "Mm."

"And you have no intention of revealing it."

"That is correct."

No answer on whether she was angry or not. No intention of telling the whole truth.

Just a smile that wasn't a real smile.

I felt as though I was watching a movie, that the lens was slowly focusing in on the protagonist's grin. Chi-chan's lips were pursed, and she gazed at me with a breathless sort of focus that forced me to stop everything else and simply look back at her. Her irises shone at me with something like starlight. The feathery eyelashes closed in on each other, touched, then parted. I felt as though I was falling into the sparkling darkness of her eyes.

When she tilted her head ever so slightly, I began involuntarily to move my head along with hers. I had been tamed. Her dimples deepened. The smile that was originally sweet now seemed saccharine—a honeypot meant to ensnare those who got too near.

It was the first time that I really noticed the beautiful rosy color of her lips.

"Hold on a second! We can't talk about anything serious if you keep looking at me like that!"

"Hm? Why not? And what can you mean, 'like that'?"

Her voice, too, was honey. I fell even deeper.

Deeper? Deeper into what?

I couldn't say.

What had we been talking about? I could not retrace the thoughts.

Instead, I turned my face toward the window and watched the waves of golden wheat flash by. After the wheat came the mountains: the ones near us looked jade, and the ones farther away looked gray-blue, like iron. Layers and layers of mountain ranges were rimmed by a motionless stretch of soft clouds. I exhaled quietly and felt my cheeks lose some of their heat.

That was when Chi-chan began to laugh—a melodic laugh that plucked at my heartstrings and made me press a palm to my chest.

"Aoyama-san, let us have some sushi when we arrive. There is a cafeteria at New Hokutō Station that sells higher-end food like sashimi and sushi. It's also not far from our hotel. You can have a glass of daytime rice wine the way you like."

"Mm."

"The cafeteria even sells ohagi mochi cakes. You mentioned before that you like botamochi cakes, but you haven't had them on the Island yet, isn't that right? Botamochi for spring, ohagi for autumn.[2] Allow me to witness the formidable feats of your appetite once more."

---

2. King: Botamochi and ohagi are essentially the same Japanese dessert, made with red bean paste and mochi rice cake. In the spring, this is called botamochi after the word botan for peony. In the autumn, this is called ohagi after the word hagi for bush clover.

I finally turned to face her again. Her face revealed no ulterior motives. She seemed sincere in her intention to please me.

"Chi-chan."

"Yes?"

"Are you a demon?"

"Ha—I shall take that as a compliment!"

When Chi-chan and I officially met on that late spring day in the Takadas' banquet room, she had cordially accepted my many requests about eating this and to try that. In that moment, I'd exclaimed with all my heart: *You—you—are you an angel?*

Little did I know back then that this interpreter—this player of word games—was in fact a little demon and a player of human hearts!

I probably never would have detected this in her had we not spent so much time together. Though she wore a placid smile, Chi-chan was in fact a worldly person capable of bending and stretching the rules. She was discreet and scrupulous, but she was also capable of complaining and chastising, as well as teasing and jesting. This made her a delightful companion and a genuinely likable person. Yet it was all a mask.

Behind the mask, Chi-chan's heart was far away.

It was thanks to this distance that she was able to be so measured and agreeable; even her protests and rebukes were an act. I wondered whether our relationship was in fact like a waltz: though I had wished for the dance, any real forward or backward movement between us had been led by Chi-chan. Could this really be called a friendship?

On our previous trip to Taihoku, I'd asked her whether we were friends. Her answer: *If you consider us to be friends, then I will do the same.*

Here, then, was the real question: *Did* I consider us to be friends?

At the cafeteria, Chi-chan and I sat across from each other and ordered sashimi, nigiri sushi with fish, inari sushi with sweet tofu skin, simmered abalone, grilled mackerel, and rice cooked with scallops and mushrooms.

The December day was chilly, and I ordered a bottle of warmed rice wine. The wine came with appetizers of oden stewed in miso and pickled silver-stripe round herring.

She filled my cup and I filled hers.

The oden came in a large bowl, and Chi-chan loaded my plate with eggs, radish, and fried tofu—my favorites. For herself, she chose konjac, baby taro, and carrots. Were they *her* favorites? I couldn't remember. But they were the items that I tended not to choose.

"If I'm remembering correctly, Chi-chan, you started teaching right after graduating from high school, correct? Did you apprentice under anybody in between?"

"Apprentice? You mean in tea ceremony or flower arranging? No, I did not."

"What about a part-time job at a restaurant or something like that?"

"No, not that either."

"Or some other sort of traditional Island skill or craft? Like how on the Mainland we have the shamisen and traditional instruments?"

"As you know, I do not possess any musical talent."

"That's not true. When you sang the koa-á folk song, 'The Song of a Dozen Dishes,' you sounded like a professional."

"But, Aoyama-san, you've never heard a professional koa-á singer."

"Hmph."

"What is it that you are really trying to ask?"

I shook my head and scarfed down my egg and radish in a few large bites.

"I beg your pardon," said the waitress bearing a large plate of sashimi. I shifted slightly to make room, but Chi-chan straightened and received the lacquer plate with both hands. When she lowered it to the table, there was no sound of contact.

She giggled at my expression. "Is it not natural for a concubine's daughter to learn to serve others?"

I dropped the fried tofu between my chopsticks. When I looked up, she seemed unflappable as usual. "That's what you really wish to ask, is it not? Why I am so skilled in serving others? Why did you not ask whether I have worked in a café or apprenticed at a yūkaku?"[3]

I stared into her smiling face—the rose-colored lips.

"Chi-chan, are you trying to insult yourself or me?"

"Do you find what I said to be an insult? As Confucius said, 'Those who are low-born acquire many skills in humble matters.'"

"You're angry. But why?"

She gave a mirthless chuckle. "What on earth can I reply to that?"

"Can you not tell me directly if there is something that bothers you?"

"But there isn't anything of the sort, so how can I tell you about it?"

This was most certainly a lie. I was at a loss for words. Chi-chan reached her hand toward my face and brushed the corner of my mouth with a finger.

"You've got a bit of miso."

She then casually licked away the sauce on her finger—as though it were nothing, nothing at all.

---

3. Yáng: Yūkaku were traditional red-light districts that were legal under the Japanese colonial government. Japanese-style yūkaku were introduced to Taiwan in the Meiji period. Compared to the sex work that took place in yūkaku, the newer and more urban cafés were adult entertainment establishments with less-explicit sexual transactions.

Hot blood rushed from my neck to the crown of my head. I blushed deeply.

"Are you all right?"

No, I'm not all right!

I leapt to my feet and tried to speak, but my tongue remained knotted in my mouth. In contrast, Chi-chan seemed entirely at ease. With my tightened chest, I looked at her—Ō Chizuru—and felt as though I was meeting her for the first time.

"Do sit down, Aoyama-san. People are staring."

"Hmph."

"You're still holding your chopsticks."

"And whose fault is that?"

"Mine, apparently."

"Hmph."

"Oh, they've served us squid sashimi. You are fond of squid, are you not? Here, please eat. Maybe we should leave the wine for now. That must be what's making you so flushed. Why don't I ask the waitress for some hot tea?"

Uncharacteristically, I ate the whole meal without tasting the food.

Afterward, we headed to the hot springs hotel on a nearby hill. The air was filled with the pungent scent of sulfur, and white steam rose even from the gutters and ditches on the side of the road. Sea bream hotpot was on the menu, for the weather was chilly enough for such delicacies. All in all, the Onsen Village did not disappoint, yet I'd lost my enthusiasm. There was a small public bath for women near the hotel, and at this point I did not even have the heart to protest about the discrepancy between the size of this facility compared to the much larger public bath for men. My sole aim was to soak myself in hot water and to follow this with an ice-cold beer.

Chi-chan objected. "We had alcohol just now—what if we were to faint in the bath? That would be humiliating. Besides,

I'm afraid I do not have the strength to carry Aoyama-san back here to your room if *you* were to faint."

"But we didn't even finish a single bottle."

"And yet your face was so red that it looked like you would start bleeding."

"But that wasn't because of the drink."

"Oh? Then what was the reason?"

She, the culprit, seemed sincere in her confusion. But how could I begin to explain? I sighed deeply and slumped down onto the tatami floor.

"Why don't I order you a cold drink before we go to the baths? Would you prefer a Calpis or lemon soda?"

I said nothing. The black haori jacket could not have suited her better. Her face seemed almost translucent from the contrasting color. A powder-white face with ruby lips—exactly like a Noh mask. Until that moment, I had never thought that I would ever feel frustration and distress when looking at Chi-chan. Yet she gave no sign of shedding her mask, and I, seeing this, felt a flame of fury stir within me.

She noticed the change in me. Her smile ebbed a little from her face.

"You don't look so well, Aoyama-san. Have you caught cold?"

She extended a hand. I blocked it before it could reach my face.

"Are you angry?"

"Yes."

"Hm. Should an interpreter who angers her employer simply resign, do you think?"

I sneered. "So *that's* why you've been trying to upset me?"

"I am sorry if you think that I have done any such thing intentionally."

Her equanimity only added fuel to my rage. "If you want to quit, why don't you just say it outright?"

"Would you accept my resignation?"

"No, I wouldn't. And that's why you want to force me to dismiss you, is that right? But that's not very strategic of you, is it, Miss Ō Chizuru?" These words were a crack in the dam, leading instantly to a full-out flood. My voice rose and rose: "Maybe to the Ō family, half a year is enough time for you to follow around a Mainlander woman, so quitting now may not be much of a loss. But what about for Ō Chizuru as an individual? Not a single person in your future husband's family nor your own family is really invested in your happiness. Am I right? So, pray tell me, what reason do you have to leave my side?"

"Ah—you are quite right. Aoyama-san is perhaps the only person in the world who treasures me as an individual."

"Liar."

"I'll swallow a thousand needles to prove myself." Her smile was unwavering.

I took several deep breaths. "Are you aware of your mask?"

"My . . . mask?"

"Can you deny that you're wearing a mask right now? You've hidden your true feelings from me ever since the day we met. Which was fine, seeing as I was a stranger. But somewhere along the way, you'd finally begun to share with me some of what you really feel. I thought that you were finally willing to lower the mask for me. What I don't understand is, why have you put it on again?"

Silence.

"My guess is that it's because I made you do something against your wishes. It's because of the kimono, isn't it? If I'd known just how much you disliked wearing it, I would never have forced you in the first place."

"Aoyama-san . . ." She watched me closely. "Perhaps you are right about the mask. Your powers of observation really are extraordinary. But, as I said, I have nothing against kimonos."

"But—"

"Liking or disliking kimonos isn't the crux of the problem, Aoyama-san. I cannot explain it well, because even though you are kind and observant and well-meaning, you have a blind spot that you cannot possibly be aware of. That is all."

"What—what's the blind spot?"

"Please excuse my bluntness, but *because* it is a blind spot, I cannot explain it in any way that you can easily understand. Such is my assessment of the situation. Therefore—"

"Therefore you have come to the conclusion to distance yourself from me without giving me a chance? But that's just—baseless and—brutish!"

Chi-chan sat up straighter. "Yes, precisely. I believe that it is most ideal for us to maintain a strictly professional relationship."

I stopped breathing. *Professional relationship.*

"I am very sorry."

"So this is a renouncement of friendship!"

"It is precisely because Aoyama-san regards me as a 'best friend' that I wish to respond clearly and honestly. I pray that you can understand my feelings."

I tried to contain the heat in my chest. We stared at each other—me with my lip quivering, Chi-chan with her ramrod-straight spine. Neither of us stirred from this stalemate for a long time.

A long, long time.

I began to feel worn down by this sustained intensity of feeling, yet Chi-chan showed no sign of relenting.

Damn it! I sighed in defeat as she grinned in victory. "You show no sign of fear!"

"That is because I know Aoyama-san is a noble-minded individual."

"That's not true at all. If this table weren't so heavy, I would have flipped it like the men in Kyūshū do."

I rapped the tabletop irritably with my knuckles, yet she

laughed and slackened her posture. I thought I caught a glimmer of moisture in her eyes when she said, "But I really wasn't lying. Aoyama-san, you are the only person in the world who treasures me."

"Then be my friend!"

"Alas, I truly cannot."

This was impossible to respond to, and I could only make some distraught cackling noises at the back of my throat. "Well, I'll be damned! Let's order some beer! Let's have sukiyaki tonight! I need meat in times like these!"

"What you call sukiyaki is made from beef, isn't it? Islanders don't generally eat beef—I don't eat beef."

"What's that, Miss Interpreter? Isn't that something only a friend can say?"

"Ah . . . but you are so noble-minded and generous. I do beg your pardon about the inconvenience."

"How—what—" I collapsed onto the table, my hair tumbling onto my face.

Chi-chan brushed it back for me, sighing lightly. "Aoyama-san really is a very kind person."

"I am. And you're taking advantage."

"It's true. I really don't know how to properly communicate my gratitude to you."

Something rippled in her gaze. I turned away.

"This is a trap, isn't it? Like how they send a beautiful woman to seduce someone in stories. Just like with the miso earlier."

"What do you mean? There was miso at the corner of your mouth, so I removed it. And—are you not a woman, too? What trap?"

"Sure, if you insist. But please—at least continue eating at the same table with me."

She dragged out her voice with a fond, lazy drawl that I'd never heard her use before: "Aaaall right."

Here she was, taking another step in our waltz, leading me

under the guise of accommodating me. The fire continued seething in my chest, but what choice did I have except to follow her?

After we returned to Taichū, there was no more talk of Noh masks or of friendship. The clock seemed to have rewound to my early days on the Island, with Chi-chan angelically preparing nutritious and delicious lunches and dinners for me on my writing days. Whether I asked for koe-kńg, kiâm-muê, cream bread, peanut candy, Hakka meat pies, bí-ko, or turnip cakes,[4] Chi-chan would make them appear on my table like some sort of omnipotent god.

A rainy season was upon us, much like when I first got here; but this was wintry rain, and though Taiwan's southern climate saw no snow except on its highest mountains, the continuous rain brought a piercing chill. I proposed sukiyaki to Chi-chan again. When she looked confused, I said, "Let's make it with pork instead of beef." I wanted to share the delicious dish with her regardless of the constraints.

Back when sukiyaki was first introduced in the Meiji era, it was known simply as beef hotpot. There were originally different ways of making the dish in Kamigata and Edo,[5] but these eventually merged in the Taishō era. The dish became known ubiquitously as sukiyaki, and the recipe became almost identical

4. King: Koe-kńg is made with minced pork, shiitake mushrooms, scallions, and bamboo shoots wrapped in deep-fried dough; kiâm-muê is salty porridge, usually stewed with minced pork, tofu, and a mix of sliced vegetables; bí-ko is glutinous rice mixed with shiitake mushrooms, pork, and shallots, and steamed in a bamboo tube.

5. Yáng: Kamigata is the former colloquial name for the region now known as Kansai, which includes Kyōto and Ōsaka; Edo is the former name of Tōkyō. Even after the names were changed in the Meiji period, the Japanese occasionally refer to the places by their former names.

across Japan, even in Kyūshū. Furthermore, there used to be one pot per person, but as time passed people began to share one large pot in the center of the table. Miso was eliminated from the sauce, which became composed of soy sauce, mirin, sugar, and rice wine.

First, beef, scallions, and onions are simmered in a flat pot. Then the sauce is added, followed by other ingredients like tofu and vegetables. A fresh egg is beaten into a small bowl. After the pot begins to boil, one removes the ingredients from the pot and dips them in the raw egg. The resulting taste is sweet and savory at once, with a springy and melts-in-mouth texture that makes it impossible to resist scarfing down several bowls of rice.

"If shutō means 'alcohol robbery,' then perhaps we ought to call sukiyaki 'rice robbery'!" I said.

Chi-chan laughed. "Is that why you made three whole cups of rice?"[6]

"I would have made four, but I wanted to save some room for the meat."

"You seem very happy."

"Well, this was one of the dishes that I really wanted to share with you. Yanagawa pot with loaches in the summer, codfish sticks with winter melon in the autumn, and sukiyaki in the winter."

In her ensuing silence, I saw that the clock had not turned back after all. The Chi-chan who had heartily enjoyed the Yanagawa pot with me would not have been silent now.

"Will you not ask me what we'll eat in the spring?" I asked.

"Spring in the Mainland . . . would it be raw noodlefish? Or hatsu-gatsuo?"[7]

---

6. Yáng: One traditional cup of uncooked rice is around 180 milliliters, which is enough to serve two.

7. King: Hatsu-gatsuo literally means "the first katsuo," referring to the first catch of skipjack tuna in the spring.

"Aha, Miss Detective has made a reappearance."

"Only because you once said that sashimi is best in winter and spring."

"Nevertheless, your knowledge is still astounding. It's my understanding that Islanders rarely eat noodlefish or katsuo tuna, so where on earth do you learn all this information?"

"Would you like to take a guess? There are certain types of people who know the answers to these things."

"Librarians?"

"Close, but not quite."

Booksellers? Train station staff? Postmasters?

Chi-chan shook her head to all.

"Don't tell me it's movie narrators from the Mainland—the people who explain silent films or foreign movies in the theaters? Like the saying 'Reading ten thousand scrolls is traveling ten thousand ri of roads'?"

"Clooooose, but not quite."

Damn it!

I began making the sukiyaki, first heating the pot and searing the sliced, fatty pork within. The point to sukiyaki is meat, so I was naturally generous with the portions. When the pork looked half-cooked, I removed it to add the tofu, which I cooked on both sides. I added back the pork, followed by green cabbage, shiitake mushrooms, julienned burdock root, konjac, carrots, and finally the sauce. Just as the sauce was coming to a boil, I added chrysanthemum leaves.

Meanwhile, Chi-chan loaded the white rice into bowls and prepared the eggs for dipping.

"Doesn't it look delicious?"

"It does smell quite wonderful."

"We don't generally bother with serving chopsticks when eating sukiyaki, so just use your own chopsticks and take whatever you like. Ah, but do start with the meat! And feel free to eat three or four pieces in one go!"

She nodded and did as I said, blowing slightly on the steaming meat.

Chi-chan was probably the only person in the world who looked good whether she was eating dojo loaches or loading her mouth with so much pork that her cheeks bulged.

"How is it?"

"Extremely delicious."

"Isn't it?"

I, too, dipped three slices of pork into the raw egg and stuffed them in my mouth.

Heaven!

"I'll concede that Yanagawa pot might not be for everyone, but surely nobody can claim to dislike sukiyaki."

"Is that so?"

"After all, everyone must 'suki' sukiyaki."[8]

Chi-chan burst into laughter, accidentally dropping the piece of carrot between her chopsticks back into the pot. "Oh, I beg your pardon."

"Never mind that. Chi-chan, do you like carrots?"

"Yes. Why do you ask?"

"When we had oden in Hokutō, I wondered whether you atc the carrots because you like them or because I don't like them."

She did not respond right away. After finishing the piece of carrot, she ate a piece of fried tofu. "You don't have to worry about things like that on my behalf, Aoyama-san."

"How can I not, when we're eating sukiyaki together?"

"I . . . I'm not sure what you mean."

"Because you can only eat sukiyaki with people you 'suki,' you see."

"Did you learn these puns from rakugo artists?"[9]

---

8. King: Suki means "to like" in Japanese.

9. King: Rakugo is a form of traditional Japanese entertainment with a single storyteller giving a humorous monologue on stage.

"Are they not funny?"

She pouted. "I do not wish to lie."

This made me laugh, and I helped myself to generous bites of pork, burdock root, and green cabbage.

"Most places use napa cabbage in sukiyaki," I said, "but green cabbage is delicious, too."

"People in Kyūshū seem to prefer green cabbage over napa when it comes to pot dishes."

"How did you know that?"

"Because many of the Mainlanders who come to the Island are from Kyūshū."

"Is that so." I picked up a piece of thin-sliced pork with my chopsticks and delivered it to Chi-chan's plate.

"Are you treating me like a child now, Aoyama-san?"

"In a strictly professional relationship, one would simply say 'thanks' for something like this."

She faltered.

"I'm only joking," I said. "Remember when I told you about how I suffered from nutritional deficiency when I was tending the lamp at the little shrine? By the time I got back to Nagasaki, I was very ill. When I finally began to recover, my aunt took me to sukiyaki restaurants. To me, sukiyaki is a dish to be shared with people who are important to me."

There was a pause.

I said, "There's nothing to say to that, is there? Don't worry about it. To me, you are an important person. That's all there is to it."

"Is that not quite 'brutish' of you as well?"

"You're a brute and I'm a brute. We're even."

"Very well . . . as you please."

"I'm the one who should be saying that."

We never lowered our chopsticks in the midst of this back-and-forth, and our first round of sukiyaki was soon gone.

I moved the pot back to the kitchen to start a second round;

sukiyaki didn't generally include water chestnuts or bamboo shoots, but these winter ingredients were so wonderfully fragrant and fresh on the Island that I tossed them into the pot. I didn't add any meat for this round, and instead sifted out any foamy remnants of pork from the broth.

While I was minding the stove, Chi-chan said, "Aoyama-san."

"Yes?"

"You are the only person in the world who has cooked a meal meant solely for me."

Her expression was tender and wholehearted. No mask. All my doubts and questions seemed to dissolve.

"It's my honor."

"I'm sorry."

"It's nothing to apologize for."

"That's true. You're right." After a pause, she said, "Perhaps I'll make clam-boiled noodles for lunch next time."

"What's that?"

"Taichū's extra-thick wheat noodles cooked in clam broth. It's not a 'dish,' strictly speaking, but somewhere between street food and home cooking. Diced pork and green onions are stir-fried in a wok, and clams are made into a broth along with dried flounder. The noodles are cooked directly in the broth, then everything is drizzled with bah-sò and topped with white pepper. The hot fragrant soup combined with the chewy extra-thick noodles can warm the stomach instantly. Two bowls would not be enough."

"What a delectable description! Oh, I remember—you've made me extra-thick noodles before, but not with clam. Are clam noodles special to you in some way?"

"Oh, yes—though not special in the wonderful way that sukiyaki is special to you. The taste of clam noodles is deeply etched into my childhood, you see. It was something that a legendary woman chef would make cheaply in large batches. Even though it was something of a mess-hall dish, she never skimped on any of the ingredients or steps, and as a child I thought it was the most exquisite dish in the world."

This little speech raised many, many questions for me. But the most pressing among these was: "So would making clam-boiled noodles for me be a form of thanks?"

"Yes, you can say that."

"Perhaps I'm being too forward here, but Chi-chan, you've never made clam-boiled noodles specially for just one person before, have you?"

"You are observant as always. No, I have not."

"Does this mean that I am special to you?"

"Yes, you are special."

A smile. A smile so sweet that it seemed as though the argument at the Hokutō onsens never took place.

Never mind, I thought. What was the point in getting to the bottom of things, really? When I brought the second round of sukiyaki to the table, Chi-chan beat in new eggs and refilled our rice bowls. We ate and ate and ate, crunching loudly on the water chestnuts and bamboo shoots.

I was tickled. "It sounds like we've turned into buffalo."

"There's nothing wrong with that. Do the Aoyama family's sharecroppers not keep buffalo? They always look so contented when they're ruminating."

"Is that so?"

"If the opportunity arises, I will take you to see them in the countryside or on a farm."

I said nothing.

"Aoyama-san?"

My tongue betrayed my earlier resolve with another question.

"Is there a difference between someone who's special and someone who's important?"

Her hands stopped.

"What I mean is," I said, "if you dislike me, you can simply say so."

"I don't dislike you."

"In that case, *especially* in that case, I don't understand why you can't be friends with me."

"I am not trying to be intentionally enigmatic. I simply do not have the words in my vocabulary right now to make you understand. If I—if in the future I find an explanation that would make sense to you, I will answer you honestly."

"Really? I would love to turn the clock forward and see that future. But is that future one in which we are still not friends?"

She was quiet for a while. Then she said, "I do not wish to lie."

We both said nothing for a long while.

"All right, all right. Let's eat."

"Thank you for your understanding."

"Well, there's nothing I can do."

"You can dismiss me."

"That is the one thing I cannot do. You still have to take me to see the water buffalo."

"Very well."

"And the sakura of Alisan."

"That will depend on the condition of the railroads."

"I also want to try the food made by this legendary woman chef."

"That will be more difficult, but I will do my best."

Eating a delicious meal from the same pot as her, I *did* feel as happy as a buffalo.

What was the definition of friendship, anyhow? I had long lost sight of the answer.

CHAPTER IX

Tshài-Bué-Thng / Leftovers Soup

"Is there anything good to eat around here?"

I started. "Huh? How did you—"

"It's been awhile since I've heard this catchphrase of yours, Aoyama-san."

"Now that you say it, that may very well be true! But only because you've been answering the question before I can ask it."

She'd caught me by surprise. I looked up from the notebook where I'd been writing shorthand notes and observed her. Did she look back on our past interactions the way I often did? Her smile seemed as placid and inscrutable as ever.

I still could not help but feel that the person sitting before me was both an angel and a demon.

In December, I'd received multiple telegrams from my aunt Kikuko about the New Year. I understood that she meant to chide me for staying away from home for so long, but the actual content of these missives was simply the traditional New Year's menu: kanro-ni glacé fish, chikuzen-ni braised chicken and vegetables, miso-pickled vegetables, pickled sea cucumber intestines, karasumi made with mullet roe, mentaiko with pollock roe, ikura with salmon roe, kazunoko with herring roe, various fishcakes, sugared chestnuts and black beans, konbu-wrapped pork, datemaki egg rolls, and mochi soup with red beans. My aunt knew my gluttonous ways well enough to deliver a heavy blow.

Some of these dishes I could find on the Island, but others

were impossible, especially the Aoyama family–style datemaki egg rolls that even I didn't know the recipe for. Just thinking of the New Year's zōni savory mochi soup was enough to make my mouth water. It would have been an outright lie to say that I didn't miss home. Yet I did not return to Nagasaki.

The Takada family had invited me to join them for New Year's Eve soba, but I'd turned them down.[1] Meanwhile, Mishima-san had come to bring me year-end gifts on behalf of City Hall, and systematically asked me whether I would like to order a New Year's meal or a hot springs trip. I replied that it would be wonderful if he could arrange for me to spend the holiday with an Islander family, which immediately sent his dark brows into a deep furrow. He said, matter-of-factly, "I'm afraid that would be difficult. Why do you not ask Ō-san?"

I did not ask her.

For Chi-chan had made her move long before Mishima-san and Madame Takada paid their visits. While the Gregorian Solar New Year was a national holiday for those of us on the Mainland, most of the Islanders still celebrated the Taiwanese Lunar New Year that this year fell in the middle of February. This would be a busy period for the Ō family, whereas the end of December and the beginning of January did little to affect their daily routines.

After explaining all this, Chi-chan asked, "Are there any Mainland dishes that Aoyama-san would like for the Gregorian New Year?"

What was the thinking behind her offer to make me a feast for the holiday? I had no intention of prying.

She'd prepared a bountiful set of New Year's dishes, including much of Aunt Kikuko's menu on top of shrimp and abalone, and I in turn had prepared two types of mochi soup: one with stock

---

1. Yáng: It is Japanese tradition to have soba noodles on New Year's Eve. The New Year's feast that Aoyama describes would be eaten on New Year's Day and the two days that follow.

made from bonito and dried flying cod, with shredded carrots and radish as well as burdock root, mushrooms, and fresh red-meat fish, into which I added mochi that had been roasted until it was browned and bloated; the other soup was brewed from a generous amount of sugar with red beans, with pieces of mochi buried within the thick red soup, to be unearthed like buried treasures.

All of the food, whether the cold New Year's dishes in lacquer boxes or the steaming mochi soup, was delicious enough to make me want to cry.

Chi-chan, with her monstrous appetite to match mine, acted as my companion on this delicious journey. We ate and drank to our hearts' content, our conversation touching on many subjects and never snagging on any hurdles. We were at the table for hours and hours, until the New Year's breakfast turned into lunch.

Yes, my New Year on the Island had been very pleasant indeed.

And yet Chi-chan was inscrutable, unpredictable. For dinner on both New Year's Eve and New Year's Day, we'd eaten soba noodles along with grated yam, shrimp tempura, raw eggs, and fishcake; as the evening cold seeped into the house, we'd set up a stove to grill mochi, dipping the swollen cakes in sweet kinako flour and peanut powder; to top off, we'd grilled nori seaweed to wrap around the mochi, which we doused with soy sauce. We'd eaten these with our hands, passing them from left to right to left hand while yelping at how hot they were.

Chi-chan's cheeks had turned red and bright before the nighttime fire. Her eyes held a warm gleam and her dimples were shallow, quiet, sweet.

Even so, when I'd asked, "Doesn't being like this make us so-called friends?" she'd only smiled and said, "You've had too much to drink. You ought to get some rest."

Smiting me, though gently.

It was just as Confucius's disciple said of his teacher: "When I look up at his wisdom, it seems to grow more lofty; when I try to penetrate his wisdom, it seems to grow more stalwart; when I seem to be approaching his wisdom, suddenly it appears behind me."

After the holiday, we resumed our hot springs tour.

The first morning, we took the train to Kīrun, where we screened *A Record of Youth* at a cinema near Kīrun Station, gave a half-hour lecture at the Kīrun High School for Girls, and took the transfer train to the Kinsan onsens. After the hot springs, we gorged ourselves on crab, octopus, and small saltwater clams.

The second morning, we returned to Kīrun to take the train to Hatto, where we stayed for barely an hour before turning back. We toured the Keian Maso temple and the Immortals' Cave, spent the night at a hotel near the port, then returned to Taichū on the third morning.

The one thing that stood out in our itinerary was the brief trip from Kīrun to Hatto and back.

Chi-chan was the one who'd arranged it. While we were discussing the trip beforehand, I'd asked why we were going to Hatto, an offshoot station that hadn't even made it into the *Travel Guide to Taiwan's Railways*.

"When we visited Takao, Aoyama-san had enjoyed the Katansui River Iron Bridge. So I thought that you might be interested in Kīrun's railroad landmark, too."

"Oh! Because Takao represents the Island's South and Kīrun represents the North?"

She was momentarily quiet. "I beg your pardon. To be honest, I made the arrangements because *I* wish to see the landmark."

"I see. Well, there's nothing wrong with that."

"You are very kind."

"Aren't I? Anyway, what is this railroad landmark? Is it also an iron bridge?"

"No, it's not a bridge. It's more like—history."

Hm?

What Chi-chan pointed out about my not saying my usual catchphrase was true; that day, for instance, we'd already eaten lunch before heading from the Kinsan onsens back to Kīrun City, and before any urge to snack had even arisen, Chi-chan was already guiding us toward an Islander dessert shop. The fried sticky rice coated in white and black sesame, peanut powder, mung bean powder, and puffed rice had the tastes and textures of nothing I'd ever eaten before. On the other hand, the Island's tshùn-tsó and the Mainland's karintō—both of which were sweet sticks of deep-fried flour—tasted almost identical.[2]

I was recording these discoveries in my notebook in the waiting room of Kīrun Station. I began packing away my writing things as the train pulled in; it would take us to Hatto in a matter of ten minutes.

The landmark that Chi-chan wished to see was a tunnel and a waterfall. On the way south, right before the train headed into the tunnel, passengers could see two columns of water coursing down from the sky, much like two white dragons. The train would seem to dive past the twin dragons into the tunnel. Heading back in the other direction from Hatto to Kīrun, the train would zoom from the dark tunnel out into the thunderous waterfalls, as though breaking through an ocean wave.

Back in the Meiji era, railroad officials had marked the

---

2. Yáng: Taiwan's tshùn-tsó and Japan's karintō, both of which are sugar-coated and -dusted sticks of fried flour, are remarkably similar. However, tshùn-tsó are made from glutinous rice flour and malt sugar, whereas karintō are made from wheat flour, eggs, and mizuame sweetener (a starch-converted sugar similar to corn syrup).

tunnel's entrance with the characters for "double dragon," and the sight became well known as the Double Dragon Waterfalls.[3]

"The waterfalls existed long before the Qīng period, but it wasn't until the railway was built that people could visit them easily. A Shina poet once wrote of the sight, 'Few knew of these waterfalls then / obscured by empty mountains for thousands of years.' Obscured by empty mountains for thousands of years! What a sight to be seen!"

How excited she must have been to have spoken with so much emotion.

Listening to her, I stopped my munching and set aside the tshùn-tsó. The train inched forward slowly, as though it was using its teeth to cling to the rails. The sound of crashing water came to us, far away at first then growing clearer.

Chi-chan stared out the window.

I stared at Chi-chan.

The cascade was now at its loudest; I blinked; the next moment, we were in boundless darkness.

Before I blinked, the sight of Chi-chan's childlike grin was borne into my eyes.

I'd never seen her smile like that before.

What could I do about such a person?

In the darkness of the tunnel, I let out a sigh.

---

3. Yáng: The Double Dragon (Mandarin: Shuānglóng) Waterfalls are also known as the Fāngdǐng Waterfalls, and were referred to as one of Kīrun/Kēelúng's Eight Great Sights from the late Qīng period to the early Japanese-rule period. After World War II, the Taiwan Provincial Highway 5 was built to connect Taihoku/Táipěi and Kīrun/Kēelúng, obscuring the view of the waterfalls. The highway further caused the water's path to redirect; as a result, the double waterfalls no longer exist.

The tunnel, too, had a name. Officially, it was the Tik-Á-Niá Tunnel, Bamboo Peak Tunnel, but it was also known as the Taki-No-Moto Tunnel, or Waterfall Origin Tunnel. The tunnel was deep and broad, but this wasn't what made it a famous landmark. I hadn't understood at first when Chi-chan called the sight "history," but she later explained to me that the story began with the Shikyūrei Tunnel, Lion's Ball Peak Tunnel, about one kilometer away.

Taiwan's railroad construction began under the Qīng emperor Guāngxù. The Qīng people had regarded Kīrun as the northern tip of Taiwan and built the first railway from Kīrun southward, passing through Taihoku and ending in what is now Shinchiku. The greatest hurdle they encountered during this time was the Lion's Ball Peak.

The peak was part of a mountain range known in the Qīng period to be a so-called dragon's vein in a fēngshŭi sense. Furthermore, the mountain itself was a great barrier that couldn't be easily traversed; the only way past it was to dig a tunnel through it. Yet the Qīng officials at the time were lacking in both resources and technology, on top of having to contend with the Islanders' superstitions. And perhaps they had simply blundered. Whatever the reason, there had been poor communication between the Qīng government and foreign engineers, leading to a great design flaw: the tunnel was dug from both ends of the hill, but when the two sides reached the center, there proved to be a great altitudinal difference between them. The route had to be revised, costing a great deal of further time and effort.

The product of all this was the Lion's Ball Peak Tunnel. From both the northern and southern entrances, the ground gradually elevated until they met in the middle; a cross section of the tunnel would look something like a long bow.

This was Taiwan's first railroad tunnel.

The tunnel's unusual form led to many inconveniences, and

the Japanese Empire decided to open a new tunnel after taking over Taiwan. Construction on the Bamboo Peak Tunnel thus began in Meiji Year 29[4] and concluded two years later. The fact that the Empire started construction when they were only in the second year of their rule over Taiwan showed just how much the Government-General prioritized the project. The site, with the Double Dragon Waterfalls, was also chosen to serve a touristic function. According to research that I later conducted, Hatto Station was mentioned in the edition of the *Travel Guide to Taiwan's Railways* published in Taisho Year 1,[5] which introduced the Double Dragon Waterfalls. One could therefore assume that the site was once a prominent landmark.

I felt more and more that the Island, with its layered traces of passing time, was a palimpsest of history that one could not help but admire. Did not both the Lion's Ball Peak and the Bamboo Peak Tunnels embody the grandiose railway dreams of both the Qīng and Japanese Empires? The former with its bow-shaped path; the latter with its flying cascades. The Qīng Empire that overcame hurdles; the Japanese Empire that crafted romance. Was it not fascinating?

"I can write a novel about this! I'll call it *The Taiwan Railway* and I'll write about the construction process of the Island's railroads starting from the Qīng period. Yes—I can start with the digging of the Lion's Ball Peak and end with the completion of the Bamboo Peak Tunnel. What do you think? Then this can catalyze the story about the whole railroad—which is really more than the history of the railroad and more like the history of the Island's pioneering!"

I said this after returning to Hatto Station, while scarfing down the desserts we'd bought. We'd taken a walk near the sta-

---

4. Yáng: 1896.

5. Yáng: 1912.

tion when we first arrived, but there was really little to see other than the Kīrun River, and dark clouds had begun looming ominously in the distance.

Chi-chan looked thoughtful.

"That sounds like it would require a lot of research."

"Very true!"

"That would make for a very different novel from *A Record of Youth*. How many years do you plan on taking to finish it?"

"That's a good point. Let me think . . . each of these tunnels took two, three years to open, right? Maybe I'll just set aside two years. I'll write a short story about it before that—maybe I'll call the short story 'Tale of the Dragon's Vein'!"

"Ah. I look forward to reading it."

"Oho, if I really were to write it, Chi-chan, you wouldn't get away with simply *reading* it."

"Meaning?"

"You'd be in charge of translating it into the Han language."

"Oh? When was that decided?"

"Why, just now!"

Silence.

"Hahahaha."

"I must remind you, Aoyama-san, that in the current political atmosphere, there is not a single Han-language column left in the newspapers."

"What? How is that possible?"

"I have always thought that when it comes to translation, whether it is translating Mainland novels into the Han language or translating Han-language literature from Shina or the Island into Japanese, an Islander translator would have an advantage. But with the war between the Japanese Empire and Shina—aigh, in the future, there might be no need for any translators in Taiwan."

"Ah . . . huh . . ."

"I apologize. I've made the conversation heavy."

“There’s no need for you to apologize. It’s true that the Island’s positioning between the Mainland and Shina is very unusual . . . I spoke without giving due consideration. I’m the one who should apologize.”

She immediately said, “There is no need to apologize.”

The mood had grown oppressive. I had no choice but to continue crunching loudly on the tshùn-tsó sticks. When I emptied the bag, I patted the powdered sugar off of my hands and made a bold declaration: “Chi-chan, let’s take another good look at the waterfalls on the way back! We’ll use the scene as an illustration in the novel. We’ll use a printmaker—with color!”

She seemed slightly surprised. Then she smiled. “Yes. Let’s get a good look on the way back.”

What happened after that?

Let me think.

Chi-chan didn’t behave in any way out of the ordinary all the way back to Kīrun. No, even after that—when we’d walked around Kīrun in the drizzling rain and eaten chikuwa fishcakes by the port, she’d behaved normally. While she hadn’t returned to her former ease, she also hadn’t been wearing her conspicuously stiff Noh mask.

It was perhaps even fair to say that she’d relaxed her guard completely at one point.

The moment had taken place at Keian Temple, an old Maso temple that had been built under the Qīng emperor Qiánlóng. Chi-chan told me about how Keian Temple exemplified the prosperity and cultural progression of Shina descendants in Kīrun, as well as how Kīrun occupies a unique place as the “entryway” to Taiwan.

“Kīrun really is the ‘tip of Taiwan’—not only because it’s the starting point of the railroad, but also because it’s the entry and exit point for ships. Both passenger and freight ships take this route between Kyūshū and Kīrun. When I was young, I dreamt about coming to this port. Taichū Station always has trains loaded with bananas, and I once asked my relatives where the bananas were going. They told me that they're going first to Kīrun, then to the Moji Port in Kyūshū, and I thought about how a port piled high with green and yellow bananas must be filled with their fragrance."

"I would have loved to see Chi-chan as a child."

"Well, unfortunately, when I later visited the port, I discovered that it smelled only of salt and seawater—not a whiff of bananas. Also unfortunately, that young child has grown up to be an unadorable adult."

"That's not true at all. You're still adorable."

"Seems like an angel but is actually a demon, isn't that right?"

"Haha! That's not something you would have said when we first met, Chi-chan! But, you know, even a demonic Chi-chan would be adorable."

When she frowned at me, it was in mock anger. There was no real ire behind it.

And what happened after *that*?

We'd taken a taxi to the Immortals' Cave, a curious, immense cave that had been naturally formed and later modified to include statues of the Kannon Bodhisattva[6] and the goddess Benzaiten. Both the sea-shaped and hand-shaped stones were impressive to behold.

What I found most interesting was a separate, smaller cave within the Immortals' Cave. The path to it was extremely narrow and dark, allowing for only one person to pass at a time. There were statues of gods to worship within the smaller cave as well,

---

6. King: The Kannon Bodhisattva is known as the Guānyīn Bodhisattva in Mandarin Chinese. She is one of the most widely worshipped Buddhist deities in Taiwan (and much of East Asia) and is known as the God of Mercy.

but one could not pray to them except by squeezing through the path with a candle in hand.

I volunteered to go first, but Chi-chan said that her stature made it easier for her to move and that she ought to go first. This made sense, so I ended up following her, clinging tightly to her hand.

"You don't have to be nervous, Aoyama-san. There's nothing dangerous ahead."

"They call it the Immortals' Cave, but it doesn't seem like a place where gods dwell. I wouldn't be surprised if a ghost appeared instead."

"And if there were a ghost, how would holding my hand help?"

"I'll summon the monster in my stomach to fight the ghost!"

Chi-chan began to laugh. Her laughter echoed and echoed in the stuffy, narrow, dark passage. It rang as clear as crystal.

After *that*? We left the cave and went to have all sorts of fish-cakes and fish balls by the port. This was followed by a one-night stay at the Funakoshi Hotel. Did I say something wrong in between? Did I do something?

I couldn't pinpoint the moment when the change began. Was it when we'd finished eating at the restaurant and struggled to share one umbrella on our rainy way back to the hotel?

When we got to our hotel room, Chi-chan handed me a towel and said, "Here." I didn't immediately understand, and she gently placed the towel on my shoulder. It was only then that I noticed that the right side of my body was drenched.

I looked at her in alarm. The sleeve of her coat was spotted with rain, with a few droplets still beaded on the cloth. I brushed these off with the towel.

It was then—

"Please don't do that anymore." Her face was solemn. "Aoyama-san treats me with more kindness than I can take."

I was lost. "What, you mean the umbrella? Or patting off the rain? That hardly counts as kindness."

She was silent. Then:

"If your interpreter today had been Mishima-san from City Hall, would you have treated him the same way?"

"*Huh*?"

I pictured Mishima-san's knotted brows, his face as sour as a plum. Just the thought of toweling his sleeve made my face, too, wrinkle like a sour plum.

"I believe you wouldn't have."

"No, I wouldn't have."

"This might seem nonsensical to you, but . . . isn't this differential treatment, then?"

What—how—what is she saying! My brain was a scramble; I could only stand there stupidly. She, too, continued standing. I felt exasperated that we had, once again, found ourselves at an impasse. But before I could sigh and concede defeat, Chi-chan left to bring a new towel.

The soft clean cloth touched my cheeks.

And then my ears.

Ah. So even my head had gotten wet.

Did this mean that it was she who had conceded defeat first?

"I don't believe that Mishima-san would help me dry my hair like this either."

No response.

After a moment's consideration, I added, "If you don't like it, I won't do things like that anymore."

She made a quiet *mm* sound. "Me neither."

Meaning the towel and the hair, I suppose.

The incident lingered in my mind long after the Kīrun trip.

For, not long after we returned to Taichū, something happened that I really, truly could not figure out—*really, truly,* even after wringing my brain for any possible clue.

The room was aglow with sunlight.

Chi-chan looked at me directly, gravely. *If you really cannot change your attitude toward me, I will have to resign my post.*

Forgive me for jumping ahead.

Let us turn back the clock a little.

At the very end of January, Chi-chan said that she would take me to visit the legendary woman chef.

Islanders call chefs tsóng-phòo or to-tsí,[7] and a head chef who is capable of spearheading a full banquet is respectfully referred to as a tsóng-phòo-sai, a master chef. This particular chef, known as Master A-Phûn, was one such master chef. She'd been born to a gentry family in Zhāngzhōu during the Qīng period, but while she was still a girl she was separated from her family during political turmoil and had since spent her life as a civilian. She never married, instead drifting between the kitchens of prominent families, learning the Hoklo and Hakka cuisines of the Island as well as the Fukien and Canton cuisines of Shina. Whether it was casual home cooking, street stall grub, restaurant banquets, or delicacies on the private menus of the wealthy, she was thoroughly versed in any and all genres.

Though she was a culinary professional, Master A-Phûn also kept the regal ways of her former life, always dining on exquisite foods, gambling freely, and indulging in fine music and theater. Whenever she earned a good sum at a given job, she would quit and go gallivanting about until the money was spent, whereby she would return to working. It was only after her fiftieth birthday that she'd finally accepted a long-term post with the Lin family, wealthy Islanders in Taichū's Ōsato Village. She had been

7. Yáng: To-tsí can be written with multiple Chinese characters, including ones that also mean knife or butcher; it carries a derogatory implication that the chef is less of a cook and more of a butcher.

cooking exclusively for the matriarch Madame Lin for about a decade.

Chi-chan and I took the bus to Ōsato on a clear winter morning.

"I can't believe you really found the master chef."

"I promised you I would."

"Chi-chan, you're also a very kind person."

She chuckled. "Not at all." Then: "If Master A-Phûn refuses to cook for you, would the monster in your stomach be able to take it?"

"Ahaha . . . if that's the case, I'll just have to cry all the way home."

"I want to ask whether you are joking, but you do not seem to be."

"Well, Master A-Phûn has cooked only for Madame Lin for almost ten years, isn't that right? If she's so adamant about her boundaries, we really can't force her."

Chi-chan watched me for a while.

"I will do my best."

What could she mean?

The Lin family mansion was an imposing Shina-style complex built in red brick. A boy servant led us to an old woman outside the outer walls, who then led us to a girl servant within the walls, who in turn led us into the complex. We passed through door after door, wall after wall, down lit and shadowed hallways and several sharp corners. Suddenly, a Shina-style gate of glistening majolica tiles rimmed with orange trumpet vines appeared before us. We stepped through it and entered a small courtyard surrounded by buildings. The girl servant said, "Please make yourselves at home" in unsteady Japanese and disappeared.

All three of the buildings—before and to the left and right of us—were delicately crafted Shina-style houses. Together with the gate through which we'd entered, they formed a neat little square. The door to the small house directly in front of us was open, and a melody sounded from within its dim depths.

A record player.

When I stopped to listen, I found that the music was European classical.

The red-brick structure looked as though it was frozen in the Qīng period, yet it was filled with Western music that had traversed oceans. The situation was too full of mystique; I found myself unable to move. Chi-chan and I stood side by side until the song ended.

A person emerged. It was a beautiful woman whose plain, red-black Taiwanese chōsan could not subdue the striking nature of her features. She looked us both up and down, then settled her gaze on my face.

"It's you, isn't it? I'll say this only once, so listen up." Her Japanese was confident, fluent. "*I don't cook for Japanese people.*"

I was shocked. My first thought: *This* beautiful woman was Master A-Phûn, who was supposedly over sixty years old?

My second thought: this master chef was not willing to cook for me. I could not help but say, loudly and from the bottom of my heart: "What?" *Hold on a second, Master A-Phûn!*

Chi-chan said in a resounding voice, "I have heard that Master A-Phûn never refuses a bet. If I win against you, might I trouble you to make just one dish for Aoyama-san?"

A bet? Where was her confidence coming from? While my tongue was tied with surprise, the two of them had switched to conversing in Taiwanese Hokkien.

"XXX, XXXXXXXXX, XXXXXXXXX, XXXXXXXXX, XXXXXX, XXXXXXXXXX?"

"XX, XXXX."

Chi-chan, who spoke first, had been decorous and sincere. Master A-Phûn's response, however, was curt. This dynamic persisted in their ensuing exchange, with Chi-chan doing her best to sound persuasive and Master A-Phûn refusing to waver in her resolve not to cook for a Japanese person. I was utterly focused on the exchange but still could not make out a single word. It was only when Master A-Phûn finally slowed down her snappish responses that I picked up one word of Japanese: kohaku, meaning amber. Even so, I didn't understand the word's significance.

After who knew how long, Master A-Phûn fell silent. She turned her electrifying gaze on me. "You! You're very lucky!"

Leaving behind this one sentence of Japanese without any context, she whipped around and went back inside the house.

What was going on? I looked at Chi-chan. She showed me her dimples, probably in an effort to reassure me. I did not have time to speak to her before Master A-Phûn reemerged. She held a large bowl in her hand.

Master A-Phûn pointed a finger at a tea table under the eaves of the entrance gate. Chi-chan moved toward it and I followed suit. It was only in turning around that I saw how the orange trumpet vines, in full bloom, cascaded down the wall to contrast magnificently with the black roof tiles and red brick.

Taiwan. What a resplendent place.

The awe was inopportune, but I could not help but fixate on the thought that this house was a microcosm of the whole island.

I picked up the Shina-style sandalwood tea table and placed it in the center of the courtyard. Chi-chan and Master A-Phûn each stood on one side of the table. The clacking in the large bowl proved to be—just as I expected—dice.

Four six-sided dice.

When Chi-chan and I played, we'd only played with three. This, the game that they were about to play, was a game that the

Islanders called sip-pat-á:[8] dice of the same number didn't count, and the other dice were bet against either the highest or lowest number. The lowest possible number in this case was three and the highest twelve; this highest outcome was called sip-pat-á. If all four dice were the same number, this was called "one color," which won over sip-pat-á. When Chi-chan and I played, the only rule was to bet for either higher or lower and add up all the numbers. It had been a much more simplified version of proper sip-pat-á.

Let us now return to the scene.

Chi-chan tossed three or four times as a warm-up. Master A-Phûn coughed lightly, and Chi-chan said, in Taiwanese, "Please."

Master A-Phûn, as dealer, tossed first.

Clack clack clack. All four dice stopped at six black dots.

"One color."

I looked toward Chi-chan, but she had already seized the dice in her hand and released them breezily.

The dice rolled along the walls of the bowl. When they stopped, all four showed a single red dot.

"One color."

My gods!

I was right after all—it wasn't simply thanks to luck that she'd won every time we'd played. But this wasn't the time for me to fuss over such details. Whose victory was it?

Master A-Phûn gave a loud laugh and said a long string of words in Taiwanese. I didn't understand a single one, but Chi-chan nodded and smiled at me.

---

8. Yáng: Sip-pat-á is now known by several other names, all of which contain the word sip-pat, which means eighteen in Taiwanese Hokkien. Many people are under the impression that this is because three dice together add up to eighteen, but this is a misunderstanding; a six plus a pair of any other two numbers is also known as a sip-pat.

A smile brighter than the winter sun. A smile radiant with pride.

"I won you one dish, Aoyama-san!"

Despite my confusion, a grin spread across my face. "Uh—what exactly happened just now? What did you talk about?"

Hmph. Master A-Phûn was chuckling from her nose. "The child wasn't raised by Kohaku for nothing. A clever one indeed. What a shame that she's chosen to befriend a Japanese! But a bet is a bet. I'll make one dish. And I want both of you out of here as soon as you're done eating!"

Wha—

Chi-chan spoke before I could: "Very well. The dish I would like to order is—tshài-bué-thng."

What on earth was tshài-bué-thng?

When Chi-chan made the request, Master A-Phûn frowned, then burst into raucous laughter.

And then we were chased out of the house.

The girl servant was waiting outside the gate.

It was as if I'd entered the Peach Blossom Spring—the ethereal utopia as written by Tao Yuanming. Like the character in that fable, I retraced our steps along the wall and lost track of how far or near things were down the long corridor; suddenly, a forest of orange trumpet blossoms, as if there was a beam of light. Perhaps I had simply blundered into an ethereal, utopian, Resplendent Island.

I was bursting with questions and was desperate to get answers from Chi-chan on the bus ride home: Who was this Kohaku, this Amber? Why was Chi-chan's dice-playing technique so impeccable? What was the relationship between Master A-Phûn and Chi-chan?

But I knew that she would not respond in any real way.

The bus dropped us off at Shintomichō Market, and we ate lunch at the nearby cafeteria. Hayashi rice, omelet rice, shrimp tempura, fried meatballs, fresh salad.

"What on earth is tshài-bué-thng?" I asked at last. But as soon as I began my questioning, I couldn't stop at one. "Did you technically win just now? And what did Master A-Phûn mean?"

A smile. "According to the rules, that would have been a draw. But Master A-Phûn had agreed beforehand that a draw would also be my win. Don't fret, Aoyama-san—in half a month, Master A-Phûn's signature dish, tshài-bué-thng, leftovers soup, will be ready for us."

"Oh, it's such a complex dish? No wonder we couldn't have it today. I'd thought that she was chasing us out of there!"

"Well, I believe she *did* want to chase us out of there." Her smiling eyes were little arches. "A Taiwanese banquet has twelve dishes. Subtracting the midbanquet small dish and the final dessert, that makes ten dishes. Every dish will inevitably have some leftover pieces on the plate, and in the past, Islander master chefs who didn't wish to waste food would mix all of the food left on the plates into a so-called leftovers soup, which would be given to neighbors and friends after the banquet. Nowadays, it is considered a delicacy in its own right—a merging of many delicious flavors. Shina, for instance, has the famous dish fó-tiào-qiáng, literally 'Buddha Jumps over the Wall,' which combines all sorts of meat, fish, and vegetables including shark fin, quail eggs, scallops, and such. And leftovers soup is the Taiwanese equivalent."

Ack! I choked a little on the meatball I'd just stuffed in my mouth.

Chi-chan pushed the water glass toward me and continued explaining: "When I was young, I once saw an old rich man hire a master chef to create a whole banquet solely to taste the leftovers soup. Aoyama-san—in order to make leftovers soup, Master A-Phûn must first prepare a full banquet."

B-b-but that means—

"Yes, indeed, Aoyama-san. In half a month, you'll be able

to enjoy Master A-Phûn's twelve banquet dishes. Ah—not only twelve. Along with the soup, that makes thirteen."

Uuuuooooaaaaah! I wanted to cry out, but the meatball stoppered my mouth. I could only make my eyes wider and wider.

I must have looked ridiculous, for Chi-chan smiled at me softly. "Miss Monster won't have to shed any tears on her way home, I imagine."

I swallowed.

"Chi-chan!"

"Please lower your voice."

We were in public; I didn't care. "No matter what you say, nothing will change the fact that I see you as my best friend. You are the only person in the whole world—in all of heaven and on all of earth—who has regarded me and the so-called monster in my stomach seriously!"

The winter daylight, filtered through the cafeteria's glass windows, shone a halo around Chi-chan's body.

Just like how, in this world, in all of heaven and on all of earth, Chi-chan is the only person who glows in my eyes.

"*That's* why I can't bear that you have to settle for a lesser life here on the Island. What can you do after marrying a man like that? If you can't work as a translator on the Island, then why don't we go to the Mainland?"

"Stop, please."

She interrupted me, but I did not stop. "It makes sense for a caged bird to seek more open lands. Besides, Chi-chan, you're no sparrow, you're a white phoenix! Isn't that right? If what you're missing is a rising wind to lift your wings, then let me be your easterly wind!"

"I said, please stop."

"Mmph!"

"What if I don't want to ride that easterly wind?" Her tone was firm.

I was dumbfounded. "But why not? I've said it before: you don't have to rely on the Ō family to move to the Mainland. I might not earn all that much as a novelist, but I am the heir to the Nagasaki branch of the Aoyama family. This is the best possible arrangement for you that I can—"

"Enough, Aoyama-san!" She cut me off, looking into my eyes with the most severe expression. "If you really cannot change your attitude toward me, I will have to resign my post."

What?! How many times had I shouted the word that day? But this "what" was the most piercing, most unforgettable of all.

"You do not know where the Ō family home is located, correct? Meaning you will not be able to find me so long as I stop going to your cottage. I am sorry, but I will ask Mishima-san to take on the duties of interpreter for the present. Please forgive me." She stood and made a formal bow. "I will take my leave now. Do excuse me."

She began walking away as soon as the words were out. I was still too dazed to react. It was the first time she'd left her seat early in our travels together.

I had enraged her.

But how?

I sat with my back straight and my mind stunned in that beautifully lit cafeteria. When and where had I incensed her so? I had not the slightest inkling about the changing workings of her heart. All I knew was that, though there was only a single meatball remaining on my plate, I had absolutely no way of finishing my meal.

CHAPTER X

Tau-Mī / Potato Noodle Stew

On the last night of the thirteenth year of Shōwa, Chi-chan and I had eaten traditional New Year's Eve soba noodles together. We had grilled mochi cakes on the stove and eaten them with sweet kinako flour, with soy sauce and seaweed, with powdered peanut. We had sipped warm rice wine and steaming hot oolong tea. The coal in the stove crackled gently. The winter had been cold and the night sky opaque; a thin mist had risen from the Yana River and seeped into the cottage. I'd proposed playing dice and Chi-chan had agreed. The highest number won. That night, and that night only, I'd tossed an eighteen while she tossed a seventeen.

The last night of the thirteenth year of Shōwa was the first time that Chi-chan had spent the night in the cottage.

We had opened the shōji doors dividing the zashiki main room and tsugi secondary room and laid out futon bedding on the tatami of both. I was tipsy and soon fell asleep, waking in the middle of the night to find Chi-chan still reading by lamplight in the tsugi room. She always removed her Noh mask when reading. Under the beam of warm light, I felt as though time had rewound and we were once again on the train returning from Shōka to Taichū, where Chi-chan had translated for me the story in her hand, reading aloud in her sweet voice.

What time is it? Keeping my voice soft, I asked, "Chi-chan, can you answer me something?"

"Hm?"

"Why did you never agree to stay over before?"

"Hm . . ."

"I want to hear the whole truth."

She lifted her gaze from the page. "Because there is a servant's room in this house."

"Is that so."

"That is so."

I climbed out from under the blankets and dragged her empty bedspread all the way into the main room, right next to mine.

"What are you doing?"

"Now we're completely equal." I felt like I was gouging out my heart and lungs and holding them out to her in my hands. "No matter what happens, I will *never* regard you as a servant. So *please*, have a little more faith in me!"

She watched me without speaking and only sat down on her futon after a long moment. There was no gap between the two bedspreads—no barriers. Satisfied, I climbed back under my blankets. "Feel free to turn on the light on this side if you want to keep reading."

"I can't possibly do something like that."

"Is that so."

"That is so."

I fell silent.

She fell silent.

"Chi-chan, I would never have guessed that you assumed I would make you sleep in the servant's room. Is that the type of person I am in your eyes?"

"It's precisely because you're so kind, Aoyama-san."

"What?"

"If even *you* regarded me that way, whatever would I do with myself? I didn't want to take the risk of discovering—"

"Chi-chan, you *do* value me, don't you!"

I reached out and held her hand. The skin was cold and soft. After a fleeting moment of hesitation, she, too, gripped my hand.

I sighed softly. "See, doesn't this make us friends?"

She made a small chuckling sound that also sounded like a sigh. She placed my hand under my blanket and tugged the corners tight.

"You've had too much to drink," she said. "Please get some rest."

Moonlight seemed to be glistening in her smiling eyes. Angel? Demon? Either way, what more could I say?

But there had been no moonlight on that New Year's Eve. I took the opportunity to memorize Chi-chan's eyes; my own figure had been reflected in them.

Was it possible that it had all been a dream?

If this were a dream, I wished I would wake. In the morning, it was not Chi-chan but Mishima from City Hall who showed up at my door. This was two days after Chi-chan bade me farewell in the cafeteria.

"Thanks to Ō-san and the Takada family's request, I have the privilege of once again acting as your guide and interpreter," Mishima said, presenting me with an official document. "I am at your service."

He handed me my upcoming itinerary. On day one, I was to visit the Tōen Shrine; on day two, I was to give a lecture at the Tōen Public Hall in the morning and another at the Shinchiku Public Hall in the afternoon, after which I would return to Taichū the same evening. It was far too tight!

I was immediately resistant. "Just two days for both Tōen *and* Shinchiku? Is that even possible? Besides, with two lectures, there's not a minute left for actual traveling. And why must I go to the Tōen Shrine? The Islanders' Keifuku Temple would be far more interesting. And wouldn't I have to miss dinner in Shinchiku if we have to come back to Taichū right after the event? This level of activity would be too much even for a tourist group. Mishima-san, please explain to me why the itinerary must be this way."

He was expressionless. "Aoyama-sensei, I am not Ō-san."

"Of course not."

"Forgive me for being forward, but Aoyama-sensei, it is your tenth month on the Island. Though the Takada family and City Hall have made no specific requirements of you, we have received heaps of letters and telegrams inviting you to give lectures, write articles, and visit various locations . . ."

"Do you intend to insult me, Mishima-san?"

"I have spoken out of turn. But please allow me to say this: Aoyama-sensei, are you aware of who has been taking external criticism in your stead?"

I froze.

He pressed on. "I am not Ō-san. Rather, I am an employee of the Taiwan Government-General who must uphold the reputation of Taichū City Hall. While I will take on the work of your secretary, there is no reason for me to take on infamy on your behalf. Pray understand my position."

My mind plunged into chaos.

"Aoyama-sensei, may I continue with my explanation?"

"Please do."

"Since you arrived on the Island, it has not only been girls' schools and women's groups interested in meeting a celebrated Mainlander writer, but also esteemed individuals all across Taiwan. The invitations have only multiplied after the well-received Taiwan Travelogue essays began serializing. I am not certain how Ō-san filtered down this high demand, but I am very certain that I do not have the same capacity, so my only option is to ask Aoyama-sensei for your assistance. According to the records, you have yet to visit Tōen and Shinchiku. The most efficient way of meeting public demand while reducing Aoyama-sensei's burdens is to arrange for large-scale lectures in public halls. Meanwhile, the Tōen Shrine was completed last year, and as it is expected of a model subject of the Empire to pay one's respects to the shrine, this may help subdue some groundless gossip. Such was my reasoning for arranging the itinerary this way."

I forced myself to clear a path in my muddled brain. "Is it true what you say about Ō-san receiving unreasonable abuse on my behalf? If so, why didn't she tell me directly? If I'd known, I would *never* have let Chi-chan endure that alone!"

Even unflappable Mishima widened his eyes when I let slip the nickname of Chi-chan. But he instantly resumed his neutral expression. "I do not know the reasons why Ō-san did what she did." When I said nothing, he added: "In fact, I would rather have thought that Aoyama-sensei, given how much time you've spent with Ō-san, would be better informed on her reasons."

"Are you mocking me, Mishima-san?"

"I would not dare."

"Hmph."

"Allow me to return to our main point of discussion. If you are amenable to this itinerary, Aoyama-sensei, I will come to meet you for departure next Saturday at ten in the morning."

"Ō-san said that this would only be short term! Why would you still be substituting for her next week?"

"Logically speaking, Aoyama-sensei, you are the one with the answer to that question."

The honorable and righteous Mishima had positively trampled on my open wounds without reservation. In any other context, his rudeness would be quite inexcusable. But I was so shocked by the news that he'd brought that I'd missed the timing to get angry.

I had plummeted into a nightmare. On Saturday morning, the person at my door was, indeed, stony-faced Mishima.

"I would like to have Hakka cuisine."

"Very well, I will do my best."

"When you said that previously, Mishima-san, I never got my tshenn-tsháu-à tea or pineapple juice."

Silence.

"Ō-san would not say that it was impossible."

"Thank you for letting me know, Aoyama-sensei."

"In which case—I want to have Hakka cuisine."

"Unfortunately, that is impossible."

"At least give me a reason, will you?"

"Very well. Because Tōen does not have Hakka cuisine."

"But there are Hakka people who live in Tōen, aren't there? I've researched this! I don't need banquet-style food, just everyday Hakka fare."

"The Hakka community is not in Tōen but in Chūreki."

"That's only one stop away from Tōen!"

"Our schedule does not allow for any additional time in Chūreki."

"Ō-san would have said yes to me."

"That is truly a shame. I hope that Ō-san will agree to continue acting as your interpreter in the future."

The above took place in Tōen. The same occurred again in Shinchiku.

"There is a Hakka community in Shinchiku, is there not? If I remember correctly, there's a Bannin tribe there as well. Even a snack will do. Do you really know *nothing*?"

"Please accept my deepest apologies for being unequipped to answer your questions, Aoyama-sensei. I am familiar with neither the Islanders' native tribal distributions nor the Island's culinary culture."

"Pardon my frankness, Mishima-san, but can you even call yourself a local guide and interpreter?"

"Pardon me as well, Aoyama-sensei, but City Hall staff are not professional interpreters. We typically recommend women guests visiting from the Mainland to purchase Shinchiku's famous perfumed powder as a souvenir."

"That's just a product made for tourists, isn't it? Don't you know anything about the unique aspects of Hakka or Bannin cuisines?"

Nothing.

"Aaah, Ō-san would . . ."

"I really do feel that it's a shame for you—a shame that there is only I to fill such shoes."

"Mishima-san, are you so blunt with your other esteemed guests?"

"No. Usually I would say, 'Very well, I will do my best.'"

The pain in my heart made even my head ache with distress. What had I done to anger Chi-chan, and what exactly was it that I needed to do in order for her to come back? I cried out to the gods within my heart: Please! Let this Mishima go back to his job at City Hall! Please!

"Aoyama-sensei," Mishima said. "I am sure that, in your eyes, Ō-san is the one deserving of the title local guide and interpreter. Perhaps it is not my place to say this, but the things that Ō-san did for you in fact far exceeded the responsibilities of an interpreter. If you continue to hold all interpreters to this standard, you will not find anybody fit to replace Ō-san even if you dismiss me."

His line of argument infuriated me. "You are quite mistaken, Mishima-san! Ō-san and I are friends, and of course I realize that she has taken care of me in ways that exceed the responsibilities of an interpreter. I've never held you to the same standard!"

"Oh? So Aoyama-sensei and Ō-san are friends. You must excuse me, for I never perceived this from what I have witnessed of your interactions."

"Mishima-san, now you are most *definitely* ridiculing me!"

"I would not dare."

"When will Ō-san return to her post? She and I have plans to eat tshài-bué-thng on Tuesday, two days from today."

"Tshài-bué-thng? If this is for work purposes, Ō-san will pass on the relevant information to me so that I might take Aoyama-san to the appointed location."

"Absolutely not!" I growled. My rage splashed forth as from a toppled bathtub. "The chef is unwilling to cook for Japanese people. This cannot happen unless Ō-san is present. Please inform Ō-san that she must be the one to take me that day. Mishima-san, this is not a matter to be taken lightly!"

He looked at me. The thick brows were drawn close together, dipping toward each other. Perhaps he was thinking *Does this woman really need to lose her temper over a meal?*

But I couldn't care less what he was thinking.

"Ō-san dedicated a lot of energy to changing this chef's mind. How can she possibly give up at this juncture? This meal ought to be shared with Ō-san. Have I made myself clear, Mishima-san?"

He nodded. "If this is not a part of work but rather your personal relationship, why does Aoyama-sensei not contact Ō-san directly?"

He had asked the question to stop me in my tracks.

Very true—why not? Because I did not have her address—because I did not even know where to send a telegram.

Am I stuck in a nightmare?

If Chi-chan doesn't return, then my days living on Taiwan Island would be no different from a dream.

When I asked Mishima about how to contact Chi-chan, he had replied only that it was inappropriate for him, as City Hall staff, to provide contact information for private citizens. Besides, it was the Takada family that had made the hire. "Please ask Madame Takada directly."

"Would that not make me a husband who goes to his wife's employer demanding where his wife has gone?"

Mishima did not respond, but his heavy gaze seemed to say *Well, aren't you?*

Since my arrival on Taiwan Island, the most disheartening trips I'd taken had all been with Mishima.

The militaristically busy itinerary in Tōen and Shinchiku came to an end. By the time a taxi delivered me back to the Yana River cottage, the sky was already bleary with night. I'd had no appetite on the train south from Chikunan Station and only ate four salted duck eggs. The moment I began peeling the eggshell, something zapped through my mind's eye—the first time I passed Chikunan while heading south, I'd also bought duck eggs. I'd missed seeing the broken Gyotōhei Bridge ruins between Jyūroppun and Taian Stations because I was so busy peeling them.

Since then, I'd taken numerous train rides north and south with Chi-chan. More than once, we'd gazed out the window at the broken bridge together.

I was sure that she'd said this to me before: the region of Chikunan and Byōritsu along the railroad was a hub for Islander Hakka people. She'd said that their cuisine and language, in particular, differed from those of the Hakka population in Taichū. She'd said *But it might be too early to go into specifics—perhaps I should save the explanations for when we visit in the future.*

She'd promised. And now—my heart somersaulted. Ah, it was just like what Lord Nobunaga once said—fifty human years is but a dream, an illusion!

Exhausted in both body and soul, I slept until the sun had climbed high overhead.

Birds were warbling both far and near. Their voices filtered past the cottage's roof tiles, past the shōji doors, past the borders of my dreams.

When I at last opened my eyes, I saw that daylight had filled and warmed the room. On the other hand, the coal in the room's stove had cooled entirely, leaving behind a somewhat lonely scent.

On New Year's Eve, Chi-chan had read deep into the night in this very room. Her eyes had been purer than moonlight.

By the time I rose, it was already ten o'clock. What could one eat at such a time? My body felt cottony, and could only muster enough energy to slice some toast from the cupboard and pair it with milk.

Taking a large bite, I tried to recall what I'd eaten the previous night. I could not.

If Chi-chan had been with me in Tōen and Shinchiku, we would have eaten a few Hakka dishes, and after taking the train back to Taichū with our stomachs full, perhaps topped off with a dessert of egg mixed into hot almond tea. Then, in the morning, Chi-chan would have opened the glass doors and ushered in cold air to clear my head. She would have peered into my study and said *Good morning, Aoyama-san.*

Good morning, Chi-chan. Let's grill mochi again today!

We would have said those things.

Yet I was alone at the dining table. The toast in my mouth was no different from a ball of crumpled paper.

Would a true daughter of Kyūshū be so downhearted?

I left the cottage with the hope of easing my melancholy, thinking that maybe I would go to the Taichū Sugar Factory on the so-called Sugar Railway, whose final stop was Nantō Station. I'd visited the Tōho onsens on my hot springs tour in the early winter, but I'd yet to venture far down Nantō Street. I hadn't traveled alone for a long time. How long did it take to get to Nantō? Perhaps half a day could be spent just swaying along on a train.

A February morning in the Southern Country. With the sun overhead, the day was not cold.

I abandoned the idea of taking a bus and instead walked on foot toward Taichū's city center. Soon it was noon and my stomach was vocalizing loudly, the paper-like toast long digested into nothing. I walked past many stalls, shops, restaurants, cafeterias, and cafés, past the thick aroma of sautéed onion and curry roux, past the rising scent of bah-sò, garlic chives, fried shallots, and pork bone broth. Past the coffee and milk, past the honey and sweet egg cakes. Ahead: bí-hún-tshá vermicelli noodles, grilled sausage wrapped in sticky rice, oyster pancakes. Farther ahead: sushi rolls wrapped in nori seaweed. Bananas and wax apples. Shredded chicken noodles and hot soup noodles. Sauce-grilled unagi. Baked sweet potato. Boiled peanuts. Red bean soup. Raw eggs over udon noodles. Lóo-bah rice. Potato croquette and fried meatballs . . .

What was going on? Why did nothing tempt my appetite?

I beelined to the waiting room for the Sugar Railway at Taichū Station without stopping for any food, a sheen of sweat coating my forehead. It was only then that I realized that the train wasn't running.

This was the type of shameful blunder I never would have made with Chi-chan by my side.

Utterly defeated, I began to make the trek back to the cottage, feeling my legs to be unbelievably frail. By contrast, the people surrounding me seemed to brim with energy. Two high school students passed me from behind, their young boyish voices as clear as the blue sky.

"Hey, that's a promise!"

"It's *not* a promise! I said I can't!"

The two young men were of similar build. One draped his arm around the shoulders of the other. They stopped at the street corner and waited for the cars and buses to file by. I came to a halt behind them.

"You said you can't in the morning, right? That's why I said to meet after lunch!"

"*No,* I said I'd be busy *starting* in the morning. Islanders have to pay all sorts of visits on the first day of the Lunar New Year, just like Mainlanders do on the Gregorian New Year, you know."

"Oh, is that so? Oh, I know—let my family's driver take you! That way, you can finish early."

"Aigh—forgive me, Master Murakami!"

"Forgive you? Why, you hateful, faithless brute!"

The Mainlander boy named Murakami wrapped his arm even more tightly around the Islander boy's shoulders. The Islander boy shrugged him off easily and, taking advantage of a gap between the passing cars, arrowed forward. His Mainlander friend chased after him, and their laughter rang loudly as they charged ahead. The boys seemed no different to me from the golden and glowing trumpet flowers that lined the walls along the street.

Look at how well they got along—an Islander and a Mainlander, friends.

My steps grew even heavier.

I dragged myself past the curtain of trumpet flowers, feeling something else gallop across my chest.

Not so long ago, I had seen trumpet flowers more striking than these.

Along the walls of that red Shina-style house, the flowers had burst into cascades of orange, red, and yellow. Between the petals, vividly colored clay and mosaic tiles peeked through. Chi-chan stood holding dice in front of the sandalwood tea table against this golden backdrop.

The confidence in her eyes had far outshone the vibrant flowers.

When the Mainlander boy had tightened his hold on the Islander boy and cried *Forgive you? Why, you hateful, faithless brute!*, I, too, imagined putting my arms around Chi-chan's shoulders. I wanted to shake her and yell *You hateful brute! Don't be faithless!*

In my dream that night, I gripped her shoulders. But the moment I began to shake her, hard, I woke.

I was in bed—in the same room where Chi-chan had been reading on New Year's Eve.

There was still a lingering glimmer in the stove. I found that my eyes were moist.

"Hateful Chi-chan . . . faithless brute . . ."

Knock knock. The sound came from the shōji door on the side of the veranda. It slid slowly open. Behind it, the glass sliding door was also ajar. Fresh, cool morning air poured into the room.

A small figure stood with its back against the mellow sunshine: Chi-chan, like a mirage.

"Good morning, Aoyama-san."

I threw off my blankets.

"Chi-chan!"

I wanted to get up, but instead she seated herself next to my futon and reached out to smooth the collar of my pajamas.

"You didn't even lock the doors. Isn't that dangerous?"

"Oh, well . . . I've forgotten before, too, and nothing's gone wrong . . ."

"Aigh. What are we to do with you?"

Was I dreaming?

I felt I hadn't seen her coaxing smile in a long, long time.

"You've risen rather late this morning. Would you like breakfast?"

"Chi-chan, does this mean you're coming back?"

"At least for today—I can't be a faithless brute, after all."

"Ahaha! So you heard me!"

Her obliging smile slowly transformed into something much more solemn as she looked at me. I looked back at her.

The room fell quiet.

What was it that I wanted her to say in that moment? Was it "thank you"? or "sorry"? Or did I want her to ask me "Have you reflected on your mistakes?"—though I still did not know where I had erred?

What she did say was, "Remember the nine-layer cake that I told you about? The Hakka people have a similar dessert called nine-layer wedge. Both are made from milled zairai rice. Hakka nine-layer wedge is colored with white and yellow sugar and built up layer by layer as a breakfast pastry. What do you think?"

Still that smiling face. Still the adorable dimples.

Although not the Noh mask.

I wanted to respond with words, but my stomach called out before my mouth could.

Soon I'd eaten two whole pieces of nine-layer wedges, each the size of my palm. My stomach's wailing eased at last, and I proceeded into my third piece, tearing off the layers of chewy rice dough and counting them while I chewed. There were indeed nine layers.

Meanwhile, Chi-chan set some watered-down milk on the stove and quickly transformed the plain toast in my cupboard into many-flavored sandwiches: butter, fruit jam, thick slices of ham. When the milk came to a boil, she put out the stove fire and added sugar and tea leaves to the pot.

Sandwiches and steaming milk tea.

Chi-chan and I sat on opposite ends of the dining table.

I could not believe that this was the same toast that had tasted like paper just the day before. The bread was now fluffy and smelled pleasingly of wheat; when I chewed, the natural sweetness of its starch instantly brightened my mood. I finished the plate of sandwiches before the tea had even cooled enough to drink.

Chi-chan, meanwhile, didn't touch the food. Sipping her tea, she said, "Your appetite is as good as ever."

"Really?"

The Chi-chan before me seemed completely at ease, as though there had never been any conflict between us—as though she hadn't left me without a word for half a month.

She, as ever, had a knack for turning back the clock.

And as for me, Aoyama Chizuko? Should I let the clock rewind, or should I press for an answer?

When the milk tea was no longer scorching hot, I drank half a cup in slow gulps.

"Chi-chan."

"Yes?"

"New Year's Eve was the only time that you've lost to me at dice."

"True."

"But you could have won, correct?"

"Yes, I could have."

"Then why did you choose to lose to me?"

"Why indeed?" She lowered her teacup. Her expression remained tranquil. "Aoyama-san, what do you think the reason was?"

"Because you wanted to have faith in me, maybe. But when we were in Kīrun—or rather, when we were in Ōsato—I did something that made you lose faith in me, is that so? But I genuinely do not understand what happened."

"Mm . . . I am sure I caused Aoyama-san great trouble. I am very sorry." She raised the cup to her lips again.

"You don't seem inclined to explain."

"It's not that I am not inclined, it's that I am still thinking about *how* to explain it to you."

"Is that so."

"That is so."

Because she smiled at me, I smiled back at her. But while one can physically turn back a clock's hands with a finger, one can never stop time from pressing ahead.

I'll be going back to Kyūshū in just two months.

This I did not say out loud.

Fleeting light, fleeting light, I beg you drink this cup of wine.

Why was it that time refused to halt in its steps?

We, too, had no choice but to tread ahead.

At noon, we arrived once more in the Lin family's utopic Peach Blossom Spring in Ōsato. The same young man, old woman, and young woman guided us from stop to stop as in a relay race. At the finish line was Master A-Phûn.

Also at the finish line was a Shina-style square table made

of sandalwood with mother-of-pearl detailing. A large canvas awning had been raised over the table to shield us from both the Southern Country's midday sun and the late-winter winds. A rich savory scent filled the air—it was coming from the small house. When the banquet began, the dishes would come one by one from that house onto our table.

A banquet that would normally be for eight people, just for Chi-chan and me. There was one catch, however.

"Even though I lost the bet on tshài-bué-thng, I *will* ask you to leave if you can't finish the whole meal!" Such was Master A-Phûn's warning, conveyed in Japanese and with a smile.

Chi-chan, too, smiled. It was a smile as arresting as the waterfall of trumpet flowers behind her. "If we cannot finish the meal, we will stay to wash the dishes for you."

Master A-Phûn, guffawing, turned and strode back into the house.

Immediately, a girl servant brought out plum juice and candied fruits. The banquet had begun.

The plum juice was just the right warmth, and the candied fruits each had a different kind of sweetness. These were followed by the first appetizers—a cold platter that included sausage, karasumi roe, chicken rolls stuffed with egg yolk, and thin-sliced pork hearts flavored with Shina medicinal herbs.

Chi-chan and I dove in with our chopsticks. Soon the dishes emptied. The girl servant skillfully caught on to our rhythm and brought out the second dish in a timely fashion.

This second dish was a full chicken. The girl used chopsticks and a ladle to split the tender meat, revealing that the bones within had already been expertly removed. The chicken had been stuffed with julienned wood ear mushrooms, bamboo shoots, daylilies, ham, and pork. When this lush stuffing was mixed in with the juice from the meat, it made for a thick, rich chicken broth.

The third dish was a steamed full fish. The outside of the fresh fish was coated in a web-like layer of pork blubber; the inside was bursting with filling. The handiwork was incredibly complex and delicate.

The fourth dish was ten large shrimps that filled a whole plate. There were bamboo shoots, mushrooms, and carrots tied to the backs of each shrimp with strips of dried bottle gourds. This showed a sense of fun, and so did the sauce, which had been simmered from tomatoes—a rather rare choice on the Island.

Just when I noticed that we'd had three soupy dishes in a row, the fifth dish arrived and was composed of five small mountains of fried foods: pork ribs, eight-treasure meatballs, shrimp balls, pork liver rolls, chicken skin rolls. Each had a dramatically different texture, and Chi-chan and I went through one round of each, then a second, then a third . . . ah, many moons ago, we had done the same thing with five different kinds of meatballs on the first night that she ever dined with me.

I looked up and happened to meet her eye.

Perhaps we were both revisiting the same memory. That time, we had just returned from Rokkō, where Chi-chan had confided in me about her family origins as we strolled down the ancient street. How nostalgic! Despite this, we only exchanged a look and silently returned to eating. We ate until the plates were empty.

The girl servant brought us the sixth dish, which was the midbanquet small dish: pleated shrimp dumplings. The translucent dumpling skin was crystalline and the taste was refreshing—a perfect palate cleanser after the oiliness of the fried items.

The midbanquet dish symbolized an intermission in the meal. Had we been in a restaurant, this would have been when Islander gē-tòa performed traditional music as a geisha would on the Mainland. There were no performers here. But the way the girl servant seemed to be anticipating the amount of leftovers required for the tshài-bué-thng recipe, deftly withdrawing dishes before we'd completely finished them, felt like a skilled performance in itself.

We were presented with warmed hand towels to clean our

hands and faces. I seized this opportunity to sneak a glimpse at Chi-chan. Was it because of the memory of the meatballs? Her expression seemed to have softened.

Seeing this, something seemed to melt within my chest.

In that instant, the girl servant silently removed the towels and presented the opening dish for the second half of the banquet. This seventh dish was a soup, called the salted egg and four-treasures soup.[1] Ingredients included pork tripe, pork cartilage, dried squid, and fresh clams, with the yolk of the brined egg acting as the primary seasoning. The soup itself was a light yellow color from said yolk, which made me assume that its taste would be intensely salty, but the reality was pleasantly fragrant and mellow.

It was this soup that truly made me realize just how much control and restraint went into Master A-Phûn's elegant craft.

The dishes were never heavy or greasy, but each seemed to linger on the palate. None of the flavors or textures were repetitive. As a result, neither the diner's mouth nor stomach felt overburdened, and one did not grow tired of the banquet as it continued.

I'd been invited to countless banquets ever since I arrived in Taiwan in the spring, including many Taiwanese banquets tailored for Mainlander guests, and initially I'd disliked such banquets for being designed to draw tourists. But Master A-Phûn had completely upended my impressions of a Taiwanese restaurant banquet.

A sense of wonder was born within me.

When Chi-chan made me the curry feast, I'd felt the existence of a distinct "Taiwanese cuisine," but I saw in hindsight that it had been but a superficial feeling. It was there at Master A-Phûn's

---

1. Aoyama: Salted eggs are raw eggs soaked in brine until the insides of the eggs turn solid.

table that I understood, profoundly, that while Japanese, Western, and Shina cuisine all constituted techniques that had been developed and honed through centuries of imperial dining, the colonial land of Taiwan *did indeed* have its own nuanced, established, unique, and finely crafted Taiwanese cuisine.

Before I could dwell on this, the eighth dish arrived: crispy duck.

This was a full duck. The girl servant pressed down on the duck's back with a hefty cleaver, and with that single motion we heard cracking all over the body—it would not have been remiss to call it a miraculous scene. As it turned out, the name crispy duck came not only from the skin and the meat but even from the bones. In terms of the sheer fun of eating, this grand dish felt more like a snack, especially as a follow-up to the broth. It would not be inappropriate to call it an appetizer to open the second half of the banquet.

As if to complement this thought, the ninth dish, savory bí-ko medley, was one that truly showcased a master chef's prowess. As in sushi, the rolls used tofu pockets to wrap bí-ko rice cake and other ingredients. These pockets were then coated in wheat flour and the whole thing was fried at a precise temperature and cut into small pieces. There were several different "medleys," including salted egg yolk, mushroom, bah-sò, and cilantro ends; diced taro, diced winter melon, and fried shallots; and a sweet version with a generous amount of peanut butter, refined sugar, and cilantro.

Two-thirds savory, one-third sweet. Savory, savory, sweet. We seemed to have been caught in a mysterious loop. Just like on New Year's Eve, when Chi-chan and I had also alternated between sweet and savory mochi—had also blown on and gulped down wonderful steaming food together.

The rolls filled my stomach to the brim, but the tenth dish had appeared.

Bamboo shoots and pork belly.

Nagasaki's pork kakuni, Shina's Dōngpō pork, and, on the Island, the Hoklo people's lóo-bah, the Hakka people's fung-ngiug.[2]

Chi-chan's and my gazes met each other again.

"The last time we had fung-ngiug was in Takao," I said.

"Do you need Master A-Phûn to make you some lóo-bah rice this time?"

"No, no. This is different, after all."

"Mm—yes, it is different."

The sauce-simmered pork was as tender as could be.

My cheeks were filled with pork and my heart filled with roiling waves, memories of days past flaring and vanishing like sea foam. The memories of eating bah-sò and sukiyaki at the same table as Chi-chan—they splashed before my eyes, then swiftly dissipated.

I picked up a piece of pork with my chopsticks and delivered it to Chi-chan's plate.

After a few moments' hesitation, she, too, set some pork on my plate.

A bittersweet current shot through my heart.

At the same time, the monster in my stomach felt satiated in a way that it had never been before.

It only made sense that I was full, because the two of us had just consumed ten dishes from a banquet meant for eight people. But what I felt was not just about quantity. It was a feeling of emancipation and satisfaction that arose from the little hidden monster finally receiving the kindness and regard that it had longed for.

When the young Aoyama Chizuko had been ostracized to

2. Yáng: This is inaccurate. In reality, the Hoklo banquet dish much closer to the other ones listed would be hong-bah instead of the casual-dining lóo-bah.

that little shrine in the mountains, the monster in my stomach had been starved not of food, but of love, of respect.

I laid down my chopsticks as though laying down an immense weight.

"Aoyama-san, are you all right?"

Had she noticed the disturbance in me?

"Mm—it *is* rare for me to feel this full. But I think I'll be all right if it's dessert next."

She chuckled. "Dessert wouldn't be a problem?"

I smiled at her. "The monster likes variety."

"How very like Aoyama-san to say something like that."

"What about you, Chi-chan? How is your stomach doing?"

"Hm—dessert wouldn't be a problem for me, either."

"See? There you go."

"Indeed."

I felt woozy, though we hadn't drunk any wine. It was the wooziness of satiation.

Chi-chan and I relaxed in our seats, supporting our chins with our hands. Light and time seemed to slow.

We began to whisper.

"I wonder what the next dish will be."

"Whatever it is, it will certainly be delicious."

"Well, most definitely."

"Indeed."

Our wishes were answered: both the remaining dishes were desserts.

The eleventh dish was a dumpling made from jujube paste and dried longan wrapped in white jade powder. The twelfth dish was a sweet soup made from peanuts, silver ear fungus, and longan. The soup glided warmly from my throat down through my chest and to my stomach—a sweetness that bore deep into the body. The banquet thus drew to a close with the most fulfilling finale.

Chi-chan and I seemed to let out small sighs at the same time.

The final soup's base hadn't been cane sugar, but sugared winter melon.

Just like the winter melon tea we drank together several months ago in the south of the Southern Country.

I watched Chi-chan and she watched me. Her expression was as gentle as it was on that day in Tainan.

"Aoyama-san."

"Yes?"

"It is the Islander New Year's Eve this Saturday. I originally wanted to make for you a traditional New Year's dish called tau-mī. It is a recipe that combines all the various ingredients of different New Year's feasts—or, in other words, all the left-overs. Everything is added to a thick, starchy mixture made from sweet potato flour and stirred and stirred until it congeals into a semitransparent cake. This is a New Year's dish from Shina's Quánzhōu and is an auspicious symbol for the gathering and bringing together of different people. Tau-mī can be made from very modest ingredients or from lavish things like seafood, meat, vegetables, and bone broth. But whether plain or luxurious, a New Year's Eve spent sharing tau-mī with Aoyama-san would no doubt have been a most joyful one."

"You said 'originally wanted to' . . . does that mean you no longer plan to?"

"That's right."

I knitted my brows in pain.

Chi-chan, however, was placid. "Remember how you were confused, back at Tainan First High School for Girls, about why Tân-san had shown resistance against Ōzawa-san's protection?"

I did not understand why she was bring up the students now, but instead of asking, I only shook my head gently.

She raised the corners of her lips: a sad smile.

"This is just my own speculation, but perhaps it was because Ōzawa-san never once asked Tân-san whether she actually wished to receive such protection. Ōzawa-san shielded Tân-san from falling flowers and from blinding sunlight—she acted like a knight in shining armor, but did Tân-san wish for this? In a girls' school where Mainlanders are the majority, it is likely that such special treatment only makes Tân-san's situation more difficult, yet Ōzawa-san may not have realized this at all. I believe Tân-san's resistance was an act of protest against Ōzawa-san's misguided treatment."

"Chi-chan, you mean—"

"You are noble, considerate, and kind, Aoyama-san—you are willing to go above and beyond on my behalf. But it is precisely *because* you would never let me sleep in the servant's room, *because* you are outraged when somebody looks down on me for my status, that I have no idea how to make you understand. How do I explain myself so that I don't seem like an unreasonable child who covets your equal treatment yet paradoxically defies your kindness? The truth is that I am the same as Tân-san. The truth is that gentle Aoyama-san never once asked me: *Do you want this protection?*"

Lightning struck me, leaving me tongue-tied.

Chi-chan once again smiled her sad, troubled smile.

"There may never be another person in this world who will cherish me the way you have. To me, you are a special and utterly unique presence. These are true, certain, and unalterable facts. As time passed and I grew closer to you, I found that if we continued this way, we would surely open our hearts to each other and play significant roles in each other's lives. But I felt afraid of this future, because the person that you treasure and care for is the docile Islander interpreter who needs your protection. Yet that person is not the real Ō Chizuru—not the real Ông Tshian-hòh—not the real me! So can Aoyama Chizuko and Ông Tshian-hòh *really* be called friends? As you know, I made the 'brutish' decision that the ideal status quo is for you and me to maintain a strictly professional relationship."

I wished most desperately to speak, but despite opening my mouth several times, I could not utter a single word.

It was then that the girl servant presented us with two small bowls of tshài-bué-thng.

Yes, she was perceptive as she had been while controlling the rhythm of our whole meal, finding an appropriate lull in our conversation to bring out the finale dish. But I felt as though I'd fallen into a Charlie Chaplin film—a tragic world in which I was isolated, different from others, and unable to communicate. Dismay drowned out all of my other emotions.

Chi-chan was still smiling at me. "I am most glad to have been able to enjoy this food with you today."

I had no idea what expression I wore as I looked at her. She reached for my hand and gave it a little squeeze, and I in turn gripped her hand tightly—just as I had on New Year's Eve. But, just like on that night, Chi-chan gently let go of my hand.

"Aoyama-san, this will be my final time sharing a meal with you. I have already extended my formal resignation to Madame Takada. Please do not think of me anymore."

CHAPTER XI

Kiâm-Nn̄g-Ko / Savory Cake

The season for lighting hearths on the Southern Island was short indeed.

The pile of charcoal in the kitchen had barely dwindled since late February. By March, cold wind only blew in the middle of the night or at the crack of dawn, dissipating completely as soon as the sun rose. New green graced the trees lining the Yana River, spring breezes brushed the branches, and golden sunlight dove and flickered between the young leaves.

I greeted spring on the Island.

Back in Kyūshū, spring is the season for hatsu-gatsuo—the first snapjack tuna of the year. But I felt none of my usual ardor in pursuit of this springtime delicacy. No, it wasn't just tuna—the longtime resident in my stomach seemed to have reached nirvana at last, taking my appetite along with it. Even as my stomach growled, I could think of nothing that I *needed* to eat. Every morning, I tossed and turned in my bed and did not rise until as late as ten o'clock. I ate only neko-manma rice, egg over rice, or white toast with sugared butter.

A stomach was but a fireplace and food was but charcoal. When one was hungry, one chomped down on rice or toast with one's teeth until one could swallow, and from there the steam train of one's body could continue chugging along. For the first time in my life, I understood that the activity of eating was truly no more than that.

In the afternoons, I would begin writing.

Without an appetite, I could only smoke. I'd learned to do it a few years prior from having to socialize for work, and while I normally had no yearning for cigarettes, during this period I could smoke half a pack in one day. But I often only took one inhale of the cigarette and left the rest to burn between my fingers, with the ashes burning smatterings of holes in my draft paper.

I wrote inside the holes.

After Tōen and Shinchiku, Mishima maintained his usual style when arranging my trips to several cities and towns in central Taiwan, including Chikunan, Byōritsu, Kiyomizu, Inlin, and Toroku, where I visited countless impressive buildings, parks, and shrines to partake in countless lectures, tea talks, and film screenings. It was a beautiful spring, yet my itineraries were so busy that they cut into my time even for walking and reading. I protested to Mishima, who said that he would pause from arranging any excursions for the time being. However: "Would Aoyama-sensei be amenable to writing one or two articles on your visits to the Island's shrines?"

No, she would not.

That was my heartfelt response, but I was so idle at the cottage's desk that I ended up writing two short pieces on the Tōen Shrine near Tōen Station and the Memorial Hall of Attendance near Toroku Station. My memories of these places were superficial at best, however, and it took a lot of flipping through the *Travel Guide to Taiwan's Railways* to fill two draft pages. With the *Guide* open to its first page of thc railroad map, I used a finger to trace the dotted lines and discovered that, while the railroad did not reach it, there was a ferry route to the small islands of Hōko.[1] I thought about going and felt a spark in my heart, but after a few more seconds my desire to travel plummeted just like my appetite.

1. King: Toroku Station is the Japanese pronunciation of present-day Dǒuliù Station. Hōko is present-day Pénghú.

Was there any need for me to stay in Taiwan for the planned duration of twelve months?

Then, after I go back to Kyūshū, I can reorganize the dispatches into a book—maybe something titled Taiwan Travelogue. *If I were to write something like that, it would be much more holistic to cover all four seasons, don't you think?*

I'd once declared these things, jubilant and smug.

Traveling is living in a foreign place. As in, experiencing all four seasons of normal life in a foreign place. Leaving behind a home environment where one's habits have settled into old, tired ways and spending one's days somewhere else, trying to find some new feeling in the mere act of being alive in this world. In this sense, traveling is a way of cleansing one's body and mind—starting afresh.

Cleansing one's body and mind, I'd claimed. Yet by this point I spent my mornings rolling about in bed and my afternoons rolling about on the tatami, heading out to sit on the veranda only when my body began to ache from all the lying around. There I sat smoking and staring at the wild ginseng flowers sprinkled across the yard. The total lack of productivity made me wonder whether there was any reason left to remain on the Island.

After writing a half-made-up article, I felt no less aggravated. I grabbed the stack of business cards sitting on my desk, stood, turned to face the open space that constituted the dining room, tatami room, and veranda, and began shooting the cards about like a ninja's shuriken daggers. *Swish swish swish swish . . .*

It wasn't the Hōko Islands that I truly longed to see.

I'd been reading that day about Toyohara in the *Guide*. I'd visited the town when I first arrived in Taiwan, but it was only while reading that I learned about a subsidiary Ishioka Line that could take me to the Meiji onsens. I did feel that it was a shame not to have gone there on my winter hot springs tour.

But it wasn't the Meiji onsens that I truly longed to see, either.

Swish swish swish—

A thought leapt forth from the bottom of my heart.

The sakura of Alisan.

The remaining business cards tumbled from my hand like rain.

Ah! How miserable!

I slumped into a chair.

Feeble limbs, hollow stomach, crowded chest.

I had spent almost a year leading a "normal" life in Taiwan—walking, eating, putting on clothes, going to bed, strolling the streets, taking buses and trains, and visiting markets, theaters, and hot springs. But this so-called normality was perhaps only a beautiful dream.

A clattering sound. I could tell from the way the side door slid open that it was Sae-san, the Takada family's housekeeper.

I did not move.

She entered and looked at the strewn business cards. "Aoyama-sensei, you're as astonishing as ever."

"I'm sorry. Just leave it—no need to clean it up."

"Very well." She returned to the kitchen.

For a while, whenever Sae-san came over, I would charge toward the side door with the force of a samurai charging the enemy, startling her. Even so, Sae-san only ever clapped her chest a little and did not comment on my behavior.

Who did I want to see instead?

Who was I waiting for when I was rolling about in the futon or on the tatami?

Who did I want to share lychee and peanuts and water chestnuts with when I sat smoking on the veranda?

I knew the answer.

How should a daughter of Kyūshū, descendant of an esteemed family, face a best friend who has decided to sever all relations?

A truly noble person ought to offer said friend their best wishes.

I abided by these principles. Even when my memories replayed like a film—*in the center of the courtyard by that opulent little house, two people sitting face-to-face at the sandalwood table inlaid with mother-of-pearl, sunlight landing on the white canvas overhead*—I could only grit my teeth and try to stop myself from behaving brashly.

Oh, how I longed to chase after her and say something more. But that was not Aoyama Chizuko's style.

Aoyama Chizuko must—*must*—continue with her daily life.

And so I decided that wherever Mishima arranged for me to go, I would go. The next trip was to Toyohara.

Toyohara had no public hall, and considering that I'd already visited previously, what could be the purpose of such a trip? If it was to visit the Meiji onsens, I had no wish to go with officials from the Government-General. I did not conceal these feelings from Mishima, but he in turn had developed an aloof method of dealing with me.

"There are royal paddies owned by the Emperor in the southern parts of Toyohara. Taitō is not the only prefecture to produce the Emperor's rice; Taichū's Toyohara is responsible as well. We hope that Aoyama-sensei can write an article on this subject."

"As part of the Southern Expansion Policy? Please ask somebody else for this sort of thing. It isn't my area."

Mishima wasn't angered by my unceremonious refusal. "I have heard that Aoyama-sensei is partial to the Island's small dishes. Then how about an article on kiâm-nn̄g-ko?"

"Kiâm-nn̄g-ko? What's that?"

"It's made by steaming, like a Western sponge cake, but with the Island's bah-sò minced pork sandwiched between two pieces of cake. Kiâm-nn̄g-ko means savory cake."

Mishima launched into a matter-of-fact explanation: The Taiwan North-South Railroad went into full operation in the forty-fourth year of Meiji, and Prince Kan'in Kotohito personally came to the Island to host the opening ceremony. When officials from all over the Island went to receive the prince, kiâm-nñg-ko savory cake was the dish that they presented to his royal highness. The dish was created in Sekkasai, a storied bakery in Toyohara. It was because the Toyohara region has had a long history of cakes and pastries that a chef would have even thought to meld together the Island's traditional tastes with Western baking. It was said that kiâm-nñg-ko gained fame in Toyohara because Prince Kan'in Kotohito had praised it profusely. It was a local specialty beloved by both Islanders and Mainlanders; it had nothing in particular to do with Southern Expansion.

"Hm—it's just like that story of anpan buns with red bean paste: how the Kimuraya Bakery became so famous after serving their invention to the Emperor that anpan became famous all over Japan and can even be found on Taiwan Island. I see—there's Kimuraya for anpan, and there's Sekkasai for kiâm-nñg-ko."

"It sounds like Aoyama-sensei is willing."

My appetite remained dismal. But then again, this savory cake included the Island's bah-sò.

I did as I was told.

No lecture, no onsen. Instead, we visited the royal paddies and Toyohara Shrine, socialized with various officials over lunch, and took a stroll to a local Maso temple. On the way, Mishima pointed out a storefront, saying that it was the very bakery that had invented kiâm-nñg-ko. As we approached, I did in fact smell the rich aroma of salted duck eggs, sugar, and freshly baked cake. Even so, the worm of gluttony in my stomach only turned on its side and let out a small whimper. I followed Mishima past the bakery and to the temple.

Maso temples in the Southern Country are a vivid crimson. Strings of red lanterns stretched across the temple as far as the eye could see, and the tiled roof and antefixes were also bright red. Intricate stone and wooden dragons encircled the structure's large columns. The gilding dazzled. The murals seemed alive; many statues were composed of elaborately arranged pieces of multicolored ceramic.

And then there were the countless idols of different gods on the altars. The Buddha, the Kannon Bodhisattva, the goddess Maso—every divine face wore a quiet, equanimous smile. But one face stopped me in my tracks. I asked Mishima: who was that god with the childlike grin?

He took one glance.

"It's Nuózhà, the Third Prince."[2]

"From Shina folklore?"

"Yes."

I stared at the youthful face. Yes, I believed there was a tale inspired by Nuózhà in that Han-language novel that I'd bought Chi-chan in Tainan. Among the stories where the author imagined the gods bickering and brawling in modern Taiwan was one about Nuózhà riding on his famous Wind Fire Wheels down to the human world, where he came upon a crowd engaged in a bicycle race. The sight horrified him—*Every one of them has a pair of Wind Fire Wheels!* Thinking back to Chi-chan's translation, I found myself grinning.[3]

On the altar, Nuózhà smiled back at me, his dimples etched deep into his cheeks.

Aigh, aigh, aigh.

---

2. King: Nuózhà's name is pronounced as such in Taiwan and as Nézhà in present-day China. As a deity, he is popularly represented as in his rebellious youth; he eventually survives a battle-heavy coming-of-age to be promoted to the deity also known as the Third Lotus Prince. Mandarin names for the other gods mentioned in the passage are the Kannon Bodhisattva, Guānyīn, and the goddess Maso, Mātsǔ.

3. Yáng: In the passage where Aoyama writes about this particular novel in chapter III, Nuózhà is not mentioned. However, said novel is likely *Little Deities* by Hsú Pǐng-tīng, whose fifth chapter, "In Which Bicycles Shock the Third Prince," would fit the description here. See page 60.

"Aoyama-sensei seems to have a lot of interest in the Island's affairs."

"Very much so. Speaking of which, isn't this quite an ancient temple? I wouldn't have known without visiting that it was so palatial, and so clean and state-of-the-art at that."

"That is because there was a renovation during the Taishō era." Mishima's voice was flat as ever. "The temple was built in the Qīng period under Emperor Yōngzhèng, and was at first dedicated to worshipping the Kannon Bodhisattva. Somewhere along the way, it was altered to focus on the goddess Maso, and for many years now it has been widely known. The Taishō renovation took many years, and as a result it has been but twenty years since construction ended."

"Emperor Yōngzhèng? That must mean the temple has been active for two hundred years, then. Centuries of people have come and gone, yet the gods continue to watch over the Island's faithful—it's quite moving when you think about it that way. But this surprises me. Hasn't the Government-General been building their own shrines everywhere? Maybe they aren't as I thought, if they've been willing to maintain the Island's temples as well!"

Mishima did not respond to these thoughts. But I was used to the boredom of traveling with him.

"Mishima-san claims not to know about Islander culture, but that's just an evasion tactic, isn't it?"

He said nothing, not even bothering to cover up his lie.

After the temple, Mishima bought some kiâm-n̄g-ko and took me to a nearby kissaten tearoom for a break.

The tearoom was plainly furbished—a far cry from the fashionable establishments in Taichū's city proper—but the leisurely atmosphere put one at ease. Further, it differentiated itself by offering pineapple juice on the menu.

I told the waitress that I would like a glass of pineapple juice and a hot coffee.

Mishima asked me to please wait. "You do not have to order on my behalf, Aoyama-sensei."

I immediately disabused him of this notion. "I have no intention of making your decisions, Mishima-san. Both orders are for me."

He gave me a look, said nothing further on the subject, and asked for a cup of coffee with milk.

In the silence that fell after we placed our orders, I lit a cigarette, took a long inhale, and exhaled as though letting out a deep sigh.

It was Mishima's and my custom not to converse unless it was absolutely necessary. A few moments later, our coffees and pineapple juice arrived, along with the kiâm-nn̄g-ko we'd brought, presented on a plate. Mishima and I began to eat in continued silence.

Kiâm-nn̄g-ko really did resemble a sandwich. I put out my cigarette and stuffed a large bite into my mouth.

So soft. My teeth sank into the pillowy, slightly moist cake. The first note to surge forth was a medley of duck egg, wheat, and sugar, shortly followed by the flavor of bah-sò. This bah-sò wasn't made simply of minced pork; it had a slight crunch, which had been smoothed out with a touch of salad dressing. I chewed carefully and thought I detected some sort of root vegetable mixed within.

I'd never had bah-sò like this.

Every family has its own bah-sò recipe depending on their financial means and dining habits.

Really? Wow. Islanders must really like their bah-sò!

Aoyama-san, when I was young, I thought that pork skin bah-sò was a rare, luxurious dish. I had a dream back then: that one day, when I grew up, I would eat as much bah-sò-pn̄g as my heart desired.

Well, then, I suppose today is that day.

The kiâm-nn̄g-ko was so soft that it soon dissolved in my

mouth. Yet somehow I found it difficult to swallow, as though there was gravel sandwiched between the layers of cake.

"Uh—Aoyama-sensei?"

"I'm fine."

I finished the rest of the cake in a few bites. "Was that bamboo shoot mixed into the bah-sò?"

"Yes." He turned silent once more after the curt response. Perhaps he'd only broken the customary silence to confirm that, yes, when a woman was stupid enough, she could in fact choke on cake.

I gulped down my pineapple juice and breathed out slowly. I racked my brain for a topic that would not be awkward.

"Kiâm-nñg-ko really is something else. It goes extraordinarily well with pineapple juice, doesn't it? The Island's flavors are truly astonishing."

"Very true, Aoyama-sensei."

I did not mind the robotic response. My long-stoppered desire for chatter had been loosened by the cake.

"It's not at all inferior to anpan buns. If someone were to import kiâm-nñg-ko to Tōkyō, it would certainly make a big splash, no? In fact, they wouldn't have to go all the way to Tōkyō—Nagasaki would be enough. The whole baked goods trend began in Nagasaki, after all. Delicious food can conquer tongues no matter where in the world it goes."

"You are quite right."

"Mishima-san, there's no need for that kind of diplomatic response here."

Silence.

"I can't write about the Southern Expansion Policy or things like that, but from time to time I do have to admit that the Empire has given rise to some wonderful things on this Southern Island. How should I put it? Like polishing raw stone into gleaming jade, I suppose. In that sense, it's true that I can think of one or two articles to write on the subject. One on kiâm-n̄g-ko, one on chikuwa."

"Chikuwa?"

"Mm—not in Toyohara, but in Kīrun. They make chi-kú-lah fishcakes there, which evolved from the Mainland's chikuwa, which originally evolved from kamaboko fishcakes. Originally, the Island's signature fish paste product was fish balls, right? But with the fresh catch of the Island's Kīrun Port and the modernized factories introduced to the Island by the Mainland, the seafood product of chi-kú-lah[4]—Taiwanese chikuwa—can now be celebrated all over the Island.[5] I learned about this when I was traveling to Kīrun during the winter. And, apparently, it's the chikuwa factories in the Kīrun area that continue to be thought of as the highest in quality."

"This must have been information from Ō-san."

"Yes."

Infinite forlornness in my heart.

"In my hometown, Nagasaki, there's a type of chikuwa where they beat tofu into the fish paste and grill it together. Meanwhile, in Kumamoto, there is the historical Hinagu chikuwa. I'd told Ō-san about my homesickness for these flavors, and she'd told me, very kindly, 'Then please try Kīrun's chikuwa,' and took me to try the local handmade chi-kú-lah that wasn't a bit less delicious than Kyūshū's chikuwa. So then I said, maybe the birth of Taiwan's chikuwa is to the Empire's credit—"

---

4. Yáng: The Taiwanese variety remains a common and popular snack in present-day Keelung (Kīrun), referred to by the Taiwanese Hokkien name chi-kú-lah, derived from the Japanese chikuwa.

5. King: Yáng, in the Mandarin edition, uses the same Han characters for chikuwa and chi-kú-lah; while researching what makes Kīrun's chikuwa different, I found the unique local pronunciation of chi-kú-lah and decided to differentiate the two foods with two pronunciations.

I stopped midsentence.

Mishima was looking at me in silence. I hadn't stopped because of his solemn expression, but rather because something had flashed within my mind yet escaped my grasp.

"I see," he said. "The same goes for kiâm-nn̄g-ko and chi-kú-lah. Both are raw stones that have been polished into jade. Both are to the Empire's credit." Mishima mechanically repeated my words, yet a displeasure that he could not conceal hardened between his heavy brows.

Ah, yes, that was it.

I'd finally located it—the smudge of light that had flickered in my mind's eye.

Chi-chan's face.

Winter, January, eating chi-kú-lah with Chi-chan in Kīrun, I'd expressed these same thoughts. On that rainy day by the port, Chi-chan's face betrayed a very fleeting trace of displeasure—just like the displeasure in Mishima's expression—yet Chi-chan had erased this so swiftly that I had not even registered it at the time.

A roll of film sprinted through my head.

That January night by Kīrun Port, Chi-chan and I had shared an umbrella while heading to the hotel, and it was on that brief walk that something changed in Chi-chan's attitude.

I paused the film.

"Mishima-san, am I right that you do not agree with what I said?"

"No, Aoyama-sensei is quite right."

Aaah. Mishima—he was not a skilled liar.

Chi-chan had evaded me similarly back at Kīrun Port.

Back then, I'd said: "The Empire's harsh methods are hateful indeed, but now I can't help but admit that the Government-General really has made the raw jade that is the Island shine with the gleam of a jewel. It's the same for the Double Dragon Waterfalls at the Bamboo Peak Tunnel and for the chi-kú-lah at Kīrun Port. Me, I absolutely despise the arrogance of this self-proclaimed Great Country, whether it's the Hinomaru flag or the Rising Sun flag of the Empire.[6] But when it comes to the Taiwanese chi-kú-lah born on the Island—for this achievement alone, maybe I can say a few good things on the Empire's behalf."

How had she responded then?

"Are you full? Then let's head back to the hotel."

Of course both the barbaric Empire and the unreasonable bureaucrats were deplorable, but if we were to objectively examine the development of the Island's infrastructure, it was undeniable that the Empire had also provided powerful assistance. Was that not so?

The overwhelming bewilderment that I had felt before now struck me again, and I had to down a whole cup of coffee to regain composure.

Mishima stood.

"I will now escort Aoyama-sensei back to Taichū and—"

Interrupting his attempt at escape, I said, "Hold on one second, please. There's something that I would like to ask you, Mishima-san. Will you answer me?"

Since I gave no sign of moving from my seat, he had no choice but to sit back down.

"Of course, Aoyama-sensei."

"First, I must ask that you answer my question with absolute honesty."

He said nothing.

"Even if you deny it, the truth is that you do not agree with what I said earlier, isn't that right? No, I am not asking for you to echo my opinions—I only wish to hear your true thoughts. At

6. King: Hinomaru literally means "the ball of the sun." This refers to the national flag of Japan. On the other hand, the Rising Sun flag with sixteen rays emanating from the sun in the center is associated with wartime and imperial Japan.

this point, only you, steadfast and upright Mishima-san, can answer my question: please, tell me, what was my mistake just now?"

"For fear of causing offense, I'm afraid I cannot answer that question."

"I swear that whatever you say, I will not take offense."

Silence.

"In the future, if any of my words or actions cause Mishima-san displeasure, you can feel free to leave your seat or cease working for me with immediate effect. I will raise no objections."

"Are you quite certain?"

"I swear on the Aoyama name."

My repeated promises seemed at last to bend the will of this unyielding Government-General bureaucrat.

"Aoyama-sensei perhaps thought that a Taiwan Government-General employee, one who supports the Southern Expansion Policy, would certainly agree with the sentiment that the achievement of forging the colony of Taiwan into a strong base for Southern Expansion is to the Empire's credit. Is that so?"

Before I could respond, he continued: "Yes, as a member of the Government-General who is loyal to the Emperor, I follow all policies initiated and promoted by the Empire and the Government-General. As such, I never criticize the national agenda."

"Then why do you not approve of my praise for the Empire?"

"What I disapprove of is not praise for the Empire, but Aoyama-sensei's tendency to judge things as you please according to your subjective and arbitrary criteria. Even if you do not state it explicitly, your unwillingness to accommodate the Southern Expansion Policy makes clear your disapprobation of the Empire. And yet, when it comes to your likes and dislikes, your position changes—you sometimes even praise the Empire's policies. Whether you choose to criticize or support these policies has little to do with whether the Empire has caused harm or done good—it has more to do with your personal preferences."

I had never heard anything like it before. My eyes bulged with shock and, seeing this, Mishima stopped speaking.

"Please continue, Mishima-san."

"That is all I have to say."

"There must be more. Please do not be uneasy. I promise that I will listen in good faith."

"In my humble opinion, Aoyama-sensei's arbitrary preferences not only manifest in your views on the Empire's policies, but also in how you regard all kinds of things and phenomena on the Island."

"Can you please be more specific, Mishima-san?"

"Aoyama-sensei is from Nagasaki. Even in our brief time together, I have felt your love for your hometown. I, who was born on the Island, likewise feel affection for my hometown." He paused, and for a moment there was a shadow of restraint between his brows, but then the resolve to speak his mind seemed to harden in his face. "'Kiâm-nn̄g-ko and pineapple juice—the Island's flavors are truly astonishing.' Those were Aoyama-sensei's words. And yet, the way in which you talk about the Island's flavors does not sound to me like you are appreciating them for being delicious, but more for being exotic, as one might appreciate a rare animal. It is only natural for Aoyama-sensei to pay attention to the things that rouse your interest and are novel to you, but then to claim that your personal preferences are proof of some greater trend in the relationship between the Empire and the Island seems to me forced and, pardon my frankness, a sign of intellectual arrogance."

I was speechless.

"Take chi-kú-lah, for example. It is true that the Island's fishing industry has expanded due to technology introduced by the Empire, but this has also altered the Islanders' culinary life as a result. Do the Islanders take pleasure in these changes? For another example, Toyohara Maso Temple was not in fact preserved due to the Empire's benevolence, but because the Imperial Army had caused great damage to the temple during the Meiji era, leading the Islander residents of Toyohara to dedicate tremendous time and energy to gain approval for a renovation in the Taishō era. Even so, when Toyohara Shrine was completed a few years ago, the government added new Japanese stone lanterns, and they added a torii gate to Maso Temple as well. How do the Islanders feel when they see these additions? 'The Empire has given rise to some wonderful things on the Island.' The so-called wonderful things are only wonderful to Mainlanders, and more specifically, they are only wonderful to you."

These were words that could be considered offensive indeed. Yet Mishima's gaze did not waver as he continued looking at me. He was, after all, a young man with a steely tenacity. As the old idiom went, 'The newborn calf knows not to fear the tiger.' But rather than a calf, he seemed to me more like a newborn tiger.

My silence deepened.

Mishima, perhaps having emptied all the words pent up within him, also fell quiet.

A blurry sort of hypothesis formed before me.

"Mishima-san, I'd thought that infrastructure that makes life more convenient and dynamic would be well received by the people."

"Taichū Maso Temple, which was even older than the one in Toyohara, was razed overnight in the first year of Taishō as part of Taichū City's urban reorganization. In exchange for the centuries-old temple, Taichū gained well-ordered and conveniently structured streets. There is no trace of that temple left today."

". . ."

". . ."

I lit my cigarette again, inhaled the smoke all the way to the bottom of my lungs, then released it in a slow breath.

Mishima remained quiet.

A second inhale. In, then out. A third. A fourth.

The cigarette burnt out in my hand.

"From Mishima-san's standpoint, even assistance offered out of goodwill is simply another form of arrogance—is that so?"

It took a moment before he replied through the smoke.

"There is nothing in the world more difficult to refuse than self-righteous goodwill."

Neither Mishima nor I said a single word on the journey back to the Yana River cottage.

His muteness, perhaps, was a result of having spoken so boldly. I sometimes caught sight of his face in the rearview mirror, looking glum and conflicted.

I felt equally confounded, equally gloomy.

By the time night fell, I still had no appetite. I ordered some sashimi to be delivered and gulped it down with chilled rice wine. I then spent the rest of the evening pacing the engawa veranda, where the sky was so dark that I could not see the small blossoms of the wild ginseng, but even as the hours passed I could not rid my chest of the occasional explosions of pain. I finished off the remaining half of my cigarette pack.

When it came to an hour where I had no choice but to go to bed, it was all I could do to toss and turn. My stomach was wailing, my heart was in a scramble, and finally I kicked off my blankets and rolled off of the futon and onto the tatami, all the way across the room.

I am but a simpleton—I am but a Great Cedar.

In the dream was a bougainvillea tree in full bloom.

Under the vivid blossoms stood Ōzawa and Sparrow. A wind rose; Ōzawa used her body to shield Sparrow from the falling flowers.

Also in the dream was a cascade of orange trumpet flowers.

An Islander boy and a Mainlander boy raced down the street, diving between the flowers. The Mainlander boy finally caught up to the Islander boy, throwing his arms around the latter.

A spring wind rustled the trumpet flowers—beautiful and blinding.

The majolica tiles gleamed.

By the little house with the red bricks and black roof tiles, there was a full wall of waterfalling trumpet flowers.

I stood across from Chi-chan.

She smiled, showing her adorable dimples.

When I reached out, she held my hand.

I could not help but bury my face in our interlaced fingers.

"Aoyama-san," she said. "The truth is that I am the same as Tân-san, no more and no less. The truth is that gentle Aoyama-san never once asked me *Do you want this protection?*"

I cried out from the pit of my gut: "Chi-chan, it's not like that!"

The bubble burst.

I woke to the light of dawn.

A dream. Only a dream.

Hunger pained my stomach. I had no choice but to rise and look for food in the kitchen.

The cupboard where I usually stored my white toast held the souvenirs I'd bought the previous day in Toyohara. In the sunlit kitchen, I ate six whole pieces of kiâm-n̄g-ko. The pillowy cake and the savory bah-sò warmed my stomach.

The sixth piece was also the last piece.

The steamed cake was ever so soft, yet while I was chewing I felt that some hard object had jammed my throat. I realized only then that my shirt was wet with my own tears.

Spring. March. Sakura blossoms on Alisan.

Last year, in Kagi, pouring wine into each other's cups, trying all sorts of sashimi and geh, I'd said this to Chi-chan: "The sakura on Alisan. Let's go see them. Together. Next spring."

She'd seemed unwilling, and I'd said, "It's brutish, isn't it, to transplant Mainland sakura and force them upon the Island's soil? You think so, too, don't you?"

"I never said that, Aoyama-san."

"But I was watching your face closely the whole time, and I don't believe I misread your expression."

". . ."

"It's true that the Empire's coercive methods are unpleasant, but the beautiful sakura are innocent of any crime. It would be a dream for me to go see sakura blossoms with you, Chi-chan. You know, I've never had any friends to go flower-viewing and picnicking with . . ."

". . ."

Back then, all the way back then, she had already conveyed her stance to me.

As for me! I am but a proud, foolish, despicable brute!

CHAPTER XII

Mitsumame / Fruit and Jelly Ice

To reach Chōkyōshitō on foot, one had to walk from Kawabata District, the northwestern corner of Taichū, to Akebono District, the southeastern corner. It was a straight-line distance of twenty chō.[1]

"Straight-line distance" referred to the road that bisects Taichū City, which ran through the Taishō Bridge that crosses the Midori River and was therefore known as the Taishō Bridge Avenue. Both the national state-run buses and the Taichū City–run buses operated on the road, making it a true artery for the city.

Though the cottage by Yana River was near this convenient thoroughfare, I'd never walked along the entire length of Taishō Bridge Avenue. Though in February I'd walked all the way to the Sugar Railway's station, back then I hadn't stuck to Taishō Bridge Avenue but instead circled the shop-lined Shinsei Bridge Avenue, my thoughts as jumbled as my footsteps. Aah—it had been almost one whole year since I began living in this city, yet I hadn't ever truly seen or inhabited it.[2]

Water rushed along the Yana River.

Was this not exactly what Confucius meant by "Passing time is rushing water, whether day or night"?

I crossed the river lined with new green leaves. To my right was Taichū Hospital and to my left was the Fruit and Vegetable

1. Yáng: Approximately two kilometers or 1.4 miles.

2. Yáng: Taishō Bridge Avenue is present-day Mínquán Road; Taishō Bridge itself is now Mínquán Lyù Bridge.

Trade Association as well as storefronts with various logos. Farther ahead was Shintomi District, with the red-and-white structure of Shintomichō Market. The restaurants from which I often ordered sushi and soba noodles were located nearby.

A few dozen steps later, I saw to my right three mansion-like buildings lined up like dango dumplings on a stick: the Governor's Residence, Taichū Prefecture Hall, Taichū City Hall . . . this was the most imposing of Taichū's streets. To the opposite side of these government buildings was a luxury hotel, the Taichū Post Office, and the Taichū branch of Taiwan Bank.

Farther ahead, past the bureaucratic buildings, was the Taichū Prefectural Library to the left and Taiwan News Agency to the right. There were law offices, fancy hotels, large stores, the Salvation Army, the Buddhist branch Hokke Shū's missionary offices, and a Tenrikyō church. People of all economic, intellectual, and social classes shared this stretch of the street. This bustling area brought a smile to my face, though I'd never made the effort to get to know it before.

Life had been but a dream to me. Eyes that could not see; ears that could not hear. Such had been my state of being.

I crossed the Midori River on Taishō Bridge, the river breeze urging my footsteps forward. I traversed the bridge over the railway, walking directly through the shadow cast by the bridge and leaving behind the avenue and the railway.

The scenery before my eyes was now completely different. The glamour of the earlier streets had been shed like a golden cloak. The buildings here were small in scale and plain in color; they stretched into the distance as far as the eye could see.

There were no large, eye-catching stores, and instead the small shops sold only food or casual clothes. Fruit vendors selling Islander produce hung bunches of bananas from the ceiling like curtains, which in these Shina-style arcade structures looked all the more fathomless. Most of the passing crowds spoke in Islander tongues.

The trilling of the steam train rang out past the clouds; I looked up to see a train chugging by. Looking back to my surroundings again, I saw that there was something of a gathering place a little ahead. It was Shikishima District Market. Compared to Shintomichō Market, known as the Second Market, Shikishima Market was known as the Third Market and was plain in appearance—it looked about half the size of the former. The streets only grew more and more bucolic after the market, with farmland on all sides, as well as tropical green-leafed trees several stories high. Buildings whose uses I could not guess at appeared on both sides of the street; the only structure whose purpose was immediately clear was the Akebono District Public School.

Farther ahead, just beyond Taichū City, was Chōkyōshitō.

Chōkyōshitō—the place that on a map fell just outside of the city—a place where I had never stepped foot despite all my travels across the Island.

Ahead of me were bucolic, empty roads. There were no official buildings or large stores with advertisements, only Islander residences, paddies and fields, distant mountains, and wispy clouds. The squarish structures of Taichū Second High School fell somewhat jarringly in the center of this rustic scene.

To think that, in just half an hour's journey from the northwest to the southeast corners of this city, the scenery could be this different. The changes were as drastic and rapid as scenes in a movie; its ups and downs were as extreme as the plot of a novel.

In the eight months during which she acted as my interpreter, Chi-chan walked this exact path two to three times a week, from the Third Market to the Second Market, step by step, all the way to the cottage by Yana River in Kawabata District.

As for me—I had never once made the trek to Chōkyōshitō.

Kawabata to Chōkyōshitō: half an hour on foot, for a distance of twenty chō. But it was as far as the unseen side of the moon.

That was the distance between Chi-chan and me.

Last summer, on our way back to Taichū from Rokkō and Shōka, Chi-chan had translated the Han-language novel to me aloud. The novel had been set in Tainan, which she and I had later visited a few months thereafter. Yet even though we had plenty of downtime, it never once crossed my mind to visit Senkan Tower, Shàngdì Temple, Maso Temple, Wénchāng Temple, or Wǔ Temple, where the gods had confronted each other in the story.

I did not even know the title of that novel.

Both she and Mishima had seen through my blind spot long ago. No—rather, they had seen through *me*. I complained about the Empire's treatment of its colonies, about men's treatment of women, about Mainlanders' treatment of Islanders—I derided and protested these ridiculous ways of the world, yet I was but another citizen of this world with all its earthly flaws, unaware even of the subconscious conceit and prejudice in my heart.

In the end, as the author of all those articles in the Taiwan Travelogue series, pontificating about the sights and scenes I've witnessed on the Island, I had never once truly understood the Island, nor held true love or care for the Island. I'd even boasted: *As a novelist, what can I do? I can come to Taiwan, write down what I observe, and preserve the state of this island before it's changed forever.* The articles themselves, written sporadically and casually from the gaze of a Mainland traveler, are ironclad proof that I had been looking down on the Island all along.

Mishima once mocked me for the same thing. *Oh? So Aoyama-sensei and Ō-san are friends. You must excuse me, for this was imperceptible to me based on what I have witnessed of your interactions.* Capricious Aoyama Chizuko and accommodating Ō Chizuru—Ông Tshian-ho̍h—who submitted to the former's every whim:

no, theirs was not an equal relationship in any sense. All my offers to be her "easterly wind" had only been a manifestation of my superiority complex.

That morning, when I'd eaten six pieces of kiâm-nn̄g-ko cake in one go, I'd stood in my kitchen for a long time. I'd stood for so long that the ray of sunlight on the silver kitchen faucet actually shifted by half an inch.

After Chi-chan left me, I had done everything in my power to suppress every urge to go beg her to return. It had felt like hugging a red-hot metal stove to my chest; it had felt like being crushed by an ice-cold waterfall.

For forty-four days, I'd gritted my teeth through the bitter pain.

Watching the golden light inch across the faucet, I wondered: What about now?

Chi-chan's words still echoed in my ear.

Can Aoyama Chizuko and Ông Tshian-hỏh really be called friends . . . ?

I thought: It's about time to answer this question.

The Ông family lived in a traditional Shina-style courtyard house located near the Taichū Second High School.[3] These were the only two things that I knew about their home from all these months. When I reached the Mainlander school, I saw that while it wasn't nearly as bustling as Taichū City proper, there was still a certain amount of infrastructure surrounding it, including a

3. Aoyama: Generally speaking, it is customary on the Island for "first" high schools to be meant for Mainlanders while "second" high schools are for Islanders. But because Taichū First High School was founded through the fundraising efforts of Islanders, its students were mostly of Islander descent. Meanwhile, the Second High School founded by the Government-General had mostly students of Mainland descent.

state-operated bus stop and light rail for handcars. There was also a general store selling household goods.

I circled the school's perimeter. There were many ancient Islander neighborhoods in the area, and I would occasionally see a burst of bamboo bushes, but not so many full-fledged courtyard houses. There were only two large and truly imposing courtyard mansions, plus two smaller-scale complexes. It could not have been difficult to find out which of them belonged to the wealthy Ông family.

But—to knock on the front gate and meet with her in a large, open courtyard?

I could not picture it.

My feet brought me all the way around the campus and back to where I'd started.

Even a spring day quickly grew hot in the Southern Country. I ducked under the shaded walkway of a building to hide from the sun and wipe away the sweat on my forehead.

The bench outside the general store seemed to beckon to me.

It must have been a general store that grew out of an oil-press shop, for the air was thick with the scent of sesame and peanut oil. I decided to enter and order a bottle of soda. The interior was small, with one wall of tin cans and glass jars, another wall of large glass urns filled with individually sold candies and snacks. Among the other available goods were grains and eggs, along with some medicines and soap displayed in a separate wooden cabinet.

The storekeeper was an Islander, and an old lady at that. This could have posed a serious language barrier, but thankfully ramune sodas in Taiwanese are pronounced similarly enough—la-mú-neh—and I managed to communicate my order to her. My throat remained dry after one bottle, and I asked for a second and a third, draining each bottle in one go on the bench outside the store.

I'd been to plenty of Mainlander dagashi snack shops on the Island, but never to an Islander general store. Thinking about this, I lined my three glass bottles on the bench and spun them around, watching the marbles clatter inside the glass.

"XXXX."

The old woman's voice came from behind me, speaking in Taiwanese. I turned and saw her approaching with a small bowl in her hand. She held it toward me, so I raised both hands to receive it.

"Eat."

This she said in Japanese. Seeing my blank expression, she urged again: "Eat, eat." Her tone was that of issuing an order.

This made me grin. I replied, in Taiwanese, "To-siā." *Thank you.*

She, too, smiled, gesturing at the bowl.

Kue-tsí.

Black-and-white striped kue-tsí.

I nodded at her, placed a piece between my front teeth, and bit down. But the shell did not split in half—rather, I'd bitten the whole piece in half.

What was this? The kue-tsí wasn't hard at all. Its texture was completely different from any kue-tsí I'd had before.

"XX, XX. XXXXXXX." The old woman slowly pinched a piece of kue-tsí between her fingers and dug one of her nails into the husk. The white kernel tumbled down into the bowl. "Eat."

Following good advice was like riding an easy wave; I did as she instructed. The kernel was thin and small, but as soon as I bit down I knew that this was unlike anything I'd eaten before—soft yet plump, with a trace of bitterness like the pistil of a flower, and a faintly sweet aftertaste.

"Is this not kue-tsí? Black-and-white striped kue-tsí are sunflower seeds, aren't they?"

"XX, XXXXX, XXXX."

"Hm? What was that?"

"XX, XX."

"Oh, that sounds familiar! Are you saying I don't have to worry about it?"

"XXXXXXX, XXXX, XXX."

"A different type of seed, is that it?"

So went our parallel conversations, back and forth.

Hehe. A gentle chuckle to my side.

"You have not changed at all."

Flawless Japanese.

I followed the voice to its source.

Standing in the shade of the building's walkway was a petite woman.

The young woman and the old woman nodded at each other and exchanged greetings. The old woman then returned inside the shop.

"I haven't gotten any answers."

"What was your question?"

"This—it looks like kue-tsí but tastes different."

"These are uncooked sunflower seeds. They are taken from the disks of dried sunflowers and are not processed with any roasting or pan-frying, which makes them fresher and softer. Uncooked sunflower seeds are usually only found on farms in the countryside. These were specially sent to the old lady by the family's tenant farmers."

"I see. The raw seed doesn't seem to have high oil content at all. I'm surprised people can even extract sunflower oil from this."

"Sunflowers are classified into types for eating and types for oilseed. This edible variety has to be specially grown and delivered here. You are quite lucky to have come upon these fresh seeds."

"I never thought I'd be able to eat raw sunflower seeds."

"I mentioned a long time ago that I would have liked you to try them if possible."

I said nothing.

She said nothing.

A wind rose. It felt like the wind that had blown the bougainvillea blossoms off of their branches. It felt like the wind that had stirred the little wild ginseng flowers while I sat smoking on the cottage's veranda.

A crystalline noise sounded in my heart. It was the tiny, tiny crackle of the ice cubes left at the bottom of our empty glasses in the suite at the Tainan Railway Hotel. At last I rose from the long bench and stood face-to-face with the lithe figure.

"I wanted to see you, Chi-chan."

"So did I, Aoyama-san."

"On my way over, I had a hunch that I would find you here."

Chi-chan smiled and replied, "So did I."

But was it a hunch, or was it simply an impassioned wish? I did not say this part out loud.

Chi-chan and I sat peeling the sunflower hulls on the two ends of the long bench. Before us, pedestrians and vehicles passed by; behind us, people went in and out of the general store. None of them seemed to have anything to do with us. Whenever the wind blew, scattered petals fell here and there from the towering trees that lined the street.

The trees were dense with blossoms, the same color as a violet sunset.

"Those are chinaberry flowers." Chi-chan, who had no doubt observed the focus of my attention, began explaining to me as always. "In the Mainland, the flower for graduation season is sakura, but here on the Island it is chinaberry flowers—khóo-līng-á. The first line in my alma mater's school song is 'Blooming khóo-līng-á / O noble, serene / purple flower.' It is also our official school flower."

"I used to assume that Chi-chan had mostly unhappy memories of school, but judging from your tone just now, it seems the reality was different from what I'd imagined."

"Most days cannot be divided so simply into happy or unhappy. I am sure that Aoyama-san's school days were the same."

"Me? I don't have any happy memories from school. My peers gave me the nickname of the Great Cedar because I was socially obtuse and out of place. I spent all my days writing and didn't make a single friend."

"Ha. That does sound like what Aoyama-san would do. But did you mind them saying those things?"

"No, I didn't mind. I read the books I wanted to read and wrote the things I wanted to write, and four years had gone by before I knew it."

"You once said that you have never had a friend to go drinking or flower-viewing with."

"True. No happy memories from school . . . but nothing that I can call an unhappy memory, either. Maybe the root of the problem is that I've always been too proud to make space for other people in my mind. Chi-chan must have felt this deeply over the past year."

She was silent.

"Chi-chan."

"Mm."

"Here is my deduction."

"Hm?"

"The daughter of a rich farming family's concubine—a child who grew up drinking muâ-ínn-thng jute soup—what must she have undergone in order to metamorphose into a knowledgeable scholar who is fluent in multiple languages and well versed in modern popular culture, and even aspires to become a rare translator of novels? What is the journey that led little Ông Tshian-ho̍h to become Miss Ō Chizuru? I've been mulling over this mystery for a long time. But if I'd asked directly, I don't believe you would have answered me."

"That's true."

"So I'd like to solve this mystery now."

"I am all ears."

"Firstly. The Ông family's ancestral home is Zhāngzhōu in

Shina, but on the day that we had Master A-Phûn's tshài-bué-thng soup, when you talked about the Island's traditional New Year's dishes, the example you gave was Quánzhōu's tau-mī noodle stew. New Year's feasts tend to be seminal childhood memories. In my case, when I spent the New Year on the Island, I thought often about the Aoyama family's datemaki egg roll recipe and Kyūshū's zōni savory mochi soup. So why was it that Chi-chan's idea of New Year was Quánzhōu cuisine?"

"Mm."

"Secondly. Chi-chan's dining preferences are very unusual. Even though some Islanders might eat white toast or other types of bread as snacks, the type of family that Chi-chan hails from must keep very conventional dining habits. I grew up in the Nagasaki branch of the Aoyama family, where our habits are much more casual compared to the strict rules and complex etiquette of our head family in Kumamoto. Given the status of the Ôngs, I'm guessing that your family's ways are likely more similar to the Kumamoto Aoyama family's. Furthermore, even in a place like Nagasaki where coffee has a lengthy cultural history, it's still rare for young women to prefer coffee over other beverages. Thus, I highly doubt that it is a favorite among young Islander women. So where did Chi-chan acquire such a taste for bread and coffee?"

"Mm."

"Thirdly. No matter how I thought about it, I couldn't fathom how you could have learned such remarkable dice-rolling skills. But thankfully, Master A-Phûn gave me an invaluable clue: 'The child wasn't raised by Kohaku for nothing. A clever one indeed.' She'd pronounced 'amber' the Japanese way. Kohaku is not a common Mainlander name, and so must be an alias. Could it be that Chi-chan had a mentor of Quánzhōu descent who'd gone by the Japanese name Kohaku? After all, you've hinted in the past of having somebody whom you can turn to with all kinds of questions! So, perhaps this Kohaku is extensively knowledgeable, fluent in foreign languages, skilled at gambling, well traveled, adept at singing Islander koa-á book songs, familiar with Han Islander culture and Hakka culture, as well as the Island's indigenous cultures, and equally versed in Shina, Mainland, and Western cultures—even in the most fashionable and avant-garde matters. But can such an omniscient and almighty mentor really exist? I later came to think it possible that Kohaku is not the name of a single person. What do you say, Chi-chan?"

"That would be quite shocking. But this is not quite deduction, just a compilation of clues."

"True, but here's the fourth point. You once said that clam noodles are a dish that made a deep impression on you as a child. You said that Master A-Phûn would make it in large batches as a mess-hall dish shared by many people at once. But where would a young Chi-chan have dined under such circumstances except at the Ông family home or at school? But you lived with your mother's family in the countryside and commuted to school. And it seems unlikely that a daughter of the Ông family would have shared a mess-hall meal with the servants at home.

"Which brought me to another question: In what situation would Master A-Phûn have made such a dish? Given her personality and clout, it seems impossible that she would have cooked specifically for a mass meal. For someone like her to be compelled into making clam noodles, it must have been a lost bet or a favor. It was only after she heard the word Kohaku that she agreed to bet on dice—which means that Kohaku is the only connection between the two of you. Finally I arrived at a possible conclusion: Kohaku is the name of an establishment, and Master A-Phûn and you must have met when she was cooking clam noodles at Kohaku."

"Mm."

"Lastly. In the tearoom in Shōka, Chi-chan's distant relatives had jeered, 'To think that even someone who grew up on muâ-ínn-thng can dine in tearooms now!' That was the one time, the *only* time that you brought up your mother. Chi-chan's mother was a girl from a jute-farming family who'd gained the favor of the head of the Ông family when she was performing as a gē-tòa entertainer. You never once mentioned her after this, which I now assume may be because she passed away young . . . I'm sorry that I didn't notice this before. But this has become my final clue. So here it is, the deduction: after Chi-chan's mother passed away young, her gē-tòa friends taught her to cultivate their many talents and skills. As for a place that can accommodate so many experts on such diverse realms . . . this Kohaku, with its Japanese name, is probably a café."[4]

"Oh dear, oh dear."

"Am I correct?"

"Aoyama-san—or perhaps I should call you the Great Detective! But, all these things have long passed. Did you come all the way to Chōkyōshitō just to present your conclusions?"

"No. What I came to say is, from the beginning, you have been on my mind."

". . ."

"You're not smiling anymore, Chi-chan. But of course you're not—that makes absolute sense. Because the Great Cedar hasn't changed. I've always done and said whatever I want without making space for others, and it took me so long to realize that I never *truly* listened to the things that you've been trying to tell me. I've been so deaf that I even drove you to ask, 'Can Aoyama Chizuko and Ông Tshian-ho'h really be called friends?' Do I have the right to tell you that you've been on my mind? I'm self-aware enough to know that even this is questionable. Even so, I have come here today to see you—and what I want to say is,

---

4. Yáng: Per the earlier footnote in chapter III, café refers to a specific type of establishment that served alcohol and was known for nightlife catered to male customers.

yes, you're on my mind, always on my mind, so I had to come tell you to your face."

I paused. After a few cautious breaths, I continued in a solemn voice, carefully separating each word: "I am sorry, Miss Ông Tshian-hȯh. Aoyama Chizuko is a despicable brute who has no regard for others, who always thinks she knows best, who is arrogant and doltish. From the beginning to end, my ignorant words and actions have repeatedly damaged our friendship. For this, I am most deeply sorry."

We didn't finish peeling the sunflower kue-tsí. Meeting my eye, Chi-chan did not try to conceal the mess of emotions clouding her mind. She did not put on her Noh mask.

I felt my shoulders relax slightly at last.

"I won't ask anything of you anymore, Chi-chan. Not to be friends, not to be your 'easterly wind,' nothing. I wanted to let you know that I've finally understood why you chose to sever our relations—that's all. I am not trying to seek your forgiveness."

Aoyama-san. She'd exhaled my name like a sigh.

"Aoyama-san . . . the first time that we dined together at the same table, you told me that we would eat our way through Taiwan Island, that we were destined to meet. To be honest, I felt indifferent back then. But later, I—and especially now, in this moment, I cannot help but marvel that, yes, you and I were destined to meet."

She smiled—a sweet but sorrowful smile. "Aoyama-san."

"Yes."

"Thank you. And sorry."

"For what?"

"You are gentle and kind, Aoyama-san—and you have taken care of me in so many ways. But it's also true that you can be a brute who has no regard for others, who always thinks she knows best, who is arrogant and doltish."

Ouch. A harsh blow indeed.

I produced a forced smile, which only made her eyes soften even more.

"But despite all that, Aoyama-san, you have always opened your heart to me. You have told me, in the most forthright terms, that you regard me as an intimate friend. I am extremely grateful to you. But precisely because of this, I am also very sorry. There were several times when I told you that I do not wish to lie to you, but the truth is that I have deceived you much earlier and in a much more foundational way. I—and I'm sorry, but I—I never once opened my heart to you, never once truly regarded you as a friend."

"Mm."

"Are you not angry?"

"No, I'm not angry. Or, rather, I knew it already."

This disoriented her. "You knew?"

"Well, yes. I've said this before, right? I'm always observing you, and so I don't believe I misread your expressions."

My words must have truly shocked her. Chi-chan's long eyelashes batted up and down, and she said nothing for a long time.

"At first, I just thought that I couldn't force a woman as reserved and prudent as you to open up to me. But after my 'deduction,' I've reached a new understanding. Your 'seductive' charms come from the same set of skills as your excellent dice-throwing. I've thought about the type of person your mentors wanted you to become. Was their aim to nurture a woman who can keep her future husband on a tight leash? No, I don't think so. I believe that their goal was to teach you self-preservation, so that whether your future husband respects you or dotes on you or not, whether he lives a long life or dies young, and whether you marry near or far, you would be able to live securely in the world. These worldly mentors have done everything they could to save you from the pain of following in your mother's footsteps. If you were raised with such an education, it only makes sense that it would be impossible for you to easily reveal your true feelings to others."

"You really do surprise me."

It took her a long time to utter this one sentence.

I replied in the same slow, soft tone: "Chi-chan, just like you have long been aware that I have another side of me that is arrogant and self-important, I have long been aware that you have another side to you that is secretive, unforthcoming, and perfectly capable of lying with a straight face—a masterful actor. It is this masterful actor whom I regard as my best friend."

". . ."

"What to do if the cuckoo does not sing?"

"In the style of Ieyasu? If the cuckoo does not sing, wait for it."[5]

"Precisely. I knew you would get the reference."

"I really am at a loss with you."

"Aigh . . . I am the one who has always been helpless."

She looked at me, straight-faced.

I looked right back at her.

"Very well, allow me to solve the long-standing mystery for you."

"I'm all ears."

"Your deduction," she said, "was almost all correct. My mother died of illness before I started public school, and three of her old friends found me, taught me, and nurtured me. I address them as my aunts. Kohaku is indeed a café, one that is still in operation in Shintomi District to this day—managed by my eldest aunt. My middle aunt lives with her husband in Sakae District, where they sell Western imports. My youngest aunt

---

5. Yáng: The question "What to do if the cuckoo does not sing?" comes from a famous Sengoku-period anecdote that delineates the respective personalities of Oda Nobunaga, Toyotomi Hideyoshi, and Tokugawa Ieyasu. Hideyoshi's answer was, "If the cuckoo does not sing, coax it"; Ieyasu's answer was, "Wait for it"; and Nobunaga's answer was, "Kill it."

spent many years in the red-light district of Hatsune as a madam for other gē-tòa.

"In my school days, I would study at Kohaku after school. It was a café where Mainlanders, Islanders, Shina people, and Westerners passed through, and among the girl servants were people of native descent. With my three aunts as my mentors, I learned how to live peacefully and securely in this world. As you know, I have no musical or rhythmic talents, and that was intentional—they did not wish me to go into the same line of work as they. Years later, the concubine's daughter Ông Tshian-hȯh grew to become the public school teacher Ō Chizuru that you know.

"You were right in that we were destined to meet, but it is a sad destiny indeed. This is my first time openly admitting to my roots, and I will never do so again to anybody else. Yet despite this, Aoyama-san and I can never become true friends—it is ultimately impossible for a Mainlander and an Islander to share a friendship of equals."

"That is simply too tragic a conclusion to draw."

"But it is the truth."

It was my turn to be straight-faced.

Before me, Chi-chan's eyes rippled with tears. How long had she carried this sadness within her?

"Chi-chan. After you solved the mystery of Ōzawa and Tân, you expressed confusion that the two of them, despite being a Mainlander and an Islander, would exchange private photos. You said then that the feelings of young women are the greatest mystery in the world. Do you remember?"

"Yes."

"The following is not a deduction, merely my imagination. In the photograph, Tân was wearing riding pants and boots, remember? Petite Tân chose to be photographed in this commanding riding suit, then chose to give said photograph to Ōzawa. Perhaps it was to convey to Ōzawa: 'I *am* strong enough, so please trust me accordingly.' If they weren't friends, why go that far? This must mean that, despite the friction between them, Tân and Ōzawa do feel true friendship toward each other!"

"..."

"Ōzawa has made very real mistakes in her treatment of Tân, but the feelings that Tân holds for Ōzawa must be equally real. Aoyama Chizuko has made very real mistakes in her treatment of Ông Tshian-hȯh, but . . ." I did not finish the sentence. I released my breath.

Chi-chan, like me, exhaled quietly—carefully.

I held my hands toward her. She took them in hers.

Then she lowered her face. Tears fell onto the kue-tsí husks below.

"You are quite right. Even though I cannot open my heart, the feelings that I hold within this shuttered heart are, nonetheless, real."

I held her hands even more tightly.

She did the same.

We clasped each other's hands with all our strength.

The spring breeze sent the chinaberry petals into flurries in the sky.

When she raised her face again, Chi-chan's eyes were glistening.

Mine must have been doing the same.

Doesn't being like this make us so-called friends? I would no longer say things like this.

We sat gazing at each other on the bench outside the general store, our reflections stirring in each other's irises. What next?

The long hand of the clock ticked forward, one dial at a time.

I announced that I was hungry.

She laughed and said, "How very like you."

"Let's go eat something nearby."

"Would you like bí-hún-tshá vermicelli noodles? There's a stall in the Third Market that used to sell bento boxes of their delicious bí-hún-tshá on the train platform."

"I bought a bento on the platform of Shinchiku Station when I first arrived on the Island—bí-hún-tshá is the first Islander food that I ever had. Have you had lunch yet?"

"Not yet."

"Then let's have something that you like. Potato croquette, curry rice, carrots, fried tofu—what else do you like, Chi-chan?"

"Aoyama-san has a remarkable memory."

"Ah—mm, can't we change that at least?"

"Change what?"

"Call me Chizuko or something."

"We've discussed this—it's strange when we have the same name."

"Or Aoko, maybe. Or Yama-chan."

"Ao . . . Aoko. Ah, no. I can't do it."

"But you did! I heard you!" Then: "Come on, let's go eat. Let's go eat and let's go drink all we want."

I hooked my arm through hers and rose to my feet.

She nudged me with her shoulder. I nudged her with my elbow.

Chinaberry blossoms fell like rain. Khóo-līng-á.

We strode forward, letting the petals rest on our hair and shoulders.

Khóo-līng-á are graduation flowers.

Sakura for the Mainland, khóo-līng-á for the Island.

The long hand of the clock ticked one dial at a time. The short hand circles twenty-four times in one day. The following day would be the first of April.

The date of my return to Kyūshū was the second Friday of April.

I refused to bring this up. Chi-chan, too, acted as though there was nothing looming ahead.

Oyster pancakes and bí-thai-ba̍k vermicelli, ham and egg sandwiches, corn chowder. Chi-chan named some things she liked, then I named some things I liked. Omelet rice drizzled with hayashi hashed beef, nigiri sushi, fried pork cutlets, almond tofu, peanut powder, edamame, cucumbers, egg floss, karasumi mullet roe.

We chuckled at each other.

Oh, and jūn-piánn rolls.

A straight road, windingly tread.

Chi-chan walked it from Chōkyōshitō to Kawabata District. I walked it the other way around.

A short road—and a long, long one.

Up and down we walked until we reached the midpoint. The Midori River District.

The winding road was treacherous; it took three hundred days traveling Taiwan and thousands of ri traversed on the railroad to reach its end. Chi-chan and I stood side by side on the Taishō Bridge of Midori River District. Nearby, whistles sounded in Taichū Station as a steam train rumbled off. Where was that train headed? The whistling grew tinnier as the train chugged farther away. A breeze rose to meet us, bringing with it the fresh scent of the Midori River. We moved neither forward nor backward. A vendor's cart by Taishō Bridge was already selling fruit and jelly ice, though it was hardly summer yet. The vendor's call was like a shepherd's song. I did not know where that train was headed.

I had no idea of the future that awaited me back in Kyūshū.

The only thing that I knew was something small—tiny.

It is this: On the last day of March in the fourteenth year of Shōwa, shoulder to shoulder on the banks of the narrow Midori River, our eyes tracing that ribbon of water into the distance, Chi-chan and I shared one bowl of fruit and jelly ice.

It was very sweet. It was very delicious.

Afterword to *My Taiwan Travelogue with Tshian-hȯh*, 1970[1]

Memories of My Mother

Aoyama Yōko (artist and adopted daughter of Aoyama Chizuko)

There is an island deeply rooted in my mother's heart.

I have known this from a very young age. How young? Around seven or eight years old. It was not long after I had started school, which was also the time when Mother was writing *Taiwan Travelogue*. Whenever I came home from school, our maid Auntie Haruno would ask me to bring an afternoon snack to Mother's study. "Yōko-san, please tell your mother about the pleasant day you had today." Whenever I entered Mother's study, however, it was she who would tell me about her days—stories from her island days.

Mother and I ate many things together: countless types of sweet breads, dorayaki pancakes, red bean paste daifuku, mochi, raisins still attached to the branches of grape bunches, fruit cakes, castella cakes . . . If the snack of the day was karintō crackers, Mother was bound to say this: "Taiwan's tshùn-tsó is far more delicious than Japanese karintō." That was when I learned about the island in my mother's heart.

Having grown up in the Aoyama home with its rich and diverse book collection, I was something of a literary fanatic even as a girl. One day, Mother asked whether I wanted to read her

1. Yáng: Aoyama Chizuko's *Taiwan Travelogue* went out of print in 1954; in 1970, it was retitled *My Taiwan Travelogue with Tshian-hȯh* and reissued. The new edition included the afterword "Memories of My Mother" by Aoyama Chizuko's adopted daughter, Aoyama Yōko.

novel. This was the manuscript for *Taiwan Travelogue*. I immersed myself in the manuscript for several days.

When I reached the ending, I went to Mother in tears, whining, "Is this a true story? But it's too sad!" I'd assumed that Mother would laugh this off as always, giving me the same response that she often gave to such complaints: "Novels are just novels." Had she said that, I would have pleaded: "Then *please* give it a happy ending."

But, to my surprise, Mother said, "Yes, it's a sad and true story."

Her smile looked so disconsolate that I felt at a total loss. In the end, it was I who began bawling at the top of my lungs.

That night, Mother did something she rarely did: she lay down with me at bedtime.

In bed, I asked her, "Did you go see Chi-chan after eating the kiâm-nn̄g-ko cake?"

"I did."

"Well, then why is that not included in the novel?"

Mother did not respond straightaway. But, later, she added a twelfth chapter to *Taiwan Travelogue*.

It was many years later that I finally read the articles that Mother wrote for the Taiwan Travelogue series. It was in juxtaposing the travel essays with the novel that I saw the differences in the author's states of mind. I never asked Mother, "Why did you write a long-form novel instead of adding to the travel essays?" Nor did I ever ask her, "Why is there no prologue or afterword to this novel?" Because I knew the answers.

Everything that she wanted to say was already within the novel.

The novel *Taiwan Travelogue* was published in Shōwa Year 29 (1954). After its publication, Mother went around asking her acquaintances from far and wide to take a copy of the book to Taiwan. She spent year after year asking people to mail or take copies with them, but nothing ever came of this. When I was at junior college, the remaining copies of *Taiwan Travelogue* were destroyed in a windstorm, leaving the novel officially out of print. It was only then that Mother ceased her attempts at fulfilling her wish.

As young as I was, I could easily guess that book's hoped-for destination was Chi-chan.

In Shōwa Year 43 (1968), Mother contracted a severe lung disease. At her sickbed, I asked whether she would like to go on an onsen trip. She shook her head and said there was no need.

"Get *Taiwan Travelogue* printed in a new edition under a new title and—Yōko, I'll have to trouble you to take it to Taiwan for me."

I was twenty-six years old that year, the same age Mother was when she visited Taiwan. Before the novel's reprint, I took a trip to Taiwan myself. I could not locate the person on Mother's mind—I could not even find a trace of the Double Dragon Waterfalls that Mother had captured in such painstaking detail in Kīrun (Kēelúng). I did track down one thing, however: tshùn-tsó.

Tshùn-tsó is, indeed, similar to karintō. But I did not find it nearly as delicious as Mother had claimed. Mother's impression of tshùn-tsó's exceptional flavor must have been amplified by the long-treasured memories from her youth.

Eating the tshùn-tsó, it occurred to me that Mother perhaps wrote the novel *Taiwan Travelogue* for Chi-chan and Chi-chan alone.

Mother died of illness in January of Shōwa Year 45 (1970).

I followed the instructions in her will and secured a reprint for the novel that had never loosened its grip on her mind.

My hope is that, through this novel, Aoyama-san and Chi-chan can at last be reunited on that beautiful island.

May, Shōwa 45 (1970)
The Aoyama ancestral home, Kumamoto, Japan

Translator's Note to *A Japanese Woman Author's Taiwan Travelogue*, 1977[1]

Noodles

Wáng Chiēn-hò

In ROC Year 64 (1976), my eldest daughter Chèng-měi told me that she received a phone call at her research institute from a Miss Aoyama Yōko in Japan.[2] Two weeks later, Aoyama Yōko-san arrived at my home in Austin, Texas, along with a book titled *My Taiwan Travelogue with Tshian-hȯh* and the news that Aoyama Chizuko-san had passed away many years ago.

"After the war ended, Mother sent someone to Taiwan every year to look for a Ms. Ông Tshian-hȯh. She never imagined that you and your family had emigrated to the United States. I am fortunate and grateful to be able to fulfill my mother's dying wish today."

Yōko-san spoke fluent English, and was elegant in both her word choice and her sentence structure. Her open and even gallant demeanor was just like her mother's.

I invited her to stay with us, and she, with that same refreshing

1. Yáng: *My Taiwan Travelogue with Tshian-hȯh* was published by Ông Tshian-hȯh's (Mandarin name: Wáng Chiēn-hò) eldest daughter Wú Chèng-měi in a self-funded and self-edited Chinese translation in a 1990 limited release, under the title *A Japanese Woman Author's Taiwan Travelogue*. The Chinese translation was done by Ông Tshian-hȯh. This new edition included two forewords, of which this translator's note is the first.

2. King: The Republic of China calendar begins in 1912, the year that Sun Yat-sen founded the republic in Nanjing. After the republic's removal from China to Taiwan, the latter has continued using the ROC calendar alongside the Gregorian calendar.

frankness, agreed to stay for two weeks. Every morning, she prepared breakfast for me.

Every morning for two weeks, I revisited Shōwa Taiwan at the breakfast table.

"What was my mother like in your eyes?"

What was Aoyama Chizuko like?

I told her that the real Aoyama Chizuko was just like the character Aoyama-san.

I told her that on our trip to Chānghuà's Bāguàshān to visit Shōka Onsen, we had some wolfberry tea at a street stall. Aoyama-san proclaimed: "This is made from the root of wolfberry, is it not? To brew tea with tree roots—only a Southern Country can have such wisdom." At this, I could not help but curse at this ignorant brute in my heart of hearts. "A nation that loves burdock roots has no right to call us root-eaters!"

Of course, I had never once voiced such counterarguments out loud.

Yōko-san bent over with laughter when she heard this. "That certainly sounds like the mother I knew," she said.

To this day, I have no intention of delineating the discrepancies between my own memories of the past and the Taiwan Travelogues recorded by Aoyama Chizuko-san. After taking two whole years to complete this Mandarin Chinese translation, however, I wish to document just one small incident as a brief response to Aoyama Chizuko-san's novel.

During a cold wave toward the end of Shōwa Year 13 (1938), Aoyama-san fell ill.

I set aside my plans for the day and brought medicine to her cottage by Yana River.

"I'd much prefer noodles over traditional medicine."

I could not argue and therefore obliged. I boiled noodles and topped them with raw egg and grated yam. Aoyama-san's appetite remained healthy despite her illness; she finished the noodles in a few gulps.

"The grated yam would taste even better with some white fish mixed in, you know."

This meant that she wished to add to her "order." I wrestled with the mortar and pestle to grind the yam along with the fish while stewing bone broth. Despite the cold, I was drenched in hot sweat. At last, I presented Aoyama-san with a second bowl of egg and grated yam noodles.

"It's just too delicious! For the next one, I would love a hot dish—noodles in the Islander style!"

The third bowl, therefore, was steaming egg drop noodles topped with flatfish, dried shrimp, and pork bone broth. After downing this bowl, Aoyama-san announced that she was homesick for her hometown's flavors.

My word! How was *I* to know what Nagasaki's flavors tasted like?

To appease her, I produced some noodles with a broth made from konbu seaweed, bonito, and sweet soy sauce.

"My nose is too congested. I can't seem to taste the subtleties of the broth."

And so the fifth bowl of noodles was of richly flavored red miso and pork. I added a sixth bowl of my own accord: dry noodles stir-fried with rice wine, pork lard, and sesame oil. I thought, with this final push, even Aoyama-san's stomach must be bursting—and, surely, her conscience must recognize that she had overexerted me with these requests.

When she finished the two bowls, Aoyama-san's expression was one of contentment at last. But then she said: "I feel hot all over. As the final dish, I would like to have ice-cold sōmen."

Aigh! What could I do but admit defeat!

I wanted to ask a servant to go buy ice and had instructions in mind for which stall in Shintomichō Market was cleanest, but ultimately my worry that others would be too careless overtook me, and I ended up running over to the market myself to secure the ice. Returning to the cottage, I diced cucumbers and okra as toppings and served them with iced noodles.

Winter winds howled outside the cottage, but the dining table looked like summer itself. Aoyama-san slurped the noodles without bothering to chew, only stopping when she was done. She laid down her bowl and chopsticks and grinned at me—the grin of a child who had frolicked to her heart's content on a summer's day.

"Chi-chan, you might as well marry me! Be my bride!"

"What good can come out of being Aoyama-san's bride?"

"Why, to be by each other's side for richer or poorer, for better or worse. And, if there's good food, I will always give you half."

"Can that be called good?"

"If there's only one bowl of rice left—no, even if there's only half of a bowl left, I would give you half. And if there is only one grain of rice left, large enough only to fit seven gods, I'd give you four of the gods, Chi-chan."

What a fool.

I don't mean Aoyama-san, but myself. In that moment, I felt as though if I had been willing to blindly follow this person, to marry her, perhaps I really would have found happiness.

I also shared this anecdote with Yōko-san at the breakfast table.

Yōko-san had smiled and said, "So Tshian-hȯh-san does like Mother back after all."

Is that so? Perhaps that is so.

Before I knew it, thirty years had passed since the day of those noodles at the Yana River cottage. *Fleeting light, fleeting light, I beg thee drink this cup of wine.* It makes sense that this poem is now on my lips. If one day we are to meet in heaven, Aoyama-san, on behalf of all the wine that we could not share in our lives, I will again raise my cup to you.

July 1977
Columbia, Missouri

Editor's Note to *A Japanese Woman Author's Taiwan Travelogue*, 1990

A Promise with the Departed

Wú Chèng-měi (literary scholar and daughter of Wáng Chiēn-hò)

The process behind publishing the Mandarin Chinese edition of *A Japanese Woman Author's Taiwan Travelogue* was one of many twists and turns. The original book, titled *Taiwan Travelogue*, was published by the Kumamoto-based publisher Hōbundō in 1945. In 1970, contemporary artist Aoyama Yōko, daughter of Aoyama Chizuko, oversaw the process of a reprint under the new title *My Taiwan Travelogue with Tshian-hòh*. In 1975, Ms. Aoyama Yōko managed to contact my office in the Department of Comparative Literature at the University of California, Los Angeles, whereupon the journey to producing this edition began.

From a scholarly standpoint, a prewar novel written by a Japanese woman author about colonized Taiwan is a rare and precious work beyond my imagination. From a personal standpoint, however, given my mother's status as one of the novel's main characters, it is naturally difficult for me to offer any profound criticism or analysis of this work—nor do I have any intention of attempting it.

The Chiǎng Chīng-kuó government announced an end to Taiwan's martial law in the summer of 1987. One sweltering afternoon, my mother called me at the university from her home in Austin and expressed her wish to translate *My Taiwan Travelogue with Tshian-hòh* into Mandarin and to have it published in Taiwan. My mother was seventy at this time; the translation of a long-form novel was a hefty undertaking, and she'd called me to request my assistance out of the fear that her health would not be able to sustain a project of such scale. However, I was a full-time professor at the time and was struggling with my own workload. I asked Mother: Why translate into Mandarin? And why publish in Taiwan?

She said, "It is a promise I have with the departed."

There was nothing I could say to object to this. Because my mother was not only my mother.

Mother was an independent individual outside of her societal role as my mother. The first time I felt that my mother was not merely a mother was when I was nineteen and she was forty-three. In a fit of teenage rebellion, I had chosen to move far from my parents in Columbia, Missouri, to attend the University of Wisconsin, Madison. In 1959, during a vacation in my sophomore year of college, my mother appeared at my dormitory out of the blue. Shocked, I asked, "Mom, how did you get here?"

She said, "I drove here." This only furthered my shock: Columbia was at least four hundred miles away from Madison.

"I left after breakfast and stopped for a sandwich and some coffee in a town on the Mississippi River at around noon. It wasn't as far as I thought it'd be, though it *is* a long enough journey to leave one's backside aching."

She'd driven four hundred miles by herself in a dress suit and an exquisite hat.

The second time that I felt this, and even more acutely than the first, was when we received *My Taiwan Travelogue with Tshian-hȯh* from Ms. Aoyama Yōko. My mother always behaved like a gentlewoman in the traditional Japanese fashion, leading a simple yet fastidious lifestyle. She referred to my father by the Japanese address "danna." With him, she was never without a smile, and she never refused any of his requests. As a girl, I once said to my younger brothers, "When Mom calls Dad 'danna,' it sounds less like 'husband' and more like 'boss,' don't you think?" My brothers both agreed with me.

Yet Chi-chan was entirely different from the mother I knew.

Reading the novel had shaken me to my core; I did not know how to begin to discuss it with my mother. When she asked for my thoughts, I stalled by saying, "So will you really give the kimono from Aoyama-san to me?" In reality, I never developed strong preferences regarding my appearance and could not care less about where the kimono would go. But my mother had smiled. "I'm sorry, but danna sold the kimono after the war. Resources were scarce back then."

I countered, "But our family was doing relatively well, weren't we? Was it necessary to sell the kimono?"

She chuckled. "You're right. Why did we have to sell it, I wonder?"

In that moment, I suddenly understood why my mother had always treated my father like an honored guest.

My mother, Ms. Wáng Chiēn-hò, had a personality like dancing flames and willpower like an iceberg, yet despite this she had always hidden her true feelings under that elegant, pleasant smile.

Now, to return to the year 1987.

Despite my secret resistance to taking on the task of translating a whole book, I still returned to Columbia to see my mother. But what she presented me with was not notes or pieces of a draft, but a translation of the whole manuscript that she had completed back in 1977. Her translator's note was only further proof that my interpretation of her true self was not mistaken.

I told her that it would take time to find and coordinate with a Taiwanese publisher all the way from the United States. Was that okay with her? She said, "Time is not of the essence. The thing that matters is to make this into a reality."

This was the same year that my only daughter, Jo, was graduating from high school, and so the three of us—three generations of women—decided to travel together to Taiwan and spend the summer in the Japanese-style house that our family still owned in Táichūng.

Mother loved the engawa veranda of that house and was always sitting there to catch a breeze. One morning in late August, Jo was reading the newspaper aloud in Taiwanese Hokkien to Mother before breakfast. When she finished reading the first page, my mother suddenly said a long string of words to Jo. Jo froze, because the words had been in Japanese, which Jo couldn't understand. She laid the newspaper on my mother's lap and went searching for me in the kitchen.

When I went out to the veranda, my mother was stretched out in the lounge chair, apparently asleep and with a smile on her face.

In the moment, I thought that it must have been lingering jet lag. Her face seemed entirely at ease; she seemed contented. Yet she was never to open her eyes again. My mother thus embarked on the next journey of her life there in her homeland.

The long and winding journey of publishing *A Japanese Woman Author's Taiwan Travelogue* in Mandarin, meanwhile, extended all the way to 1990. We spent three years searching for a publisher willing to accept the Mandarin translation to no avail. After discussing with Ms. Aoyama Yōko, I decided to re-edit the manuscript and self-publish it.

The published product *A Japanese Woman Author's Taiwan Travelogue* that you now hold in your hand, dear reader, has been cut down with consideration to Taiwan's current sociopolitical landscape, which is still easing its way out of martial law and the strict censorship on the subject of its colonial history. Along with the changes to the title, this edition is really but an abridgement of *My Taiwan Travelogue with Tshian-hòh*. This is a regret that I must bear despite my best efforts.

It is my wish that one day, when Taiwan's future has been reshaped by democracy, a complete version of this book will at last be able to reach readers of Mandarin. Perhaps, in that future, there will be another scholar who is willing to pick up this book and delineate all the many points that make it a unique work.

With hope—

August 1990
Táichūng City

Translator's Note to *Taiwan Travelogue*, New Mandarin Chinese Edition, 2020

Amber

Yáng Shuāng-zǐ

The story of the new Mandarin Chinese edition of *Taiwan Travelogue* begins at the end of 2014. My late elder sister and I had taken a brief trip to Kitakyūshū in Japan, also traveling through Fukuoka, Moji, Kumamoto, and Yufuin, among other places in the region. There, we visited the Hayashi Fumiko Memorial Reference Room located in the historical building of the Former Moji Mitsui Club. The exhibits showcased many of the letters between the feminist writer Hayashi Fumiko and her contemporaries, including famous Japanese writers such as Yoshiya Nobuko and Kawabata Yasunari. My sister does not understand Japanese, so I paraphrased everything for her in Mandarin under my breath. But, when I saw a postcard from a certain Aoyama Chizuko, I cried out, "Someone once wrote a book called *Taiwan Travelogue!*"

My sister leant over and likewise cried out. "Who's this Aoyama Chizuko? Why haven't we heard of her before?"

Thankfully, we were the only two people in the room.

The postcard's contents were, in translation: "What a joyous thing to have been able to discuss my time in prewar Taiwan with you the other day. My new book *Taiwan Travelogue* was recently published and a copy will arrive at your residence shortly. Aoyama Chizuko, July 11." The postcard's label added: *Mailed on July 11, Shōwa Year 29.*

At that time, in December 2014, my sister and I were mired in a swamp of research and fact-checking for a historical novel set in Japanese colonial Taiwan. The discovery of such a postcard was a pleasant surprise indeed. After returning to Taiwan, I began looking out for the name Aoyama Chizuko and the title *Taiwan Travelogue* while continuing to conduct research, and to my surprise found some fragmented excerpts of a Mandarin translation online. At the bottom of the web page was yet another wonderful surprise: a brief note that read, *A portion of this manuscript is in the collections of the Museum of Taiwan Literature.*

In February 2015, I contacted the Special Research Division of the Museum of Taiwan Literature. I will save the reader the details of the long and complex logistics that ensued. Eventually I received a call from an administrator who explained, "This data does not exist in the Museum of Taiwan Literature inventory, but there is a Japanese researcher who informs us that she is in possession of the complete manuscript. She has said that you may contact her directly if you are interested."

This Japanese researcher was Ms. Hiyoshi Sagako. From her, I received electronic scans of the 1970 Japanese edition of *My Taiwan Travelogue with Tshian-hȯh* as well as the 1990 Mandarin edition of *A Japanese Woman Writer's Taiwan Travelogue* via email.

My work on a new Mandarin edition began on June 19, 2015. But my ailing body was far from reliable, and for every hour that I spent concentrating at my desk, I would have to spend double the time recovering in bed. This sluggish pace meant that the translation took four whole years to complete. If there are any readers out there who have been awaiting this book, I thank you for your patience.

Why, despite my illness, did I insist on completing this work?

There have been many hands on this book: Aoyama Chizuko's novel (1954), Aoyama Yōko's afterword (1970), Wáng Chiēn-hò's translation and translator's note (1977), Wú Chèng-mĕi's editor's note (1990), and this latest 2020 translation. What are our goals—mine and my four predecessors'—for this work?

I believe that, from 1954 to 2020, this book in all its forms has always brought forth its translators' internalized feelings about the vicissitudes of life as well as inspired the hope to at last fully piece together this ineffable and true affection that took place on Taiwan Island and under the dictates of history and fate.

Why did Aoyama Chizuko choose to rewrite the story as a novel instead of publishing her travel essays on Taiwan as a collection? And, building off of that question, would travel/historical writing have been more "real"? Are novels/fiction "made up" by comparison? I have no plans to write a dissertation on these questions, so please allow me a sentimental answer instead: a novel is a piece of amber, one that coagulates both the "real" past and the "made-up" ideals. It is something that can be visited again and again in its unparalleled beauty.

There are many people whom I must thank for the realization of this new Mandarin edition. I am grateful to Ms. Hiyoshi Sagako, who provided the invaluable manuscripts; to Xiaō Siāng Shén and Cyǔ Chén for their assistance during the translation process; to my forever buddy Guō Rú Meí; to Patience Chuang, editor in chief of SpringHill Publishing, and to deputy editor Wú Fāng Shuo.

Very special thanks go to my late older sister, the Jò-tzū half of the name "Shuāng-zǐ." I, the Jò-hūi half of "Shuāng-zǐ," may have held the pen that translated this book, but it is in fact a product of our shared work.

As I prepare to lay down my pen, the thought that seizes my heart is: this book can very much be described as our piece of amber.

On the spring equinox of 2020
At home in Yǒnghé, Taiwan

Translator's Note to *Taiwan Travelogue*, English Edition, 2024

Lin King

When I first began working on *Taiwan Travelogue* with my Graywolf Press editor, Yuka Igarashi, we had envisioned adding yet another layer to what we referred to as the "onion" of story premises. Yáng Shuāng-zǐ and SpringHill Publishing originally published the novel with "written by Aoyama Chizuko, translated by Yáng Shuāng-zǐ" on the cover, a decision that stirred up some controversy in the Taiwanese literary world. Some readers complained that they'd purchased the book expecting it to be a translation of a 1930s Japanese text and felt tricked. Subsequent printings of the book showed "written by Yáng Shuāng-zǐ" on the cover.

Between the covers, the novel's premise remained the same: that it is a Japanese text translated by Yáng into Mandarin Chinese. At the suggestion of writer, translator, and mentor extraordinaire Jeremy Tiang, Yuka and I had planned on making up an additional premise for why the English edition *had* to be translated from Yáng's Mandarin translation instead of from the "original" Japanese text—all existing Japanese copies were lost in a warehouse fire, for example. We needed a reason to keep Yáng's footnotes and postscripts; we also wanted to do it for fun, since so much of the novel is about the fun of translation.

In the end, we decided that this may be one suspension of disbelief too many. But we did make use of Yáng's "translator's" footnotes conceit to add another layer of "real" translator's footnotes. I was therefore able to provide historical, cultural, and literary context for English readers, and even explain some of my translation decisions early on; this has been a luxury that I wish more English literary translations would allow.

There are a few notes that I'd like to share about this English translation of a text that is about translation between Japanese and Mandarin.

First, because Mandarin, Japanese, and Taiwanese Hokkien all use Han characters, Yáng doesn't have to specify the pronunciations of words. When Yáng writes, in Mandarin, that Aoyama says the word 台中, Mandarin readers understand that Aoyama is talking in Japanese about the place known in Mandarin as Táichūng. While I was rendering this into English, however, it felt discordant to me to use Mandarin pronunciations in supposedly Japanese speech and thoughts. I therefore chose to use Japanese colonial pronunciations, and therefore Aoyama stays not in Táichūng but in Taichū, visits not Mātsǔ temples but Maso temples, and mostly calls her interpreter not the Mandarin name Wáng Chiēn-hò or the Taiwanese Hokkien name Ông Tshian-ho̍h, but the Japanese name Ō Chizuru. (Mandarin names for key places mentioned in the text can be found on the map at the front of this book.)

Second, I decided to keep accents and tones. Yáng Shuāng-zǐ, not Yang Shuang-zi; lóo-bah-pn̄g, not loo-bah-png; Tōkyō, not Tokyo. These may seem visually cumbersome to an English reader, but as a user of these three languages, I always find it frustrating when accents and tones are omitted in romanization, which often means that a reader who knows the original language can't determine how to pronounce the words.

Third, special thanks are also due to the Graywolf team for making this translation a reality and for their kindness and patience; Susan Bernofsky for her guidance; Jenna Tang for her help; and Director Huichun Jo Chang and Shan Sandy Chang-Chien at the Taipei Cultural Center in New York for their continued support.

Lastly, I would also like to thank Miura Yūko, the Japanese translator of *Taiwan Travelogue*. Her translation, published by Chūōkōrōn-Shinsha in 2023, was of great help to me for fact-checking my Japanese transliterations of names and places. Surely Aoyama and Chi-chan would be tickled by this: a Taiwanese translator, while bringing the book to the ultimate colonial language of English, has struggled to determine how the Japanese colonial government would have pronounced Taiwanese terms and therefore consulted the Japanese translation of a Taiwanese novel that claims to be a Taiwanese translation of a Japanese novel. *Oh dear oh dear oh dear!*

Autumn 2023
New York City